BO

BRIDES

Three novels from international
bestselling author

HELEN BIANCHIN

brought to you

With Love

BOUGHT
BRIDES
HELEN BIANCHIN

All the characters in this book have no existence outside the imagination of the author, and have no relation whatsoever to anyone bearing the same name or names. They are not even distantly inspired by any individual known or unknown to the author, and all the incidents are pure invention.

M&B™ and M&B™ with the Rose Device
are trademarks of the publisher.
Harlequin Mills & Boon Limited, Eton House,
18-24 Paradise Road, Richmond, Surrey TW9 1SR

BOUGHT BRIDES © Harlequin Enterprises II B.V./S.à.r.l. 2009

The Greek's Bought Wife, Purchased by the Billionaire and
The Marriage Deal were first published in Great Britain by Harlequin
Mills & Boon Limited in separate, single volumes.

The Greek's Bought Wife © Helen Bianchin 2005
Purchased by the Billionaire © Helen Bianchin 2006
The Marriage Deal © Helen Bianchin 2000

ISBN: 978 0 263 87545 4

010-0809

Harlequin Mills & Boon policy is to use papers that are
natural, renewable and recyclable products and made from
wood grown in sustainable forests. The logging and
manufacturing processes conform to the legal environmental
regulations of the country of origin.

Printed and bound in Spain
by Litografia Rosés S.A., Barcelona

The Greek's Bought Wife

HELEN BIANCHIN

A collection of bestselling novels
from some of our favourite writers,
brought to you

With Love

August 2008
BOUGHT BRIDES HELEN BIANCHIN

September 2008
VIRGIN BRIDES LYNNE GRAHAM

October 2008
ROYAL BRIDES LUCY MONROE

November 2008
PASSIONATE BRIDES PENNY JORDAN

Helen Bianchin was born in New Zealand and travelled to Australia before marrying her Italian-born husband. After three years they moved, returned to New Zealand with their daughter, had two sons, then resettled in Australia. Encouraged by friends to recount anecdotes of her years as a tobacco sharefarmer's wife living in an Italian community, Helen began setting words on paper and her first novel was published in 1975. An animal lover, she says her terrier and Persian cat regard her study as as much theirs as hers.

Bride, Bought and Paid For by **Helen Bianchin** is a new **Modern**™ romance available in October 2009.

With sincere thanks to
Samantha Bell

CHAPTER ONE

NIC LEANDROS eased the powerful Lexus down into the underground parking area beneath a luxurious apartment building located in Sydney's suburban Double Bay, slid into a reserved bay and cut the engine.

His cellphone rang, and he quickly checked the caller ID, uttered a husky oath, and let the call go to MessageBank.

Sabine...*again*. How many times had she called today? Four...five? The woman was becoming obsessive, he admitted with a wry grimace. He hadn't expected an easy end to the relationship. But how long would it take for Sabine to understand *no* meant precisely that?

It had been months since he'd cut the ties, politely refusing her veiled invitations until her protestations reached desperation point, whereupon he refused to take any of her calls. For the past several weeks she'd virtually stalked him, resorting to SMS text messaging several times a day and turning up wherever he happened to be...in his favoured Melbourne restaurants, at two parties and a fundraiser.

He'd issued a warning, followed it with legal action. Yet Sabine still persisted.

Nic crossed to the bank of lifts. He had no need to check the apartment number or the floor on which it was situated, for it was one of several owned by the Leandros Corporation and occupied until very recently by his young half-brother.

Sixteen years his junior, Vasili had been a much-loved addition to the Leandros family twenty-one years ago. To his father Paul, a delight, and the apple of Nicos' adored stepmother Stacey's eye.

Nic reflected on the affection they'd shared, despite the gap in their ages. Vasili's upbringing had followed an identical path to his own...strict and loving. How else could it be beneath Stacey's guiding hand?

Yet Vasili had developed a recklessness Nic had never aspired to. He'd sailed through scholastic studies, gained a degree in business management, and entered the Leandros Corporation at the bottom of the corporate ladder...as Nic had, succeeding without any seeming effort.

Vasili had remained in Sydney acquiring corporate skills, while Nic was based in the Melbourne head office, in between extensive travelling between America and Europe.

Yet their bond had remained a close one, despite the vagaries of distance.

Good-looking, fun, Vasili had had a love of life, girls, and fast cars...in that order.

Tragically, it had been the fast car—a Lamborghini—that caused Vasili's death little more than two weeks ago.

Nic had been aware of the numerous girls who sought Vasili's company, his bed, and his share of the Leandros fortune. Although Tina Matheson had been the first girl Vasili had invited to move in with him.

What Nic hadn't known was news of Tina's pregnancy. Stacey had been Vasili's only confidante in that piece of information, the day before his untimely death.

There had been no mention of it...hell, no visible sign of it as the slender auburn-haired girl had stood at Vasili's grave-side ten days ago.

Among the grief-stricken, Tina had stood apart. Cool, controlled, with a fragility he'd instinctively felt the need to ease.

Yet he'd been polite on introduction, distant as befitted the solemnity of the occasion, and had stood in silence as Stacey had issued Tina with an invitation to join the family in a private wake.

Tina's refusal had surprised him. Given the circumstances, he'd thought she'd use any advantage to further her relationship with the Leandros family.

If he was honest, he'd have admitted he wanted to see her again in less sombre surroundings, for there was some indefinable quality about her that intrigued him.

Her stance, the way she held herself aloof. The classical, fine-boned features, cream-textured skin. Eyes the colour and brilliance of emeralds, deep, unfathomable.

Untouchable, he'd reminded himself.

His half-brother's woman. The mother of Vasili's unborn child.

The existence of a Leandros grandchild had provided an element of hope for Paul and Stacey Leandros. The child of their child. A child who would share Vasili's inheritance, and take its rightful place in the Leandros family.

Both Paul and Stacey had assumed Tina would welcome their support, their help. Dammit, their unconditional affection and love.

Except Tina had politely refused Stacey's, then Paul's advances. Something that merely accelerated Stacey's grief to an inconsolable level.

Now it was Nic's turn to attempt to sway Tina's decision. *At any cost*, Paul had determined.

Money. Sufficient of it could buy most anything, anyone, Nic decided with wry cynicism as he passed through security and rode the lift to the penthouse level. Besides which, he was a shrewd judge of character, a lauded strategist…and he had a few contingency plans.

It was simply a matter of determining the one most likely to succeed, and putting it into action.

Seconds later he crossed the marble-tiled floor to a set of ornate double doors.

Nic pressed the call button, then held it down when no one answered.

Nic wondered at Vasili's fascination with the woman carrying his child, for at twenty-seven Tina was almost six years Vasili's senior, and the only child of a widowed mother whose remarriage five years ago had resulted in a move to Noosa on Queensland's Sunshine Coast.

Tina had a record of average scholastic achievements, a love of sport, life. A flair for fashion had led to a managerial position in an up-market Double Bay boutique owned by her mother. A collection of friends, but no long-term boyfriend.

Dammit, why didn't she answer?

Impatience creased his features as he withdrew his cellphone, hit auto-dial, and queried Paul as to when the apartment had last been checked.

His father's answer brought forth a frown. The morning following Vasili's death.

Two weeks ago?

'Given the current situation,' Paul relayed, 'Stacey refuses to interfere with Tina's live-in arrangement.' His voice sharpened. 'Give me a few minutes and I'll call you back.'

Nic didn't have to wait long for Paul to relay the building manager was on his way with a master-key.

The apartment offered stunning views over the bay, but Nic took little notice of the sparkling nightscape beyond floor-to-ceiling glass as he thanked the manager and closed the door behind him. Instead he walked through the lounge, eyes alert for any signs of occupation, only to discover there was none.

Vasili's clothes hung in one of two large walk-in robes, and there was an assortment of male toiletries atop a double marble vanity unit in the master *en suite*.

The sight of them hurt, like a stake through the heart. Curiously more so than when he'd received the tragic call from Paul; more so even than the funeral. For now there was the visual attestation Vasili would never return to claim what was his…clothes, possessions, or the joy of holding his child.

A muscle bunched at the edge of his jaw as he

crossed to the second robe, only to discover on opening the door that it was empty.

Nic moved through the apartment, checking a second bedroom, a third...and discovered both were empty. There were no clothes in either wardrobe or chest of drawers. No sign of any feminine possessions in each adjoining *en suite*.

A husky oath escaped from his lips.

Tina Matheson had moved out.

It was obvious Paul hadn't considered keeping tabs on her. Dammit, *he'd* only given the need a fleeting thought, then dismissed it, sure she'd milk the situation, eagerly taking whatever Paul and Stacey offered. Hell, even demand more in a quest to set herself up for life by virtue of the child she carried.

He checked the dining-room, the kitchen, spotted a set of keys resting on the marble bench-top and reached for them, examining each before weighing the set in one hand. Then he slid them into his jacket pocket and made a phone call.

The name *Leandros* garnered respect. It also opened doors to data not easily available to the general public.

Within fifteen minutes Nic had the information he needed.

It didn't take long to drive the few kilometres to a small private hotel where Tina Matheson was registered as a guest.

Locating her room took mere minutes, and when there was no answer to his knock he repeated the action, harder, more forceful than before.

He was about to give it another try when the security chain was removed, the lock disengaged, the door opened sufficiently for him to glimpse a female clutching a large bath-towel around her slender form.

Nic registered damp auburn curls piled high on her head, pale features, and a pair of brilliant emerald-green eyes.

Eyes that hardened somewhat as they ascertained his identity.

'Go away.'

The door slammed shut, and he stifled a lurid oath.

'Do that again,' he warned with dangerous silkiness, 'and I'll disregard common courtesy.'

He heard the security chain engage, then the door opened a fraction. 'I could take that as a threat and call the police.'

'Go ahead.'

'Don't tempt me.'

'Aren't you going to ask me in?'

'Not if I can help it.'

'We can have a conversation now,' Nic offered with deceptive mildness, 'in relative privacy. Or,' he paused slightly, 'I'll arrive at your place of business tomorrow and hold it there.'

There was a perceptible silence, then Nic heard the locks disengage, and the door swung open.

She was more petite than he recalled, but then she was barefoot. The bath-towel had been discarded in favour of a towelling robe.

She looked tired, and there were dark smudges beneath her eyes. The result of grief, lack of sleep...or both?

'Another Leandros emissary?' Tina took in the tall,

broad male frame clothed in superb tailoring, forced herself to meet and hold those dark, almost black eyes…and felt all her protective self-defence instincts rise to the fore.

'We have been introduced.'

The voice held a faint American-inflected drawl, and she suppressed a shiver of unease. Nic and Vasili Leandros might share the same father, but as men they were as chalk to cheese.

Whereas Vasili had borne an air of insouciant youth, Nic Leandros possessed an indefinable quality that meshed ruthlessness and power…and combined it with a sexual chemistry no woman could successfully ignore.

Raging hormones had to be the reason why she felt vaguely off balance. It couldn't be the man unsettling her.

'You want to conduct this conversation on the doorstep?'

Oh, Lord. She'd just emerged from the shower. 'You'll have to wait while I get dressed.' And she shut the door in his face.

It took only minutes to step into underwear, jeans, add bra and tee shirt. She didn't bother with her hair. As for make-up…forget it.

He was there when she pulled back the front door, his tall frame seeming even more threatening than before.

Men of Nic Leandros' ilk weren't used to having doors shut in their faces, she perceived with a certain wry humour as she silently indicated he could enter.

'Thank you.' His voice was dry, and held a degree of impatience as he followed her into the suite.

Tina turned to face him, aware of the need to take control.

'Let's get this over with, shall we?'

One eyebrow rose, and his gaze remained steady. 'Dispense with polite conversation?'

She lifted a hand and smoothed back a wayward fall of hair, only to silently damn the visible indication her nerves were twisting every which way but loose.

'Why pretend civility when we have opposing agendas?' Tina queried, and saw those dark eyes harden fractionally.

'Can you blame Stacey and my father for wanting to share a part of their grandson or granddaughter's life?' he queried quietly.

'Do you think I don't know where this is leading?'

'Enlighten me.'

'Let's see.' She tilted her head and began listing probable possibilities. 'What comes next? Any minute soon you'll present several attractive reasons why I should agree to your parents' desire to assign the Leandros name to Vasili's child.' She paused and drew in a deep breath.

Nic Leandros dominated the room, his presence a compelling entity that disturbed her more than she was prepared to admit.

'If I agree, the heat will be on for it to be raised and educated according to Leandros tradition.'

'And that's a problem…*because*?'

He didn't get it. 'I'll lose control.'

'Any decisions made will, of course, be reached by mutual agreement.'

'Oh, please.' Tina raked his features with evident cynicism. 'Give me a break.' Her gaze speared his. 'How long will it take your parents to lodge an *unfit parent* complaint after the birth?' She closed her eyes, then opened them. 'Deny that's the master plan.'

A muscle tensed at the edge of his jaw. 'I doubt anything of the sort has entered Stacey's mind.'

'But it will, eventually.'

Her fierceness and her fragility were a contradiction in terms, something he found intriguing.

'When I return to work and put the babe into a day-care nursery?' She felt as if she were on a runaway train. 'Employ sitters on the rare occasion I feel the need to socialise?'

'It's my parents' intention to provide handsomely for the child's welfare.' He waited a beat. 'The ball is in your court. Name your terms.'

'And they'll be met?' She lifted a hand and ran it wearily over her hair. 'Thanks, but no, thanks.'

He'd tabled each stumbling block and had a strategy for every one of them. It was just a matter of time... 'Perhaps you'd care to elaborate why?'

'I don't see how a one-night stand qualifies the right for the child to assume its deceased father's name.' If she'd hoped to shock, she gained no visible reaction from his expression. 'Especially when I had no intention of making it my own.'

Nic's eyes became hooded. 'Vasili meant nothing to you?'

Tina took her time with the question. 'We played

the boyfriend/girlfriend game.' She paused fractionally. 'It was…convenient. For each of us.' She had no obligation to relay *why*.

'The age difference didn't bother you?'

Her chin tilted a little and her eyes acquired a dangerous gleam. 'Are you implying Vasili was my *toy boy*? We were *friends*.'

'Yet you moved in with him.'

Explanations tended to become complicated. Yet Nic Leandros was entitled. How else would her decision make any sense?

'I sold my apartment,' Tina defended. 'I was in negotiations to buy another. Vasili suggested I move in with him instead of securing a hotel room or renting short-term.' It had seemed so logical at the time, and she'd insisted on contributing towards food and utilities.

'And shared his bed,' Nic accorded in a hateful drawl.

Her chin tilted a little, and her eyes blazed green fire. 'Once.'

Dammit, that was all it took. *Once.* A little too much champagne, a friendly kiss that had become more, and somehow they'd ended up in the same bed.

She dimly remembered voicing a half-hearted protest as instinctive wisdom had fought against the persuasiveness of Vasili's mouth, his hands. Then it had been too late. The sex had been less than noteworthy. Not that she'd had much experience to compare it with.

All the pent-up emotion of the past few weeks caught up with her. 'I should disillusion your mother…sorry, stepmother?' she offered the correction. 'Your father? Paint a false picture of a relationship that was only *friendship*?' She was on a roll, unable to stop. 'Enlighten them that the conception of their coveted grandchild was a mistake? Dammit,' she said forcefully, 'a meaningless, *forgettable* mistake.' She wanted to hit something, throw something. Anything to rid the impossible anger that burned within…at herself, for being so senseless.

'Obviously there were no precautions taken.'

Tina heard the words, and only just refrained from hitting the man who uttered them. *'Obviously.'*

'Yet you've taken no steps to abort the foetus.'

She drew in a sharp breath and pressed a protective hand to her waist. 'No.'

Nic's eyes narrowed. 'Would you have, if my parents had been unaware of the pregnancy?'

Tina didn't hesitate. 'No.'

The insistent ring of a cellphone sounded loud in the silence of the room, and Tina watched as he withdrew the unit, checked the caller ID, and registered his irritation as he thrust the cellphone back into his jacket pocket.

'Have you eaten?'

Her eyes widened. 'Excuse me?'

'Dinner.' His voice held an element of impatience.

He was talking of *food*? 'I don't see that's a relevant question.'

'It's relevant if you haven't eaten.'

'Why?'

'I'm suggesting we share a meal.'

'Again…*why*?'

She irritated and fascinated him at the same time. She was also the first woman in a long time to refuse his invitation.

'Go change. I'll make a reservation.'

Tina closed her eyes, then opened them and shot him a fierce glare. 'Are you usually this dictatorial?'

He extracted his cellphone, and hit a speed-dial button. 'I'm known to get what I want.'

'Really?' She was singularly unimpressed. And remained so at the ease with which he secured a table.

Nic regarded her steadily. 'You want to argue with me?'

'Heaven forbid any female would dare,' Tina offered facetiously, and caught a glimpse of something that was almost humour in those dark eyes.

'You being an exception?'

'Count on it.' She glared at him, then she crossed to the door. 'I want you to leave.'

His expression remained unchanged, except there was a sense of innate power, a strength of will, evident beneath the surface.

Her gaze arrowed in on his, and didn't waver. She could feel her spine stiffen...literally. 'I don't want to share a meal with you.'

'Same destination,' Nic stated. 'Separate cars.'

'That's a persuasive ploy?'

'A compromise. It's almost seven, neither of us have eaten, and we've yet to reach a satisfactory resolution.'

'*My* decision is made.'

'One that concerns *you*. However, there's a child's

life at stake. Your child.' He paused slightly. 'But indisputably also my brother's child.'

She *was* hungry. In the past few days she'd developed a heightened sensitivity to the smell of food. The thought of ordering a meal of her choice that she didn't need to prepare or cook was enticing. Besides, it was clear Nic Leandros wouldn't let up any time soon.

'Go wait outside while I change.'

'And have you lock the door behind me?' His expression held wry cynicism. 'Collect what clothes you need and get dressed in the *en suite*.'

She wanted to kill him...or at best do him physical harm. Yet it was no contest. A venue they drove to in separate cars was preferable to the intimacy of a hotel suite.

At least she'd be free to walk out of a restaurant undeterred. Whereas *here* it would be a different matter entirely. And, while his presence was unlikely to pose a threat, she had the distinct feeling he'd play any game by his own rules.

'There's a problem?'

Tina sent him a scathing glare. 'I'm deciding what method I should use to render you physical harm.'

His mouth quirked in silent amusement, and she bit back an attempt at childish retaliation as she crossed to the storage unit.

With quick, economical movements she collected black silk evening trousers, an emerald green silk camisole, matching jacket, and headed for the *en suite*.

A few minutes, minimum make-up, a vigorous

brush through her hair, and she was done. When she emerged it took only seconds to step into stiletto heels, then transfer money and keys into an evening purse.

Tina was conscious of his appraisal, and deliberately arched an eyebrow. 'Shall we leave?'

They rode the lift down to the basement car park, and within minutes Tina followed Nic's black Lexus to the trendy heart of Double Bay, parked, then accompanied him into a small, intimate restaurant filled with patrons.

The *maître d'* greeted Nic with the obsequious fervour reserved for a favoured patron, personally escorted them to a table, saw them seated and summoned the drink steward.

Prestigious, known for its fine cuisine, and expensive, Tina acknowledged as she cast the room a casual glance.

The service was excellent, and she requested mineral water, chose a starter as a main meal, and settled back in her chair.

The steward brought their drinks, served them with deferential good humour, then retreated.

'You eat here often.' It was a statement, not a query, and Nic subjected her to a solemn appraisal.

'Whenever I'm in Sydney.'

Uh-huh. The Leandros corporation had its main base in Melbourne. Vasili's parents resided there. So did Nic, Vasili had relayed...in between business trips to New York, London, Athens and Rome.

'I imagine you'll acquaint your parents with my decision?'

He fingered the stem of his wine goblet with deliberate distraction. 'When we're done with it.'

She held his gaze. 'There is no *when*.'

'What if I were to suggest an alternative option?' Nic paused, then added, 'Or two.'

She took a sip of icy liquid. 'There are none.'

'Adoption,' he presented with deceptive mildness. 'For a mutually agreed sum.'

Tina froze, temporarily unable to utter so much as a word for several long seconds before anger ignited and threatened to explode. 'You have to be joking.'

'One million dollars.'

She opened her mouth, then closed it again as she found her voice. 'Go to hell,' she managed in a fierce undertone as she collected her evening purse and stood to her feet.

'Two million.'

Tina registered the calmness apparent in his voice, and barely controlled the urge to throw something at him.

'Three.'

Incredulity was uppermost. She turned, only to come to a halt as her arm was caught in a firm grasp. She directed him a vehement glare that would have felled a lesser man. 'Let me go!'

His eyes held hers, their expression impossible to read. 'Sit down. Please,' he added with chilling softness. 'There are other options.'

'I don't see how you can top it,' Tina ventured savagely.

'Marriage.' He paused fractionally. 'To me.'

For a few heart-stopping seconds she remained

transfixed with shock. It took her time to find her voice. 'Are you *insane*?'

She picked up the glass and tossed the contents at him in a wildly spontaneous action, watching as he dodged the icy mineral water, and saw it hit his shoulder and cascade down his jacket, his shirt.

In the next instant the glass slipped from her fingers, hit the table, and slid onto the tiled floor to splinter into countless shards.

Tina was vaguely aware of the steward's presence, his concern, the removal of glass and mopping up operation. She even recalled offering an apology.

And heard Nic's drawling explanation. 'It's not often a man receives such an unusual reaction to his marriage proposal.'

She was vaguely aware of the steward's effusive congratulations, and the news took wing and spread.

Somehow she was no longer standing, but seated opposite the arrogant, ruthless man who had, she strongly suspected, stage-managed precisely this scenario.

'Retract it, and do it *now*,' Tina said in a fierce undertone.

'A marriage mutually convenient to both of us,' Nic continued silkily. 'It will give Vasili's child legitimacy and a legal place within the Leandros hierarchy.'

Her voice dripped ice. 'Haven't you forgotten something?'

A cameraman appeared out of nowhere and a camera flash temporarily blinded her.

'I won't be a part of it.'

'No?' Nic ventured silkily. 'Be warned, I can be your friend...or your worst nightmare.'

CHAPTER TWO

SUDDENLY it all fell into place, and Tina hated him. Truly *hated* him.

'This is the ultimate manipulative manoeuvre, isn't it?'

Everything about the evening up to this point had been a farce. The child she carried was of prime importance. The *only* importance.

'A process of elimination.' His drawled admission caused the breath to catch in her throat.

'You thought I was a money-grubbing bitch with an eye to the main chance?' Anger tore at her control when he didn't answer. 'You bastard.' The accusation whispered silkily from her lips.

His expression didn't change, nor did his gaze waver from her own. 'It was a possibility I had to consider.'

Tina attempted a deep calming breath, and cursed softly when it had no effect whatsoever. 'Should I surmise you've also run a routine check?'

She had nothing to hide, except one incident on record. He couldn't have delved that far, surely?

'Private schooling, love of sport, father killed in an accident when you were seventeen.' He paused for a few seconds. 'Assaulted a year later by an intruder during a home invasion.'

Tina felt the colour leach from her face as she

fought to control the vivid image obliterating her vision. In an instant she was back there in her bedroom, home alone in the apartment she'd shared with her mother, waking to an unusual sound close by, scared out of her wits in the knowledge someone was in her room.

The guttural voice, the stale smell of unwashed clothing…one hard hand clamped over her mouth while the other tossed aside bedcovers and ripped the thin nightshirt from her body. She'd fought like a demon, lashing out with her feet, her hands…

Nine years had passed since that frightening night. She'd had therapy, learnt coping mechanisms and acquired combat skills.

Her determination to be a survivor not a victim had left her with an almost obsessive need for security measures, a mistrust of men…and a legacy of infrequent nightmares.

'Assaulted, but not raped,' Tina managed quietly. Although it had come close. Too close. He'd hurt her, broken her arm, fractured three of her ribs.

'You were hospitalised.'

So he'd gained access to the medical report.

'Did you also unearth a speeding ticket, a few parking violations?' She was like a speeding train, unable to stop. 'Run a check my taxes are paid to date?'

His steady gaze was unnerving as the silence stretched between them.

'I'm suggesting a marriage in name only,' Nic offered in a faintly accented drawl.

'A sham? Separate rooms, separate lives?'

'A mutually convenient partnership,' he elaborated. 'A shared social existence.'

'Isn't that taking familial duty and devotion just a little too far?'

'Vasili would want his child to be well cared for...to legitimately bear the Leandros name. I can at least do that for him.'

'Regardless of *my* wishes?'

'You'll be more than adequately compensated. Houses at home and abroad, frequent travel, jewellery, an extremely generous allowance.'

'For which I should be duly grateful?' If looks could kill, he'd fall dead on the spot. 'And *you*?' Tina demanded. 'What would you get out of such a marriage?'

'A wife, a legitimate Leandros heir, a social partner.' He waited a beat. 'And one very persistent woman out of my life.'

'I very much doubt you need protection from anyone. Especially a woman!'

Tina was so impossibly angry she didn't pause to think. 'I imagine your wife would be expected to turn a blind eye to a mistress discreetly set up in an apartment somewhere?' She leaned forward and sharpened a mythical dart, just for the hell of it. 'Or does your taste run to same-sex lovers?'

She glimpsed something hard in the depths of those dark eyes, then it was gone.

'Are you done?'

Tina paid no heed to the dangerous silkiness in his voice. 'What about my needs?'

His eyes locked with hers, and she couldn't look away. 'All you have to do is ask.'

She swung her hand towards his face. Except it didn't connect.

Instead he used her momentum to pull her into his arms and silenced her by covering her mouth with his own in a kiss that tore her composure to shreds.

Nothing she'd ever experienced came close to the frankly sensual plundering he subjected her to. It was an invasion of the senses, a flagrant, devastating attempt to suppress her will.

When he released her she could barely stand, and she was hardly aware of the notes he tossed onto the table, or that he followed as she turned and walked from the restaurant.

It was impossible to ignore him, for he was *there* as she unlocked her Volkswagen...a funky bright yellow sedan, with a sunroof, that she'd fallen in love with on sight.

'Tomorrow,' Nic inclined as she slid in behind the wheel.

'Go to hell.' Fierce, angry, *foolish* words, she perceived as she fired the engine and sent the car towards the exit at a speed in excess of the marked restriction.

Nic Leandros was the most impossible man she'd ever met. If she never saw him again, it would be too soon.

A sharp horn-blast startled her, and she swore beneath her breath at her failure to notice the traffic light had changed from red to green.

Focus, Tina silently berated as she sent the car forward.

In a determined bid, she attempted to dismiss Nic Leandros from her mind.

Except it didn't work. She could still feel the pressure of his mouth on her own, the taste of him. Dammit, the sensual sweep of his tongue.

Oh, for heaven's sake! *Get over it.*

Nic Leandros was merely exerting male dominance in a spontaneous attempt to still her angry tirade.

Tina slept badly, and woke feeling as if she'd run a marathon. The beginnings of a headache threatened an emergence, and her stomach didn't feel as if it belonged to her at all.

Sweet tea and dry toast...or was that merely an old wives' tale?

The temptation to bury her head beneath the pillow and tell the world to go away was uppermost. Except it wasn't going to happen.

There was work...and some time during the day she had to face Nic Leandros. The hope *he* might go away was as unlikely to be realised as a snowfall in summer.

What time was it? She checked the digital clock and groaned. Another hour before room service would deliver breakfast.

Okay, so she could do the sweet tea, and there was probably a snack-pack of dry biscuits in the complimentary mini-bar. The day's newspaper should already be outside her door...

If her stomach decided to revolt, better sooner than later, she determined a trifle grimly.

Ten minutes later she cast the newspaper aside and took a leisurely shower, then dressed; she ate a healthy breakfast, tidied the suite, then she cast a glance at the time.

It was early, yet the need to keep occupied prompted the thought of work. Better to be at the boutique than sit twiddling her thumbs in a hotel room.

She would dust the fittings, vacuum, then check the floor stock before opening up at the usual time.

Early mornings tended to be slow, with few patrons making an appearance much before ten, when Lily reported in for the day.

With that in mind she collected her laptop, caught up her bag and went down to collect her car.

Double Bay was only a matter of kilometres distant, and she parked at the rear of the building, activated the car alarm, then crossed to the entrance out front.

Tina took great pride in the boutique with its elegant salon, beyond which lay a small back room where extra stock was stored, as well as the usual utilities.

There was a need to be in familiar surroundings, she acknowledged as she crossed the salon. To *think* and rationalise Nic Leandros' proposition. She'd be damned if she'd term it a *proposal*.

She hadn't thought of children; she definitely hadn't considered marriage.

It was the reason she socialised within the safe company of a few selected and trusted friends. Vasili used to tease that while *he* protected her from male predators, *she* protected him from female fortune hunters. A mutually satisfactory relationship.

At least it had been until that fateful night when a friendly kiss had led to more. A tenderly concerned

Vasili who had suggested it was time she made the final leap to sexual intimacy with a friend for whom she held affection and trust. Add the enhancement of wine...and it had seemed so *logical* at the time.

Ironic that the act should result in pregnancy. Yet she wanted this child...an unexpected gift in living memory of a fun and caring young man.

Was she right in keeping the child solely *hers*? If Vasili were alive, they'd share parenting and the child would assume the Leandros name.

So why did she baulk at Nic Leandros' proposition?

Because Vasili's half-brother was an unknown quantity. Older, ruthless...*dangerous*.

Yet she had to concede there were advantages. The child would have a father figure, a legal right to its heritage, grandparents, *family*. A stable, loving environment in which to grow.

On a personal level she'd have a steady male companion whom she could trust not to hit on her at the end of an evening.

Another plus was the knowledge Nic travelled extensively on business. A lot of the time he wouldn't be in the same city, the same country.

The vacuum hummed as she ran it over carpet and marble tiles, then she carefully smoothed a dusting cloth over shelving, polished the mirrors before standing back to admire her handiwork.

The salon held the restrained elegance of an upmarket boutique, its design and fittings...so exactly right for the Double Bay location renowned for its fashionistas, the wealthy women who could indulge their expensive tastes in imported and Australian designer apparel.

Tina possessed a natural love of clothes, and had done so for as long as she could remember, mix and matching outfits as she'd dressed her dolls…Barbie, of course, in each of her guises. As a teenager, she'd helped out in her mother's boutique, proving she had a keen eye for fashion, accessories, and an instinctual flair for putting things together.

There was no hesitation in which field she'd make her career, and she'd learnt the retail clothing trade from the floor up…initially through her mother's expert tutelage, then in one of Sydney's large city stores for three years before returning to co-manage her mother's Double Bay boutique.

Until five years ago when Claire had met and married Felipe, the second love of her life, shifted base to Noosa, leased her apartment and left Tina in control.

The Double Bay social set employed a reasonably routine shopping pattern, meeting around nine-thirty for coffee, electing to begin browsing the various boutiques around ten-thirty, followed by a long lunch at one of the trendy restaurants, before doing the air-kiss thing and departing for homes cleaned by professionals.

Lily arrived promptly at ten, almost bursting into the boutique, modifying her excitement as Tina finished dealing with a patron who'd bought the entire outfit displayed in the front window…including shoes and handbag.

A folded newspaper was placed onto the glass-topped island counter.

'Have you *seen* this?' Lily demanded, *sotto voce*, following it with an irrepressible grin.

Tina glanced at the newsprint and felt the breath catch in her throat. Strategically placed centre page was a reasonably sized photograph taken the previous night at the restaurant, together with a bold caption speculating a date for Nic Leandros' forthcoming marriage to Tina Matheson.

'How come you kept this to yourself?' Lily teased. *'Give.'*

The truth was a credibility stretch…even for a friend. 'It represents a gross misinterpretation by the media.' Initiated by a determined manipulative man, Tina added silently, and met Lily's speculative gaze.

'That's all you're going to say?'

'For now.'

The electronic door buzzer provided a timely interruption, and she turned to discover the courier delivery guy with a packing box.

'Where do you want this?'

Three patrons entered the boutique, one serious buyer, Tina judged, and two browsers idly riffling through the racks.

With a quick word she excused herself and crossed to the courier's side. 'Out back.' She silently signalled Lily to take over while she checked the invoice.

Minutes later the courier clipped the signed invoice onto his clipboard and departed, leaving Tina to cross to the two women checking out a garment, whereupon she offered assistance, complimenting the designer, the fabric and style.

Another sale, followed soon after by another, adding to a productive morning, Tina reflected as she took a moment to complete the unpacking of new stock.

'Oh, my.'

The hushed tone in Lily's voice had Tina shooting a glance in her direction. 'As in?'

'Serious eye candy about to walk through the door.'

Male, Tina deduced. An attractive husband intent on buying his wife an expensive gift? She didn't bother glancing up. 'Go for it.'

'I wish.'

Lily's reverence brought forth a slight smile. Lily was equally *friend* as valued employee, and considered herself to be a connoisseur of men.

'However, he's *yours*.'

Tina's gaze shifted to the salon entrance and the breath caught in her throat in recognition of the man engaging Lily in conversation.

Nic Leandros…*here*?

If he thought she'd walk over to him and play *pretend* in Lily's presence, he could think again.

With outward calm Tina extracted the last garment from the box, deftly inserted a clothes hanger and transferred it onto a rack so it could air for a while. After lunch she'd freshen today's delivery with the steam-iron before transferring the garments onto display racks in the salon.

She was acutely aware of the muted background music whispering through strategically placed speakers, creating a relaxed ambience that was reflected in the elegant combination of delicately blended cream, wheat and beige utilised in the furnishings. A luxurious setting to display the exclusive range of designer garments for which the boutique was known.

'Tina.'

It was a voice she'd recognise anywhere. It was also one she didn't want to hear. Yet good manners forced her to school her features into a polite mask as she turned to face Nic Leandros.

Her gaze was silently challenging. 'Is there something I can help you with?' Cool...she could do *cool*, despite the fact her nervous system was in direct conflict. It was insane the way one glance at that well-shaped, sensual mouth brought a vivid recall of how it had felt possessing her own.

'Lunch,' Nic informed her with deceptive calm. 'Your assistant is happy to take charge for an hour.'

He really was the limit! 'I already have plans.' She didn't, but he wasn't to know that.

'Change them.'

'Why should I do that?'

'We can discuss arrangements here,' he informed steadily. 'Or over lunch. Choose.'

The electronic door buzzer sounded, signalling the arrival of a client.

'This is neither the time nor the place,' Tina protested quietly, silently hating him for placing her in such an invidious position. She made an instant decision. 'Give me five minutes.'

She made it in four, spoke briefly to Lily, preceded him from the boutique, and waited until they reached the pavement before demanding, 'What do you want?'

She kept her voice low, but her pent-up anger was an audible force.

'To continue the discussion you walked out on last night.'

His drawled tone held a steely quality she chose to ignore. 'You're giving me a choice?'

There were a few trendy cafés and restaurants dotting the street, and Nic indicated one close by.

She wanted to turn and retrace her steps, and almost did. Except he'd probably follow.

Within seconds he caught a waiter's attention, sought a table, and waited until they were seated before venturing, 'It's possible the media will make contact with you at some stage this afternoon.'

Tina was unable to prevent a cynical element tinging her voice. 'For this I need your help?'

Nic's gaze remained steady. 'Regarding my statement announcing our imminent marriage.'

A waitress crossed to their table and stood with pen and pad poised as Nic placed an order for two.

'I may not *want* the chicken Caesar salad,' Tina stated, and fixed Nic a deliberate glare before turning towards the waitress. 'Don't you just hate it when a man thinks he knows a woman's mind?' A double-edged query, if ever there was one.

The waitress, having undoubtedly witnessed the behaviour of numerous patrons during her employment, merely flicked Tina a glance that clearly queried Tina's sanity.

What woman wouldn't give her eye-teeth to have a man of Nic Leandros' ilk appear so...in control?

Damn. She liked Caesar salad. 'Make mine spinach

and fetta tortellini with the mushroom and bacon sauce.'

Tina met Nic's hooded gaze. 'We can argue this back and forth for ever.' She wanted to hit him...or, failing that, go several rounds in verbal battle. 'Give me one good reason why I should agree to marry you, aside from being pregnant with Vasili's child.'

He regarded her thoughtfully. 'Protection.' He could promise her that. 'Loyalty. Trust,' he endorsed quietly.

Sans love or fidelity.

Get real, a silent voice taunted. Neither love nor fidelity enter the equation. Nor do you want them to. So why even go there?

'And the child? You intend claiming it as your own?'

Nic's eyes narrowed. 'Foster the illusion I'm the child's biological father?'

Her chin tilted a little. 'Yes.'

'I will delight in my wife's pregnancy, and initiate adoption proceedings immediately following the birth.'

Ensuring the legalities were neatly taken care of.

'You avoided answering the question.'

'The child will be born a legitimate Leandros, with two parents.' His eyes speared hers. 'No one, apart from Paul and Stacey, need know personal details.'

'And Claire.' Dear heaven, she had yet to enlighten her mother of the pregnancy. She eyeballed the man seated opposite. 'I won't keep the truth from her.'

'I wasn't going to suggest you do.'

There were a few other conditions she needed to

voice, and she paused as the waitress presented their meals.

'Claire's boutique is my responsibility,' Tina insisted as soon as the waitress was out of earshot. 'Don't expect me to give up work and assume a social butterfly persona.'

'No objection, with one proviso.' Dark eyes lanced her own. 'Unless the medics advise otherwise.'

She wanted to argue, and her eyes darkened to a deep emerald-green. Something that fascinated him. She was fire and ice, and a complex mix of strength and vulnerability.

'I want a prenuptial agreement protecting my interests.'

That was his criterion, surely? 'Anything else?'

'What if either one of us chose to file for divorce?'

'I doubt the possibility will occur.'

'But if it does?' Tina persisted, and met his hard, level look.

'Be aware I'd fight you in court to assume full custody of the child.'

'You'd never get it,' she said with certainty. 'The courts generally favour the mother, especially when the male parent is not even the child's biological father.'

One eyebrow arched in silent cynicism. 'You doubt my ability to prove a case against you?'

A chill shiver feathered its way down her spine. Nic Leandros had both wealth and power in his favour. Sufficient of both to employ the finest legal brains in the country.

'No.' She paused imperceptibly. 'But don't underestimate my determination to oppose you.'

Brave words from a brave woman. He selected his cutlery and indicated she should do the same. 'Let's eat, shall we?'

The tortellini looked and smelt delicious, but Tina's appetite had gone on strike. Instead, she cast an envious glance at the crisp cos lettuce in Nic's bowl, the croutons and sliced chicken, the delicate sauce...and caught the faintly humorous twist at the edge of his mouth.

Without a word he signalled the waitress, ordered another chicken Caesar salad, and met Tina's glare with equanimity.

'What do you think you're doing?'

'Ensuring you have what you'd prefer to eat.'

Her glare intensified. 'And you know this *because*?'

One eyebrow rose. 'Can I look forward to a battlefield with every meal we share?'

'Count on it if you intend overriding every choice I make!'

Nevertheless the Caesar salad, when it arrived, was too tempting to resist, and she ate in silence while steadfastly ignoring the man seated opposite.

'No polite conversation?'

Tina offered him a level glance. 'I was trying to avoid indigestion.'

His soft laughter surprised her, and her eyes widened fractionally as she caught a gleam of humour in those dark eyes.

'Our relationship will be an interesting one.'

His drawled observation attacked her equilibrium,

and she fought to retain it. 'A qualification…I've yet to agree.'

'But you will.'

'Why so sure?'

'Because in your heart you know Vasili would see our liaison as an ideal solution.'

It didn't help Nic Leandros was right. 'Together with your assurance the alternative isn't something I'd want to contemplate?'

He took his time. 'Precisely.'

Tina wanted to throw something at him, and almost did. 'I don't like threats.'

'Believe it's a statement of fact.'

The icy certainty in his voice was a vivid reminder she didn't stand a chance against the wealth and influence of the Leandros family.

This…*marriage*, Tina qualified, was merely a business arrangement, with advantages for her, a child who surely *deserved* a stable upbringing…as opposed to a tug-of-war custody battle.

She didn't want to give in. Especially to this man, whose powerful presence disturbed her more than she was prepared to admit.

Yet a marriage based on mutual convenience among the wealthy wasn't so unusual. It forged a legal partnership, built wealth and provided heirs. A beneficial arrangement, legally documented and containing clearly defined boundaries.

'I want everything in writing.' She rose to her feet and sent him a long direct look. 'Subject to my legal advisor's perusal and approval.'

Nic followed her actions, extracted notes from his

wallet and tossed them on the table. 'The document will be delivered to you by courier late this afternoon. A copy of which will be despatched to your lawyer.' He waited a beat. 'Whose name is?'

Tina gave it, and battled the apprehension curling deep inside.

An instinctive omen? Don't be ridiculous, she silently derided as she made her way out of the restaurant. This isn't personal…it's business.

She paused as she reached the pavement. 'We'll be in touch.' Then she turned and walked away from him without so much as a backwards glance.

Outward composure, when inwardly her nerves were threatened to shred into a tangled mess.

Lily could barely contain her curiosity as Tina re-entered the boutique. 'Details,' Lily begged without preamble.

Truth wasn't an option, so she went with ambiguity. 'We're still working them out.'

A call from her lawyer a few hours later insisting on a personal consultation at day's end didn't surprise her. Nor, as she sat opposite him, did his cautionary advice.

He agreed, however, that each of her concerns had been adequately dealt with from a business aspect.

Tina signed, her signature was duly witnessed, and she walked out into the cool evening air, aware she'd just sealed her fate.

An hour later her cellphone rang, and she discovered Nic Leandros on the line.

'I've arranged an intimate ceremony at the weekend

in my home, immediate family only.' He barely
paused. 'Any further media queries, refer them to me.'

Her heart leapt into her throat. 'So soon?'

'Why delay?'

She closed her eyes, then opened them again. *Because I'm not ready for this.* But then it was doubtful
she'd *ever* be ready.

CHAPTER THREE

THE following few days passed in a blur of activity as Tina dealt with everything that needed to be done.

First and foremost had been a lengthy call to her mother, together with a wedding invitation.

Work became a welcome distraction as she fielded media enquiries, perused and signed relevant paperwork, and applied considerable effort towards choosing something suitable to wear on *the day*.

A day that came around far too quickly for her peace of mind, and one that began with a leisurely shared breakfast with Claire and Felipe at their hotel. Followed at her mother's insistence by a pampering session, massage, lunch, facial, hair treatment...the works.

A thoughtful gesture, gifted with the intention of helping her relax and unwind, after which they returned to Claire and Felipe's hotel suite in order to change and drive to Nic's Rose Bay home.

Tina had chosen an ivory silk dress with a beautifully crafted bodice, spaghetti straps, whose skirt was a dream in layered chiffon. There was a stylish matching ivory silk jacket. Stiletto heels in matching ivory completed the outfit, and she added an emerald drop pendant and ear-studs.

A small intimate family wedding involved Stacey and Paul Leandros, Claire and Felipe, the celebrant, together with the bride and groom, and was held in the large study of Nic's elegant Rose Bay home.

A setting that added formality to the occasion as Tina stood at Nic's side.

The wide diamond-encrusted wedding ring felt strange on her finger, and she hid her surprise as Nic held out a gold band for her to slide onto his finger. Somehow it seemed an unexpected gesture, given the nature of their union.

So too was the brush of his lips to her cheek...until she registered the camera flash and realised both Stacey and Claire had taken photos.

Afterwards there was champagne, which she declined, and she sipped something light and innocuous as she stood beside the tall, immaculately suited man who was now her husband.

It was too late for second thoughts...and, heaven knew, she had plenty! Such as where was her sanity when she agreed to become Tina *Leandros*.

Already she was playing the *pretend* game. So too, she observed, was everyone else in the elegant lounge room.

Nic, because he'd achieved his objective. Stacey and Paul, for now the child of the son they'd had together would legitimately become part of the Leandros family. Claire, because she loved her daughter and wanted only for Tina to be in a caring relationship.

Claire, the eternal optimist, who undoubtedly held the hope *care* would develop into affection and become *love*.

As if that were going to happen!

'Shall we leave?' Nic suggested smoothly, and received murmurs of assent.

Dinner at an exclusive city restaurant where the façade would continue, Tina accorded. Although was it a façade? Claire and Stacey seemed to have struck up a friendship, and Felipe appeared at ease in Paul and Nic's company.

In hindsight it was a pleasant evening. The venue, the food were superb; so too was the service.

Nic had inherited his father's genes, for both men shared a similar height and breadth of shoulder. There was a camaraderie between them, an equality and evident respect.

Apparent, too, was the love Paul had for his wife. It was there in the way he smiled, the light touch of his hand, the gleaming depth in his eyes.

To an onlooker their tableau would appear a convivial gathering of three couples who were very good friends.

Which simply went to show appearances were deceptive, for who would guess the bride and groom were barely acquainted, or that until this evening each set of parents had never met?

It was late when they left the restaurant, parted with affection, and went their separate ways.

Nic unlocked the Lexus, saw Tina seated, then walked round to slide in behind the wheel. Within seconds he fired the engine and eased the car into the flow of traffic.

'Nothing to say?'

Tina cast his profile a measured look. In the semi-

darkness of the car's interior his facial features were
all angles and planes.

'I'm all talked out.'

'That bad?'

Bad didn't work for her, for the evening had been
superficially pleasant. Except she'd been all too aware
of the well-hidden undercurrents associated with the
marriage and its celebration.

'Everything was absolutely fabulous.' She transferred her attention to the scene beyond the windscreen, focusing on the well-lit street and the cars traversing it.

'Definitely overkill.'

Did his voice hold a tinge of humour, or was it just
her imagination?

The day began to catch up with her...the trepidation, doubts, together with several nights of insufficient sleep. It became almost impossible to keep her
eyes open, and after a few minutes she didn't even
try.

Tina recalled stirring, and settling into a more comfortable position...then nothing as she sank into deep,
dreamless slumber.

When she woke sunlight was edging through the
wooden shutters, and for a few seconds she had no
idea where she was. Then memory returned, and with
it the knowledge she was in a large bed in the suite
Nic had allocated her in an upstairs wing of his home.

The first shock was registering the time...the next,
becoming aware she'd been divested of her clothes,
with the exception of bra, briefs, tights and half-slip.

Dammit, he must have carried her indoors and put her to bed.

Great. So much for personal privacy.

Shower, dress, something to eat, then she'd be out the door and on her way to Double Bay…in less than an hour. Hopefully without encountering Nic Leandros.

She almost made it. Would have if she hadn't encountered Nic in the kitchen about to pour what was presumably his second coffee for the morning.

'Sleep well?'

No one had the right to look so darn good at this hour. Freshly shaven, hair groomed, dark trousers, blue shirt and dark blue tie, suit jacket loosely folded over the back of a chair: Nic projected an enviable aura of power.

Tina sent him a telling look. 'You should have woken me last night, instead of putting me to bed.'

'You don't believe I tried?'

'Not hard enough.'

She hadn't stirred once…as he'd lifted her from the car, carried her upstairs, nor when he'd laid her down onto the bed and carefully removed her shoes and outer clothes. Tiredness related to pregnancy?

He indicated the carafe. 'Coffee?'

The aroma teased her senses, taunted her with anticipation of how it would taste, and she shook her head. 'Can't have caffeine.'

His gaze narrowed fractionally as he took in her pale features, the dark smudges beneath her eyes.

'You'll find several blends of tea in the pantry.' He

swept a hand towards the refrigerator. 'Fix whatever you want to eat.'

'Don't have time.' Memo to self: unearth or buy an alarm clock.

His gaze sharpened. 'Make time.'

Tina rolled her eyes. 'I'll grab some fruit and yoghurt when I open the boutique.'

'Ensure you do.'

She offered a mock salute. 'Yessir.'

Sassy...definitely sassy, Nic decided.

He drained his coffee, caught up his suit jacket and shrugged into it, then collected his laptop.

'I'll be in Melbourne all day. Don't wait dinner.' He indicated a set of keys and two modems on the table. 'Yours. Security codes to the house, garage, gates.' His cellphone rang, and he checked caller ID and rejected the call. 'I employ staff to take care of the house and gardens.' He turned towards the door. 'Have a good day.'

Tina watched his departing form, drew in a deep breath and released it slowly.

Married one day, and flung abruptly into reality the next.

What did you expect?

Nothing, absolutely nothing.

A quick glance at the time spurred her into action, and five minutes later she slid into her car, eased it free of the driveway and took the street leading to the main arterial road.

Traffic at this hour was at a peak, and, although Double Bay was only two suburbs distant, it was a few minutes past nine when she unlocked the boutique.

Food was a priority, and hot sweet tea. The small bar fridge out back held a few tubs of yoghurt, a few apples and bananas, and Tina snacked in between setting up.

Lily arrived early, which was just as well, for the day became extremely busy.

Genuine interest for the clothes, or merely an opportunity to check out Nic Leandros' new wife?

Somehow Tina suspected it was the latter.

'Are you going to tell me?' Lily began when there was a brief lull. 'Or do I have to drag it out of you word by word?'

'The wedding?'

'Love the ring…definitely in the *ohmigod* range,' Lily accorded with an impish grin, then added sternly, 'I want every little detail.'

'Armani ensemble in ivory, killer heels.' Tina ticked each finger in turn. 'Celebrant, Nic's parents, mine. Followed by dinner in the city.'

'That's it?'

'Pretty much.'

'*And?*'

'There is no *"and"*.'

'Nic Leandros is one sexy-looking beast.'

In spades, Tina agreed silently, relieved at the sound of the electronic door buzzer.

'We're not done,' Lily warned *sotto voce* as she went forward to greet the two elegantly clad women who entered the salon.

Lunch was something she sent Lily out for, and

managed a ten-minute break in which to eat the chicken salad sandwich. Lily did likewise, foregoing her usual half-hour in order to help with the influx of customers.

Consequently by day's end all Tina wanted was a leisurely shower, dinner, followed by an early night.

'What *was* that?' Lily queried as Tina locked up and they walked to their respective cars. 'A day in the life of Nic Leandros' new bride?'

'Got it in one.'

'What's up, Tina?'

Lily's quiet sincerity brought a slight catch to her throat. 'I don't know what you mean.'

'Yes, you do,' Lily said gently. 'Just…I'm here for you if needed.'

Oh, dear heaven. She'd have to brush up her acting skills if Lily could sense not all was what it was purported to be!

'Thanks,' she managed gratefully. 'I'm fine. Really,' she added with a bright smile. *And cut,* a silent director ordered. Don't overdo it.

'Uh-huh.'

The truth was stranger than fiction, and not something she intended to divulge. Yet Lily was a friend, insightful, intuitive and caring.

'It's been a hectic, emotional week. Nic—' She almost added *Leandros*, and just stopped herself in time.

'Swept you off your feet?' Lily's grin was infectious.

'Yes.' She offered a smile of her own. 'And now I get to go home and play *wife*.'

'Like that's a hardship?'

It was a game, she justified as she eased the car from its parking space. All she had to do was maintain the pretence.

How difficult could it be?

Nic Leandros' home was situated in a tranquil tree-lined street where magnificent mansions of varying design and age offered the established luxury of wealth.

Tina released the ornate wrought-iron gates guarding entrance to the elegant structure ahead.

Set in sloping, immaculately kept grounds with a semi-circular driveway bordered by miniature topiary, the house itself was impressive. Double-storeyed, with cream-plastered walls, large timber-shuttered windows, a cream and terracotta tiled roof, the entrance gained via a set of large panelled double doors.

A four-car garage lay to the right, with an internal entry to the house.

Tina activated the module and the doors slid up to reveal a luxury Porsche SUV parked in one bay.

She parked alongside and cut the engine. The garage had been empty when she'd left this morning. A new acquisition? Had to be, she determined as she retrieved her laptop and crossed into the house.

Travertine marble floors, a wide curving staircase, exquisite light fittings, elegant furniture, large rooms… There was a formal lounge and dining-room plus informal dining area, kitchen, and utilities on the ground level. Five bedrooms, each with *en suite*, plus a master suite, large study and a private lounge on the upper level.

A row of French doors led from the formal lounge

and dining-room onto a large terrace, which offered magnificent harbour views. Wide steps led down to sculptured gardens and a beautifully designed infinity pool.

It was pleasant to be able to explore at her leisure. Yesterday hadn't offered much opportunity.

All her clothing had been unpacked and placed in the walk-in robe, folded in drawers, and suitcases presumably stored elsewhere. After a busy day and a particularly hectic week it came as a welcome surprise. No doubt due to the invisible household help.

A shower and change of clothes made her feel almost human again…and hungry, she realised as she made her way down to the kitchen.

A handwritten note signed by *Maria* was attached to the refrigerator door advising there was a cooked casserole ready to be heated.

Tina extracted a portion, heated it in the microwave and decided to eat out on the terrace.

The evening was clear, the sun's light diminishing as the deep orange orb sank slowly towards the horizon. In the distance street lights were beginning to spring on, and the temperature cooled, turning the sparkling harbour waters to a dark, gun-metal grey.

There were ferries crossing towards Manly, fast hydrofoils carrying working passengers to the North Shore. A large tanker lay anchored way out past the Heads, and a passenger ship was being led in to berth by two tugboats.

Dusk fell and Tina collected her plate and returned indoors, locked up, and began switching on lights as she moved through to the kitchen.

The day's boutique sales were loaded onto computer disk ready for her to check through and assess stock.

A desk in her bedroom would be ideal, together with access to an internet connection. Nic's study? Not an option without his permission. Meantime the dining-room table would have to suffice.

Tina was still there when Nic walked into the room, and his gaze narrowed at the naked fear evident for a few shocking seconds before she successfully masked her expression.

He bit back a savage imprecation. 'In future I'll put a call through to your cellphone when I reach the gates.'

'Why?' she managed steadily. It had taken years of practice to recover her guard so quickly. 'You have state-of-the-art security. I doubt anyone could enter the house undetected. You have the tread of a cat,' she observed and tried for humour. 'So, next time whistle "Dixie".'

The edge of his mouth twitched at the implication. She was something else. He crossed to the coffee-maker and set it up. 'Busy day?'

'Polite conversation?'

Nic sent her a searching look. 'A simple enquiry.'

'The boutique was host to curiosity seekers bent on a discovery mission.'

He didn't pretend to misunderstand as he loosened his tie, and shrugged out of his jacket. 'That bothers you?'

'Sydney was Vasili's scene,' she clarified quietly. 'Now it has become mine.'

People would speculate why she'd partnered one brother, yet married the other. A fact that was already garnering interest.

So…she'd deal with it.

'How was your flight?'

Nic poured coffee into a cup, added sugar, and crossed to the table. 'Uneventful.'

His close proximity unsettled her. His choice of cologne was subtle, yet it stirred her senses. Blatant sensuality and elemental ruthlessness were a potent mix. Possessed of a steel-muscled body, broad sculptured facial features…the result was dynamite.

A force to be reckoned with, she added silently, aware just how indomitable he was to oppose.

What would he be like as a lover?

Dear God…*where had that thought come from*?

She couldn't *want* to find out, surely? The thought alone verged on insanity.

Hormones, she decided unsteadily. Had to be. Anything else was madness.

Tina quickly diverted her attention to the laptop. 'I'm almost done.' The sooner the better, then she could escape to her suite. 'There's a casserole in the fridge, courtesy of Maria, if you haven't eaten.' She keyed in the last of the data, pressed 'save', closed down and rose to her feet.

'I've accepted an invitation to dine with close family friends Thursday evening. Naturally you'll accompany me.'

She wanted to refuse, and almost did. Except declining wasn't really an option.

'It's a given,' he said quietly.

Was she that transparent? Without a further word she collected the laptop and vacated the room, unaware of the speculative expression in the man's dark eyes as he watched her go.

Surprisingly sleep came easily within minutes of sliding between the bedcovers, and she woke to the sound of her newly acquired alarm clock, rose, showered and dressed, only to discover the kitchen empty and Nic had already left for the day.

A day that was equally busy as the one preceding it, with good sales in accessories...women who were prepared to purchase in order to qualify a reason for checking out the Leandros' sole heir's new wife.

Don't knock it, a sage voice silently advised. Just smile sweetly and thank them for their patronage.

Tina's cellphone beeped with an incoming SMS message as she closed the boutique. *Business meeting. Home late. Nic.*

What did she expect? Company? Conversation?

Nic Leandros led a high-profile business life...even more so now, given he'd taken control of the Sydney office.

Hadn't she expressed silent relief at the thought she would hardly see him? So what was with the slight air of disappointment?

Get a grip.

She'd lived alone for several years and liked her solitary existence, as well as her ability to *choose* how she socialised and with whom. There was the boutique, her love of clothes, the constant striving to continue in Claire's footsteps and maintain one of the top-selling designer clothing boutiques in Double Bay.

She was providing her child with two parents and a brilliant future. What more could she ask?

CHAPTER FOUR

CHOOSING what to wear caused several indecisive minutes as Tina mentally selected and discarded clothes at random. Close family friends indicated a need for smart casual attire. Yet if they numbered among the social echelon, dressing to kill would be more appropriate.

She opted to go with a slim-fitting, classic black dress with a wide scooped neckline and black chiffon three-quarter ruched sleeves.

Make-up was understated, with emphasis on her eyes and warm pink gloss highlighting her lips. Diamond drop earrings completed the look, and she slid her feet into soft kid-leather stilettos.

Done. Tina caught up a mohair wrap, evening purse, and made her way downstairs.

Nic was waiting in the large entrance foyer, his tall, broad-shouldered frame clothed in a superbly tailored dark suit, white cotton shirt and silk tie.

He looked…incredible. A white-hot sexual animal. All he needed to do to complete the picture was *prowl*.

'Why the faint smile?'

His slight drawl held a tinge of humour, which she matched in response. 'Our first foray into the social jungle.'

'It bothers you?'

It bothers me I'm playing pretend with *you*. With Vasili it had been a game. *Fun.* Nic was a different and totally unpredictable animal.

She walked at his side to the car, slid into the front seat and waited until he gained the street before querying, 'Anything I should know in advance about the people we're visiting?'

'Dimitri and Paul have been friends and business associates for years. Like Stacey, Eleni is Dimitri's second wife. Dimitri has a son from his first marriage, and they have a daughter together. Son married and lives in London; daughter single and lives in New York.' He spared her a quick glance before returning his attention to the road ahead. 'Dimitri and Eleni divide their time between London, New York and Sydney. They flew in from New York last week.'

'Got it.'

What she didn't get was several cars lining the sweeping driveway leading to a magnificent residence high on a hill at Vaucluse.

'I imagined it was dinner for four,' Tina said quietly as Nic slid into a parking bay.

'Dimitri didn't mention anything to the contrary.'

Oh, my. She was being flung in at the deep end. 'Party time.' She sent him a steady look. 'Just spell out the agenda. Am I supposed to appear pensive and quietly secretive? Or shall I gaze at you adoringly?'

'Secretive?'

'As if I'm reflecting on really great sex. Which obviously everyone will imagine we've recently shared.'

'Let's play it by ear, shall we?'

His voice held amusement, and she deliberately widened her eyes.

'Trusting, aren't you?' She opened the passenger door as he slid out from behind the wheel.

'Just remember it takes two.' He crossed to her side and they moved towards the brightly lit entrance.

Within minutes they were shown indoors by an impeccably suited manservant and led into an elegant lounge, announced, and almost immediately enveloped by their host and hostess who greeted them both with affection.

'Tina. Such a pleasure,' Eleni said with a warm smile. 'We have waited a long time for Nic to take a wife.' Friendly, gregarious, she indicated their guests. 'A small gathering of dear friends.' Her features assumed great sadness. 'Vasili...such a tragedy. We were devastated when news reached us.'

'Thank you,' Nic acknowledged, and Tina masked surprise as he placed a casual arm along the back of her waist.

An action that merely projected an expected image, she rationalised as Eleni swept them into the large room. Yet having him so close did strange things to her composure.

Was he aware of it? She fervently hoped not!

Introductions ensued, some of which were unnecessary as Tina was already familiar with a few of the women...some of whom frequently made the social pages of the city's newspapers.

Speculative interest regarding Nic Leandros' new wife was evident. She could sense it, almost *feel* it.

Two uniformed staff offered drinks and hors

d'oeuvres, and she hid her surprise as Nic took two flutes of mineral water and handed her one.

'Solidarity?' Tina queried quietly, and met his warm gaze.

'Of course.'

'Should I thank you?' Her voice held a teasing quality, and her smile resembled warm sunshine.

'I'm sure I'll think of some way.'

'Dinner at the Ritz-Carlton?'

His soft laughter curled round her nerve-ends and tugged a little.

Why *this* man? It didn't make sense. She hardly knew him...his likes and dislikes, his flaws.

'A date?'

She offered a sweet smile. 'Whenever you can fit it into your busy schedule.'

'Nicos!'

A large, jovial, middle-aged man clapped Nic's shoulder while the man's wife drew Tina to one side in what appeared to be a deliberately orchestrated movement.

Divide and conquer?

'Eleni tells me you manage a boutique at Double Bay. My daughter is getting married soon. You must give me the address, and we'll come by.'

'Of course.' She gave the required details with polite warmth, recognising the imported designer label the woman was wearing, the Italian handcrafted shoes, the jewellery, the subtle but oh-so-expensive *parfum*.

Tina's trained eye did the maths. Serious money...*very* serious money. Most likely it wasn't spent locally, but on overseas buying trips and direct from the designer's Milan salon.

'We must lunch together.'

'Thank you.'

'Vasili...such a tragic end. You knew him, of course?'

You could say that. 'We were good friends,' Tina managed quietly, aware the gossip grapevine was about to go into overdrive.

'So *young.*' There was polite curiosity evident. 'A little wild, perhaps?'

Fun-loving, believing life was meant to be *lived*, Vasili had nevertheless possessed a keen mind and acute business nous.

'I didn't find him so.'

'Nic has the advantage of maturity,' came the confident reply.

And therefore the better choice? She resisted the urge to gnash her teeth. What was the percentage of women who consciously chose a man because of his wealth, maturity, social position?

Yet *she* had. Although *choose* wasn't quite the right word!

Unbidden, her gaze skimmed the room until it came to rest on Nic's sculpted features. He was deep in conversation, and she watched idly for a few seconds, noting the strength apparent, the well-defined bone structure. Aware, even from a distance, of his physical impact, the almost primitive aura he managed to exude without any effort at all.

At that moment he glanced towards her, almost as

if he sensed her light scrutiny, and she saw him say a few words, then move across the room to her side.

'Toula.' His smile held genuine warmth. 'I see you've taken my wife beneath your wing.' He cast Tina a fond look as he reached for her hand and threaded his fingers through her own. 'Darling, there's someone I want you to meet.' He shifted his gaze to the older woman. 'If you'll excuse us?'

Tina barely registered Toula's polite response as she crossed the room at Nic's side.

Darling was definitely overkill. So too was holding her hand so firmly. She tried to pull free, only to have him ease a thumb gently back and forth across the veins at her wrist. An action that momentarily rendered her speechless.

Then she aimed her lacquered nails and dug in, without gaining the slightest reaction. Almost in reflex action he lifted their joined hands and brushed his lips across her knuckles.

Only she could glimpse the expression in those dark eyes, witness the teasing indolence…and something she couldn't define. A vague threat? Or a silent dare?

Well, she could play the game…and play it well. Hadn't she become adept at adopting a façade?

'Careful, *Nicos*.' Her smile was wide, her eyes sparkled, and her voice held a teasing warmth. 'You might be in danger of biting off more than you can chew.'

'Now there's a fascinating thought.' His drawl was pure silk. 'Are you offering a challenge?'

'As long as you're aware it stops the instant we walk out the door.'

It was as well Eleni's manservant drew the guests' attention and announced dinner would be served in the dining-room.

'A reprieve?'

Tina deliberately tilted the edges of her mouth. 'Don't bet on it.'

The dining-room was huge, the table set with fine bone china, cut-crystal goblets, exquisite silverware, with stunning floral decorations placed at precise intervals.

Place-cards indicated seating arrangements, and Tina found herself seated next to an attractive young man whose name she failed to recall.

'Alex,' he enlightened. 'Toula's son.' He waited a beat. 'Formidable, isn't she?'

She didn't pretend to misunderstand. 'Your mother is charming.'

His smile acquired a degree of cynicism. 'Politeness becomes you.'

'A compliment?'

'Of course. If I tell you you're beautiful, will it offend you?'

He was playing with her, teasing in a way that reminded her of Vasili. 'Do you intend offence?'

He looked mildly shocked. 'Of course not.'

She smiled. 'In that case…thank you.'

'You must sample the Chardonnay,' Alex enthused. 'Dimitri has one of the best cellars in Vaucluse.'

'I don't drink.'

His disbelief was barely masked. 'You don't know what you're missing.'

Oh, yes, I do!

Staff began serving the entrée, and she watched Nic fill her goblet with iced water.

'Thanks.'

'You've made a conquest,' he commented quietly.

'Jealous?' It was a light parry that earned her a musing smile.

'Should I be?'

The edge of her mouth twitched a little. 'I guess a new husband might be proprietorial.'

Nic forked a morsel from his plate and fed it to her, giving her little option but to part her lips and accept the food.

'Thank you, darling.'

'My pleasure.'

He was good, so good even she could almost believe he meant it. Except it was just a game…one she could play equally well. As she had done with Vasili. They'd even had a name for it…*flirting mode*.

So what's the difference? she queried silently.

Except Vasili had been both friend and confidant. As familiar as a brother she could trust. She'd known his mind, his thoughts, almost as well as she knew her own.

Nic, on the other hand, was an enigma. Instinct warned there was much beneath the surface…like an iceberg. Although *ice* in its true interpretation didn't apply. The man was hot, effortlessly projecting a sensual heat that had a devastating effect on the opposite sex.

Apart from his physical attributes, there was something about his eyes—their depth—almost as if he had seen much and *knew* the intricacies of the human mind. A rare and special quality coveted by many and possessed by few.

And as a lover? She had the instinctive feeling he knew it all. Where to touch to drive a woman wild beyond reason…and catch her as she fell.

Wasn't that how lovemaking was supposed to be? Two people so in tune with each other that what they shared together was uniquely *theirs*.

Indulging in thought-provoking reflection at a dinner table filled with a complement of guests wasn't conducive to clarity of mind.

'My dear, you must tell us where Nic intends taking you for the honeymoon.'

The words were accompanied by a light feminine laugh, and Tina offered a faint smile. 'It's difficult to get away right now.'

'Of course. But soon, surely?'

Tina turned towards Nic. 'The Greek Islands would be nice, darling.'

His eyes met her sparkling gaze. 'You must allow me to surprise you.'

'How lovely.' Her voice was almost a feline purr, and she managed to keep her expression intact as he smiled and brushed light fingers across her cheek.

The soft pink suddenly colouring her features was uncontrived, and she concentrated on finishing the last morsel of food as staff began collecting plates prior to serving the next course.

One of several, each served with a different wine. Talk was convivial and it seemed hours before Dimitri suggested they adjourn to the lounge for coffee.

'Tired?'

Tina met Nic's dark gaze with equanimity. 'A little.'

'We'll leave soon.'

He managed their departure with ease, and within minutes the Lexus was traversing the arterial road down towards Rose Bay.

'You managed to charm everyone,' Nic drawled as they entered the house.

She sent him a measured look as he reset the security system. 'Should I thank you for doing likewise?'

They gained the curved staircase and ascended it together.

'I imagine you've gained a few new clients.'

'You think? Friends tend to want a higher than usual discount.' There was an edge of cynicism apparent, and she tempered it with a slight smile. 'I have a firm discount policy. No exceptions.'

He wouldn't mind observing her in action… managerial youth versus cashed-up matrons well versed in driving a hard bargain.

They reached the upper floor and Tina turned towards the wing where her suite lay. 'Goodnight.'

'You forgot something.'

She gave him a puzzled look. 'What?'

'This.' He leant in and fastened his mouth over hers in a brief, evocative kiss that tore her composure to shreds.

His eyes speared hers, their expression unfathomable. 'Sleep well.'

Then he moved towards the opposite wing without so much as a backward glance.

Tina stood immobile for several long seconds. *What was that?*

A salutatory gesture?

Sure, and piglets fly!

Attempting to analyse his agenda…if indeed he had one…occupied her mind until sleep provided a welcome release.

CHAPTER FIVE

'Oh, wow,' Lily voiced quietly. 'What I wouldn't give to look like that.'

Tina glanced up from checking an invoice and saw a stunningly beautiful young woman move into the salon. Tall, waist-length sable hair, incredible facial features, exquisite make-up, and attired in avant-garde couture very few women could get away with.

Sultry, Tina accorded. Of the jungle feline variety. A woman who could devour a man, then spit out the pieces.

Wow didn't come close.

'Yours or mine?'

'Oh, please,' Tina declared *sotto voce*. 'Be my guest.'

Lily was the consummate fashion consultant, possessed of an incredible knowledge of fabric, design, local and international designers. She also had a flair for putting things together, how the positioning of a silk scarf could turn a beautifully crafted garment into something spectacular.

Tina was aware of the young woman's voice, the rather haughty air and the faint sting of criticism as she examined and discarded one garment after another.

She gave Lily another five minutes before going into rescue mode.

'Is there anything I can help you with?'

Up close the woman's beauty was even more stunning, for her skin was flawless beneath skilfully applied cosmetics, and her hair... It was like a river of sable flowing loose down her back, shifting like satin with every movement.

'The list of designers embracing your window cites you stock Giorgio Armani.'

Tina knew Lily would have shown what stock they had. 'We carry a limited seasonal range.' She indicated the appropriate rack. 'This is what we have to offer for summer.'

She received a cool sweeping glance. 'Presumably your salon cannot afford to offer a comprehensive selection?'

Tina ignored the urge to rise to the bait. 'We cater exclusively to our existing clientele base and aim to be appropriate to the Sydney social scene.'

'Hmm,' the beautiful one dismissed. 'This—' she indicated the rack with a dismissive gesture '—is hopeless. I shall have to wait until I'm in Paris next month.'

'You have that option.'

An elegant hand indicated three pairs of stiletto shoes with matching bags displayed at intervals along one wall. 'Are these all you have?'

Difficult, *picky*...and, Tina suspected, filling in time before meeting a friend for lunch.

'They're merely suggestions, and, if you check the printed card, available in the exclusive shoe boutique in the arcade adjacent the Ritz-Carlton hotel.'

'I expect personalised service.'

Okay, so this was going to be a doozey. Time to sugar-coat business facts. 'Should you purchase an outfit, Lily will only be too pleased to help you with any further selections within the immediate area.'

Cool dark eyes swept Tina's frame, resting momentarily on her hair. 'You would do well to add highlights and wear your hair loose.'

'It's my day for the upswept look,' she responded without missing a beat, and received a pitying glance in return.

With a scornful, dismissive gaze, the woman turned and walked...*glided*, to the door and exited the boutique.

'*Well.*' Lily's voice was a long drawn-out descriptive that said it all.

'Oh, yeah, in spades.'

The rest of the day settled into a customary routine, with a phone call from Nic relaying he'd be home late.

The thought of returning to a large, empty house didn't hold much appeal.

'Feel like taking in a movie?' It was a spur-of-the-moment suggestion, and caught Lily's interest.

'DVD or the cinema?'

'Big screen,' Tina elaborated. 'Dinner first?'

'You're on. What time and where?'

She named a café, gave a time, and sent Nic an SMS message when she raced home to exchange her elegant suit for dress-jeans, tee shirt and jacket.

Pizza washed down with a cold drink satisfied them perfectly, and the movie was pure escapist fun from which they emerged relaxed and light-hearted.

'Want to go somewhere for coffee?'

Lily arched an eyebrow. 'No rush to get home to your hunk of a husband?'

At that moment her cellphone pealed, and she picked up to discover Nic on the line.

'I'm leaving the city now.'

The advance call, Tina realised. 'Lily and I are stopping off for coffee.'

'Tell me where, and I'll join you.'

She looked at Lily and mouthed, *Where?* Heard her friend's response, and relayed the venue.

'Be there in ten.'

The café was within a short walking distance, and well patronised. Finding a table involved being exceedingly quick the instant one became empty, which they managed, and no sooner had they given their order than two young men asked if they could share.

'Sorry, there's someone joining us,' Lily refused, only to have them pull out two chairs and sit down.

'They're not here yet.'

Tina looked from one to the other. 'If that's a pick-up line, it needs work.'

'Maybe you could help me improve on it.'

It was difficult not to laugh at his overt suggestive tone. 'Why don't you go practise on someone else?'

'An excellent idea,' a familiar voice drawled silkily, and she turned to see Nic standing immediately behind, his expression polite, although only a fool would ignore the silent threat lurking in those dark eyes.

He rested a hand on her shoulder and lowered his

head to brush his lips to her temple. 'Problems, darling?'

'Nothing Lily and I can't handle.' Sensation feathered the length of her spine, and she inwardly cursed her own vulnerability.

It's merely an *act*, nothing more. For the love of heaven, she didn't want it to be *real*...did she? To tread that path would lead to a madness she could ill afford.

In the guise of deception she gifted Nic a warm smile, and watched with interest as the two young men wilted beneath Nic's steady gaze and promptly vacated the table.

'Lily,' Nic acknowledged as he slid into the seat at Tina's side and ordered coffee from the hovering waitress.

Afterwards Tina had little recollection of their conversation, except that it touched lightly on the movie they'd just seen and Lily's amusing anecdote regarding the day's difficult client.

'He's to die for,' Lily said softly as she brushed her cheek to Tina's when they parted. 'See you tomorrow.' She turned towards Nic. 'Thanks for coffee.'

'My pleasure.'

Tina stood at Nic's side as Lily slid into her car, and Tina lifted a hand in farewell.

'Where are you parked?'

She told him, and they walked half a block to where her bright yellow Volkswagen stood beneath a streetlight.

'I'm on the next corner,' Nic informed her as she unlocked the door. 'Wait and I'll follow you.'

'Why?'

'Just do it, Tina.'

Her chin tilted. 'You're being ridiculous.'

He touched a thumb to the centre of her mouth. 'Wait.' Without a further word he turned and walked with fluid ease towards the corner.

She slid in behind the wheel, ignited the engine and headed towards Rose Bay, uncaring of his reaction. For years she'd driven home alone. Why should now be any different?

A steady flow of traffic occupied the main arterial road, and she refrained from checking her rear-vision mirror until she reached the gated entrance leading to Nic's home.

Impossible to imagine he wouldn't have caught up with her, and she wasn't surprised to see his car slide into the garage beside her own.

Two engines died simultaneously, closely followed by the closing of two car doors as the garage doors automatically whirred shut.

'Wilful defiance, or determination to oppose me?' His tone was deceptively quiet and too controlled.

Tina met his steady gaze with unflinching disregard. 'Why not both?'

The atmosphere suddenly became highly charged... electric...as she fought a silent battle for supremacy.

'Let's go inside, shall we?'

She lifted her shoulders in a careless gesture. 'The garage has a certain...ambience, don't you think?'

'You want to walk, or be carried?'

The silky tones sent a sudden shiver down her spine. 'You might drop me.' Facetiousness was one way of dealing with the situation.

Was that a quick gleam of humour in those dark eyes...or a figment of her imagination?

'I managed perfectly last time.'

Nevertheless she preceded him to the house and entered the foyer. 'Where do you want to hold the inquisition?'

'The kitchen?'

'Ah...informality,' Tina quipped. 'It could have meant serious trouble if you'd suggested your study.'

Minutes later she turned to face him in the large, modern, well-equipped kitchen. 'Do I get to have a glass of water before or after the lecture?'

The edge of his mouth twisted a little. 'I need you to identify a woman from a clipping in last month's Melbourne newspaper.'

He was serious, she perceived. 'You think I might know her?'

'It's possible you may already have met.'

'And you've deduced this...how?'

'From Lily's description of your difficult customer.'

Oh, boy. 'The drop-dead gorgeous person with waist-length dark hair?'

'The same.'

'She has a name?'

He pushed a hand into his trouser pocket. 'Sabine Lafarge.'

'A lover?' There was nothing she could do about

the painful sinking feeling deep within. 'Past or present?'

His eyes met and held hers. 'Past.'

'And you're telling me this...because?'

'I ended the relationship months ago.'

'She doesn't want to let go?'

'No.'

How was it possible for one small word to hold such a wealth of meaning? 'She's obsessed with you.' It was a statement rather than a query. It was hard to inject humour into her tone as she tilted her head. 'Must be your charm, wealth and sexual prowess.' She even managed a faint smile. 'My bet is on the last two...in that order.'

'This from someone who has no knowledge of the latter?'

She didn't allow her eyes to wander from his. 'For which I'm eternally grateful.' She told herself it was the truth. The emotional disturbances of late were re-lated to pregnancy hormones.

'Go show me the news-clipping.'

'It's in a file in the study.'

He had a *file* on the woman?

Minutes later she watched as he unlocked a filing cabinet, extracted a slim folder and lay it open on the large executive desk.

There, captured on photographic celluloid, was the woman who'd visited the boutique. The pose in the shot was practised, the facial features perfectly aligned, the eyes wide and luminous. She bore the confidence of a woman who had everything...and knew it.

'Yes,' Tina said simply. 'Is she likely to be a problem?'

Nic closed the file and replaced it in the cabinet. 'I sought legal counsel. Stalking,' he elaborated as he turned to face her. 'Hence the file.'

'And now you think she's intent on targeting me?'

A muscle bunched at the edge of his jaw. 'It looks that way.' He waited a beat. 'As from tomorrow a live-in bodyguard will occupy the self-contained living quarters over the garages. Ostensibly his presence will be perceived as butler and household help.'

'Isn't that overkill?'

'I'll curtail travelling interstate and overseas to a minimum.'

'What on earth do you think she's going to do? *Attack* me?'

His eyes hardened. 'She has a perfidious *modus operandi*. I won't have you exposed to it.'

Well, *really*. 'I'm capable of defending myself.' Lessons learned, she admitted silently.

He reached out a hand and trailed light fingers down her cheek. 'I'm not prepared to take the chance.'

Because of the child she carried.

A wild thought raced through her head...what if she miscarried?

Cold, hard fact provided an answer. Nic would end the marriage.

Then she could go back to living the life she'd led before Nic Leandros turned *life*, as she knew it, upside down.

A degree of anger rose to the surface at his obdurate

stand. 'What if I don't *want* someone shadowing my every move?'

'Tough,' he stated with a finality that sent shivers feathering down her spine.

She glared at him. 'Right now, I don't like you very much.'

'I guess I can live with it.'

Tina picked up the closest object to hand—a crystal paperweight—and threw it at him, watching in detached fascination as he fielded it easily and carefully replaced it out of her reach.

Then he looked at her, and she almost died at the silent threat in those dark eyes. 'Go,' he bade in a dangerously soft voice. 'Before I do something regrettable.'

She wouldn't run. Instead she raked her eyes over his tall frame from head to toe and back again, then turned and walked from the room, shoulders squared, her head held high.

It wasn't until she reached her bedroom suite and closed the door behind her that she permitted herself to reflect on what had just happened. She sank back against the door.

She had to be insane to try to best him. Mad to think she *could*.

CHAPTER SIX

SATURDAY was one of the busiest trading days of the week, and the day didn't disappoint as clients visited to check out new season's stock.

Spring was evident in early blooms: trees that had lain bare during winter were sprouting new growth, and the sun's warmth fingered the earth, bringing promise of a mild summer.

There was no sign of Sabine, for which Tina was grateful. Although she considered it unlikely the woman would appear again so soon.

Two guests who attended Eleni and Dimitri's dinner called in to browse. Toula, Tina recalled, who, after much deliberation and consultation with her friend, finally reached a decision to purchase the expensive ensemble.

'You arrange a discount for me?'

The haggling was about to begin. Tina offered the customary percentage, and saw Toula's eyebrows lift.

'But we are friends. Thirty per cent.'

Friends? I've met you *once*. 'This item is new season stock,' she explained. 'Not a sale item.'

'But you would discount at least twenty per cent if it were.'

'If the garment is still in stock by January, you would be welcome to twenty per cent,' Tina managed evenly.

'So we consider it is January and you give it to me less thirty per cent. Twenty per cent sale and ten per cent for a friend.'

With a light laugh and a teasing shake of her head Tina collected the garment from the counter and began transferring it onto the clothes hanger. 'You're good at this, Toula.' But not good enough. 'My original discount stands.'

'But that's outrageous!' Toula leaned in close. 'I can bring you plenty of business.'

Time for the hard word, politely couched. 'I manage the boutique on behalf of the owner,' she said quietly. 'It is she who sets the percentage scale.'

'I will go elsewhere.'

'As you wish. However the garment you've chosen is a designer original, for which this boutique has exclusivity.'

Toula's lips pursed. 'I shall think about it.'

'Would you like me to put it aside for an hour?' She checked her watch, then proffered a gracious smile. 'If you're not here by three, I'll return it to stock.'

'Very well.'

'She'll be back,' Lily declared when the two women exited the shop.

'Maybe.'

'She loved the garment, she looks good in it, she has money...ergo, she'll buy it.' Lily's grin had an impish quality. 'Latte on me after work if I'm wrong.'

'Done.'

Toula swept into the boutique at precisely one minute to three and handed over her credit card. 'You drive a hard bargain.'

Was it Tina's imagination, or did she detect a measure of respect? 'I run a successful business,' she corrected gently. 'I'm sure you have the right shoes and bag,' she added, drawing Toula's attention to the items on display. 'But these are splendid, don't you think?'

Toula inspected both and made a snap decision. 'If you can organise the shoes in my size, I'll take them.'

'Allow me to phone and check.'

Five minutes later she'd made a commission on the sale, Toula was a satisfied client, and Tina owed Lily a latte.

It was almost five when they shut down the boutique, and within minutes they were sharing a table at a nearby café with two decaf lattes on order.

'Nothing planned for the evening?'

How could she admit she had no idea? 'A quiet meal at home.' That should cover it.

Lily wriggled her eyebrows and her eyes acquired a teasing gleam. 'A little wine, fine food…and an early night?'

'Uh-huh.' It was a sufficiently noncommittal response.

'Sunday tomorrow,' Lily ventured with an impish grin. 'You can stay in bed and enjoy each other.' A wistful sigh whispered through her lips and her eyes acquired a dreamy quality. 'I bet he's just fabulous.'

Probably, but let's not go there.

What if she were to confide the marriage didn't

involve sex? Worse, that she was pregnant with Nic's brother's child?

Tina Matheson, well educated with strict moral values, *friend*...was paying big time for one foolish mistake.

Yet there were those who'd argue, given Nic's rugged attractiveness, wealth and social status...*what's your problem*?

Because it's not who I am, nor who I want to be.

A complex answer that wasn't any answer at all.

A waitress delivered two lattes, and Tina sipped the steaming milky brew with appreciation.

'Nothing to say?' Lily quizzed, and Tina summoned a faint smile.

'There are some things which should remain private.'

'Oh, damn,' Lily denounced good-naturedly. 'Just when I thought the conversation was going to get interesting.'

'Let's focus on *you* for a change, huh?'

'One word encapsulates it all. *Waiting*. For the right man, the right life, all my dreams fulfilled. I keep looking, and there's no one out there. At least, no one who wants to commit.'

'Maybe you're looking in all the wrong places.'

Lily leaned forward. 'I want the shooting stars, clashes of cymbals...all that to-die-for stuff. Maybe I'm just going to have to settle for *comfortable*.'

'And that would be so bad?' Tina teased.

'Easy for you to say when you have Mr Gorgeous.'

A cellphone pealed, Tina checked her own and when she picked up Nic was on the line.

'About done for the day?' Video digital ensured she could glimpse a lazy smile broadening his generous masculine mouth.

She panned the cellphone towards Lily. 'Grabbing a latte and some down time after a busy day.'

'SMS me when you leave.'

'See you soon. Bye.' And closed the connection.

'The main man?'

'How did you guess?'

Lily grinned. 'Calling you home, huh?'

Playing check-in Charlie, she corrected silently. 'Reminding me I'm no longer a single woman.'

Lily rolled her eyes. 'As if you'd forget!'

Enough already. Tina extracted a note to cover the bill, and rose to her feet. 'Let's go, shall we?'

Dusk was falling as they walked to their respective cars parked alongside each other in a staff bay. 'Have a great weekend,' she bade fondly as Lily unlocked her vehicle. 'See you Monday.'

The Volkswagen's engine ignited like a charm, and Tina headed towards the arterial road leading to Rose Bay.

The traffic lights were against her as she paused at a major intersection, and an inexplicable prickling sensation crawled over both shoulders and centred at the base of her neck.

Weird, definitely weird. It was Saturday evening, for heaven's sake, there were cars in every direction.

Yet the prickling sensation remained despite an effort to dismiss it.

Auto-suggestion, she rationalised as she activated the mechanism releasing the front gates. There wasn't anyone following her…hadn't she checked her rear-vision mirror several times since turning into Rose Bay?

Tina garaged the car and entered the house. A shower, change of clothes, and something to eat would be good.

She moved towards the stairs, only to come to an abrupt halt as Nic descended from the upper level.

Jeans and a dark polo shirt gave him a whole different look. One that warranted a second glance. His breadth of shoulder was impressive, so too was the tight musculature of his upper torso, the bunched biceps.

'Hi.' The greeting sounded inane as they met midway.

'Tough day?'

She met his gaze with equanimity. 'Just busy.'

'Steve has prepared dinner.'

'The bodyguard *cooks*?'

'Weekends,' Nic relayed. 'If we decide to eat in.'

'Just one of his many talents?'

'Why not ask him?'

Tina's eyes flared wide. 'He's not in the kitchen?'

'Right behind you, ma'am.'

The *ma'am* did it. Tall, muscle-bound, young…and Texan, Tina surmised as she turned to face him.

How wrong could you be? The man who stood facing her was of average height, possessed of a lean, wiry build, nondescript and in his mid-forties.

'Not what you expected?'

'Please tell me I got the Texan bit right?'

Blue eyes crinkled with humour. 'Dallas born and bred.'

'Thank heavens.'

Steve shot Nic a musing glance. 'I think we're going to get along just fine.'

'Next, you'll tell me you're old friends.'

'We go back a while,' Nic revealed, and she lifted a hand and trailed fingers along his jaw-line.

'More obsessive women among the skeletons in your closet, darling?'

He caught her hand, brushed his lips to the centre of her palm...and watched her eyes flare with shocked surprise. And an emotion she was quick to hide.

'Why don't you go change?' he queried evenly. 'Dinner will be in half an hour. Afterwards Steve will take a run-through with you.'

Tina retrieved her hand and eyeballed both men. 'I kick-box and have a black belt in karate.'

'A definite advantage,' Steve conceded with a lazy grin.

There was dignity in retreat, and she managed it with ease, only to hear Nic's voice as she reached the upper level. 'I'll be there in a few minutes.'

'To scrub my back?' The words slipped out before she gave them thought.

'You have only to ask.'

As if.

Warm colour tinged her cheeks at his drawled response, and she silently cursed her wayward tongue.

Twenty minutes later she'd showered and changed into dress-jeans and a soft cotton top. Her hair was a slightly damp mass of curls, which she swept into a knot atop her head and secured with a series of broad clips.

A tantalising aroma teased the air as she neared the kitchen, and she entered on impulse to see Nic leaning a hip against a bench-top nursing a glass of wine while Steve spooned what appeared to be a succulent beef stew into a serving dish.

'That smells great. Need any help?'

Steve indicated a dish of assorted vegetables. 'You can take that through to the dining-room. Nic and I will bring the rest.'

It soon became apparent the two men were friends rather than employer and employee, and their exchange of several anecdotes during the meal made for a relaxed, convivial atmosphere.

If Steve's aim was to put her at ease, he succeeded, Tina admitted silently. Although as much couldn't be said for Nic, whose mere presence was sufficient to set her nerves jangling in self-protective mode.

Why *was* that? She couldn't be attracted to him, surely? At least not in any sexual sense. Yet pheromones were working a subtle magic, tugging at her sensual heart and causing havoc of a kind she could well do without.

Just the look of him did it for her. The way he moved, his strong profile, the tiny lines fanning from his eyes and the sensual curve of his mouth.

She had instant recall of how it felt, the fleeting touch, the brief slide of his tongue over her own.

There was a part of her, buried deep inside, that wanted more, much more. The touch of his hands on her body, cupping each curve, exploring each indentation...bringing her *alive*.

Except such thoughts were the stuff of dreams; reality was a bad memory and issues of trust.

The stew was delicious, and so too was the apple crumble dessert. She gave Steve the compliment he deserved.

Tina declined coffee and settled for tea, then she insisted on clearing up, despite Steve's protestations.

As it was, the three of them made short work of kitchen duties before retreating to Nic's study where the scene became strictly business.

'We need to set down a few fail-safe rules,' Steve outlined as soon as they were comfortably settled in three leather chairs. 'No exceptions.'

'Don't you think all this is over-the-top?'

'We're not dealing with a rational person. Sabine's psychotic delusions lead her to believe the unbelievable, and she'll do almost anything to gain her objective.' Steve's gaze became inflexible. 'To date, Sabine has already broken an existing Restraining Order in Melbourne. Nic's recent move to Sydney and his marriage have merely escalated the situation. She has already relocated here.'

'So, what do you propose?'

'I want you to carry an electronic tracking device. One in your car, one on your person.'

Tina closed her eyes and opened them again. 'You have to be kidding?'

Steve didn't answer. 'You check in when you arrive at the boutique each morning, and check out when you leave at the end of each day.'

She couldn't help herself. 'Next you'll tell me we're to share a secret code.'

'That, too. Linked to me, Nic and a private security firm.'

Tina looked from one to the other. 'I'm not buying into this.'

'It's not negotiable,' Nic stated with chilling softness.

'The child I carry is so important?'

'Mother and child.'

Of course, for without the mother there is no child.

If she didn't get out of here, she'd say something reprehensible. Plus there was dignity in silence. It didn't stop the resentment...*rage*, she amended as she rose to her feet and walked to the door, paused, then turned to direct Nic a searing glare.

To hell with dignity. 'I hate you.'

The temptation to slam the door behind her was almost irresistible, except she showed great restraint and pulled it closed with an almost silent click.

Dear heaven. She needed to feel fresh air on her face and walk off some of her anger.

Dammit, there was so much of it. Aimed at herself, Vasili, *Nic*. Not to mention the intruder whose actions caused such emotional damage.

Damage she'd thought she'd dealt with. And she *had*, she reassured herself silently as she unlocked the front door and stepped out into the night.

She didn't need a therapist to confirm that she was fighting a mental battle with her emotional heart. One she'd buried deep beneath so many protective layers;

the dispensing of each was proving the cause of her self-anguish and pain.

The day will arrive when you'll discover love and need to conquer the last barrier.

To which she'd responded *Feel the fear, and do it anyway?*

You'll need to let go.

At the time, and in the years since, she was convinced she'd never allow herself to become emotionally involved. It was all about control, and she'd learned the lesson well by playing safe. Until one unguarded moment had resulted in the unforeseeable.

Now she was thrust into a situation she didn't want, and some fickle imp was intent on turning her life upside down.

Tina hugged her arms close over her chest as she walked the perimeter of the grounds. There was a moon high in the dark velvet sky, casting sufficient light for her to see where she stepped. The large wrought-iron gates guarding the property were closed and electronically locked. Not that it mattered, for she had no intention of venturing out onto the street.

Physical attraction wasn't love, not even close, she rationalised as she trod dew-damp grass. Heavens, she didn't even *like* Nic.

He was everything she disliked in a man. Ruthless, powerful, *relentless*. Sensitivity? She doubted he had one sensitive bone in his body.

She made a second turn around the perimeter, uncaring of the cool evening air. After the fourth turn she retraced her steps to the front entrance and re-entered the house.

Nic stood leaning indolently against the balustrade at the base of the staircase, his expression inscrutable as she drew close.

'Are you done?'

Tina lifted her chin and threw him a look that would have felled a lesser man. 'It was either a walk in fresh air, or do you an injury.' She drew herself up to her full height and glared at him. 'And if you dare suggest I take myself off to bed, I'll hit you.'

'I was about to recommend a hot drink.'

She derived immense satisfaction from telling him exactly what he could do with his recommendation, then she moved past him and ascended the stairs.

The fact she went to her suite, undressed and slid into bed had nothing to do with it, because *she* made the decision.

CHAPTER SEVEN

IT BEGAN as it always did…Tina was in a darkened bedroom, night, asleep and dreamless. Then the sound, so soft it barely lifted her from the subconscious.

It came again, a slight swishing noise as if someone or something brushed against the drapes at the sliding door leading onto her small apartment balcony.

She opened one eye, fractionally, caught a faint movement, and knew in that frightening second she was no longer alone in the room.

Her heartbeat went into overdrive as fear raced through her body. Surely he must hear it. She could.

Close your eyes, breathe evenly. He'll think you're asleep. Isn't that what the police advised…don't confront?

The silence ate at her. Where was he? Apart from heavy movable objects, anything of value was in her room.

Each second seemed like an hour, yet still she couldn't detect the slightest sound.

He was close. She could sense him, smell the odour of cigarette smoke…and something else. Body sweat.

Please, *please*, she silently begged. Just take what you want and go.

There was a whisper of sound as he slid open the

drawer of her bedside pedestal, the faint rustle as he removed her jewellery box and emptied the contents.

Go, she urged. *Go.*

The next instant the covers were torn from the bed, and she cried out as hard hands caught hold of her body, holding her down.

Dear God, *no*. It was a silent scream that didn't find voice.

Then she did scream as he gripped the hem of her nightshirt and dragged it over her face, pinning it there as he sank his teeth into her breast.

She fought like a demon, kicking out, flailing her fists anywhere she could connect, and she cried out as he captured one, then the other and wrenched them high above her head.

Bitch. The word was a guttural snarl as he rose above her.

Instinct, self-survival, was responsible for the desperate knee she dug into his groin. The mixture of elation and fear as it connected, his grunt of pain, her release as he rolled onto the floor.

Escape was uppermost in her mind. Out of the room, the apartment. *Go.*

'Tina.' Hands were on her shoulders, and she fought like a wildcat.

'For the love of God. Come out of it.'

Still she fought, so caught up in the nightmare it had become reality.

Except it began to change, shifting to a scenario she was unfamiliar with. She knew what followed...and it wasn't *this*.

The intruder in her nightmare didn't carry her. Nor did he call her by name. What…

She opened her eyes, only to close them momentarily as realisation hit. It was no longer dark. She wasn't in her apartment or a hotel room. She was in Nic Leandros' home. It all came flooding back, and with it…relief. Relief that was short-lived when she saw she wasn't in her suite…but *his*. What was more her nightshirt was riding high beyond decency. And Nic didn't appear to be wearing anything except a towel hitched at his waist.

'How often do you get these nightmares?'

Dammit, he could still hear her screams. The first one had shaken him to the core as he'd hit the floor running, and he'd witnessed the second, seen the fear, the shock etching her pale features. Her eyes. As long as he lived, he'd never forget the expression etched in those beautiful green depths, or how dark they'd become.

'Put me down.'

Not yet.

'Please.'

The *please* did it. Except he merely let her slide to her feet and he curved his hands over her shoulders.

'I'm fine. I'll go back to my room now.'

She was far from fine. What was more, he didn't want her tucked away in a suite on the opposite side of the house, any more than he wanted to be jolted out of sleep by her distant screams.

'Do you want to talk about that night?'

Nic watched her eyelids flutter down, then sweep upwards. 'I was all talked out years ago.'

'Yet the nightmares still persist.'

A shiver ran over the surface of her skin. 'Occasionally.'

'You're cold.' Without a word he slid his hands down her back and pulled her in, all too aware how she fitted against him.

He sensed the clean, fresh smell of her hair, the faint lingering touch of her perfume, and pressed his chin to her forehead.

For a few seconds she stood absolutely still, almost afraid to move. He felt so...good. Being held by him, the slight muskiness of his skin against her cheek, the gentleness beneath the hard musculature.

She had the strangest desire to sink in against him, to lift her hands and clasp them at his nape, then pull his head down to hers.

Except such an action was tantamount to madness.

'I want you close. Where I can see you...hear you in the night.' He felt her stiffen, and he released her, stepping back a pace. He leant down and tossed back the covers on the bed. 'Tonight you sleep here.'

Tina looked at him, and almost wished she hadn't, for there was too much smooth skin stretched over muscle and sinew. He was altogether *too much*. The powerful shoulders, washboard stomach, too *male* for any woman's peace of mind...much less hers.

Share a bed with him? Was he insane?

'Sleeping with you isn't part of the deal.'

His dark eyes held hers. 'The operative word is *sleep*.'

Her chin tilted a little. 'You expect me to trust you?'

'You have my word.'

She'd lived alone for years, with no one there to hold, comfort, help soothe a vivid memory as it returned to haunt her.

'I'd prefer to go back to my room.' She moved away from him and nearly died when he turned her round to face him. Stark fear chased across her expressive features for an instant, then it was masked.

His husky oath sounded vicious.

'For the love of heaven.' He swept an arm beneath her knees and slid onto the large bed with her, caught up the covers, curved her body in against his own and anchored her there.

'Relax.'

Please. As if that were going to happen any time soon.

If she were to struggle, what would he do?

'Don't go there.'

He read minds?

'Mistake me for someone else through the night, and I won't be responsible for my reaction,' Tina vowed quietly.

'Go to sleep.'

She silently damned him to hell.

Minutes later she felt his breathing settle into a deep, rhythmic pattern, and she waited, counting the minutes until she felt it was safe to inch her way slowly from the bed.

At least, that was the plan. Except it didn't happen, for each time she made a surreptitious move, his arm tightened.

He was asleep…she was sure of it. That deep, steady breathing couldn't be faked. Or could it?

There was something incredibly comforting about being held like this. The human warmth, security…feeling *safe*. It was nice.

Oh, for goodness' sake, she mentally derided. *Get real.* She'd never been so aware of a man in her life!

There was little she could do to control the wild images racing through her head. How would it feel to have his lips brush her nape and seek the vulnerable hollow at the edge of her neck? Turn her in his arms and trail a path to her breasts and linger there, savour each tender peak before tracing a line to her waist, and edge lower to taste, caress.

Then ease inside her…would he fit?

Enough! *Get a grip.*

What was the matter with her? This *feeling*…it was just chemistry. Nothing to do with the man himself.

She had every reason to hate the way he'd intruded, threatened, and taken over her life. And she did hate him for what he'd done. So, too, for what he was about to expose her to with Sabine.

To remain here, quiescent, was impossible. Five minutes, and she'd give easing out from his arms another try.

That was the last thing she remembered, and when she woke it was morning, an early silvery light filtered into the room…and she was alone in the large bed.

There was no *ohmigod* moment. She remembered with vivid clarity the nightmare and its aftermath. Just as she recalled falling asleep in Nic's arms.

However, it wasn't going to happen again.

With resolve she slid from beneath the covers, returned to her suite, showered, dressed in jeans and top, and went down to the kitchen to get something to eat.

Of Nic there was no sign, for which she told herself she was grateful. Steve sat out on the terrace drinking coffee, and she lifted a hand in greeting.

He rose to his feet and entered the kitchen. 'I'll make you breakfast.'

'Please,' Tina protested. 'I can fix it myself.'

'Nic asked me to tell you he took the early flight to Melbourne. He'll be back tonight.'

The prospect of a carefree day held definite appeal, and her heart felt lighter as she gathered fruit and yoghurt, popped toast and made tea.

'Do you have any plans?'

She read him in an instant. 'Like going out beyond the locked gates?' An expressive eye-roll said it all. 'Maybe, in a few hours.' First she had some data to check on the laptop, then she'd call her mother. After that, the day was hers. 'Do I need permission?'

Her frivolous query was met with Steve's steady gaze.

'I've already fitted a tracking device to your car. There are just a few things I need to explain, then you're clear to go.'

Tina lifted both hands and mimicked quotation marks. 'The secret code.'

'I suggest you treat this seriously.'

'Got it.' She carried her breakfast to the table.

He took on a stern, almost military persona. 'Do you think Nic would put me here at considerable expense on a nebulous whim?'

She had to agree, and admitted reluctantly, 'I guess not.'

'So.' He drew the word out. 'Remain alert. Don't be a hero.' He paused for a few telling seconds. 'And report the slightest incident. Even if you think it's irrelevant.'

She reflected on the goose-bumps while driving home from work... No, it was nothing.

'Spell it out.'

'What is it with you and Nic? You read minds?'

'Faces,' Steve enlightened.

'And mine is particularly transparent?'

'Unguarded.'

And she thought she was doing so well! 'It was just a feeling,' she offered slowly as his eyes sharpened.

'Never ignore an instinct. You didn't see anything untoward? A car following you into this street?'

Tina shook her head. 'No. I checked.'

'We'll talk when you've had breakfast.'

She took time to update data into her laptop, rang her mother for their usual Sunday morning chat, then she grabbed a jacket, bag, caught up her keys and went in search of Steve.

There was effectiveness in simplicity, and, mindful of his caution, she set off for Darling Harbour where she browsed for a while, bought a pair of earrings that caught her eye, picked up a falafel and bottled water and demolished both as she wandered through the maze of lower-level shops.

It was almost five when she headed towards Rose Bay, and on impulse she stopped by her apartment, saw the painting was finished, the tiling completed, and the new carpet had been fitted. There was only the electrician to connect new kitchen white goods, install new light fixtures, then she could move her furniture in from storage.

The question rose to mind as to whether she should keep the apartment empty or lease it out.

She shook her head at the prospect of it being tenanted when she'd gone to considerable expense to refurbish.

Decisions, she reflected as she returned to her car. Something caught her eye as she unlocked the door. Paper, undoubtedly a flier, was tucked beneath a windscreen wiper, and she removed and tossed it onto the passenger seat to dispose of later.

Nic's Lexus was in the garage when she reached home, and she ran lightly upstairs to change before joining the men for dinner.

Tailored trousers and a loose light woollen top, she decided. Five minutes to freshen up, and she'd be done in ten.

Or would have, except when she opened the walk-in robe it was empty. What...? She crossed to the chest of drawers and pulled out one, then the others...all empty.

Where?

'I've moved it all down to my suite.'

Tina turned slowly to face the owner of that drawling voice and saw Nic leaning against the door-jamb, casually dressed in jeans and thin woollen jumper that moulded his muscular frame to perfection.

Calm, she should remain calm, she admonished silently.

'Why did you do that?'

'Because that's where you'll be sleeping from now on.'

He watched as those green eyes acquired a fiery tinge. They mirrored her every mood, and right now there was no question as to her anger.

'You can just move them back again,' she managed tightly. 'Or, better yet, I will.'

'By all means.' He straightened and stood to one side as she brushed past him. 'Just be sure I'll move them back again.'

She flung him a stormy look. 'Then we're both going to be busy.'

'It would seem so.'

Of all the dictatorial, pitiless men, Tina fumed as she entered the master suite...and came to an abrupt halt at the sight of Nic's large bed moved off centre to accommodate another bed, not quite as wide, but close.

Clearly intended for *her*.

Well, he could think again. No way was she sharing his suite.

She crossed to the nearest walk-in robe, swore briefly beneath her breath when she discovered it was *his*, and crossed to the other, gathered up everything on hangers and carried them to the opposite wing of the house where she thrust them into the wardrobe.

It took three trips to return everything, by which time her anger level had moved up a notch or two.

For a moment she almost decided against dinner, except she was hungry, and, besides, she refused to give in to a fit of the sulks. It wasn't her style.

Steve was tending a barbecue on the terrace when she joined the men. Steaks on the grill smelt delicious, and there were salads to choose from, together with crunchy bread rolls.

Tina took a small steak, added a serve from each salad, and crossed to Nic's side, intent on playing the part of polite wife. 'How was Melbourne?'

'An urgent trip at Paul's request.' A smile curved the edges of his mouth. 'You were asleep when I left.'

'No problems, I hope?' Should she care?

'A few minor hiccups which needed sorting out in private.'

A stand-alone outdoor gas-fired heating unit gave off warmth, tempering the cool evening air, and she watched the light flicker across Nic's strong features, highlighting the angles and planes, the broad cheekbones.

'As from tomorrow, I want you to use the four-wheel drive.'

'I have a perfectly good car of my own.' One she'd chosen with care, loving the bright yellow paintwork, the sunroof, and the ease of driving, parking.

The very classy, stylish Porsche sitting in the garage wasn't *her*, and she said so.

'Take it,' Nic directed. The vehicle's specs possessed plenty of grunt, lightning acceleration, plus protection and safety. It would also help maintain his peace of mind in caring for her.

'And if I don't?'

Hell, she was a piece of work. 'You want to argue?'

'You want meek compliance?'

He was torn between laughing, or shaking her.

Instead he resorted to drawled cynicism. 'Heaven forbid.'

'Just so we've got that straight.'

Steve busied himself with clearing the barbecue, and when they finished the food Tina gathered up plates, utensils and took them through to the kitchen.

'I'll do that.' Steve had followed her in, and she shook her head.

'You cooked, I get to clean. Go do the man-talk thing with Nic.'

'He's on a call.'

'So take a break. I can rinse and load the dishwasher.'

He lifted both hands in a gesture of mock self-defence and backed off. 'Okay. But when you're done, I get to introduce you to the dog.'

Dog? Impossible it might be a cute, fluffy little house dog she could hug. Visions of a Bichon Frise came to mind, a miniature poodle...

'What breed?' Alsatian, Doberman—

'German Shepherd.'

Tina offered a stunning smile. 'Of course.' Then felt remorse. Steve had done nothing to deserve a facetious response. 'Does it have a name?'

'Czar.'

Another male. She was surrounded by them. 'Give me five minutes.'

He was a beautiful animal, strong, receptive, intelligent. She fell instantly in love, and delighted when the admiration appeared mutual.

'Let's take a walk, shall we?'

Well-trained, Czar obeyed every command, and

gazed at her adoringly when she complimented him and held out her hand...which he immediately licked, then offered a front paw. She laughed, an uninhibited, genuine sound as she fondled his ears. 'You're just gorgeous.'

'And yours.'

Tina sobered and spared Steve a steady look. 'Another protective measure?'

'It bothers you?'

Maybe because until weeks ago her life had revolved around her work, leisure, and sporting pursuits. It had been a good existence, she had been happy, there had been satisfaction in running a successful business that she loved.

Now, by misadventure, she was pregnant with Vasili's child, married to his brother, and under possible threat from her husband's former mistress.

'That's something of an understatement.'

They walked in unison around the perimeter.

'The friendship between you and Nic...'

'Where, when and how?' Steve anticipated.

'Yes.'

'New York, ten years ago, through mutual friends.'

'Succinct.'

'It's my Navy SEAL training.'

She looked at him. 'That clarifies it.'

'Thought it would.'

Together they turned towards the house, where Steve bade her goodnight before retracing his steps.

To his rooms above the garage? A further exercise with Czar?

Tina checked her watch as she ascended the stairs.

A leisurely shower, followed by an early night with a good book seemed a reasonable way to end the day, and with that in mind she entered her suite, crossed into the *en suite*…and stopped.

The toiletries she'd set out on the vanity table were no longer in evidence.

Nic wouldn't have shifted her things *again*, surely?

A quick inspection of the walk-in robe clarified that he had. The chest of drawers had also been emptied.

Damn him!

Anger rose like a tide as she turned and stormed to the master suite and began gathering up her clothes. When she turned, he was standing inside the room.

'Going somewhere?'

She wanted to hit him, and would have if her arms hadn't been filled with clothing. 'Don't you get it? I'm not sleeping in this room with you.'

Nic pushed hands into the front pockets of his jeans and lifted his shoulders in an imperceptible shrug. 'You want to waste time and energy…' He left the words hanging in the air. 'For every time you take those to the guest suite—' he inclined his head towards the clothes she held '—I'll bring them back again.'

She lifted her chin and shot him a dark glare. 'It'll be interesting to see who tires first.'

'Indeed.' He watched with a degree of musing irritation as she walked around him and disappeared through the doorway.

Nic wasn't there when she returned minutes later, and she scooped lingerie out of drawers, balanced toiletries, cosmetics, and managed without anything slipping to the carpeted floor.

Third time round and she was done, and she muttered beneath her breath as she restored everything. Of all the male chauvinistic... Words failed her.

Well, that wasn't strictly true, Tina dismissed as she adjusted the water temperature and stepped into the tiled cubicle. She had a repertoire of unflattering descriptives she'd like to rain on his unsuspecting head.

The warm beat of water began to soothe her temper, and she stayed there, enjoying the feel of water cascading over her body.

It was a while before she turned off the dial and caught up a towel, blotted the moisture from her skin, and tugged a brush through her hair. She reached out a hand for her nightshirt, then cursed beneath her breath when she discovered she hadn't brought it into the *en suite*.

In one swift movement she wrapped the towel, sarong-fashion, around her slim curves and emerged into the bedroom to find her nemesis leaning a hip against the chest of drawers.

'Looking for something?'

If he'd taken her clothes...

She closed her eyes, then slowly opened them again. 'You're enjoying this, aren't you?'

'Not particularly.'

Her eyes flashed green fire. 'I want to *kill* you.'

One eyebrow lifted in silent mocking query. 'You're not exactly dressed for fighting.'

Tina launched herself at him, and cried out as he scooped her into his arms and carried her from the room. She aimed a fist at his shoulder and felt it connect. 'Put me down, you fiend!'

'Soon.'

Tina lifted a fist for a second attack.

'Don't.'

It came as a dangerously silky warning that gave her the sense to pause. Seconds later he released her down onto the carpeted floor in his suite.

She was a tightly coiled feminine ball of fury, with her hair a mass of damp curls, bare shoulders and legs, and a towel that was in danger of slipping low.

'You might want to hitch that towel.'

His musing drawl had her reaching to fasten the edges in double-quick time, and she was helpless against the warmth colouring her cheeks.

It was a long time since he'd seen a woman blush. Most women in his social circle were adept at attracting a man's interest. Subtle flirting was a game they played well, and he recognised all the sophisticated moves.

'I don't want to be here.'

'You can choose,' Nic began with silky indolence, 'between this bed and mine.'

She fought for control, and managed it…barely. 'I hate you.'

'So you've already said.' He raked fingers through his hair and regarded her steadily. 'I have to tend to some paperwork.' He paused for a few seconds. 'Don't plan a repeat trip to the other side of the house. I'll only fetch you back, and then you won't have a choice.'

The thought of spending another night anchored to

his bed was sufficient for her to decide it was infinitely wise to comply.

Tomorrow, however, was another day, offering a further battle.

On the edge of sleep a tiny voice teased...*But who will win the war?*

It was late when Nic re-entered the room. The lights were dimmed low, but not sufficiently low that he couldn't see the small feminine figure curled up in the smaller of the two beds.

She didn't move, except for the steady rise and fall of her breathing, and he let his gaze roam over her delicate features, the cream-textured skin, the slightly parted mouth.

Beautiful, he acknowledged silently. Individual, fiercely independent, with an inner strength that was admirable. Vulnerable, he added, aware of the unusual mix.

He'd consciously chosen to make a life with her. Because of the child she carried. Yet that wasn't strictly true. He'd been intrigued and challenged by her, captivated in a way that surprised him.

There was a part of him that wanted to soothe the pain in her past; to rebuild her trust and have her view him as her friend. Explore what the future might hold.

Something that would take time.

Control...he had it.

And he was a very patient man.

CHAPTER EIGHT

TINA woke to the sound of the shower running. It took a second's orientation to realise where she was. Not her suite. Nic's. Mercifully, not his bed.

The push-pull contretemps of the previous evening came back to haunt her, and she grimaced a little.

What time was it?

Sufficiently early, she determined, not to have to rise for another twenty minutes. However, there was no way she wanted to be *here* when Nic returned from his shower.

She slid to her feet, quickly gathered up fresh underwear, shrugged into a towelling robe, crossed to the empty *en suite* and she didn't emerge until she was showered, partly dressed and her make-up complete, bar lipstick.

Nic was in the process of fixing his tie, and she met and held his steady gaze.

Act, she bade herself silently. You can do it. 'Hi.'

He looked far too *male* for her peace of mind. Dark tailored trousers, the white shirt emphasising his breadth of shoulder, the inherent vitality he managed to exude without any seeming effort.

A power to be reckoned with in the boardroom.

And in the bedroom?

She didn't want to think about it.

A smile teased the edges of his mouth. 'Sleep

well?' He had, knowing she was within reaching distance.

'Yes.' There was surprise, for she couldn't recall waking. With that she disappeared into the walk-in robe, part-closed the door, selected a smart business suit and finished dressing.

Minutes later she caught up her bag, laptop, keys, and made her way down to the kitchen.

'Nic's already left. An early meeting,' Steve explained as she set about organising her own breakfast.

She felt surprisingly well rested. It was Monday, the sun was shining, and the week lay ahead. Another delivery of new stock was due in, and she needed to check out autumn catalogues from several European designers on the net.

There was also a need to check her diary and factor in an appointment with her obstetrician.

Czar lay outside the French doors leading onto the terrace, and she crossed to greet him. His magnificent tail thumped in recognition and he sprang into a sitting position.

'You're to take the four-wheel drive,' Steve reminded her as she made ready to leave, and she gave an expressive eye-roll.

'I'd feel more comfortable if I took it for a test-drive before I face the usual morning rush-hour. Tonight?' she cajoled. 'I promise I'll use it tomorrow.'

'Nic—'

'Pass?' She kept on walking before he had a chance to answer.

Traffic seemed heavier than usual as she traversed

the New South Head Road, and it wasn't until she reached the boutique and began collecting her bag and laptop that she noticed the folded sheet of paper she'd discovered tucked beneath her windscreen the previous evening.

An advertisement for local discounted pizza? Buy-a-coffee-get-one-free offer?

She almost scrunched it into a ball ready to bin it, when something—curiosity, instinct?—made her unfold it.

Instead of the expected bulk printing, the page was blank, except for one word scrawled in bright red lipstick. *Bitch.*

Doing the maths was easy.

Sabine. Had to be.

What got to her was that she'd been watched, followed.

For how long? Since the photograph of her sharing dinner with Nic had appeared in the newspaper? Or had it begun when Nic had re-located from Melbourne to Sydney?

For a moment it gave her a creepy feeling, then common sense offered rational thought.

Sabine was unlikely to try anything in public. All Tina had to do was be extra vigilant whenever she was alone.

As to the note…she'd hand it over to Steve tonight.

The day ran to schedule. Lily bubbled with excitement at having met a new man on a blind date with friends.

'He's nice,' Lily relayed dreamily.

Nice was good. 'I'm happy for you.'

'Thanks. We're taking in a movie tonight.'

Tina was relieved when the day ended and she could close up. A slight edgy feeling had niggled at her composure all day, and she'd found herself checking the entrance each time the electronic door buzzer had sounded, wondering if or when Sabine would show.

She queried the wisdom of asking Lily to stay longer, only to dismiss the request.

For the first time in ages she experienced a feeling of trepidation as she locked up and walked to her car. The area was well lit and there were people around.

Everything went smoothly. No paper tucked beneath the car's windscreen wipers, and no one appeared out of nowhere to surprise her. Although traffic was heavy, no car tailgated her own, nor did anyone follow when she turned into Nic's street.

His Lexus was in the garage when she pulled in, so too was the four-wheel drive.

Paramount was the need to change into something comfortable. Clothing that fitted well was beginning to pull at her waist. And she felt the need for food, a snack, fruit, anything to quell the faint queasiness that seemed to linger.

Nic was in the process of discarding his business suit for jeans when she entered the room, and she quickly averted her attention from the bare muscular chest, powerful thighs, the black hipster briefs…

This room-sharing was going to have to stop. She valued her privacy, and, besides, she'd never survive emotionally if she continued to bump into him at every turn.

'Good day?'

How did she answer that? Go for the kill, or delay a confrontation until after dinner?

'So-so,' Tina managed cautiously as she mentally weighed her options, and she was unprepared when he crossed the room and caught hold of her chin, tilting it so she had no choice but to look at him.

'Explain *so-so*.'

He'd pulled on jeans, which was a relief, although the wide expanse of lightly tanned musculature up close did nothing to prevent the way her pulse jumped to a rapid beat.

'Can we save the report until after dinner? I'd like to change, then eat first.'

Some expression moved across those dark eyes, but she was unable to pin it down. 'Five minutes. The condensed version,' he bade silkily.

'I'm not going to share this suite with you. Someone left a note on my windscreen.'

'Sharing isn't negotiable. Explain the note.'

'In a word—*bitch*.'

He brushed a thumb along her jaw-line, and back again, watching her eyes dilate at his touch. He wanted to pull her in, savour that delicious mouth and ease the fine tension darkening her eyes. Almost did, except she'd react like a spitfire, and any ground he might gain would be lost.

'Tell me you didn't throw the paper away.'

'It's in the car.' She moved back a step, relieved when he let her go. 'And I insist on having my room back.'

His gaze seared hers. 'We've already done this.'

'Your house, your rules?' she flung at him.

'Call it what you will.'

Tina uttered a frustrated oath, one that saw his eyebrow lift as she crossed to the walk-in robe.

When she emerged the room was empty, and in a fit of pique she collected her clothing and transferred them. Just for the hell of it.

Dinner had been prepared in advance by Maria, and afterwards at Steve's bidding she caught up the keys to the four-wheel drive, familiarised herself with it, then she took Czar for a walk around the grounds.

It was after nine when she went upstairs to shower and prepare for bed. Of Nic there was no sign, and she didn't know whether to swear or cry when she discovered her clothing had once more been removed.

Give it up. Except it wasn't about winning or losing. But independence…hers.

Yet persistence, in this case, was proving futile.

Besides, she was tired, she no longer felt inclined to fight him…at least, not tonight, and she'd meet whatever tomorrow would bring.

Wondering when Sabine might show her hand next was a game Tina didn't want to play, and although the woman's appearance was inevitable, waiting for it to happen wasn't doing her nervous system any favours.

An invitation to attend a foreign film première didn't exactly thrill her, for her knowledge of French was limited to a few phrases and words, none of which related to any fluency with the language.

The evening was, however, a social event, with the

proceeds going to a nominated charity. One the Leandros conglomerate supported.

Dress-up time, Tina accepted as she entered the glittering foyer at Nic's side.

His presence drew immediate attention, and she could understand why. Apart from the fact he was the Leandros heir and numbered among the echelon of wealthy benefactors, he possessed an exigent chemistry, which combined with elemental sexuality succeeded in garnering attention. Especially from women.

Attired in a black evening suit, white linen shirt and black bow-tie, he was something else.

Attractive didn't come close, she admitted as she accepted a flute of orange juice from a passing waiter.

Tina had chosen her outfit with care, electing to wear elegant evening trousers with matching camisole and jacket in deep jade green. Jewellery was confined to a diamond drop pendant and matching earrings.

The *in*-crowd, she perceived, recognising several familiar faces. She observed the air-kiss greetings, admired the women's eveningwear, aware she could put a name to most…and tell the difference between a genuine designer original and a copy.

Mixing and mingling was a refined art form, and there were the society doyennes, some of whom delighted in displaying public affection while in private thought nothing of aiming a figurative dagger.

The games people played, Tina mused, and wondered what they were really like when the social masks were removed.

'Having fun?' Nic's amused drawl brought a sparkling response.

'Of course, darling.'

His eyes gleamed with latent humour as he threaded his fingers through her own. 'You're doing so well.'

'Why, thank you.'

Wit and practised charm. Fire and ice. Vulnerability. It was the latter that curled round his heart and tugged a little. For her determination in becoming a survivor.

'Nicos.'

Tina heard the sultry voice, recognised it on some remote level, and turned to face its owner.

Beauty at its zenith, she accorded, and striking in a way few women ever achieved. The gown was Versace, the make-up perfection, and the hair...a waist-length river of dark silk.

Sabine. In person.

It was a public place with numerous guests. Nic would be forced to play *polite*.

Except he barely inclined his head.

Oh, my.

'Aren't you going to introduce me to your wife?' Sabine purred.

Talk about eating a man alive! The woman was having sex with her eyes...if that were possible.

Tina wanted to turn and walk away. Nic's fingers curled round her own, almost as if he sensed her intention.

'We've already met,' Tina managed calmly, hating being placed in such an invidious position.

Sabine spared her the briefest glance. 'Really?'

Dared she confront? 'You visited my boutique last Friday.' Once begun, why not go for broke? 'Followed me on two occasions, and left an inflammatory note on my windscreen.'

'I don't know what you're talking about.'

Yes, you do, Tina concluded silently. 'It'll be interesting if the police match fingerprints on the note to your own.'

Not so much as an eyelash moved on those exquisite features. 'Jealousy is such an unattractive trait,' Sabine opined with saccharine sweetness.

'Yes, isn't it?' The *touché* was deliberate, and Sabine's eyes narrowed for an instant before she turned her attention to Nic.

'I'm quite disappointed you haven't answered my calls, darling.'

'Why would I do that?'

His voice was as cold as an arctic floe, and Tina suppressed a slight shiver at the thought he might ever use that tone with her. Quiet, deadly, *lethal*.

'We have a history.' Sabine laid a lacquered nail on the sleeve of his jacket, and offered a seductive pout as he removed it.

'You possess a vivid imagination.' His chilling disregard would have cut another woman to shreds. Except Sabine appeared to be immune.

The pout increased. 'Should I go into detail in front of your wife?'

'It would be a wasted effort,' Tina ventured in a deceptively soft voice. 'You see, I don't *care* about Nic's past, or what he did with whom.'

'How remarkably...generous of you.'

'Isn't it?' she parried sweetly, and complied as Nic drew her away.

'I didn't need rescuing.' The protest was genuine, and he lifted their joined hands to his lips.

'It was going nowhere.'

Sensation spiralled from deep within, heating the blood in her veins as it encompassed her body. A sweet, bewitching sorcery that stroked her nerve-ends and brought them to quivering life.

It wasn't fair. She didn't want to feel like this. Couldn't *afford* to, she amended. Needing him would be akin to a living death…a place she refused to visit, even briefly.

At that moment the buzzer sounded as a reminder for guests to take their seats, and Tina looked forward to the cinema's dimly lit auditorium, for then she could relax in the knowledge there was no need to maintain a façade.

Surely Sabine hadn't been able to organise a reserved seat close by. Heaven forbid it might be next to their own.

The seats quickly filled, none of which within immediate proximity appeared to be occupied by Sabine.

Subtitles provided a translation as the film got under way, although the actors' lip synchronicity didn't match, and provided a slight distraction.

Tina became so fascinated by the pathos of unrequited love, the gestures and body language, that it was several minutes before she realised Nic's fingers remained entwined with her own. Something she attempted to rectify, except his hold tightened imperceptibly, making it difficult for her to slip her hand free.

A further attempt was equally unsuccessful, and she pressed her nails against his knuckles in silent warning. To no avail.

So what was the big deal? Maintaining her equilibrium, for one thing.

There was no intermission, and, instead of a happy-ever-after ending, the couple parted and went their separate ways.

'You didn't enjoy it?' They reached the main lobby and began moving towards the main entrance.

'Different to what I expected. Very *noir*.'

'Instead of light and happy with all ends nicely resolved?' Nic teased.

'Of course. However, the cinematography was good.'

There was no sign of Sabine as they made the pavement, nor did she make an appearance as they walked to their car.

Gone, but not forgotten, Tina surmised, and wondered what the woman's next move would be…and when.

'I think you owe me an explanation,' she began as Nic eased the four-wheel drive into the stream of traffic.

He spared her a quick glance. 'Sabine?'

'Who else?'

'We met through mutual friends, shared dinner, met up again at a party. After that she began appearing at whatever social function I happened to attend.' He paused as he negotiated an intersection.

'You shared a relationship with her.'

'For a short time.'

'Which you ended.'

He didn't attempt to disguise the facts. 'It proved difficult.'

Tina could only imagine. She persisted. 'Phone calls, text messages, invitations...all of which you ignored. Then the stalking began,' Tina surmised as she took in the scene beyond the windscreen.

The sky was a dark indigo sprinkled with stars, with the promise of a fine day in sight.

'Did any of that feature in your decision to—?'

'Marry you? No.'

Should she be relieved? The jury was out on that one.

'Sabine wants you.' Is obsessed with you, she added silently.

'I'm taken.'

Now why did that generate a swirl of emotion? It was crazy, *insane* to fall prey to the sensual heat this man managed to project without any effort at all.

All evening he'd been close, too close for comfort. His cologne acted as a sensory aphrodisiac, teasing her senses, creating wanton thoughts that had no place in her life.

She wanted to maintain control...over her emotions, her well-guarded heart. If she lost it, there was no one to catch her when she fell.

'In a marriage that's merely a sham.'

'One which suits both of us.'

Did it? She was no longer so sure.

As Nic drove through the gates the lights came on

in the house, welcoming them home. It was...comforting, Tina admitted as they entered the lobby.

'Go on up,' Nic bade. 'I need to check emails. Time difference,' he added in explanation.

It was an hour before he climbed the stairs and entered their suite. For a moment he wondered if she'd enforced independence and retreated to the other side of the house. Yet the bed next to his own was occupied, her slender frame curled beneath the covers.

She looked defenceless in sleep, her features pale against the rich auburn hair spread over the pillow, and he fought down the urge to slip beneath the covers and gather her in.

Except such an action would bring her sharply awake and heap feminine ire on his head. It would also lose him any ground he'd been able to gain.

CHAPTER NINE

THERE was a sense of relief apparent when the day reached its end without mishap. Business at the boutique had been brisk, the drive home didn't give Tina cause for concern, nor did it faze her to learn Nic was entertaining business associates over dinner in the city.

Home *late* could mean anything. She decided to walk Czar around the garden before fixing a salad and, after eating, taking a shower then sliding into bed with a book. She read for a while, then closed the light and fell into a deep, dreamless sleep from which she didn't wake until morning.

Nic was seated at the breakfast table when she entered the kitchen, and he glanced up and shot her a level look as she moved between refrigerator and counter in easy synchronised movement. Yoghurt, fruit, toast and tea. The latter two first, in case her stomach decided to play revolt.

'Successful night?' Tina posed as she drew out a chair and joined him.

He looked rested, energised, and incredibly male in dark tailored trousers, blue pinstriped shirt and tie. A jacket lay folded over an empty chair.

His smile was vaguely cynical. 'We managed to iron out a few kinks and agree to disagree on a few aspects.'

His subtle cologne teased her senses. 'So-so, huh?'

'It could have been better,' he alluded drily.

There was no time like the present. 'Are you free this evening?'

Nic leaned back in his chair and regarded her with a degree of curiosity. 'What do you have in mind?'

The toast was good, so too was the tea. And her stomach appeared to behave. 'Dinner at the Ritz-Carlton,' she elaborated, adding, 'I don't welsh on a bet.'

'Our date.'

Tina silently awarded him high marks for instant recall. 'On condition I get to drive, order, pay, then deliver you home.'

'Role reversal?' She amused him as no other woman did.

'Are you going to object?'

'Not at all.'

Tina checked her watch, gathered up the tub of yoghurt, fruit, then she rose to her feet. 'I'll make a booking. Will seven suit you?'

'Of course.'

She collected her bag, laptop and balanced both as she walked to the door. 'Tonight.'

It would, Nic decided as he shrugged into his jacket and prepared to follow her, prove an interesting evening.

He was waiting for her in the entrance lobby as she descended the stairs shortly after six-thirty, wearing a multi-layered chiffon dress in a subtle floral pattern. Her hair was swept high with a few loose tendrils curling either side of her face, and her only jewellery was a pair of stunning drop earrings.

'I do like punctuality in a man,' Tina managed as she reached him. 'Shall we leave?'

Nic extended an arm. 'After you.'

Choices, she mused as they entered the garage. She'd prefer her Volkswagen, but she doubted it would comfortably accommodate his lengthy frame.

The four-wheel drive won out, and she released the alarm, opened the passenger door and indicated he should get in.

'Isn't this taking role reversal too far?' he drawled as she slid in behind the wheel.

'I promise I won't embarrass your masculinity in public,' she said solemnly, and heard his husky chuckle.

'Thank heaven for small mercies.'

Parking at the Ritz-Carlton wasn't a problem. She simply drove into the entrance and requested valet parking.

The restaurant was well booked, with several guests occupying bar space, and given the choice Tina opted to be taken directly to their reserved table where, once seated, she conferred with the wine steward, requested Nic's preference, and ordered accordingly.

'You've done this before,' Nic said, and watched as she inclined her head.

'Of course.'

'Let me guess,' he ventured lightly. 'Vasili was your partner in crime.'

'True.' She sobered a little, remembering the fun

they'd shared, the laughter in playing the flirting game.

The wine steward delivered the wine and went
through his little spiel, allowing *sir* to sample a taste
when *madam* declined.

When it came to the menu, she dutifully perused it,
suggested a starter, and provided an experienced run-
down on the selection of mains.

'May I have some bread?'

She almost laughed at Nic's deferential tone. 'Naturally. Herb, garlic, bruschetta, Turkish?'

'Turkish, I think, with hummus?'

Tina summoned the waiter and placed the order.

'You're getting a kick out of this,' Nic declared,
and met the vaguely impish expression evident in her
eyes.

'And you're not?'

'It provides a refreshing change.'

'I'm glad you're enjoying yourself.'

He wanted to laugh, and settled for a soft chuckle.
'You really intend to see this through?'

Tina inclined her head as bread was brought to the
table.

'Tell me about a day in the life of Nic Leandros.'

'The man, or corporate executive?'

She lifted her glass and took a sip of chilled water.
'The latter.' The *man* was ever-present, invading her
thoughts, her dreams, her life. Too close, too much.

She no longer possessed a safety net, and she'd
never felt so exposed in her life.

'Meetings, in and out of the office. Conference
calls, decisions,' he drawled, watching her expressive

features. 'Dealing with hiccups, delays, the frustrations associated with differing time zones around the world.'

Associates, managers, personal assistants, secretaries…some of whom had to be women. Attractive? Did they have a *thing* for the boss, flirt with him? Aim for something more?

'Yes,' Nic agreed with drawled indolence. 'And no.'

Tina arched a deliberate eyebrow. 'Not for the want of trying, I imagine.' She too could play the mind-reading game.

The waiter delivered their starter, and Tina ate with relish. Lunch had been a snatched bite of a sandwich as and when she could manage it.

'Your turn.'

She dealt with a succulent slice of stuffed mushroom, and followed it with a sip of water. 'A day in the life of Tina—' She almost said 'Matheson'. 'Leandros?' Nearly a *faux pas*.

'Pleasant clients,' she continued. 'Picky customers, delayed deliveries, unavailable stock. The occasional shoplifting attempt,' she added, recalling a few. 'And handling the customer who buys an outfit, wears it that night, then returns it the next day with the excuse it's not suitable and demands a credit.'

'The mantra ''the customer is always right'' doesn't apply?'

'Not when the customer has been photographed wearing the outfit in public,' she elaborated drily.

The food was divine, and they took their time, enjoying the ambience, the music filtering softly in the background.

During the main course Tina brought up the subject of travel, countries she'd visited, those she'd like to explore.

'Paris is to die for,' she offered wistfully. 'Austria, skiing. London. Milan for the fashion shows,' she added. 'Venice, Rome. New York.' She cast him an enquiring glance. 'I guess you travel so frequently it's no longer an adventure. Just long flights, hotel suites, intense business meetings, with little or no time out for social activities or pleasure.'

He took a sip of wine, then reached for water. 'That pretty much covers it.'

'Wheeling and dealing, surviving the vicious cut and thrust of it all?'

'Yes.'

'You don't take a break…ever?' she queried. 'One that involves little or no contact with the business world?'

'Rarely.'

'All work and no play?'

The corners of his mouth twitched with humour. 'You want details of *play*?'

Affairs? There had to be a few. He bore the look of a man who *knew* women and had bedded many. The thought disturbed her more than she imagined possible.

'I doubt you can remember them all,' she managed sweetly, and heard his quiet laughter.

'You think there have been so many?'

'I'd rather not answer that on the grounds that anything I say…' She let her voice trail deliberately, smiled graciously as the waiter appeared to remove their plates, then she requested the dessert menu and perused it.

'If you have a sweet tooth, the sticky date pudding is to—'

'Die for?'

'Mmm,' Tina agreed with a sunny smile. 'I'm going to settle for the fresh fruit compote.'

They took their time over coffee…tea, in Tina's case, and when the waiter presented the bill she preempted him by indicating it should be given to her.

'If you insist.' Nic's voice held mild amusement, and she spared him a severe glance as she tendered her credit card.

Minutes later she signalled the concierge to collect the four-wheel drive.

'Thank you for a pleasant evening,' Nic said with unruffled ease as she drew the vehicle to a halt in the garage.

'You're welcome.'

They entered the house together, and she made for the stairs.

'You forgot something.'

She turned, faint surprise etching her features as he moved towards her.

'Isn't this where you get to kiss me goodnight?'

He was kidding…wasn't he?

Tina hesitated, then reached up and pressed her lips to his cheek. At least that was her intention. Except he moved and her mouth connected with his own.

He didn't allow her the opportunity to pull back.

Instead he captured her head between both hands and took her fleeting touch and turned it into something more.

Much more. A slow, exploratory dance, wholly sensual...dazzling in its intensity. A taste of passion, electrifying and as intoxicating as fine vintage champagne.

Dear heaven, she registered on some deep level. If this was how he kissed, what would it be like if he made love?

Don't go there.

She had no idea how long it lasted. Thirty seconds, a hundred...more.

When he released her she could only stand there looking at him in stunned silence.

He trailed gentle fingers down her cheek and let them rest fleetingly on her mouth. 'Sleep well.'

She remained standing there as he turned towards the study, and it was only when she heard the imperceptible click of the door closing that she made her way to their suite.

Sleep was never more distant. Her lips, her mouth...dammit, her entire body was incandescent with sensual heat.

It wasn't fair.

Work provided a necessary distraction, and with each passing day Tina became a little more at ease in sharing the large master suite.

It helped that there were two *en suites*, two spacious walk-in robes. Individual privacy could be maintained...and was, she reflected with relief.

Although living in such close proximity meant she

was constantly aware of his presence. The thrown-back covers on his large bed, the clothes he'd worn during the day draped over a valet frame. The faint lingering scent of his cologne. The fresh smell of soap drifting from his *en suite* after each shower.

The occasional glimpse of him in a state of semi-undress was enough to send her pulse racing to a rapid beat.

Tonight wasn't any different as she put the finishing touches to her make-up, then crossed into her walk-in robe to dress.

Nic stood, naked from the waist up as he pulled on trousers. One glance was all it took for her nerve-ends to go completely haywire. Gleaming tanned skin stretched over strong muscles that flexed with every move he made.

At that moment he lifted his head and their eyes locked, fused for a few infinitesimal seconds. Then he smiled, and every bone in her body went into serious meltdown.

No one man deserved to look so ruggedly attractive, or effortlessly project more than his fair share of sexual chemistry. Primitive, intensely sensual. Lethal.

Tina forced herself to utter a casual, 'Won't be long,' before disappearing into the walk-in robe.

The gown she'd chosen to wear was a dream in deep blue chiffon silk, with a beaded fitted bodice, spaghetti straps, and a layered skirt. There was a matching beaded jacket to complete the outfit, and she slid her feet into hand-crafted stilettos, then added the finishing touch of delicate diamond drop earrings.

With a few dextrous strokes she fixed a few stray

tendrils of hair, then she crossed into the bedroom to discover Nic standing indolently at ease, looking, she determined, far too compelling for any woman's peace of mind.

Especially hers.

'Ready to go?'

Tina caught up her evening purse and offered him a stunning smile. 'Showtime.'

'There's just one thing.'

He crossed to her side and she resorted to humour as a defence mechanism. 'Lipstick on my teeth? Smudged mascara?'

'You look beautiful.' A beauty that came from within, he added silently.

Oh, my. Did he have any idea how he affected her?

'Thank you.' She let her eyes skim his impeccably suited frame. 'Believe you'll have the women vying for your attention in droves.'

'You're verging on overkill.'

She shot him a witching smile as they descended the stairs. 'Really?'

Traffic was heavy as they made their way into the inner city and joined a queue of cars lining up for valet parking at the prestigious hotel.

The Royal Children's Hospital benefit was a glittering annual event, patronised by many and attended to capacity, Tina mused as she stood beside Nic in the foyer of the hotel's grand ballroom.

Anyone who was *someone* was there, and she recognised a few society doyennes, the titled few, and some of her clientele.

The women wore designer gowns, a ransom in jewellery, while the men looked resplendent in black suit and bow-tie.

Waitresses plied guests with champagne and orange juice, and the muted music was almost eclipsed by the buzz of conversation as guests mixed and mingled.

Premonition or a finely tuned instinct? Tina wondered silently as her gaze idly skimmed the room.

Would Sabine make a last-minute appearance?

The charity had been booked out for weeks, and the only way Sabine could gain entrance was an ability to persuade an existing ticket holder to part with their own.

At that moment doors to the huge ballroom were thrown open, guests were invited to take their seats, and Tina allowed herself an inward sigh of relief as they reached their reserved table.

Ill-timed, given Sabine's appearance scant minutes before the Master of Ceremonies took the podium.

The woman's magnificent hair stood her apart from every other woman in attendance. If that wasn't sufficient to garner notice, Sabine had chosen to wear black...a strapless backless creation that moulded her perfect curves. The effect was so exceptionally stunning it doubtlessly quickened every man's pulse...as well as another part of their male anatomy.

Scarlet lipstick and gloss, matching lacquered nails, Sabine epitomised the ultimate sexy seductress.

Her male handbag for the evening was a polished escort whose model looks and body probably came at a high price.

There were two vacant chairs at an adjacent table,

and Tina watched with idle fascination as Sabine slowly threaded her way towards them.

Amazingly, the Master of Ceremonies delayed beginning his speech until Sabine and her companion were seated.

There was no one word in any dictionary to do Sabine justice.

Worse, Sabine sat directly in Tina's line of vision. A line of vision Nic also shared.

It was, Tina concluded, going to be one hell of an evening.

An understatement, for Sabine played every trick in the book...and then some. Without doubt solely for Nic's benefit.

A reminder of what he'd shared...and still could?

Tina told herself she didn't care.

Instead, she sipped chilled water, forked small morsels of food into her mouth with no recollection of their taste or texture.

She also conversed with fellow guests sharing their table. Although afterwards she could remember neither the topic nor her contribution.

The faint niggling back pain that had persisted on and off through the day suddenly intensified into a deep spreading ache, and she subtly shifted a little in the hope of easing it.

Had she slept awkwardly? Inadvertently stretched a muscle? It couldn't be something she'd eaten, surely?

Perhaps it would help if she stood up and moved a little. A visit to the powder-room?

It took a while, as several other women guests de-

cided to take advantage of a lull in the evening's proceedings.

Coffee had already been served when she finally
re-entered the ballroom, and various guests were exchanging seats at different tables while others made
slow progress towards the main doors.

Tina bore Nic's swift appraisal as she slid into her
seat. 'Time to leave?'

'Please.'

His gaze sharpened as he took in her pale features,
the darkness lurking in those beautiful green eyes.
'What is it?'

If only it were something as simple as a headache,
but she was afraid it was more than that. 'I'm not
sure.'

Nic didn't hesitate as he made a swift call to the
concierge, then he led her out to the lobby where their
car was already waiting for them.

'I'd rather go home first,' Tina protested as Nic
headed for the nearest private hospital. The next instant a spasm of pain temporarily suspended her
breathing, and any doubt she might have had gave
way to sickening certainty.

Everything after that became a blur as she was
wheeled into the emergency ward, admitted, ques-
tioned, put on an intravenous drip, then examined.

Miscarriage, or spontaneous abortion as it was
termed. Quite common. They'd run some tests, do a
scan, give her pain relief, and check her throughout
the night. All being well, she'd be released late tomorrow.

'Go home,' Tina directed when Nic remained after the medics were done.

His expression was bleak, his eyes dark and unfathomable as he pulled a chair close to the bed. 'I'm staying.'

'You can't.'

'Watch me.'

She felt too drained to argue with him, and she simply closed her eyes, unwilling to think. Not *wanting* to think as she began to drift. Had they given her something to make her sleep? What *time* was it?

Dammit…what did it matter? *Nothing* mattered any more.

Uninterrupted sleep was an impossibility as nursing staff seemed to appear at frequent intervals through what remained of the night. Once, when she turned her head to check, Nic was still there.

The hospital's quietness was broken with the early morning nursing shift change, the appearance of the tea lady, and general fussing in preparation for the various doctors' rounds.

Of Nic there was no sign, and when she queried she was told he'd gone home to change.

Tina showered and put on a fresh hospital gown, then, at the nurse's urging, slid back into bed.

'Are you comfortable, dear? Breakfast will be served soon.'

There was a remote unit to activate the television set mounted high on the wall. Magazines to choose from. She wasn't interested in either, but anything was better than reflecting on the miscarriage.

It was as if she was locked into a state of ambivalence, where few or no emotions existed.

Another nurse breezed in, took her temperature, checked her blood pressure, the intravenous drip, then asked how she felt.

'Fine.' The blank answer was automatic. The truth was she didn't know how she felt.

Her mind was whirling with thoughts. There was vague guilt that the pregnancy had been a mistake; not a planned event conceived out of mutual consent and longing for a child. She recalled her initial shock, decisions, Vasili's accidental death. Tina's head spun with it all, her thoughts intensifying as she remembered Nic's insistence that they share a marriage of convenience for the sake of the Leandros heir.

Except now there was no child.

So where did that leave her?

Breakfast arrived, and she picked at it, choosing fruit and cereal, toast, then drank the tea.

Tina glanced up and saw Nic framed in the door for an instant, then he crossed to the bed and leaned down to brush his lips to her forehead.

'How are you?'

He'd changed into tailored trousers, open-necked shirt and jacket. He indicated the holdall in one hand. 'I've brought you some clothes. Things I thought you might need.' He had flowers, an enormous sheaf of them. 'The nurse said she'd find a vase.'

'Thanks.'

She looked…fragile. And her eyes held shadows he could only begin to guess at. 'I checked at the nurses' station. The obstetrician will be here soon.'

'So they said.'

He beat the urge to collect her from the bed, settle with her in the chair and hold her close. Except she'd probably resist the move. His eyes locked with hers, but she was the first to look away.

Hell. Did she know how helpless he felt? How words…any words…seemed inadequate?

The obstetrician came and went, organised a follow-up consultation, and sanctioned her discharge later in the day.

She could go home.

A good suggestion…except, where was home *now*?

No pregnancy meant there was no need for the marriage to continue. When could she expect Nic to file for divorce? For divorce was inevitable…wasn't it?

'I've made a few necessary calls,' Nic relayed quietly. 'Lily will take charge of the boutique, and Claire will be here around midday. I've invited her to stay for a few days. Stacey will call you tonight.'

Claire? There had never been a time when she'd needed her mother more.

Nic remained until it was time to go and collect Claire from the airport and he brought her directly to the hospital.

Tina held out her arms and enfolded her mother close. 'It's so good to see you.' She patted the bed. 'Sit.'

Nic smiled at the sight of them, two women who looked more like sisters than mother and daughter.

'I'll go leave you to it.' He leaned in and brushed his lips to Tina's cheek. 'Be back at four.'

'Thanks,' she said quietly.

It was wonderful to catch up with her mother, and they talked up a storm…about everyone and everything, except the most pressing aspect of all. How the miscarriage would affect her relationship with Nic.

Tina found it impossible to put her fears into words, and Claire, with a mother's intuition, left the subject well alone.

'How long are you staying?'

'Until Tuesday. I'll get the late flight back, stay in Brisbane overnight, and leave for Noosa at dawn.'

Two days. It wasn't long enough, and she said so.

Dinner that evening was a convivial meal. Steve had outdone himself with a superb roast chicken and various salads, and he produced a delicious cheesecake, which he admitted he'd collected from a local bakery.

There was coffee, and Tina savoured it with the appreciation of one denied the pleasure for several weeks. A tiny bonus, but one nonetheless. And right now, she'd take any bonus she could get.

Stacey's call, when it came, proved difficult for them both. There were no *right* words, nothing to ease Stacey's pain of a double loss within a matter of weeks. It served to intensify Tina's guilt…unfounded, she knew, but there nonetheless. Not only for the loss of the child, but the fear of losing Nic.

'Darling, why don't you go up to bed?' Claire suggested gently around nine. 'I can't imagine you had much sleep last night.'

'You just want to get rid of me, so you can charm these two men,' she teased, and heard her mother's light laugh.

'How did you guess?'

Nic rose to his feet in one easy movement and accompanied her into the foyer.

'You don't need to come with me,' she said quietly. 'I'm not going to fall in a heap between here and the bedroom.'

Inner strength and fragility. It was her fragility that threw him, for he could see her closing up, distancing herself, and he felt powerless to prevent it.

'No,' he agreed with studied ease as he began ascending the stairs at her side.

They reached the upper floor and traversed the hallway to the master suite.

Inside Tina turned to face him. 'So why are you here?'

'Ensuring you take prescribed medication.' He crossed into the *en suite*, filled a glass with water and returned to hand her the pills.

'I don't need a nurse.'

'I wasn't aware I suggested you did.' Tina swallowed them down, then watched as he walked to the door.

'I'll be up later.'

Then he was gone.

She was fine, she told herself as she undressed and slid into bed. What was more, she'd read for a while...

When Nic re-entered the room she was asleep, and the book lay on the carpeted floor.

He scooped it up and placed it on the bedside table, then he stood looking down at her for a few minutes as she slept.

The temptation to slide in beside her and gather her close was almost irresistible.

Instead he crossed the room, shed his clothes and slid into his own bed to lay staring at the darkened ceiling as he became locked into contemplative thought.

CHAPTER TEN

'WHAT do you feel like doing today?'

It was after nine, the morning was clear with a hint of spring warmth in the air, and there was a sense of relaxed pleasure in having shared breakfast with Claire and taking the opportunity to enjoy a second cup of coffee without needing to hurry.

'Spending time with you, darling.'

'Why don't we go check out the boutique?' Tina suggested. 'Take in lunch and do a little retail therapy?'

'Cabin fever, so soon?' her mother teased.

'Got it in one.' How could she explain that she had a burning need to get out of this house? A house she might very soon be asked to leave?

'You don't think you should rest?'

Tina shook her head. 'I did that yesterday, remember? At your and Nic's insistence.' With Steve as back-up guard, she hadn't stood a chance. But today...well, today was a different matter.

'The obstetrician—'

'Assured me I'm fine to ease back into a normal routine.'

Claire's eyes twinkled a little. 'I'm all too familiar with that determined streak of yours. Four hours, tops,' she cautioned. 'Less, if I think you're beginning to fade.'

They left at eleven, despite Steve's voiced reluctance, with Claire at the wheel and Double Bay as their destination.

The boutique was Tina's first priority, and Lily's delighted greeting and warm hug made her day.

'It's great to see you,' Lily enthused. 'But should you be here?'

'That's what I told her.'

Lily offered Claire a mischievous smile. 'Didn't listen, did she?'

'I have her on a leash.'

'Ready to rein her in?'

'If you don't desist in talking about me as if I'm not here…' Tina protested in a light voice. 'Any problems?'

'None I can't handle,' Lily assured, and reeled off stock deliveries, sales, orders.

'Want to take a break while Claire and I mind shop?'

Claire stepped forward. 'I mind, you sit,' she directed briskly. 'Lily, go take half an hour.'

It was good to be back, Tina mused. Anyone would think she'd been gone weeks instead of a day. Tomorrow she'd come in for several hours, maybe ten-thirty until three-thirty or four. If the going got tough, she could always leave.

'I like what you're doing here,' Claire complimented as she riffled through stock. 'It's well organised and beautifully displayed.'

'Thanks.'

It was pleasant to see her mother work the clients who intended to browse, and bought due to Claire's superb salesmanship. Definitely an art, Tina acknowledged, and one her mother possessed in spades.

'I learnt from the best,' she applauded when the boutique emptied, and caught Claire's smile.

'The item looked good, complimented her figure and colouring...it sold itself.'

'Sure.'

They were both smiling when Lily returned, and she offered with a quizzical lift of one eyebrow, 'Are you going to share, or do I have to guess?'

'Claire just sold the Saab ensemble.'

Lily's expression was comical. 'That only went out into stock this morning. Maybe you should stay awhile.'

Claire collected her bag. 'I'm taking my daughter to lunch.'

'Hey,' Tina protested. 'My invitation, my treat.'

'You don't stand a chance, darling. The only decision you get to make is the choice of venue.'

Tina glanced from her mother to Lily. 'I'll be in tomorrow.'

'Better check with Nic first,' Lily warned, and ignored Tina's expressive eye-roll.

It was early, most of the lunching crowd didn't congregate till late in the day, and although reservations were heavy, Tina managed to secure a table at an elegant restaurant well known for its fine cuisine.

They settled on a light main, declined wine, and opted for mineral water.

'Lily seems to be managing very well.' Claire took a sip of water and leant back a little in her chair. 'You could easily take a break away.'

'Maybe.'

'Think about it,' her mother encouraged, and Tina inclined her head, only to dip it quickly on recognition of *whom* the *maître d'* was bent on ushering towards a vacant table.

Sabine.

'Something wrong, darling?'

An understatement, if ever there was one.

'Why, *Tina*.' The soft, purring voice was definitely feline. 'I didn't expect to see you here.'

Believe me, neither did I. 'No,' she managed in a noncommittal tone.

Sabine turned towards Claire. 'I don't think we've met. Sabine Lafarge. An—' she deliberately effected a telling pause '—old friend from Nic's past.'

Not so *old*, and determined to intrude on the present.

'Perhaps I could join you?'

Pushy, definitely pushy, Tina determined and was about to refuse when her mother beat her to it.

'No.'

Ah, Claire hadn't lost her touch for summing up a person in seconds flat.

'The restaurant has no spare tables.'

Tina waited expectantly, and wasn't disappointed with her mother's firm response. 'We're having a private conversation.' Lifting a hand, she summoned the *maître d'*, explained they were not inclined to share and heard his voluble apology.

'But madam insisted she is a friend.'

Claire's smile was pure honey. 'Madam is wrong.'

Sabine's killing gaze held a laser quality as she turned and walked from the restaurant.

'You owe me an explanation,' Claire began evenly.

Tina offered the condensed version, only to see her mother's eyes narrow.

'That's one dangerous female. Watch your back, darling.'

'Watching,' she said obediently. 'More coffee?' Having been denied coffee for several weeks, she seemed bent on making up for lost time.

'Nic's reaction to this is…?' Claire pursued and Tina stifled an inward groan. When Claire took the bit between her teeth, there was no stopping her.

'Tightened security,' she enlightened quietly. 'Steve doubles as a bodyguard. I carry a tracking device. My Volkswagen stays in the garage and I get to drive the fastest, most sophisticated grunt machine on four wheels. There's also a guard dog.' She took a deep breath and expelled it slowly. 'Enough, already?'

'I'm impressed.'

'One can only wonder how long it'll last.'

Claire offered a thoughtful look. 'Because?'

'There's no longer a Leandros heir.'

Her mother appeared to take a moment. Concentrating on a careful assemblage of words, perhaps?

'Is it not feasible at some stage in the future you and Nic might consider having a child together?'

Tina was temporarily lost for words. 'You know—'

'Yes, I do,' Claire said quickly. 'Only too well. I was there, remember?'

'Then why would you—?'

'Suggest it?' Claire posed. 'Isn't there a part of you that wants to love and be loved? To feel secure in a relationship? To grow old with a man who is not only your lover, but your best friend?'

'And as a marriage to Nic already exists, why not kill two birds with one stone?' She couldn't begin to describe how the thought affected her. 'Haven't you forgotten one small detail?' She aimed for calm, and almost didn't make it. 'Maybe that's not what either of us might want?'

Claire looked thoughtful. 'Don't *you*?'

'I don't need the complication.'

That hardly answered the question, but at this point it boded well not to comment, Claire decided, and signalled for the bill. 'Retail therapy?' she suggested with a smile.

They arrived home two hours later with several brightly emblazoned carry-bags, which they had fun separating and re-examining.

Maria had prepared minestrone soup and a delicious lamb roast for dinner, and Tina insisted on preparing the table while Claire retreated upstairs to pack.

Nic entered the dining-room as she placed the last glass, and she stilled the faint fluttering sensation in her stomach as he came close.

'Good day?'

She stood back a pace and offered a slight smile. 'Claire and I checked the boutique, did lunch and engaged in some retail therapy.'

He caught hold of her chin, lifted it, and examined her features. 'You were supposed to rest.'

'I've already done this with Claire.'

Nic decided not to pursue it. 'Any problems?'

He'd hear about it anyway, so she might as well spill it out. 'Sabine entered the same restaurant and did her best to join us.'

His eyes sharpened. 'I gather she was unsuccessful?'

Tina attempted to move free from him, and failed miserably as he cupped her face between both hands.

She didn't want to be this close to him, for all it took was a look at that sensually curved mouth to remember just how it felt on her own. 'Please, I need to go freshen up before dinner.'

He lowered his head and kissed her…a slow, gentle sweep of his tongue over hers, then he let her go.

It was enough he'd felt the quickened pulse-beat, sensed her quick intake of breath an instant before his mouth had settled on her own.

Nic watched her leave the room, then he crossed into the kitchen and conferred with Steve. Today's rebuttal would have increased Sabine's need to strike back. The difficult part was predicting how, when and where.

Steve joined them for dinner, and conversation was kept light as anecdotes were exchanged and commented upon.

Normal, Tina judged as they drove Claire out to the airport.

It was hard to say 'goodbye' when it came time for her mother to pass through to the departure lounge, and Tina fought against a sudden bereft feeling as Claire disappeared from sight.

Tiredness descended like a shroud as Nic drove home, and she simply leaned her head back against the cushioned rest and closed her eyes.

She felt all talked out and incredibly weary.

Did she actually fall asleep? She couldn't be sure.

When Nic brought the car to a halt in the garage she undid her seat belt and preceded him into the house. Bed, she decided. But first a shower.

A muscle bunched at the edge of his jaw as he ascended the stairs at her side, and she uttered a faint protest when he swept an arm beneath her knees.

'I can walk.'

'Indulge me.'

She really didn't want to, but struggling for independence would gain nothing.

'I'm fine,' she assured him as they reached the bedroom.

'Sure you are.' He let her slide down to stand on her feet, and he reached for the buttons on her shirt.

'What do you think you're doing?'

'Undressing you.'

He sounded almost…caring. And despite her tiredness, it put a whole different context on his ministrations. One that caused faint alarm bells as his fingers skimmed her skin.

She didn't want to feel like this. Dammit, to stand here quiescent was a madness she couldn't afford.

'Don't.' Was that her voice? Pleading, almost begging him to desist.

He took little notice and continued with the task until she stood in bra and briefs. 'Go.'

Tina escaped into the *en suite*, and returned a while

later to find the lights dimmed low, her bed turned down, and a glass of water together with two pills on her nightstand, which she ignored. She wasn't in any pain and she didn't need anything to help her sleep.

She'd always thought it a fallacy that anyone could fall asleep the instant their head hit the pillow. Yet all she remembered was closing her eyes.

Later she had no idea of the time or how long she'd been asleep. All she knew was that it was dark, and she was locked into a familiar nightmare...where she was in bed in her apartment, the faint sound, the muffled movement, then the hand clamped over her mouth.

She couldn't breathe, couldn't see, and she began to struggle, fighting against a strength much stronger than her own...

'Tina.'

Strong hands held her flailing arms as a male voice penetrated her subconscious. Yet still she fought him, kicking out in an effort to find any slight advantage in her quest to best him.

Her name sounded clear, close...and the nightmare faded as she returned to the present.

She took in the large room, and experienced a mixture of consternation and relief with the recognition of where she was and with whom.

She had a haunted look, her eyes, wide dark pools, mirrored unspoken terror...and Nic transferred her from her bed into his, in spite of her protest.

'Shut up,' he chastised quietly as he anchored her close. 'Just...shut up.'

She shouldn't be here, shouldn't stay. Except it felt

so *good*. His body was warm, his arms strong, she felt safe. Secure, she amended silently as she gave in and let herself drift.

Tina stirred into wakefulness through the night, moved slightly and became aware she lay curved against a warm, muscular chest. What was more, she was held in position by a strong male arm.

Then she remembered…and felt her senses quicken.

It would be so easy to stay. To snuggle in against him and enjoy the closeness, breathe in his warm male scent, and feel the slide of his hand…

What was she thinking?

She couldn't go where he might lead. Told herself she didn't want to. And knew she lied.

In the night's darkness it was possible to indulge the mind, to allow herself to believe anything was achievable. Even love.

Claire's words whispered through her brain, adding to the fantasy of what her life might be like with Nic, children…a future.

Except it wasn't going to happen.

What was more, to remain in the same bed with him was *impossible*.

She'd die if he stirred in his sleep and mistakenly thought she was someone else, and began making a move on her.

Out, a silent voice urged. *Now.*

The thing, she determined several minutes later, was achieving her escape. Not easy when every inch she gained was lost as the arm draped over her waist tightened.

An involuntary action, or deliberate?

Involuntary, she decided. Had to be.

What next? The bold approach? That might work.

It did, and she slid into her own bed with a sense of relief.

There was no sign of Nic when Tina woke, and she went down to breakfast prepared to do battle regarding her decision to return to work. Only to have Steve relay Nic had already eaten, and was on his way into the city.

'Do you think you should?' Steve queried when she voiced her intention.

Assertiveness was the key. 'Yes.'

'Be alert,' he warned. 'Sabine—'

'May increase the nuisance factor,' she finished for him, and received his succinct confirmation.

'Got it,' Tina assured him as she collected her keys.

The morning proved busy, and there was a sense of normality in slipping back into a familiar routine. The stock looked great; Lily had shown herself to be more than capable in the few days Tina had been absent. Sales receipts were good, there had been one or two minor hiccups…but nothing Lily wasn't able to handle.

Around eleven Lily answered the phone, spoke quietly, then handed Tina the receiver. 'Your gorgeous husband.'

'What do you think you're doing?' His voice was pure silk.

'Working.'

'Ensure it's not for the entire day.'

She wasn't in the mood for over-protectiveness. 'We're busy,' she managed quietly. 'I have to go.'

She cut the connection, cast the salon a quick glance...and realised the day had just taken a turn for the worse.

Sabine. On a mission. With no doubt as to who was her target.

'We need to talk,' the woman began without pre-amble as she reached the counter.

'There's nothing to discuss,' Tina responded evenly.

Sabine offered a searing look meant to turn her vic-tim to ash. 'Get out of Nicos' life. Or I'll take you out.'

Tina could see Lily surreptitiously keying digits into her cellphone in the background.

'I'd like you to leave,' Tina voiced with deceptive calm, doubtful *polite* would work.

'When I'm done.'

Don't take your eyes from hers. An essential cau-tion.

Yet the attack came out of nowhere, lightning quick and deliberately vicious as Sabine's hand connected with Tina's cheekbone.

'Nic is *mine*,' Sabine hissed as Tina steadied her-self.

Without a further word the woman turned and strode to the door...which didn't budge. Whereupon Sabine yelled in fury, 'Open the door.'

'It'll stay closed until the police arrive.'

Sabine turned on Lily. 'Open it!'

The scene could go any which way, but two against one had to provide some advantage.

Sabine's howl of outrage was almost animalistic in tone when Lily didn't move, and in a fit of rage the woman began to run amok through the salon, pushing over an antique cheval-mirror, then she snatched up a bag from display and hurled it at Tina...who ducked, then successfully tackled Sabine to the carpeted floor.

It wasn't the smoothest move. But then the salon wasn't a *dojo* where carefully orchestrated manoeuvres were made with skill and expertise.

Down and dirty was never pretty!

Steve arrived minutes ahead of the police, and everything after that took on an unreal quality.

Tina endured Steve's scrutiny and waved aside his insistence the cut on her cheekbone needed an ice-pack.

She also attempted to avoid being photographed, and was in the midst of voluble protest when Nic entered the salon.

His presence resulted in an outraged plea from Sabine, which he ignored, nor did he offer the woman so much as a glance.

Instead he crossed directly to where Tina stood and subjected her dishevelled form to a sweeping appraisal.

'It's not as bad as it looks,' she managed, aware her hair had escaped from its smooth pleat and was all over the place. Her skirt didn't exactly sit right, her shirt was out and, when she checked, a few buttons were missing.

He took in the cut and swelling on her cheek, the

gouges on her hands from Sabine's lacquered nails, and turned towards the attending officer, offered a few succinct words and added, 'Throw the book at her.'

A bright flash, and Steve had his photograph. It coincided with one the police photographer took of Tina, the fallen cheval-mirror.

'I should go tidy up,' Tina inclined, and it was only when she checked her mirrored image that she realised just what a sight she presented.

Nic's image appeared behind her own, and she offered a token resistance as he turned her to face him.

He lifted a hand and touched her cheek with gentle fingers, saw her wince, and let them trail down to rest at the edge of her mouth.

His eyes were dark, his expression unfathomable, almost as if he didn't trust himself to speak.

She had to say something...anything was better than the silence that stretched between them.

'Sabine finally made a physical move,' Tina offered, and glimpsed a muscle bunch at the edge of his jaw.

'At considerable cost to you.'

'It could have been worse.'

'I'm taking you to get this—' he indicated her swollen cheek '—checked out. Then we're going home.'

She rotated her jaw. 'You want to play nurse...fine. But I'm staying here.' She needed to keep occupied, not spend time on reflection.

'On one condition. Steve stays with you.'

'Isn't that going just a tad overboard?'

'No.'

Tina filched a brush from her bag and tidied her hair, fixed her clothes, retouched her lipstick and returned to the salon in time to see Sabine escorted into a police car.

The salon presented its usual tidy appearance, doubtless due to Lily's efforts, and an officer was busy recording Lily's version of events.

'This is so unnecessary,' Tina voiced as a medic probed her cheek and swabbed the cut.

'You're going to have a beautiful bruise,' came the breezy response.

'I'll put ice on it,' she promised.

'That'll help.'

Then they were out of there, and she turned towards Nic as they reached the boutique. 'Satisfied?'

'No, but it'll keep.'

A police officer had remained to record Tina's account, and he expressed a need to access the boutique's security cameras, explained both Tina and Lily's statements would be ready to sign late that afternoon, then he left.

Nic followed after exchanging a few words with Steve, who in turn indicated he'd remain out back.

'Don't want to frighten the women away.'

Lily put her head to one side and cast him a wicked smile. 'Oh, I don't know. We could camp you up a bit, add some unisex shades, and there you go…we've gained a new assistant.'

'I don't think so.'

'Pity,' Lily teased.

It was fortunate the incident had occurred close to midday when most of their clientele lunched, and Tina downplayed it for those few who expressed curiosity at witnessing police moving in and out of the boutique.

They sent out for lunch and ate during alternate short breaks. Together, they contrived to keep busy, and bade each other an affectionate 'goodnight' at day's end.

Tina drove towards Rose Bay with Steve following close behind. Nic's Lexus was parked inside the garage, and there was nothing she could do about the sensation curling inside her stomach as she ascended the stairs.

It was crazy to feel like this, to be so aware of a man who had taken control of her life, turned it upside down…and was doubtlessly going to pitch her out of *his* life very soon.

The question was when, not if. And waiting for the figurative axe to fall was akin to walking a tightrope with no safety net.

Sabine Lafarge would be dealt with…but how long before a team of lawyers filed for her release on bail? What then?

Tina entered the master suite and came to an abrupt halt at the sight of Nic emerging into the bedroom with a towel hitched at his waist.

His dark hair was damp from his recent shower, and there was too much muscular flesh exposed for her peace of mind.

All it took was a glance for her to vividly recall what it felt like to be held close against him for several hours through the night.

Worse, how much *more* she wanted from him.

To know she could walk up to him and pull his head down to hers, to savour his kiss, initiate intimacy and luxuriate in his response.

The mere thought of him as a lover sent the blood racing through her veins. He had the look, the touch that could drive a woman wild. It was there in his eyes, his stance…a magnetic quality that exuded sensuality at its zenith.

'Hi.' As a greeting it was incredibly inane.

He crossed the room and stood close. Much too close, for she could inhale the clean smell of the soap emanating from his skin.

'Hi, yourself.'

His voice held a teasing quality as he brushed gentle fingers along the edge of her jaw. 'How's the pain threshold?'

'Bearable.' In truth the left side of her face ached.

'In other words, it hurts like hell.' He traced the slope of her nose. 'Take something for it.'

Tina inclined her head and made for the shower, emerging a while later to don tailored trousers and a knit top. She left her hair loose, added moisturiser and pink gloss, then she ran lightly downstairs.

Food…whatever it was smelt good. What was more she was hungry. Which had to be a first for more than a week nursing a lacklustre appetite.

Maria had prepared lasagne, a crisp salad, and there were crunchy bread rolls. Ambrosia, Tina admitted silently as she tucked into her portion.

'Any update on Sabine?'

'Out on bail,' Steve informed. 'Nic has filed

charges, and taken out a Restraining Order on your behalf. You need to confirm and sign your statement.'

'I'll do it on the way to work in the morning.'

'Early,' Nic informed. 'On our way to the airport.'

She was in the process of forking a morsel of lasagne and her action stilled as she cast him a puzzled look. 'Would you care to run that by me again?'

'We're spending a few days on Hayman Island in the Whitsundays.'

Tropical north Queensland. Sunshine, warm temperatures, sandy beaches, clear waters.

'You made this decision...*when*?'

'This afternoon.'

'Had your PA clear your schedule and make bookings?'

'Yes.'

'There's just one thing,' Tina offered solemnly. 'You forgot to ask if *I* could factor in a few days away.'

Nic tore a piece of bread from his roll and ate it. 'It's a done deal,' he relayed with deceptive quietness. 'Lily will take care of the boutique with a little help from her cousin Annie...whom Lily assures me you like and trust.'

She replaced her cutlery with care. 'You achieved this in—' she lifted a hand and clicked thumb and finger together '—a matter of minutes. A few phone calls, an offered bonus...phfft, and it's done.'

He looked vaguely amused. 'Something like that.'

'And if I refuse?'

His gaze hardened. 'I'm not giving you that option.'

'Short of manhandling me onto the flight, how do you expect to get me there?'

One eyebrow rose. 'Opposing me just for the sheer hell of it?'

She sounded ungracious. And heaven knew, she didn't mean to be. It was just...everything. The worst was not knowing what the next step would be.

'No. Unsure whether the two of us together twenty-four hours a day is a good thing.'

'Oh, I don't know,' Nic drawled. 'You might be pleasantly surprised.'

CHAPTER ELEVEN

THERE could be no doubt that in terms of *wanting to get away from it all*, a magnificent private island was the place to be.

The sunshine, clear blue skies and sparkling ocean waters provided a tranquil air.

One Tina coveted as she familiarised herself with the luxury suite they'd been assigned. Splendid views greeted her from wall-to-wall glass doors, shaded in part by bi-fold wooden shutters.

'Thank you.' She turned towards Nic.

'For what, specifically?'

'Bringing me here,' she said quietly. Putting a distance between what the past several weeks represented. To each of them, she added silently.

Maybe, just for a few days, she could pretend there were no shadows between them. Simply enjoy the *now*, and face the future when they returned to Sydney.

'Let's change and go explore the place.'

It was a large suite, with a lounge area, a spacious bedroom housing two king-size beds, and a luxurious *en suite*.

'That could be a plan,' Nic agreed with unruffled ease.

Cargo pants, Tina decided, a cotton top, and runners, filching each from her travel bag.

Sunglasses did much to shade the emerging bruise colouring her cheek, and minutes later she caught up a fun beach-hat, her camera, and preceded Nic from the suite.

The corporate executive persona disappeared as they traversed the large pool area, then began exploring the sandy beach.

He looked as relaxed as she felt. Different, she determined, intuitively aware it wasn't just his casual attire.

'Stand over there,' she directed, and held up her camera.

'You want photos?'

Memories, she accorded silently, I can take out and look at when all this is over. Something to remind me of a small slice of my life with a man who came to mean much to me.

She took several, fast, one after the other, and grinned when another couple passing by offered to take photos of them together.

It was easy to get into the act and place an arm along the back of Nic's waist. To laugh up at him when he curved his arm over her shoulders.

The laughter died as he leant down and fastened his mouth over hers in a brief, tantalising kiss...which was also recorded on celluloid.

'Thanks.' Nic took the camera and indicated the one the other couple held. 'Want me to return the favour?'

Honeymooners, Tina deduced, and couldn't help feeling envious. It must be wonderful to love and be loved, to gift up your soul to a man and receive his in return. To know there was unconditional trust.

It was easy to fall into friendly conversation for several minutes, to part with a 'see you around' comment as they went their separate ways.

Tina expected Nic to remove his arm from her shoulders, but to her surprise he left it there as they walked along the foreshore.

It was…nice. Sharing relaxed companionship, aware there were no sexual overtones.

This was what she wanted…wasn't it?

It was what she'd thought she wanted. What she'd conditioned herself to accept. Yet now she wasn't sure it was enough.

Are you insane?

This brief interlude is the last goodbye. A pleasant lead up to the moment when he'll inform me the marriage is over.

How could it be anything else?

Don't go there, a silent voice agonised.

Did Nic sense her insecurity? She hoped not.

At some point they turned and retraced their steps, re-entered their suite, showered and changed for dinner, then went down to the restaurant.

Most all of the guests wore casual gear, although some of the women had opted to dress up. It was a mixed crowd, some obvious honeymoon couples, families, maybe a stolen weekend for a few. People-watching was an interesting pastime, as long as it wasn't overt.

'How long are we staying?' Tina queried lightly as

she sipped a delicious Chardonnay between the starter and main.

'Until Sunday.'

Four days, total. A light shivery feeling raced over the surface of her skin, raising all her fine body hairs in instinctive awareness. Of the man, and the danger of being constantly in his company.

What if…?

Stop it. There is no *what if*.

But don't you want there to be? an inner voice posed.

They ordered coffee at the end of a leisurely meal, then wandered along the beach. The moon was clear, painting the ocean with a river of silver, and the faint light bathed the surroundings, etching them in varying shades of grey from palest pearl to almost black.

It was almost possible to believe in magic, Tina mused as Nic threaded his fingers through her own.

'Let's go back, shall we?'

She heard the faint drawling quality in his voice, and felt a wave of sadness roll over her. He was merely indulging her, and it hurt.

Stupid tears welled in her eyes, and she blinked rapidly to dispel them. Only to have them spill over and run slowly down each cheek.

This was crazy. What was the matter with her?

Emotional reaction, she rationalised. Let's face it, the past month hasn't exactly been a cakewalk!

She kept her head down as they entered their suite, and she missed Nic's sharp look, his slight frown. It was only when he barred her passage into the *en suite* that she became aware he'd moved across the room.

Dammit, he had the tread of a cat.

He stood close, much too close, and there was little she could do to prevent him catching hold of her chin as he tilted it towards him.

She lowered her eyelids in protective self-defence, and silently cursed the convulsive swallow of an imaginary lump in her throat.

He eased a thumb-pad over her cheek in a gentle gesture that caused another tear to spill.

'Suppose you tell me, hmm?'

Should she even begin?

'It's easy,' Nic said quietly. 'One word after the other.'

She managed a faint smile. 'You think?'

Was there ever going to be a better time? Avoiding and evading the issue would only delay the inevitable.

Okay, so what was there to lose?

'When do you want to file for divorce?' There, she'd voiced the query that had tortured her for days.

He didn't move. 'What makes you think that's my intention?'

'Isn't it? The loss of Vasili's child negates the reason for the marriage to exist,' she managed quietly. 'You'll want to be free to choose someone else.' This was becoming more difficult by the minute. 'Have children of your own.' She was grasping for words and the courage to continue. 'Provide the Leandros heir.'

He was too quiet. Dangerously so, and it unnerved her.

'You perceive that to be a logical solution?'

'Don't you?' she demanded, sorely tried.

'It would be inconceivable I might want to remain married to you?'

'Why?' she asked baldly. 'To keep the female predators at bay?'

'That, too.'

'And children? How do you propose to have them?'

A faint smile tugged the edge of his mouth. 'The usual method.'

Dear Lord in heaven…make love with him? 'You can't be serious.'

'Very serious.'

It solved the divorce, a financial settlement…a child and heir, children.

'You're wrong,' Nic offered softly as he read and defined each fleeting expression. 'On all counts.'

'Then…*why*?' The demand came out as an agonised plea.

'Because of this.' He pulled her in and fastened his mouth over hers in a kiss that took hold of her heart and sent it soaring high.

A deep, frankly sensual taking like nothing she'd experienced before. Hungry, compelling, it almost blew her mind.

He took her tentative response and led her towards something more, stoking her hunger until there was only the man and an electrifying emotion so intense it threatened to spontaneously combust.

Nic brought her down slowly, softening his touch until his mouth merely brushed hers, then he drew back a little.

'You want to deny what we share?' he queried gently.

She was almost trembling, and he stroked light fingers down her uninjured cheek.

Tina closed her eyes, then let her lashes sweep open.

'I'm not very good at this.' Let's face it, my one foray into intimacy was a disaster.

He caught her chin between thumb and forefinger. 'Do you trust me?'

She gave him a haunted look, one that took hold of his heart and squeezed a little.

'It's not fair,' she managed at last. 'If I ask you to stop.'

Nic brushed his lips to her forehead. 'Let's meet that when and if it happens.'

His mouth was gentle as it covered hers, subtly coaxing in a way that made her want more, and she wound her arms around his neck and leaned in, savouring his touch as he slid one hand down to cup her bottom while the other captured her nape.

A faint groan of protest emerged from her throat as he let his mouth trail to the sensitive cord at the edge of her neck, and sensation speared through her body as he traced the soft indentations, the hollows at the base of her throat, before edging lower.

She wanted to touch him, explore his naked flesh, caress him as he caressed her. Except he was wearing too many clothes, and she tugged at his shirt, freeing it from the waistband of his jeans, and he drew back a little and pulled the shirt over his head.

'Your turn.' He gave her no time to think as he took hold of the hem and tugged off her top. A deft movement and her bra followed.

With incredible gentleness he caressed each peak until they burgeoned beneath his touch, and she gasped out loud as he lowered his head and took one peak into his mouth and suckled there.

Dear heaven. She felt her body tremble as he moved to render a similar supplication to its twin, and she arched involuntarily to allow him easier access.

His hands travelled lower and dealt with the fastener at her waist, then he slid her jeans down and held her as she stepped out of them.

A lacy black thong was all that separated her from total nudity, and he shucked off his own jeans, then caught her close.

Not before the sight of him fully aroused captured her attention. For a moment she couldn't breathe, then she gasped as his fingers traced the lacy brief to her groin and slid beneath the silk.

She couldn't think as he teased the sensitive clitoris, and she groaned out loud as sensation spiralled through her body, all-consuming, electric.

He didn't stop, and just when she thought she'd *die* he began an intimate exploration that had her biting her lip in an effort to maintain some vestige of control.

Tina was hardly aware of Nic sweeping aside the bedcovers, or of being drawn down onto the bed.

He took his time, using his mouth, his hands, to bring her to climax, and she sobbed out loud as she went high...so high she caught hold of him and held on.

This, *this* was the emotion lyrics attempted to capture, together with poets and masters of every language.

She closed her eyes and let her breathing settle, her heart slow a little from its racing beat.

Except he was far from done.

Slowly and with infinite care, he entered her, feeling the silken tissues expand to accommodate him, and he covered her mouth with his own, absorbing the way her breath hitched, her soundless gasp as he eased back a little, then slid forward in gentle rocking movements until he reached the hilt.

Then he began to move, slowly at first, each thrust a little deeper until she caught his rhythm, matched it, and he let go of control as she soared with him, teetered at the brink, then fell with him in a climax that shattered them both.

Nic buried his mouth in the curve of her neck and held her close. His heartbeat matched hers, strong, fast, until it settled, and he felt her body quiver as he lightly traced her hip, the length of her thigh, before sliding up to cup her breast.

Afterwards Tina had no idea how long they lay entwined together, only that it felt good. Better than good. Right now she couldn't think of an adequate word in description.

At some stage they rose from the bed and took a leisurely shower, indulging in a slow, intimate exploration that led to an erotic coupling and the release of some of her inhibitions.

Towelled dry, Nic drew her down onto the bed and within minutes she slid into a dreamless sleep from which she didn't stir until the pre-dawn hours.

There was something incredibly sensually satisfying in feeling the slight pull of inner muscles, the sensation of having been possessed by a man and loved well, Tina reflected as she stretched a little and attempted to slip from the bed.

Except the arm at her waist tightened, and a warm, seeking mouth caressed the sensitive hollow at the edge of her nape.

'Where do you think you're going?'

'To make coffee, then ravish you.'

Nic's husky laughter sounded low in his throat as he turned her to face him. Dark eyes gleamed close to her own as he rolled onto his back. 'Skip the coffee.'

She was an apt pupil, he mused, who delighted him at every turn. A tentative lover, shy, and intensely fascinating.

'Are you just going to lie there?'

'If you need help,' he drawled. 'Just ask.'

This was no practised partner skilled in the art of gifting pleasure, who mostly faked each manoeuvre and sighed on learned cue.

This woman, his wife, delighted in discovering each indentation, hollow, muscle ridge, and displayed genuine enjoyment at each hitch of his breath, each groan as she lingered a little longer, teased a sensitive exploration of his penis, and the swollen pouches beneath.

She was having fun, and she gave a wicked chuckle as he pulled her on top of him and slid his hands up to her breasts.

'Now let's see how brave you are, hmm?'

'What do you call this?' she queried huskily. 'The early morning ride?'

He proceeded to show her, and it was she who cried out and held on. She, who almost collapsed as she lay sobbing against him at the extent of emotion she'd experienced.

'Enough,' Nic said gently as he traced a soothing pattern down her spine. 'Sleep a little, hmm? We have the day to explore the resort.'

Tina woke late to find Nic had already showered and dressed as he sat in the adjoining lounge reading the day's newspaper.

He glanced up as he heard her move from the bed, and the sensual warmth evident in his smile made her want to sit down again. 'Breakfast?'

She checked her watch and grimaced a little. 'Don't you mean lunch?'

'Go dress,' he bade easily. 'Then we'll eat and decide what we're going to do with the afternoon.'

CHAPTER TWELVE

THE ensuing three days numbered among the happiest in Tina's life.

At Nic's insistence, she took in relaxation therapy, visited the masseuse, had a manicure and enjoyed a session with the hairdresser.

Together they went wind-surfing, hired a catamaran, and played tennis.

The nights were something else as they drew out the anticipation by lingering over the evening meal, taking a walk along the beach, or the paths surrounding the resort itself.

All it took was an exchanged look, a touch of the hand, a murmured word, and they returned to their suite to indulge in a long, sweet loving that reached the heights and beyond in a magical, sensual world uniquely their own.

If *this* is happiness, Tina mused, why would she think of giving it up?

Anything seemed possible. A lasting marriage, children, a contented and fulfilling life with a man she adored.

What more could any woman ask?

It wasn't until they landed in Sydney late Sunday evening that a few doubts began to surface.

A return to Sydney meant a return to routine, work, a busy lifestyle.

Steve remained in residence, and with Sabine out on bail the woman was a looming spectre they couldn't afford to ignore.

'Hey, you look…incredible,' Lily pronounced when Tina arrived at the boutique. 'Bruise is something else, but the swelling has subsided. So,' she cajoled with a wicked grin. 'How was your break?'

'Really great.'

'That's it?'

She met Lily's teasing gaze and tilted her head to one side. 'What do you want me to say?'

'Oh…just, Nic was fantastic, it was the honeymoon you never had, the sex was off the Richter scale.' She offered an irrepressible grin. 'Stuff like that.'

'You're not going to give it up, are you?'

'Only if I have to.'

'Yes,' Tina said simply, and laughed as Lily executed a mock swoon. 'You're incorrigible, do you know that?'

'Of course. But we're friends…we walk the walk and talk the talk. It's what girls *do*.'

'There's the door buzzer,' Tina managed, and watched Lily morph into a serene, helpful salesperson as she turned towards the client.

It was a good day, Tina reflected as it reached time to close up and go home. Sales had been steady, expected stock arrived on time, both she and Lily had managed a reasonable lunch break, and she'd set up a stunning display for the front window.

Business was on track, and after four days of rest and relaxation she felt refreshed and vital again. True, there were moments of sadness and guilt. For the loss of a good friend in Vasili, the loss of his child, and for Stacey and Paul, to whom the child would have meant so much.

Steve entered the boutique just as she was ready to lock up, and minutes later he accompanied her to the four-wheel drive, saw her seated, then followed her home.

Nic's Lexus was in the garage when she drove in, and she ran lightly upstairs to their suite, deposited her laptop and bag, then she stripped off her clothes and walked naked into his shower.

'Well, now,' Nic drawled as she slid her arms round his neck and pulled his head down to hers for a soul-destroying kiss. 'That's some greeting.' He cupped her face between his hands and leant in. 'Want to try for a repeat?'

Her witching smile melted his heart. 'Mmm, what about dinner?'

'Dinner can wait.' With those few words he lifted her high against him and curved her thighs over his hips.

'But you can't,' Tina teased, loving the way he moved against her, the touch of his hands, his lips. Everything about him.

As long as he lived, he'd never get enough of her. Her generosity of spirit, her gift of giving so much of herself. It almost made him feel afraid.

Dinner was something they went down to the kitchen for around ten, fed each other morsels, washed it down with superb red wine, then returned to bed…this time to sleep.

Nic's breathing soon settled into a deep rhythm while Tina lapsed into contemplative thought.

A week ago she'd have given anything to have reached this level of understanding, trust and intimacy.

It was the realisation of her deepest dreams. Something she'd thought she would never achieve.

How had they come so far, so fast?

Don't analyse it, she admonished silently. Just accept life as it is.

Which was fine. She could do that. Except there was a part of her that longed for it all.

Love...the everlasting kind.

To *know*, deep in her heart, her soul, that what Nic felt for her was love, not lust.

Was that asking too much?

'I gather I'm meant to impress,' Tina teased as Nic negotiated inner city traffic.

'You manage to do that without any effort at all.'

His tolerant response held a musing drawl, and she sent him a brilliant smile.

'A compliment. How nice.'

She'd taken considerable effort with her appearance, taming her hair into a smooth knot with a few escaping tendrils framing her face. The Saab gown was a masterpiece in soft floral silk chiffon, draped bodice with spaghetti straps. Understated make-up with emphasis on her eyes, the pink gloss colouring her lips, and jewellery was a favoured diamond drop pendant and matching earrings. A light touch of perfume with floral tones added a final touch.

It was a mild spring evening, the sky a clear indigo with a soft sprinkling of pinprick stars. Soon the days would lengthen with the advent of seasonal summer, becoming more noticeable as daylight saving crept into the mix.

Sydney was a beautiful city, with its harbour, many coves and inlets, notable landmarks. Bright flashing neon signs, street lights, lit shop windows. The constant ebb and flow of city life…the good, the bad and the ugly, as it was with cities anywhere in the world.

Tonight's event was a formal dinner held in honour of a high-ranking Greek government minister, whose presence in Australia was designed to bolster trade between the two countries.

The venue was a major inner city hotel, and six-thirty for seven meant a steady stream of guests converging in the ballroom lobby as they sipped champagne.

Nic's presence created an effect among several of the women, and while some were circumspect, others were more blatant in their interest.

'Ah, there you are,' a vaguely familiar voice greeted, and Tina turned to see Eleni and Dimitri welcoming them into their circle of friends.

'Tina, so beautiful as always.' Eleni did the air-kiss thing, then caught hold of Tina's hands as she conducted a searching appraisal. 'My dear, your face. Is that a bruise? What happened?'

And there she was, thinking she'd done a great job with the concealer! 'I ran into something a few days ago.' The force of a feminine hand bent on inflicting damage, she added silently.

Eleni looked askance of Nic. 'An unfortunate accident,' he confirmed in carefully measured tones.

'Of course, an accident,' Eleni concurred with the knowledge of one who knew it couldn't possibly be anything else.

Tina decided to have a little fun, and she tucked a hand in his, then offered Nic a wistful, adoring smile. 'We've decided to delete that particular move from our—' she paused deliberately '—repertoire, haven't we, darling?'

Would he run with this and play?

He lifted their joined hands to his lips in a gesture that reduced her bones to water. 'Definitely.'

The look on Eleni's face was priceless.

'I've shocked her,' Tina said with a tinge of remorse as Eleni murmured an excuse and led Dimitri to greet a fellow guest.

'Doubtful,' Nic drawled, and gave her a quizzical look. 'Repertoire?'

'It sounded good.'

'Remind me to take you to task.'

'Can I count on that?' She sobered a little. 'Maybe I should go touch up my face.'

'The bruise is barely noticeable.'

Except Eleni had picked up on it, and Tina drew her hand free from his. 'I'll be back.'

He followed her slender frame as she threaded her way through the mingling guests, and stood outside as she entered the powder-room.

Was he being over-protective? Without doubt. He'd yet to relay Steve was staying on, combining bodyguard duties with those of general factotum.

Wealth and a high profile lifted the stakes for hostage situations, kidnapping of children, and worse.

Sensible precautions had become a fact of life.

Tina emerged within minutes and she merely lifted both eyebrows as he fell into step at her side.

Guests were already moving into the dining-room, and the evening began on time, with introductory speeches, some light entertainment in between the various courses, followed by a lengthy and detailed address by the Greek foreign minister.

The surprise of the evening came when Nic was called to the podium, and Tina watched in fascination as he delivered a flawless speech detailing the benefits of trade to both Australia and Greece, then proceeded to cite examples.

He stood perfectly at ease, and didn't refer to notes.

There was a round of applause, and as he descended from the stage he was swamped...yes, *swamped* was the right word, Tina mused, by a few society doyennes, a photographer and journalist.

'You didn't tell me,' she murmured as he returned to their table.

'It was a last-minute request. The corporate CEO scheduled to speak was unexpectedly rushed to hospital this afternoon.'

He'd come up with such a superb speech in something like an hour or so? 'I'm impressed.'

His smile held a degree of amusement. 'Thank you.'

'Yet another of your talents.' It was a genuine compliment, and he lifted a hand and brushed light fingers over her lips.

'We'll leave soon.'

It took a while. Coffee was served, and the guests began to move from table to table as the evening drew to a close.

Nic garnered attention as several fellow guests took time to offer praise, and he handled it with effortless charm.

Tina smiled a lot as she stood at his side, although the smile became a little fixed as a few of the women elected to show their enthusiasm with affection. No air-kisses there!

'Nic's new bride,' one woman guest trilled with obsequious gaiety...brought on, Tina guessed, by a little too much wine. 'Who'd have thought?'

'That I'd be a bride?' Tina queried politely. 'Or that Nic would marry me?'

'Oh, my dear, *no*. I mean of course who'd have thought Nic would *marry*?' There was that laugh again. 'I mean, he's such a catch. You must tell me your secret.'

It was too much for Tina. 'Sex,' she revealed with a very straight, even, earnest expression. 'Lots and lots of sex.'

The woman's eyes almost crossed as she made a valiant attempt at recovery. 'Really?'

Tina's expression remained unchanged. 'Yes,' she managed quietly. *'Really.'*

'You do realise,' Nic drawled much later as he eased the car into the flow of traffic, 'your musing banter will be circulated among the social set.'

'And that's a problem?' She shook her head. 'What it is to have earned a reputation.' She sighed, and sent him a sideways glance. 'Your wild sexual animal meter will go right through the roof,' she mocked lightly.

He laughed, a low, husky sound that liquefied her bones.

'Perhaps you should give it a test run.'

'I live to please,' she assured him solemnly.

And she did please him. As she helped divest him of his clothes after first shedding her own. As she pushed him down onto the bed and played the vamp.

Yet as she drove him wild it was he who took control and led her on a journey of discovery along a path she'd never travelled before.

Just as she thought it couldn't become more magical, he took her higher, until she cried out and begged for his possession.

It was wicked sorcery at its peak. Unrestrained, and transcending mere passion. A raw, primitive hunger that tore at the heart, the soul, and left them each sheened with sensual heat, breathless from the force of what they'd just shared.

Lust, Tina accorded on the edge of sleep.

But *what about love*?

CHAPTER THIRTEEN

'SPECIAL delivery for Tina Leandros.'

Tina glanced up from the client she was attending, murmured an apology, crossed to the counter, signed the proffered clipboard and cast the attractive gift-box a puzzled look.

Nic? Claire? She couldn't think of anyone else who might send an unexpected gift.

The morning was busy, so much so Lily transferred the box into the back room where it remained untouched for several hours. Lunch came and went, and it was almost mid-afternoon before Tina had a chance to check it out.

Beautiful wrapping, she mused as she slid off the elaborate bow. No visible card. Probably tucked inside somewhere.

Lots of tissue paper. Her fingers parted it all as she dug in deep. Ah, there it was…a second small gift-wrapped box.

Jewellery?

The wrapping undid easily, and she slid open the expensive velvet case, unsure quite what to expect.

The breath caught in her throat, and her eyes widened with shock as the contents lay revealed. A miniature baby doll, naked except for a gauze nappy, with a pin piercing its heart. The accompanying card read, 'Sorry for your loss'.

Deliberately cruel, it could only have one source.

'What is it?' Lily queried with concern.

Had she uttered a strangled sound? She wasn't sure.

Lily joined her, took one look, muttered something vicious beneath her breath, caught up the phone and hit speed-dial.

'What are you doing?'

'Calling Nic.'

'Don't. He has important meetings all day.'

Lily shook her head. 'I was given specific instructions.'

'Cut the connection,' Tina insisted. 'I'll tell him tonight.' Without good cause, for Lily blithely ignored her. Seconds later she handed over the phone.

'I'm on my way.'

'There's no need—' Except Nic had already hung up.

She sent Lily a telling glare. 'Please. Do I *look* like a fragile flower?'

'I'll make some tea.'

'Enough, already,' she dismissed with very real exasperation. An emotion that was evident a short while later when Nic walked through the door.

'I'm fine,' Tina reiterated, and barely caught her breath as he pulled her in and fastened his mouth over hers in a kiss that took hold of her suspended emotions and made her temporarily forget where she was.

'Uh-huh.' His gaze searched her features, glimpsed the bruised hurt apparent in the depths of those dark emerald eyes, and brushed his lips over hers. 'We're going home.'

'I can't—'

'Lily will lock up.'

'What *is* it with you two?'

'A conspiracy.' He kissed her again, and she leaned in against him, savoured his warmth, strength, the security he offered...and so much more. 'Taking care of you,' he added quietly. 'Let's go.'

She gave an eloquent sigh that was part smile, part resignation. 'Do I have a choice?'

'No.'

The police would collect the box, wrapping and contents. Steve was already on it, as well as conducting a search of the city's delivery agents.

It was highly probable Sabine had outsmarted them by using gloves to avoid any fingerprint evidence. But the delivery was traceable...and if Sabine could be positively identified, conviction and sentencing would follow.

Not before time, he thought grimly.

Tina collected her bag, laptop and keys, and gave Lily a hug. 'Thanks. I'll see you tomorrow.'

'You go first,' Nic directed as they reached the staff car park. 'I'll follow.'

'Where?'

'Home.'

Well, there you go. *Home* had a nice ring to it. And the elegant house set in landscaped grounds *had* become home...her personal sanctuary with the man who was the love of her life.

Nic saw her seated in the four-wheel drive, then he crossed to the Lexus, waited until she eased her vehicle onto the road, and followed close behind.

Steve was in the lobby when they entered it.

'A minor breakthrough. I have the delivery firm, they're checking their staff. There's one possible, but the pick-up point doesn't match Sabine.'

'She could have used someone as a front.'

'Highly likely. I'm on it.'

Tina moved towards the stairs. A shower and a change into comfortable clothes was a priority. Afterwards she'd walk Czar, check what Maria had left for dinner, and relax.

In the suite she slid off her stilettos, stripped off her clothes and walked into the *en suite*, adjusted the temperature dial and stepped beneath the warm, pulsing water.

Heaven. She closed her eyes and let the heated spray wash over her. Any minute soon she'd scoop up the soap...but for now she'd *enjoy*.

A faint sound caused her eyes to spring open and they widened measurably as Nic stepped in to join her.

Her lips formed a witching smile, and her eyes...dear Lord, a man could drown in those brilliant emerald depths.

'You have your own bathroom,' Tina teased, and saw the indolent warmth apparent as he pulled her close.

'Sharing yours is so much more fun.'

'I'm partial to rose-scented soap.' She caught it up and ran the bar over his chest, his stomach, lower, only to have the breath hitch in her throat as he returned the favour.

'And that's a problem?'

It was a game, a delightful play by lovers, and one in which she exulted. 'It might fight with your cologne.'

'You think?' His lips nuzzled the sensitive edge of her neck, and felt her pulse kick in to a faster beat.

'Uh-huh.'

He trailed gentle fingers down the length of her spine, caressing each indentation, and felt her body quiver.

'Want me to leave?'

Her hands settled on his hips and drew him against her. His arousal was a potent force, and hers, all hers. 'Not if you value your life.'

He fastened his mouth over hers, savouring the taste and feel of her, the moist, sweet tissues, her generosity as his tongue swept hers, bit gently, then possessed in a manner that left her in no doubt as to the degree of his passion.

And matched it, wanting more, so much more, as she clung to him and held on as if she'd never let go.

'You want to take this in the bedroom?'

'What's wrong with the shower?'

A soft, husky chuckle emerged from his lips. 'It'll do for a start.'

He lifted her high and she wound her legs over his hips, then arched back a little. 'Hmm, you learn something new each day.'

Her soft laugh became a faint groan as he eased her into a gentle rocking movement, then lowered his head to her breast.

Her breath quickened as he savoured one peak, then took it into mouth and grazed it with his teeth.

Heat surged through her veins, encompassing every nerve in her body until she was on fire, mindless in passion that demanded more, so much more than pre-coital play.

'Please.'

Yet he was far from done, and she cried out as he

used his hands to caress and stroke, stoking the fire
to fever-pitch.

Then he positioned her carefully and drove deep in
one slow thrust, feeling her silken body stretch to accommodate him, hold him fast, before she began to
move, easily catching his rhythm and matching it, taking them both high to a place where sheer sensation
ruled.

Quickened breathing and soft groans were masked
by the pulsing water, and just as she began to ease
back a little he took her so high she simply held on
and rode the sensual storm, exulting in it, *him*, and
the love they shared.

It was more, so much more than she had ever hoped
to have in her life...the man, the all-consuming passion. And *love*. It took her breath away.

Nic held her close, then angled his mouth down to
hers in a lingering kiss so incredibly sweet she wanted
to weep from the sheer joy of it.

He was the other half of her soul. The air that she
breathed. Her life.

Every day, each night, her love for him seemed to
grow. Just when she thought it couldn't be *more*, it
moved up another notch.

There was trust, unequivocal and enduring. All the
doubts, the insecurities were gone. In its place was
something so special, so unique to each of them, it
brought tears to her eyes.

'Hey,' Nic chided gently. He caught hold of her
chin and lifted it, then pressed a thumb to the sensitive
curve of her lower lip. 'What's this?'

'You,' she said shakily, and saw his eyes flare a

little. Oh, God, there were words she wanted, *needed* to say, and she hardly knew how or where to begin.

She touched his lips, trailed light fingers across that sensual curve and held them at its edge.

The ghost of a smile shook her lips. 'I love you.' There, she'd said it. 'I never thought I could feel this way.'

She brought him undone. Totally. He cupped her face with his hands and glimpsed the naked emotion in the depths of her eyes.

'Tina.'

'Don't. Please, not yet.' She was oblivious to everything, except the man. 'There's so much...' She bit her lip, unsure where to begin.

'Vasili's baby,' she managed shakily, and trembled as he smoothed a thumb over her cheek. 'Just as I was dealing with the guilt associated with the how and why of its conception, Vasili died. The baby represented an extension of his life. I couldn't take the easy way out.' The next part was painful. 'There was Stacey and Paul,' she managed. *'You.'* A lump rose in her throat, and she swallowed it. 'Marriage as a viable solution for the child's benefit.'

Her eyes were large emerald pools as she silently begged him to let her continue. Nic smoothed away the slow trickle of tears and felt his heart clench at her visible distress.

'The pregnancy became the glue that held us together.' She faltered a little. 'A child who didn't ask to be conceived, but one who meant so much.' It hurt, but she needed to get it all out. 'When I miscarried, it wasn't only the loss of the child that upset me. It was the prospect of losing you.' Her eyes searched his. 'For without the child, there was no need for the marriage to continue.'

'Fool,' Nic chided gently.

'You were so…supportive. Caring,' she added. 'In hospital, afterwards. I wanted the affection you displayed to be real. Not just a result of misplaced duty.'

Oh, hell, this wasn't easy. 'Every day I expected you to tell me the lawyers would be called in, the marriage annulled, and we'd each go our separate ways.'

She wasn't done. 'Then when you suggested we consummate the marriage and produce our own child…' Words momentarily failed her. 'I realised it wasn't me you wanted. It was a Leandros heir.'

'When we made love…how could you not know the effect you had on me?'

Truth, honesty. If ever there was the right time for it, it was now.

'I rationalised it was just sex.' Very good sex. Right off the Richter scale. 'And you were very practised in the art of pleasing a woman.'

'And my reaction? That was due simply to *practice*? Not because of the woman I held in my arms? The way I felt for her, *loved* her?'

Tina thought her heart stopped. Everything seemed suspended…time, place.

Her voice was little more than a whisper. 'What did you say?'

'*Love,*' he reiterated quietly. 'My love for you. Only *you*.'

It was almost too much. More than she had ever hoped for, or believed she would ever have.

'The first time I laid eyes on you was across an

open grave at my brother's funeral. The solemnity and pain of the occasion, the fact you were pregnant with Vasili's child...' He took a moment, then continued, 'None of it diminished the instant attraction I instinctively fought against.'

He brushed his mouth against her own, lingered, then reluctantly drew back a little. 'You fascinated me. Your strength, unswerving loyalty. Vulnerability,' he added quietly. 'I could have torn limb from limb the man whose vicious attack almost destroyed your emotional heart.'

He watched her swallow the sudden lump that had risen in her throat, and resisted the temptation to pull her close. Soon, he vowed silently.

'I wanted you in my life. Marriage was the only option. I just had to convince you of it.'

He'd used considerable skill in achieving his objective. But then, hadn't *she* condoned the marriage for similar reasons she was unwilling to identify with at the time?

'There was a need to stand back,' Nic relayed gently. 'Allow you time to trust me.' He waited a beat. 'To trust yourself.

'I silently wept with you when you miscarried,' he continued gently. 'For what the child would have meant...to Stacey, Paul. To each of us, for much the same reasons. But for you, especially,' he added. 'As much as it was Vasili's child, it was also yours.'

They were so nearly there. Only a few loose ends remained. 'Sabine—'

Tina pressed a finger to his mouth. 'She's a beautiful seductress who became unhealthily obsessed with you.'

How could she voice what she wanted to say, and have it sound right? 'Very few people escape without accumulating some baggage in their lives. It's the way you deal with it that makes the difference.'

'She could have harmed you.' The thought had kept him awake nights, seen him carry security measures to the extreme.

'She didn't get the opportunity.'

He'd made sure of it.

'I've cleared my diary,' Nic enlightened as he dropped a kiss to the tip of her nose. 'As from Monday.' Delegated, assigned, organised with cut-throat precision. 'For a month.'

A *month*? 'You have?'

'Aren't you going to ask why?'

Her eyes gleamed with soft humour. 'Surprise me.'

'We fly out late Monday *en route* to Athens, then we'll spend a few weeks touring the Greek Islands.'

A delighted smile curved that delectable mouth. 'Santorini? I've always wanted to visit there.'

'Naturally.'

'I think I love you.'

He lowered his head to touch her forehead with his own. 'Only *think*?'

Her smile widened. 'You want a rundown on my innermost thoughts?'

'Sounds like a plan.'

His voice was light, but there was a seriousness apparent, one that sent a quivering sensation through her body.

'Don't you think we should get out of here first?'

Nic reached out and closed the water dial, then he filched a towel and began blotting the moisture from her body, loving the silky texture of her skin, the slight curves...the way she quivered at his touch.

'My turn,' Tina said gently when he was done. The flex of muscle and sinew fascinated her, the hard ridges, his tight butt. The narrow waist, washboard midriff, the strong breadth of his shoulders.

'We should get dressed.'

He skimmed his hands over her body and cupped her face. 'You think?'

Held like this, she was past thinking. 'You have a better idea?'

He drew her into the bedroom, tossed back the covers, and showed her, very thoroughly, just what it meant to be loved and adored as he led her on a sensuous witching journey that fragmented her control and turned her into a shameless wanton.

Magic, she sighed a long time later. Mesmeric, intoxicating, primitive.

'Thank you,' she said huskily from within the sanctuary of his arms.

'For what, specifically?' He pressed lips to her forehead, and was unable to resist the urge to tease a little. 'Good sex?'

'For caring, believing in me.' Having the patience to ride out the emotional storm.

'A given. As it will be for the rest of my life,' he added quietly.

'I love you.' He was everything...all she could ever wish for, and more. She had a burning need to show him how much, in a way words never could.

It took a while, and it was he who groaned beneath her touch, loving the witching siren she became as she pleasured him...until he could take no more. He didn't wait to reverse their positions, he simply caught hold of her waist, lifted her to straddle him, and proceeded to take her on the ride of her life.

Afterwards she wasn't capable of moving so much as a muscle.

Nic curved an arm round her waist and traced a finger down the slope of her nose. 'Sleepy?'

'Uh-huh.'

'I didn't thank you.' He paused imperceptibly. 'For gifting me the most precious gift of all. *You.*' Truly a gift from the heart, and one he would treasure for as long as he lived.

Eternity.

'Same goes,' Tina said quietly, smiling a little as she caught hold of his hand and pressed it to her lips.

This was one of the most precious moments of her life; she was aware there would be many more as the years unfolded.

The birth of a much-wanted child or three. Celebrations and anniversaries.

One entity would remain a constant.

Love. Theirs for each other.

The for-ever kind.

Purchased by
the Billionaire

HELEN BIANCHIN

CHAPTER ONE

'YOU did…what?'

Kayla's features paled as consternation meshed with disbelief, then magnified into a sense of dread.

'You think it was easy for me to go to Duardo Alvarez and *beg*?' Defensive anger rose to the surface, and something else…rage.

Jacob's words fell with hammer-like pain, and for a few brief seconds she hovered between retaliatory anger and despair.

Duardo Alvarez.

The mention of his name was enough to send ice slithering down the length of her spine.

Bad boy made good, now billionaire entrepreneur with homes in several major cities around the world.

Her ex-husband…and the last person on earth likely to help her, or her brother.

'Why in hell would you do that?'

'I had no choice!' Jacob's expression revealed a torment that twisted her stomach muscles into a painful ball.

Oh, dear God.

The last time she'd seen her ex-husband had been at her father's funeral. A deeply sorrowful occasion with few genuine mourners, several curiosity-seekers…and she'd been too stunned with shocked grief to do anything other than act on autopilot.

She hadn't had contact with Duardo since. Didn't want any.

'Dammit, Jacob! How *could* you?'

He didn't answer. But then he had no need.

And right now there was no time for further argument or castigation. In nine minutes she had to catch a train into the city. Or be late.

Kayla caught up her jacket, slung the strap of her bag over one shoulder and turned towards him. 'We'll continue this discussion later.'

Jacob offered a slip of paper. 'Duardo's number. Call him by midday.'

Hell would freeze over first.

'Please.' Jacob's eyes were dark, desperate, and she pocketed the number.

'You ask too much.' Way too much. More than she could give.

Without a further word she left the small two-bedroom walk-up for the hard inner-city pavement in one of the city's less salubrious suburbs. Old terraced houses lined the street, each in various stages of decay and neglect.

A far cry from her former life.

Five years ago the Enright-Smythe family had numbered high among Sydney's rich and famous. Kayla, at twenty-two, held a degree in business management and had took out a handsome salary for a token position in the 'firm'.

A member of the 'young social-set', she attended every party in town, spent an outrageous sum on clothes, travelled, and was seen on the arm of a different man every week.

Until Duardo Alvarez entered the field.

In his mid-thirties and cloaked in sophistication, on the rise within the city's financial sector, his youthful past hinted at association with the shady underbelly of New York.

He was everything Kayla's parents didn't want for their only daughter.

All the more reason, in her year of tilting at windmills, coupled with boredom, for deliberately setting Duardo in her sights.

He excited her. So, too, did a sense of the forbidden. Winning him over became a game. Holding him off took enormous self-restraint. She succeeded, and in a moment of sheer madness she accepted his proposal to fly to Hawaii and marry him.

Seventy-two hours later the marriage was over.

Courtesy of Benjamin Enright-Smythe's ultimatum and her mother's death…a heart attack which put Blanche Enright-Smythe into Intensive Care and took her life.

A tragic loss for which Benjamin attributed the blame to his daughter, referring privately and publicly to the marriage as *Kayla's folly*.

Her father's denunciation speared a stake through Kayla's heart and left her racked with guilt at the thought that her whirlwind marriage might have contributed to Blanche's death. Confidante and friend, Blanche had always been there for her, frequently acting as a calming buffer between two clashing personalities…Benjamin's arrogance and Kayla's defiance.

In the devastating numbness that followed Blanche's funeral, she stood at her father's side, comforted Jacob and somehow managed to get through each day. Wanting, needing the comfort of the one man who could help ease her grief…her husband.

Medical results indicated Blanche had been dealing with heart disease for some time, evidence Benjamin refused to accept in his demented quest to wreak revenge on the man he blamed for Blanche's death.

It proved a heart-wrenching time, with divided loyalties whittling away at Kayla's emotional heart. She was painfully aware of Benjamin's fragile mental state and Jacob's need for comfort and stability.

How could she give her personal life priority at such a time?

Yet how long could she expect Duardo to be patient? Benjamin's ultimatum—*Leave this house, and you'll never be welcome inside it again*—almost tore her in two.

Family. Something her mother had considered to be sacrosanct.

Except Benjamin was hell-bent on denigration, dredging up written proof that acquisition of the Enright-Smythe empire was part of Duardo's agenda. And that Kayla had merely been a pawn in his game plan.

That day something within her withered and died.

She refused Duardo's calls, acceded to her father's demands that Duardo be forbidden entry to the family home.

Then Duardo issued an ultimatum of his own.

Choose. Your husband or your family.

She didn't utter so much as a word beneath Benjamin's torrent of anger. Instead, she slid off her wedding band and handed it to the man whose name she'd taken as her own. And watched him turn and walk away.

Then she witnessed, in the ensuing months, Duardo Alvarez's acquisition of the Enright-Smythe business empire, with Duardo now firmly labeled a predator with one goal in mind.

Absent was the desire to party, and Kayla's friends

gradually gave up issuing invitations as she refused each and every one of them. The association with frivolity and flirtatious fun seemed firmly embedded in pain. The kind of pain she never wanted to suffer again in her lifetime.

The only social occasions she attended were those instigated by her father: dull, boring business dinners where she was forced to watch Benjamin's decline among his peers.

Within a year, the firm of Enright-Smythe held a list of unfulfilled contracts, union problems, and was the subject of a takeover bid by none other than Duardo Alvarez.

By then everything had been auctioned off…the family home, staff, the Bentley, her mother's jewellery, works of art.

The media made much of it at the time.

Benjamin proceeded to gamble his way into bankruptcy, only to compound his fall from grace by committing suicide. This tragic act devastated Kayla and sent Jacob into a downward spiral of despair.

For the past three years she'd worked her day job, waitressing in a local restaurant five hours each night and on weekends in an effort to keep a roof over their heads and help pay off a mountain of debt.

Jacob put in similar hours, quitting university at nineteen and abandoning all hope of entering medical school.

Yet it wasn't enough. It would never be enough. And the money-lenders were closing in. No thanks to her brother, who in an act of desperation had played the casino, and lost.

Forget the banks, she had no collateral. Everything she'd owned of any worth had been sold. And her working hours were at a maximum.

The entrance to the subway loomed, and she rode the escalator, saw the train and watched with a sense of fatalism as it pulled away from the station.

A hollow laugh rose and died in her throat.

How much worse could the day get?

It was unwise to tempt Fate, even in humour. Add cynicism, and it could turn round and bite you, Kayla reflected as she dealt with irate phone calls, negotiated a peaceful solution between two aggressive staff members and soothed a client who threatened to take his business elsewhere unless his demands were met.

Yoghurt and fruit eaten at her desk sufficed as lunch, and the afternoon involved a series of meetings, both in-house and via conference calls.

It was after five when she shut down the laptop, relieved this part of the day was over.

Not the night, Kayla reflected wearily as she collected her bag and slung the strap over one shoulder.

A forty-five-minute time-frame was all she had in which to catch a train and report for work at an Italian restaurant in her local shopping centre. Working there offered the bonus of supplying her with a meal, usually eaten on the run between serving customers, and it was within walking distance of home.

The phone on her desk rang, and she hesitated over answering it. Whoever it was, she decided as she picked up the handset, she'd give them two minutes, tops, then she was out the door.

'Thank God I caught you,' a familiar male voice breathed in relief.

'Jacob?' Something was wrong. She could sense it, almost feel it.

'I won't be home tonight.' His voice was jerky. 'Hospital. Smashed kneecap.'

'Which hospital?' She stifled an inaudible groan as he cited one on the other side of the city. 'I'll be there as soon as I can.'

'Call Duardo, Kayla. I don't need to spell out *why*.'

Ice ran through her veins as he cut the connection.

A smashed kneecap as a warning? What next, broken ribs, damaged kidneys, wrecked spleen? How long would the thugs wait before they meted out another *lesson*? A few days? A week?

Her financial situation wasn't going to change. Heaven knew how long it would take for Jacob to return to work. Without his wages to complement her own, together with a swathe of medical bills…it was hopeless.

Kayla closed her eyes, then opened them again.

The slip of paper Jacob had handed her this morning was in her jacket pocket. She retrieved it, punched in the series of digits and waited for Duardo to answer.

What if he knew where she worked, and recognized the number on caller ID? Worse, what if he chose not to pick up?

'Alvarez.'

The sound of his voice curled round her nerve-ends, tugged a little and almost robbed her of the ability to speak.

'It's Kayla.' Oh, dear heaven, how could she go through with this?

His silence seemed to reverberate down the line.

'I need your help.'

Would he agree, or sever communication?

'My office.' He gave precise directions. 'Ten minutes.' And he ended the call.

She reconnected, only to have the call go to voicemail.

He was pulling her strings. It irked unbearably that he *could*. Dammit. She had the irresistible urge to throw something, preferably at *him*.

Given it was impossible for her to be in three different

places at once, she rang the restaurant, relayed the reason why she'd be late, promised to be there as soon as she could and listened to a heated response.

It was all she needed right now to be in the firing line of rapidly spoken Italian ire, soothed only in conclusion by expressed sympathy for her brother's accident.

Kayla emerged onto the pavement and cast an eye at the leaden sky. *Rain*, why don't you? Make my day!

Almost in direct response, the first raindrops fell. Great big fat ones, increasing with a speed and intensity that showed no intention of abating any time soon.

Great. So now she'd face her ex-husband looking very much like a drowned rat.

The price of an evening newspaper helped ward off the worst of the downpour, and some ten minutes later she entered the impressive marble lobby of one of the city's glass and steel architecturally designed office buildings, ditched the sodden paper and rode the lift to the top floor.

Alvarez Holdings occupied an executive suite, which at first sight appeared to cover the entire floor, Kayla perceived as she took in the thick tinted glass, luxurious fittings, furnishings and the latest technology.

A perfectly groomed young woman manned Reception. Moonlighting as a model for *Vogue*?

Stop with the cynicism.

Image, she reminded herself, was everything, and Duardo Alvarez could afford whatever image he chose to project on planet Earth.

'Kayla Smythe.' She'd left off the preceding hyphenated *Enright* some time ago. 'I have an appointment with—' she hesitated fractionally. This was business, not personal— 'Mr Alvarez.'

The answering smile held polite warmth…practised, and tuned up or down according to client importance. In this instance, down a notch.

'Mr Alvarez is unavoidably detained in conference.' She indicated the bay of comfortable chairs. 'If you'd care to take a seat?'

Kayla felt her stomach tighten with nervous tension. Now that she was here, she wanted it over and done with.

Each passing minute seemed like ten, and she had to make a conscious effort not to constantly check her watch. She idly flipped the pages of a complimentary magazine, with no recollection of absorbing script or pictures.

How long would she have to wait?

Was Duardo Alvarez stretching out the time to deliberately unnerve her?

If she could walk out of here, she thought darkly… Yet doing so would achieve nothing. And this wasn't about *her*, she reminded herself.

'Kayla.'

She glanced up at the sound of her name and saw the receptionist move out from the console.

'Mr Alvarez will see you now.'

Stand tall and project a semblance of aloof confidence. The latter was almost impossible, given the state of her nerves.

She'd seen his image on the television screen, in newspapers and photographs in glossy magazines. But it was *years* since she had come face-to-face with him.

Would he look the same?

The silent query arose in a moment of sheer hysteria, and she beat it down as she followed the receptionist along a wide passageway to a set of imposing double doors.

Calm. She had to remain calm and in control.

Who was she kidding? She was as nervous as a kitten about to walk on hot coals, and at that moment she hated him, herself…most of all she hated the situation which had brought her here.

The receptionist placed a discreet knock on one of the doors, turned the knob and pushed the door open, announced Kayla's presence with smooth efficiency, then retreated.

She stood frozen, limbless, as she focused on the dark-suited figure standing silhouetted against the wide floor-to-ceiling plate glass.

From this distance, with the late-afternoon light behind him, it was difficult to define his expression.

Then he turned towards her, and the breath caught in her throat.

Tall, with an admirable breadth of shoulder, he projected an enviable aura of power most men coveted, but few possessed.

Well-defined facial bone structure, harshly chiselled, portrayed an elemental ruthlessness that visibly warned he was a force to be reckoned with in any arena.

'Come in and shut the door.' His drawl held a hint of cynicism, his appraisal ruthlessly unequivocal as he took in her petite stature, the blonde hair swept high and damp from the rain.

What happened to *hello*? But what did she expect…polite civility?

'You must know I don't want to be here.'

'Point taken.' He indicated a button-backed leather chair. 'Sit down.'

And have him tower over her? 'I'd prefer to stand.'

His expression didn't change, yet she gained the fleeting impression something deep within him uncoiled in readiness to strike.

'I don't have much time.' Oh, hell, she didn't want to sound defensive. Yet everything about him screamed out for her to turn and run as far and as fast as she could.

He crossed the room to stand within touching distance, and this close she saw the tiny lines fanning from each corner of those dark, almost black eyes. The grooves slashing each cheek seemed to etch a little deeper than she remembered, and that mouth…

Dear heaven, don't even go there.

One dark eyebrow rose in silent query, and she found herself almost stumbling in speech. 'Jacob is in hospital.' Pride kept her chin high. 'I'm sure you have no difficulty imagining *why*?'

Each passing second seemed to stretch until the silence became a palpable entity. 'Your brother isn't going anywhere in a hurry.' He waited a beat. 'Neither are you.'

Sapphire eyes flashed with brilliant blue fire. 'I beg your pardon?'

Down, but not cowed, Duardo perceived. She didn't disappoint.

'Let's dispense with the pretense, shall we?' When it came to game-playing, he was a lifetime ahead of her. 'You have a mountain of debt you can't hope to clear in a lifetime. Thugs have served the first of a few painful lessons for late payment. And you have no one else but me to turn to.'

Her eyes hardened. 'Does it give you pleasure to know that?'

'You can choose to walk out that door now,' he intoned with deceptive quiet.

'And if I do?'

'You'll never walk through it again.'

His words held a frightening finality, leaving her in no doubt he meant every one of them.

She had a mental picture of Jacob lying in an open coffin, instead of a hospital bed, and she was unable to control the shiver of fear slithering down her spine.

'Perhaps we can start over?'

Benjamin had done a number on her. His own daughter. At the time Duardo had wanted to haul her over his shoulder and take her away. Vilify her father, and sue for defamation of character. Instead, he'd worked behind the scenes, and achieved what Benjamin had falsely accused him of at the time.

Because he could.

Now he moved to lean one hip against the edge of his desk, and watched her struggle for composure.

'Jacob told me you're aware of our…situation.'

He wasn't going to make it easy. But then, why should he?

What they'd shared…what once had been…was now long gone. Destroyed by complex circumstances.

'You want my help,' Duardo prompted with silky smoothness, and caught the glitter of helpless anger in those brilliant blue eyes. It gave him no pleasure to see it there.

'Yes.'

Would he make her beg? *Could* she?

For Jacob. Survival. Because she had no choice.

'We need money.' Oh, hell, this was hard. 'To pay some debts.'

'Debts which will soon accumulate and escalate to a repeat of this situation within a very short space of time.'

He knew. He had to know. Jacob would have told him, and it wouldn't take much to access the true state of their miserably dire state of affairs.

She wanted to weep, but strong women don't succumb to emotional distress.

'Please.' Desperation fractured her voice.

'There are conditions.'

She expected no less. 'What do you propose?' Inside she was a mess of jangling nerves.

'I clear all debts, and fund Jacob through medical school.'

Millions of dollars.

Her brother's discarded dream fulfilled.

A substantial financial package, for which payment in one form or another would have to be made.

She needed for him to spell it out. 'In return for...what?'

'I want what I once had.' He watched the realization sink in, then hammered it home. '*You*. As my wife.'

Colour leeched from her face, and for a few seconds it seemed as if the room took a slight sideways tilt.

Wife?

She had a sudden need to sit down, yet to do so would betray her vulnerability. And she refused to give him the satisfaction.

Yet there was nothing she could do about the way her heart raced to an accelerated beat at the thought of that hard, muscular body entwined with her own in intimate possession, enticing, sharing...gifting the ultimate tactile pleasure, with his mouth, his hands.

As it had been during those brief few days of their marriage, when he'd introduced her to the sensual delights of the flesh, and she'd believed herself to be *in love* and loved.

Even now she experienced dreams so exquisitely sensual she woke bathed in sweat...and *wanting*.

Kayla could only look at him, aware to a frightening degree of his strength of will and the power he wielded.

'Revenge, Duardo?'

He took his time in answering. 'Everything has a price.' Eyes as dark as sin seared her own. 'My terms,' he enforced with dangerous silkiness. 'Accept or reject them.'

Commit herself to him, accept him into her body, play at being *wife*…

'For how long?' The query fell from her lips.

'As long as it takes.'

Until he tired of her? Live on a knife-edge, waiting for the figurative axe to fall?

She couldn't do it.

Yet what choice did she have?

None. Zilch. *Nada.*

A pulse hammered at the edge of her throat as she fought the temptation to turn and walk out the door, out of his office…his life.

It didn't help that he knew. Or that he was intent on playing a deliberate game, pushing her buttons…simply because he could.

'I hate you.' Her voice was a vengeful whisper dredged up from the depths of her soul.

'For reclaiming you as my wife?'

'For using me as human collateral.'

'Careful, *querida.*' His warning held a dangerous silkiness that mocked the endearment.

She almost told him to go to hell.

Almost.

Only the vivid image of Jacob lying injured in a hospital bed, and the very real implication of what would inevitably follow without a large injection of cash stopped her wayward tongue.

There was only one way out of this mess. Only one man who could help.

'You want me to write it in blood?'

He didn't pretend to misunderstand. 'Your acceptance?'

Her eyes flashed with brilliant blue fire. 'Yes, damn you!'

Duardo pushed himself away from the edge of his desk in a single fluid movement and closed the space between them. 'Your gratitude is underwhelming.'

'What did you expect? For me to fall on my knees at your feet?'

'Now, there's an evocative thought.' His drawl held a degree of cynical humour, and brought a rush of colour to her cheeks.

Dignity. She reined it in and with her head held high she moved back a pace. 'Are you done? I need to go see Jacob, then get to work.'

She walked towards the door, pausing halfway to look back over her shoulder. 'I imagine you'll be in touch when the legalities are in place?'

He hadn't moved, yet she had the impression his hard-muscled body was coiled, ready to spring.

'There's just one thing,' Duardo declared with hateful ease. 'The deal is effective immediately.'

'Excuse me?'

He extracted his cellphone and extended it towards her. 'Call the restaurant and terminate your employment.'

His eyes hardened as she opened her mouth to protest. 'Do it, Kayla. Or I will.'

When she refused to take the cellphone, he flipped it open and made two consecutive calls which effectively left her jobless.

The fact he knew where she worked and who to call made her want to hit him. 'Bastard,' she bit out in husky condemnation, watching as he pocketed the cellphone and moved towards her.

She was totally unprepared for the slide of his fingers

through her hair as he held fast her nape and used the flat of his hand at the back of her waist to draw her in close.

Then his mouth was on hers, taking advantage of her shocked surprise to gain entry and begin wreaking havoc with her senses in a kiss that captured and staked a shameless claim.

For a few brief, heart-stopping moments she forgot who she was, or *where*... There was only the man, his sensual power, remembered desire and an instinctive need to meet it.

Recognition, in its most primal form.

Except a part of her brain, her heart, provided an intrusive force. That was *then*...not now.

Oh, dear God.

Realisation caused her to wrench free...an action that was all the more galling because he made no attempt to stop her.

Anger, unuttered rage, showed in the glittering depths of her eyes, the tinge of colour heating her cheeks and her heaving chest as she sought to regain a degree of control.

'Now you have something to curse me for.'

She opened her mouth, but no sound emerged, and she closed it again. Wanting, needing to rail against him...physically, emotionally.

To what end?

Duardo took in her expressive features, defined each fleeting emotion and resisted the temptation to take that fine temper and tame it a little.

It helped to know that he could.

Kayla just looked at him. He wasn't even breathing deeply. How could he appear so *calm*, when she was a total mess?

'Shall we leave?'

Jacob, hospital... For a few seconds she felt stricken that both had temporarily fled her mind, and she stepped quickly into the passageway, aware Duardo easily matched her footsteps to Reception, where he bade the *Vogue* model lookalike 'goodnight', and summoned the lift.

There were words she wanted to fling at him, an inner rage threatening to eclipse rational thought. So much so, her body almost shook with it as she rode the lift down to ground level.

She told herself she should feel relieved the financial nightmare would soon be at an end. Instead, all her nerve-ends frayed into shreds as reality began to impact.

Life as she'd known it for the past few years was about to change dramatically.

The electronic cubicle came to a halt and the doors slid open to reveal the basement car park.

She needed the lobby, and she pressed the appropriate button, only to have Duardo reach forward and counter-mand her action.

'You're coming with me.'

'The hell I am.' Kayla's eyes flashed brilliant blue fire. 'Tomorrow is soon enough for me to be shackled to you.'

'The hospital,' he intoned with chilling softness. 'After which we transfer everything from your apart-ment to my home.'

'Dammit! I—'

'Walk, or be carried. Choose.'

That he meant every word was evident in those harshly chiselled features, and she almost defied him...just for the sheer hell of it.

Almost.

Instead she walked at his side, slid into the passenger seat of his top-of-the-range Aston Martin, and maintained an icy silence as he drove across town.

CHAPTER TWO

JACOB was in a large ward, his leg strapped in protective padding, and receiving pain management via a drip.

He looked pale, dejected and almost fearful in the initial seconds before Kayla entered his line of vision, then his expression lightened and he smiled as he sighted the man at her side.

Duardo Alvarez. Their white knight in shining armor. Although *dark angel* was more appropriate, she acknowledged with wry cynicism.

'Hi.' Her greeting was warm with concern as she leaned in close to brush her lips to her brother's cheek, and heard his barely audible 'thank God' seconds before she lifted her head.

In the space of what appeared to be a very short time Duardo organized for Jacob to be transferred to a private suite, engaged a team of orthopaedic surgeons and scheduled surgery.

Omnipotent power, Kayla perceived, backed by unlimited money.

She knew she should be grateful…and she assured herself she was, for Jacob's sake. It didn't mean she had to like the deal or the man who'd made it.

The Orderly arrived to effect Jacob's transfer, and she bade her brother a reluctant 'goodnight'.

'I'll be here in the morning before they take you into Theatre,' Kayla promised as the Orderly wheeled Jacob down the corridor.

It was after seven when Duardo eased the Aston Martin from the hospital car park, and the evening light was beginning to fade, tinging the pale sky with streaks of pink that gradually changed to orange as he negotiated traffic.

Soon it would be dark, and she wanted nothing more than to return to her apartment, hit the shower and fall into bed.

Except that wasn't going to happen any time soon, and the bed she'd sleep in wouldn't be her own, but *his*.

The mere thought sent heat flooding her veins, and she consciously focused on the scene beyond the windscreen in an effort to divert attention from what the night would bring.

Streetlights sprang on, vying with brightly coloured neon signs, and traffic banked up as main arterial roads linked to traverse the Harbour Bridge.

A short while later Duardo brought the car to a halt and switched off the engine.

Nothing looked familiar—not the locale, the street. 'Why did you stop here?'

'Dinner.' He freed his seat belt and climbed out from behind the wheel. 'We both need to eat.'

'I'm not hungry.'

He crossed round to her side and opened the door. 'Get out, Kayla.' When she made no effort to move he leant forward to release her seat belt.

The simple action had the breath lodging in her throat as his arm brushed her breast. He was close, much too close, and she froze, unwilling to so much as *breathe* for the few seconds it took him to complete the simple task.

Arguing with him would get her nowhere. And there was such a thing as sheer cussedness. It had been a while since lunch, and no way could the yoghurt and fruit she'd snacked on be termed a *meal*.

With that thought in mind she slid to her feet and crossed the street at his side, entering a small restaurant where the maître d' greeted Duardo by name and personally ushered them to a secluded table.

Kayla refused wine, chose soup as a starter, an entrée as a main, followed by fresh fruit.

'Would you prefer silence, or meaningless conversation?'

Duardo spared her a faintly mocking smile. 'You could begin by filling me in on the last few years.'

'Why, when you already know everything?' She lifted her water glass and took a sip of the iced liquid. 'Did you employ someone to watch my every move?'

Duardo leaned back in his chair and regarded her steadily. 'Last time I heard, it wasn't a crime for a man to retain interest in an ex-wife.'

The waiter served their soup, offered crusty bread then retreated as Kayla raked Duardo's compelling features with something akin to scorn.

'A wife you deliberately sought with an eye to the main chance.'

His expression hardened, and there was an almost frightening element evident in the depths of those dark eyes.

'Perhaps you'd care to explain that comment?'

'The Enright-Smythe consortium.'

'Indeed?'

His voice was like ice slithering in a slow slide down the length of her spine.

'Benjamin showed me written proof.'

'Impossible, given there was none at the time.'

'You're lying. I saw the letters.'

'Which you read?'

The scene flashed vividly to mind, ingrained in her mind as the moment love had died. Papers, Duardo's name. Her father's voice, loud and accusing in denunciation.

She'd skimmed the text, sightlessly, before Benjamin had flung the papers onto his study floor and stamped a foot on them.

'You can't deny you succeeded in a takeover bid for Benjamin's company.' She was like a runaway train, unable to stop. 'Did it give you pleasure to watch him sink into bankruptcy?'

His gaze didn't waiver. 'Your father's financial decline provided me with an opportunity to add to my investment portfolio. I'm a businessman. If it hadn't been me, it would have been someone else.'

'Of course,' she acknowledged with facetious intent, only to lapse into strained silence as the waiter appeared at the table to remove their soup bowls; soup she hardly remembered tasting.

'A deal brokered after the dissolution of our marriage.'

The tension escalated into a tangible entity. 'I don't believe you.'

'Any more than you can accept your father might have fabricated a tissue of lies and manufactured supposed *proof*?'

Shocked anger widened her eyes. 'He wouldn't have done that.' Her voice rose a fraction. 'I was his daughter!'

Their main meal was delivered, and served with a polite flourish.

'Benjamin's most prized possession.' Duardo waited a beat. 'One he would have done anything to remove from my orbit.'

Kayla looked at the artistically displayed food on her plate, and felt suddenly ill. 'You're wrong.'

'I, too, can produce documented proof.' He picked up a fork, speared a morsel and held it suspended for a few seconds. 'The comparison with Benjamin's papers should prove—' he paused almost perceptibly '—interesting, don't you think?'

Except there were no papers. At least, not those. When she'd asked, Benjamin had insisted they were with his lawyers. Who, on enquiry, could find no record of them.

It seemed unconscionable that Benjamin would contrive to destroy her marriage. Had his personal grief over Blanche's loss tipped him over the edge?

'Eat,' Durado commanded quietly.

'I'm not hungry.' For even a mouthful would choke her, and she pushed her plate to one side, her appetite gone.

It had been a doozy of a day. One that was far from over. She wanted to walk out of here, away from this inimical man, what he proposed…everything.

'Don't even consider it.' His tone was a silky threat, and, without thinking, she picked up her glass and flung the contents in his face.

In seeming slow motion she watched Duardo collect his table napkin, glimpsed the startled attention of the waiter, who rushed to his aid, and she stood to her feet, collected her purse…and fled.

She made the pavement, lifted a hand to flag a passing cab, only to cry out as strong hands closed over her shoulders and swung her around.

Duardo's features looked hard in the dim reflected streetlight, the structural bones etched in controlled anger.

'You're hurting me.'

'Believe me, I'm being extremely careful not to.'

For a moment the tension between them was electric, stretched so taut the slightest movement would result in an explosive shower of sparks.

'I can't do this.' It was an agonized cry dredged from the depths of her soul.

His hands slid up to cup her face, tilting it so she had no recourse but to look at him.

'I need time,' she said.

'Time won't change a thing.'

'Please.'

He traced the outline of her mouth with the edge of his thumb. 'No.'

Kayla bit him…*hard*. Heard his muffled oath, tasted his blood and cried out as he hefted her over one shoulder.

'Put me down!'

'Soon.'

She curled her hands into fists and pummelled them against his back. To no avail, as he strode easily to his car, unlocked the passenger door and bundled her into the seat.

He was close, far too close as he caught the seat belt and clipped it in place. 'Move, and I won't answer for the consequences.'

She hated him…didn't she? Hated him for placing her in this invidious position.

Yet…what if he was telling the truth?

Had her father lied and connived to his own ends?

She shook her head in disbelief. It was almost too much for her to take in.

She watched as Duardo walked around the car and slid in behind the wheel.

It was difficult to see his expression in the dim interior of the car, and she stared blankly at the night scene beyond the windscreen.

'I want to see the paperwork detailing your takeover.'

She had to *know*.

'I'll instruct my lawyer to supply you with a copy.'

The Aston Martin purred to life, and she sat in strained silence as the car traversed the city streets. Duardo offered the opportunity for a life free from debt, the fulfillment of her brother's dream.

Jacob was all she had, and he *deserved* this chance.

So, too, did she. She closed her eyes, then opened them again. For the love of God…*didn't she*?

The alternative…

Don't go there. It serves no purpose.

There was only *now*. And she'd deal with it. She *had* to.

The car drew to a halt in the narrow inner-city suburban street where she lived.

A late-model four-wheel-drive was parked nearby, and she stood still as Duardo paused to speak with the driver before indicating the entrance to her apartment.

Dim lighting didn't disguise the dingy surroundings, or the well-trodden wooden stairs as she ascended them ahead of him. Chipped paint, and the faint but distinct smell of decay.

Double locks on the door protected a pitiful space with minimal furniture, worn furnishings and the lack of personal touches. It was simply a place to sleep, not to live.

'Collect what you need.'

It didn't take long to transfer her meagre belongings into one bag and place Jacob's possessions into another. 'The landlord—'

'Spence has already dealt with it.' He indicated the small foldaway table. 'Leave the key.'

Kayla looked at him in silent askance as he caught hold of both bags.

'I made a few calls from the hospital.'

To people who were paid to jump instantly to attention at his slightest command.

Wealth…extreme wealth, she mentally corrected, had its distinct advantages.

It took only minutes to descend the stairs and pass through the shabby entrance onto the pavement. Almost instantly, a dark figure moved forward to take both bags from Duardo's grasp and deposit them in the rear of the four-wheel-drive.

'Spence.' Duardo clarified and completed the introduction before turning towards her. 'Let's go.'

Was it too late to change her mind? *Could* she?

Yes…and no.

She was barely aware of Spence sliding behind the wheel until she heard the engine engage and saw the four-wheel-drive ease away from the kerb.

There went all her worldly possessions.

Kayla spared Duardo a vengeful look that lost most of its effect in the dim evening light. 'Mind-reading is one of your talents?'

'You want to argue?' His voice was deceptively mild, yet she sensed steel beneath the surface.

'Not particularly.'

He crossed to the car, disarmed the alarm, opened the passenger door and stood waiting for her ɔ get in.

Which she did, with considerable grace ˙nd no apparent reluctance. A lesson in the game of pretense, she accorded, aware it was the first of many she'd be required to play in the coming months.

Oh, tell it like it is, she chided silently as the car whispered through the busy streets.

Duardo had specified…*wife*.

A warm and willing body in his bed. A social hostess. What if she fell pregnant?

A groan rose and died in her throat. Protection…she had none. Hadn't used or needed it.

'Nothing to say?'

Kayla spared his profile a steady glance. 'I'm plotting your downfall.'

His soft chuckle curled round her nerve-ends.

'You don't believe me?'

'I believe you'll try.'

'Count on it.' She glanced idly at the changing scene as the Aston Martin entered the eastern suburbs, where the inner-city shabby abodes were replaced with classy apartment buildings, well-kept homes guarded by walls and ornate gates.

Duardo, according to the media, resided in a luxurious Point Piper mansion overlooking the inner harbour, bought at the time of his marriage, but never lived in by *her*.

It was purported he'd brought in a team of builders, gutted the interior and virtually redesigned the internal structure before spending a veritable fortune on fittings and furnishings.

A fortress, Kayla observed, guarded by hi-tech security, and accessible only to those authorised to enter.

Well-positioned lighting revealed beautifully tended lawns and gardens, a curving driveway leading to an elegant mansion, and it was impossible not to feel the acceleration of nervous tension as Duardo brought the car to a halt beneath the wide portico.

One of two large double doors opened to frame a slender middle-aged woman.

'Maria,' Duardo indicated quietly as he released his seat belt. 'My housekeeper.'

Spence, Maria—

'Her husband, Josef, takes care of the grounds and maintenance.'

And Josef comprised the complement of staff. Live-in?

'There are two self-contained flats above the garages. Maria and Josef occupy one, Spence the other.'

Kayla slid out from the car, and, introductions complete, she entered the magnificent marble-tiled lobby.

Huge, with a curved double staircase leading to the upper floor, exquisite lighting, gleaming dark furniture and a number of beautifully carved wooden doors guarding various rooms.

There would, she determined, be panoramic views over the harbour during the day, with a fairyland of lights at night.

'There is coffee, or tea if you'd prefer,' the housekeeper relayed quietly and incurred Duardo's thanks. 'The bags have been taken up to the master suite.'

Kayla's stomach took a backwards flip…at least, that was what it felt like! She didn't want to *think* about the bedroom, much less go there.

'Tea would be lovely.' And a delaying tactic. 'Perhaps I could freshen up, first?'

Duardo indicated the staircase. 'Of course.'

Two different wings, one comprised of a few guest suites and an informal lounge, while the other held three bedrooms each with adjoining *en suites*, with the master suite in prominent position overlooking the harbour.

A large room, with a spacious alcove containing two comfortable chairs, an antique desk and a television cabinet. Two *en suite* bathrooms, two walk-in wardrobes.

She avoided looking at the bed…the very large bed.

'You have a beautiful home.'

'A compliment, Kayla?'

'You doubt I can gift you one?'

He shrugged out of his suit jacket and spread it over a valet frame, then he tugged off his tie and loosened the top button of his shirt before moving to the door. 'When you're ready, take the second door on your left at the base of the stairs.'

There was a sense of relief in being free from his presence. But not for long…

It would be bliss, absolute bliss to take a leisurely shower and shampoo her hair with the high-end market products lined up in the *en suite*. To use the hair-drier, wrap her body in the luxurious towelling robe, then slip into that comfortable bed…and sleep.

The temptation was too great, and with quick, economical movements she discarded her clothes, then stepped into the large marbled-tiled shower stall to luxuriate in an endless supply of steaming hot water.

The delicately scented body-wash was heaven, so, too, the luxury shampoo…neither of which she'd been able to afford to use for years.

Had Maria been instructed to stock up the *en suite*? Or were the products a complimentary gesture to whichever female Duardo took to his bed?

A man of his calibre had women falling all over him. Attracted to his wealth, his social status…and tantalized by his former bad-boy reputation.

Kayla tilted her head and let the water's needle-spray course over her face. Dammit, it felt so *good* not to have to consider a tiny heating system that permitted three-minute ablutions before the water ran cold.

It was a while before Kayla turned off the dial, then, towelled dry, she pulled on the robe before tending to her hair.

Bed had never looked so good, and she turned back the top cover, touched the feather pillow with something akin to reverence…

She should unpack—but who was she kidding? The contents of her bag were so basic it would take only minutes to stow them.

As to pulling on clothes…the idea had little appeal. Nor did returning downstairs.

The weight of the day and its outcome descended on her slim shoulders, and she slid between the fine percale sheets with care.

She wasn't going anywhere.

Duardo could come find her when *he* was ready.

Kayla slept, unaware of Duardo's presence, more than an hour later, or that he stood looking down at her pale features in repose.

She didn't register that he left the room and returned close to midnight, nor did she hear the shower or sense him slide into bed.

It was only when her hand came into contact with a solid, warm ribcage in the early hours of the morning that she freaked out, subconsciously unaware of where she was in those initial few seconds.

She knew only that it was dark, the bed wasn't her own…and *who* in hell was controlling her frantic need to escape.

She heard her name…then movement, and the room became bathed in soft light.

Son-of-a-bitch. Duardo bit back the muffled curse as he took in the tumbled hair, the heated cheeks, her heaving body, the stark fear in those brilliant blue eyes…and witnessed the moment comprehension hit.

'You forgot where you were.'

Oh, dear lord. 'Yes.' The simplicity of it seemed ludicrous.

He was close, much too close. The warmth of his skin covering hard muscle and sinew, the clean masculine scent of soap...the sensual heat that was his alone.

Physical awareness as strong as it had ever been. Riveting, hypnotic...*pagan*.

The need to put some space between them was imperative, and she moved a little, aware of the stillness apparent in the dark depths of his eyes.

He could easily reach for her, draw her in against him and cover her mouth with his own. Soothe, seduce...and have her go up in flames.

As he had, many times, during their magical time in Hawaii. An apt and willing pupil, she'd exulted beneath his skilled hands, his mouth, the feel of him deep inside her.

How many nights had she lain awake, cursing herself for allowing him to walk away? For not having the courage, the perspicacity to stand up against her father.

Now she was back in Duardo's bed for all the wrong reasons, and she hated him for it.

'Go to sleep.'

As if!

'Unless you need some help?' His drawled query was unmistakable, and she made no attempt to disguise the slight bitterness in her voice.

'Do I have a choice?'

'For now.'

'Thank heaven for small mercies.'

'Cynicism doesn't suit you.'

'Pity.' She paused as she speared his gaze with her own. 'I'm not big on warm fuzzies at the moment.'

His soft chuckle was almost her undoing. 'I seem to recall you being quite talkative at this hour of the morning.'

In the afterglow of exceptionally great sex. When she lay curled into him, her cheek nestled against his chest. A time of dreams, love, hope.

'I'm surprised you remember.' Kayla's response was deliberately tart. 'With all the women who followed me.'

'You imagine there were so many?'

Thinking about just how many was like being stabbed in the heart. 'They would have stood in line for the privilege.'

'A back-handed compliment, Kayla?'

'A statement of fact.'

'Derived from experience?'

'A trick question, Duardo?' She was damned if she'd reveal she'd taken no one to her bed…since, or before him.

A silent laugh bubbled up in her throat, almost choking her. The original virgin…a one-man woman. If it wasn't so tragic, it would be hysterical.

'Which you'd prefer not to answer.'

'Got it in one.'

His mouth curved into a slight smile. 'Are you done?'

She borrowed his words without compunction. 'For now.'

'Let's make the most of the few hours before dawn, hmm?'

For a brief few seconds her eyes held uncertainty, followed by a degree of wariness.

'To sleep,' he added with a tinge of amusement before settling onto his back, and he proceeded to do just that within a very short period of time.

Much to her relief.

Or, so she told herself as she deliberately banished the slow-curling desire insidiously invading her body.

CHAPTER THREE

KAYLA came awake to morning sunshine filtering through the curtains and the knowledge that she was alone in the vast bed.

A quick glance at the time, and she hit the floor running.

The hospital… She'd promised Jacob she'd be there before he went in for surgery. Forget breakfast, she decided as she took care of bathroom necessities…she'd grab something later.

Clothes…jeans, a singlet top, jacket. Hair caught into a practised knot and secured with a large clip, minimal make-up, lipstick…and she emerged into the bedroom to see Duardo in the process of adjusting his tie.

Well-groomed, attired in impeccable tailoring, he looked every inch the executive entrepreneur. And far too ruggedly attractive for any woman's peace of mind.

Especially hers.

'You should have woken me.' The words were almost an accusation.

'What happened to *good morning*?' His New-York-accented drawl held indolent amusement, and she threw him a heated glance.

'Thanks to you, I'm going to be late.'

'Maria has breakfast ready for you.'

'I don't—'

'I've already phoned the hospital. Jacob won't be transferred down to Theatre until nine.'

'—have time to eat,' she concluded.

'Yes, you will.' He subjected her to a raking appraisal, noting the fine bone structure, a slenderness that was almost too lean. How many meals had she missed in the past? 'Spence will drive you there.'

She opened her mouth to protest, then closed it again.

His expression remained unchanged. 'It's his job description.' Only part of it. He extracted a cellphone from his jacket pocket and handed it to her. 'Yours. The essential numbers are already programmed in on speed-dial.'

Kayla thrust it into her shoulder bag, and looked in silent askance as he withdrew a sheaf of papers.

'Your signature is required on the marriage-licence application.'

Duardo handed her a pen, indicated where she should sign, then handed her a legal document. 'A copy of the prenuptial agreement for you to read. You have an appointment with my lawyer at midday to sign the original.'

Oh, my. She felt her stomach twist into a painful knot. All legalities taken care of. Somehow she didn't feel inclined to thank him.

Calm, she had to remain calm. 'I imagine you've arranged a date for this marriage?'

'Tomorrow. A Celebrant will conduct the ceremony here at the house.'

'Tomorrow.' She swallowed the sudden lump that had formed in her throat.

He withdrew his wallet, extracted several notes and handed them to her. 'I'll organize a bank account and charge-card in your name this morning. Spence will ensure you tend to the necessary paperwork.'

'You're not afraid I might abscond?' The query emerged with more flippancy than she intended, and his gaze narrowed fractionally.

'Be warned, you wouldn't get far.'

A chill settled deep in her bones. 'I made a deal,' she voiced quietly. 'There's too much at stake for me not to honour it.'

Duardo collected his briefcase in one hand and picked up his laptop. 'I'll see you tonight.'

'Late,' Kayla qualified, and at his raised eyebrow she added in explanation, 'Jacob. Hospital.'

'Spence will drop you there this afternoon.'

'I can use public transport.'

'But you won't.' There was an underlying hint of steel apparent, which she chose to ignore.

'Why not?' Besides, she wanted some degree of independence.

His eyes seared hers. 'You want to draw battle lines?'

Her head tilted a little as she held his gaze. 'Yes.'

'We'll discuss issues over dinner.'

'Let's do that.' Without a further word she made her way downstairs, aware he descended them at her side, and she didn't so much as spare him a glance as they reached the foyer and went in different directions.

Kayla found the informal dining room, and greeted the hovering Maria with a smile.

Orange juice, coffee, cereal, fruit, eggs benedict…it was a veritable feast. Her appetite, which had taken a dive, was sufficiently tempted to have a little of each.

For years, breakfast had been a gulp-and-go affair as she inevitably raced to meet the train. To sit down and savour food without the immediate need to rush proved something of a rarity.

Spence appeared as she drained the last of her coffee, and she grabbed her bag and followed him out to the four-wheel-drive.

They struck peak-hour traffic, which slowed their progress down, and although she had a host of questions, she asked only one. 'Did you know Duardo in New York?'

An easy smile parted his mouth. 'For a number of years. When I expressed a desire to move to Australia, he suggested I take care of security for him.'

Had they worked the streets together and kept one step ahead of the law? Moved on and up by the skin of their teeth and sheer luck before exchanging the shady deals for legitimate ones? Taking risks no sensible person would touch, gambling both life and limb in the driven desire to succeed?

That Duardo Alvarez had reached the pinnacle of success was no mean feat.

'Ensuring his life runs smoothly.' It was a statement, not a query, and Spence chuckled.

'I guess you could say that.'

Security covered a whole range of possibilities, of which bodyguard and driver were only two.

It was almost eight-thirty when Spence drew the four-wheel-drive into the hospital's main entrance. 'Meet me here in three quarters of an hour. Duardo suggested we undertake a shopping expedition until your midday appointment with the lawyer.'

Shopping? *We*? 'You're joking, right?'

His gaze remained steady. 'You have a problem with me accompanying you?'

Oh, my. 'Not if you're authorised to use Duardo's credit

card.' Kayla checked her watch, then offered a dazzling smile. 'Nine-fifteen.'

It took only minutes to reach the upper floor and locate Jacob's room, a single suite with a view from the window.

'Hi.' Kayla crossed to the bed and brushed her lips to his forehead.

'Right back at you.'

His voice was drowsy with the faint huskiness of sedation, and her heart ached for him.

He was all she had. The one person who'd been there for her, unconditionally, since their mother's death.

Together they'd shared the grief, weathered the despair and fought to regain a modicum of dignity through Benjamin's fall from grace.

And afterwards, when the grim reality of poverty made itself felt, Jacob had given up everything…as she had…to work every waking hour in an effort to survive.

She noted the bruises to his jaw, his cheek…much more noticeable than they had been last night. How many more were there, marring his young body?

His leg…his shattered knee. It sickened her to think of the surgery he had to undergo, and she worried if it would be totally successful. If he'd be left with a limp…not be able to run or play sport.

His welfare brought vividly to mind just what Duardo's proposition meant in *real* terms. And why she'd accepted it.

'How are you feeling?'

A faint smile parted his lips. 'Almost out of it.'

'You're going to be fine.' Words, sincerely meant in reassurance.

He squeezed her hand. 'Thanks.'

Tears momentarily blurred her vision, and she blinked rapidly to dispel them.

Within minutes a nurse appeared, took his vital signs, then signalled for an Orderly to take the patient to Theatre.

'There's a visitors' lounge at the end of the corridor where you can wait. A cafeteria on the next level.' She checked her watch. 'Given surgery, recovery, he won't be back in his room much under five hours.'

Jacob managed a slow smile as the Orderly trundled the bed from the suite, and Kayla walked at his side until they reached the lift.

She left her cellphone number with the sister-in-charge, together with a request to call should Jacob recover from the anaesthetic sooner than anticipated.

Spence was waiting when she emerged from the main entrance, and his choice of venues soon became apparent when he entered Double Bay.

Exclusive *expensive* boutiques, and once, in another life, her preferred shopping mecca. An area where serious money could be spent on designer originals...apparel, shoes, bags, jewellery.

'Wedding attire is a priority,' Spence informed as they hit the pavement.

Was she supposed to display joyous anticipation? Enthusiasm? Just how much did Spence know of her connection with his boss?

Enough. It couldn't be any other way.

'You'll need to enlighten me.'

He didn't pretend to misunderstand. 'A small, intimate ceremony, with myself and Duardo's lawyer as witnesses.'

No guests. Well, that narrowed it down. 'Classy, but not over-the-top.' And not *bridal.* She could do that.

Elegant boho-chic, white or cream, stilettos, a single,

long-stemmed red rose held in one hand? Too fashionable-of-the-moment?

Maybe she should go for formal black, or deep scarlet. Although she doubted Duardo would appreciate or approve of the irony.

She found the perfect outfit in the first boutique she entered. In pale cream, it was a nineteen-twenties-style dress with a delicate crystal-beaded skirt overlay reaching just below her knees, and a sleeveless beaded top. It was elegant, outlined her slender curves, and felt *right*.

Different, so very different from the long white fitted gown she'd packed to take to Hawaii for her first wedding.

Then she'd married for love, and had melted into Duardo's bed with willing fervour.

Now…now it seemed as if a hundred butterflies had taken up residence in her stomach at the mere thought.

Could she slip easily into intimacy? Close her eyes and pretend? Enjoy what they'd once shared together?

The vivid memory of how it had been heated her blood and caused sensation to pool deep inside.

Don't *think*, a silent voice bade. Just…deal with it.

Kayla took a deep breath and spared her mirrored image another critical look. Yes. The dress more than met the required criteria for a quiet civil ceremony.

The price tag sent her into a momentary state of shock. So, too, did the matching stilettos.

How times had changed. Five years ago she wouldn't have given the cost a second thought. Now she stood to one side while Spence presented Duardo's credit card and the boutique *vendeuse* packaged the purchases.

She spared the lingerie boutique a quick glance and walked on by…only to pause when Spence redirected her inside.

It was akin to being shown Aladdin's cave. Exquisite silk and lace in abundance. She could have had a field-day. Instead she selected a matching bra and brief set, and ignored Spence's encouragement to add more to a steadily growing collection of glossy carrier-bags.

There was time for a restorative coffee before dealing with the bank, the lawyer to sign the pre-nuptial agreement…whereupon she was handed a manila envelope.

'Duardo instructed me to give you these copies.'

For a moment she looked startled, then realisation hit. Documented proof of Duardo's takeover bid of Benjamin's company.

It was after two when Spence drew the four-wheel-drive to a halt outside the hospital entrance.

'I'll take the shopping home and have Maria put it in your room.'

'Thanks.' Kayla reached for the door clasp. 'And thanks for today. I appreciated your help.'

His smile held genuine warmth. 'You're welcome.'

Jacob's suite was empty when she reached it, and she sought out the sister-in-charge, who, on enquiry, relayed the reconstructive surgery had taken longer than anticipated and it could be another hour before Jacob was returned to the ward.

The cafeteria seemed a good choice, and she filled in time with a cool drink whilst leafing through a few complimentary magazines.

Although her mind kept wandering as she reflected on the day…and wondered what the night would bring.

Get a grip. It wasn't as if she hadn't been to bed with him before. Dammit, she'd lain at his side through last night…and woken with the knowledge he only had to make the slightest move for her to go into meltdown.

It didn't make sense. The mind and body should be in sync…yet hers seemed to be two separate entities with different agendas.

Speaking of which, there was one glaring error in her purchases, and she went in search of the medical centre, secured a prescription for the contraceptive pill then sought out the pharmacy dispensary.

Jacob had just been trundled into his suite when she entered it, and she stood to one side as the Orderly and nurse tended to routine.

'Your brother is heavily sedated and on pain relief,' the nurse informed. 'He'll be very drowsy for some time.'

An understatement, for over the next few hours he stirred momentarily, acknowledged where he was, smiled at her then he lapsed back to sleep.

A nurse checked him on the hour. 'I think it would be wise for you to go home and visit tomorrow,' she advised kindly.

'An excellent idea,' a familiar male voice drawled from the doorway.

Duardo, Kayla perceived, aware of the forceful image he presented as he entered the suite. His eyes were dark and faintly hooded as they met her own.

'I've spoken with the surgeon. The reconstruction has been successful. He endorsed the level of Jacob's sedation and pain control.'

She was reluctant to leave, and said so. 'Visiting hours aren't over yet.'

'It's doubtful Jacob will do more than stir through the night.'

Two against one. Common sense won out, and she addressed the nurse as she stood. 'Please make sure he knows I was here.'

'Of course.'

Kayla exited the ward at Duardo's side, and rode the lift down to ground level in silence, waiting until they reached his Aston Martin before offering, 'There was no need for you to come collect me.'

'We've already done this.'

She sent him a dark glance which lost much of its impact in the dim night light. 'Thoughtfulness and consideration, Duardo?' She waited a beat. 'Or taking care of a debt owed in human form?'

'Get in the car, Kayla.' His voice held a dangerous silkiness. 'And curb your acerbic tongue.'

'Is that a threat?'

'Open to interpretation.'

She had to be insane to best him. It simply wouldn't happen…unless he allowed it. And that was about as likely as a cow jumping over the moon!

Kayla slid into the passenger seat and secured the safety belt as he set the car in motion.

She chose silence as they traversed the suburban streets, and her nerves frayed a little as Duardo entered Double Bay. An area where some of the city's social echelon elected to dine in exclusive restaurants favoured for their boutique cuisine. If you wanted to be *seen*, this was the place.

'I'm not very hungry.' She became very conscious of her attire…jeans and a jacket didn't really cut it.

He slid into a parking space and switched off the engine. 'We both need to eat.' He spared her a sweeping glance. 'And you're fine as you are.'

She had one advantage, she decided minutes later as the *maître d'* greeted him with obsequious beneficence and promptly found them a table. She was with Duardo Alvarez…and that, she perceived wryly, said it all.

She declined wine, selected a starter as a main with fresh fruit to follow, while Duardo ordered an exotic seafood pilaf.

'You mentioned issues,' Kayla began. 'Shall we discuss them?'

Duardo shot her a faintly musing look. 'Let's eat first, hmm?'

She could do polite…she'd had years of practice. 'I should thank you for Spence's services today.' And gratitude, where it was due. 'We shopped.'

'At my instigation.' He sank back in his chair. 'You object?'

'What woman would?' she parried lightly.

The waiter brought their meal, and she forked small morsels of food from the decoratively arranged plate, extremely conscious of her surroundings and fellow patrons.

Duardo Alvarez bore instant recognition, and without doubt there was covert speculation as to her identity. Something that would intensify as her position in his life became known.

Sordid details would resurface and be rehashed by the gossip-mongers, creating an emotional storm she'd be forced to weather beneath the glare of publicity.

OK, so she'd get to smile a lot and play *pretend*.

'You're very quiet.'

Kayla pushed her plate to one side and took a sip of iced water. 'You want scintillating conversation, Duardo?'

'Not particularly.' It was a pleasant change to sit opposite a woman and not have her indulge in the flirting game. The subtle and often not-so-subtle prelude to an invitation to her bed.

'Then perhaps we should move along to the issues we need to discuss.'

He viewed her with speculative amusement. 'You have a list?'

'And you don't?'

The waiter delivered a platter of artistically displayed fresh fruit, and took their orders for coffee.

'You have household staff who run your home like clockwork,' Kayla ventured. 'I'd like to resume working. Part-time, flexi-time.' When this was greeted with silence, she continued, 'I need to know where Jacob will convalesce.' Oh, why not go for broke? 'I don't want—'

'Duardo! *Amico.*'

Duardo rose to his feet and took the man's extended hand. An older man, in his mid- to late-fifties, with a young woman at his side.

With accustomed ease Duardo effected an introduction. 'Darling…Benito Torres and his wife, Samara.'

Darling?

Benito's smile held musing indulgence as he indicated Kayla. 'And this charming young lady is?'

'Soon to become my wife.'

Was it her imagination or did Samara's eyes harden a little?

'However did you manage to get Duardo to put a ring on your finger?' The woman's voice held warm amusement, but there was something in the tone that didn't quite match up.

'By refusing to sleep with him.' There, make of that what you will!

Samara gave a disbelieving laugh. 'How…quaintly old-fashioned.' She pressed a brightly lacquered fingernail against Duardo's forearm and fluttered heavily mascaraed lashes at him. 'And…risky, surely?'

'He's taken, *querida*,' Benito drawled. 'And he doesn't share.'

'Shame.'

The coy seductiveness was a mite overdone, and Kayla viewed their departure with interest.

'A past lover?'

Duardo's gaze remained level. 'No.'

The truth? Did it matter?

She told herself she didn't care…and knew she lied.

The waiter brought their coffee, and she took hers black with sugar, aware he matched her actions.

'We were discussing issues,' Kayla ventured. Before the interruption of Benito Torres and his wife.

'I gather you don't want to be a social butterfly, filling your days with luncheons, charity functions, shopping and personal maintenance?'

'Not particularly.'

'You no longer have cause to work.'

She sipped her coffee, savoured the rich caffeine then carefully replaced her cup onto its saucer. 'Don't you get it?' Her eyes sparked with brilliant blue fire. 'I don't want to be beholden to you for every cent I need!'

Duardo sank back in his chair and regarded her with speculative interest. 'You'll have a monthly allowance.'

Her anger didn't diminish. 'A *clothing* allowance,' she agreed, aware she'd never be able to afford the designer gear worn by the city's fashionistas who formed part of Duardo's social circle.

'Jacob—'

'Will move into an apartment when he leaves hospital.'

'What apartment? Where?' She'd thought, *hoped* Jacob would convalesce in Duardo's home. Dammit, the house was big enough to accommodate several guests.

'Rose Bay.'

'Don't tell me. You own it.'

'The building,' he illuminated in dry, mocking tones.

'He'll need care, physiotherapy—'

'Which he'll have. Until he's fully mobile, Spence will transport Jacob wherever he needs to go.' Duardo finished his coffee.

'Divide and conquer, Duardo?'

He regarded her thoughtfully. 'Your brother has the opportunity to lead his own life. I suggest you allow him to do so.'

'When he's fully recovered,' Kayla qualified, and met the lurking cynicism in those dark eyes.

He signalled the waiter, requested and paid the bill. 'Are you done?'

'No,' she managed sweetly as she rose to her feet and preceded him from the restaurant.

The close confines of the Aston Martin made her acutely aware of his presence…and the slow burn of heat filling her body.

It shouldn't *be* like this. Dammit, she didn't *want* to feel this way. Nor did she want to be sexually possessed by him.

She'd been there, briefly, and had never fully recovered from the encounter. In those few halcyon days of marriage he'd taught her so much…too much, she reflected as the car traversed the short distance to Point Piper.

It had made her want only *him*. The mesmeric, electrifying ecstasy…wild, driven need in its most primitive form. But it was more than primeval coupling…sensual magic, where two minds, two bodies were in perfect accord, each the other half of a whole.

The whole deal. Not just sex.

Get a grip, why don't you?

That was the past.

Now, through circumstance, she had no recourse but to forge some form of future with Duardo Alvarez.

Live with him, lie with him.

A slight shiver feathered its way down her spine.

She hadn't escaped emotionally unscathed from the divorce. How could she hope to survive in a loveless marriage?

Kayla became conscious of the sudden silence, and realized the car was stationary in the garage.

A large area housing two late-model four-wheel-drive vehicles. A gold Lexus and dark blue BMW.

With slightly shaky fingers she released the seat belt and slid out of the car.

Duardo loosened his tie as they hit the lobby, and she watched as he shrugged out of his suit jacket and hooked it over one shoulder.

'I need to access emails and make a few international calls.'

'OK.' Kayla made for the stairs, and on reaching their suite she shed her clothes and headed for the shower. When she was done she pulled on a towelling robe and checked out the television console in the adjoining bedroom alcove.

She channel-surfed, settled on an episode of *Law & Order* and curled up in one of the comfortable leather sofas.

It was there Duardo found her, asleep, with her head nestled against the arm of the sofa, her hair spilling free like a curtain of pale silk.

For several minutes he stood observing the steady rise and fall of her breathing, aware of her fragility, her latent strength.

A contradiction in terms.

She felt light in his arms. Too light, he determined as

he moved towards the bed, and his grasp tightened as she began to stir, then came fully awake.

'What are you doing?' A half-hearted query, if ever there was one. She had instant recall of viewing TV…then blissful oblivion.

'Taking you to bed.'

'No.' Too late—they were already there. 'Please.' Her face was only inches from his, and she became aware of the gaping edges of her towelling robe…the fact he'd showered and pulled on a robe of his own. 'Put me down.'

Duardo complied, his eyes narrowing at the flood of pink tingeing her cheeks as she quickly fixed her robe and put some distance between them.

He looked strong, *vital*, and far too disturbingly male for any woman's peace of mind. Especially hers!

Sensation spiralled deep inside, meshing sensual heat with unwanted desire as she recalled all too vividly what it felt like to have him touch her.

The light brush of his mouth against each sensitive pulse-beat, the curve of her breast and the sensual pull of his tongue as it laved its peak.

How he had adored to explore her body, and gift her the most intimate kiss of all, driving her wild until she begged like a craven wanton for release…savouring her climax, before sending her to the brink again, holding her there, then plunging deep to take her with him.

Sensual sexual magic so incredibly exquisite it almost defied description.

For those beautiful few days, she had loved with her heart and soul…and believed herself loved in return.

Fool. Days were all she'd had before the bubble burst.

Now *love* no longer existed, and what they'd once shared could never be resurrected.

It gave her the nerve to voice the words tumbling around inside her head. Get it over and done with. Now.

'I want you to wear protection when we have sex.'

His expression didn't change, although she had the distinct impression there was anger lurking beneath the surface of his control. 'Your reason being?'

Her eyes met and held his with fearless disregard. 'I don't think it's fair to have an unplanned pregnancy.'

'Have I asked you to have my child?'

'No.' It was impossible not to visualize a boy infant in his father's image: a strong, forceful, dark-haired imp.

'You're concerned about health issues?'

'Not on my part.' That came out too quickly, and his eyes narrowed.

'You think I may have disregarded the wisdom of safe sex?'

The thought of him being with other women, indulging, sharing the sensual delights he'd gifted *her* was almost more than she could bear. 'I doubt you've remained celibate during the past three years.'

Brave fool. He wanted to shake her. 'And you, Kayla?' His voice was as silk-smooth and held a dangerous edge.

Damn him. There was no way she'd give him satisfaction of the truth. 'Our divorce absolved us from the vow of fidelity.'

'That doesn't answer the question.'

She met his gaze and held it. 'It's one you don't have the right to ask.'

Duardo took a step towards her, and she stood her ground despite every instinct warning her to turn and run.

'There's something else,' she continued, ignoring the muscle bunching at the edge of his jaw. 'Blood tests.'

Pushing him to the edge was the height of folly. Yet she was besieged with a host of emotions, not the least of which was a volatile mix of anger and desire.

She didn't want him. Couldn't need him. Yet the dictates of her body warred with rationale…and she hated him for it. Most of all, she hated herself.

'My word is insufficient?'

Was it? She no longer knew.

When she didn't answer, he crossed to a bedside pedestal, withdrew a slip of paper and handed it to her.

It took only seconds to scan the pathology report.

Should she thank, or condemn him?

Neither, she decided, hating that he was light-years ahead of her.

'That takes care of all the issues?'

His voice was deceptively mild, and she controlled the faint shiver threatening to slither down her spine.

'For the moment.'

'Good.' He reached out a hand and slid his fingers through her hair, holding fast her nape as he angled his head and closed his mouth over hers.

Evocative, intensely sensual, he played her with shameless ease, tasting the soft inner tissues, probing her tongue with his own, teasing, until a silent groan rose in her throat.

Kayla clenched a hand and aimed it at his shoulder, with no effect whatsoever.

Their bodies weren't even touching, yet it felt as if she was being absorbed by him, with any resistance fading into insignificance.

He knew how to please, with an eroticism that swept away any clarity of thought until there was only the moment, the man and the need to respond.

It would be so easy to slide the robe off his shoulders, shuck aside her own and lean into him.

Skin on skin, to taste and pleasure him, seductively explore until he lost his breath, his mind.

Except she did none of those things, and the breath caught in her throat as he loosened her robe and slid a hand to cup her breast, then tantalise its peak.

She closed her eyes, successfully veiling their expression as he trailed an unerring path to its twin, caught the hardened bud between thumb and forefinger and rolled it gently until she fought back an inaudible groan.

His hand slid to her navel, lingered there, then trailed over her trembling belly, seeking her sensitive clitoris in an intimate exploration that sent her high on a tide of exquisite sensation so acute she sank into him.

His mouth left hers and settled at the edge of her throat, savoured the delicate hollow and absorbed the vibration as she held back a silent scream.

It was almost more than she could bear as he urged her to the brink again, kept her there then held her as tiny shockwaves shook her body.

With slow, deliberate movements he put her at arm's length, then traced gentle fingers over her slightly swollen mouth.

'I hate you.' It came out as a husky whisper, and her lips trembled beneath his touch. Her eyes were large blue limpid pools, and he watched as moisture welled and threatened to spill.

'At this precise moment, I imagine you do.' He tucked wayward strands of hair back behind each ear, then let his hand slide down her jaw to cup her chin. 'And hate yourself even more.'

He dropped his hand and crossed round to the other side

of the bed, shed his robe and slid in between the sheets. In one easy movement he snapped off the bedside lamp, plunging the room into shadowy darkness.

Kayla wanted to throw something at him, and caught up a pillow ready to hurl at his hapless head.

Strong fingers closed over her wrist. 'Don't even think about it.'

The air between them was electric, yet she was too angry to take much heed as she attempted to wrench her hand free. 'Let me go.'

'Drop the pillow.'

'Like hell.'

In one fluid movement Duardo dispensed of the pillow with one hand and exerted sufficient leverage to tumble her down on top of him.

'Don't.' The word escaped as a helplessly torn plea an instant before his mouth took possession of her own.

This was no exploratory dance. Intense, hungry, it became a prelude to more, so much more than she wanted him to take.

She was barely conscious of movement as he reversed their positions, until he began tracing a path to her breast, savoured one, moved to tease the tender peak, then travelled low to seek the sensitive core at the apex of her thighs.

Oh, dear God.

She didn't want him there. Didn't want the primitive ecstasy his touch would bring…or his possession.

Because then she'd be lost. Driven by a hunger so acute, she'd no longer belong to herself…but to him. Spiritually, emotionally, physically…*his*.

Liquid fire ran through her body, heating it to fever pitch as he bestowed primeval pleasure so intense she cried out, tossing her head from side to side in a puny attempt at control.

Except she had none.

He made sure of it, and when he eased into her he covered her mouth with his own, swallowing her faint cries as her inner muscles stretched and began to convulse as she accommodated him.

He held himself there for timeless seconds, then he began to move…slowly at first, coaxing her to match his rhythm until they were in sync.

Driven wild, it was she who rose up against him, taking him even deeper inside. She who reversed their positions in a need to ride him hard, fast…until everything splintered in tumultuous climax.

Tears of emotion welled in her eyes and she held them back with sheer effort of will. The temptation to cry was almost more than she could bear, and a silent sob shook her slim form as Duardo traced the contours of each breast, focusing on the swollen peaks rendered tender from his mouth, the edges of his teeth.

Her throat convulsed, and she attempted to swallow the sudden lump that had formed there.

She was still joined with him, exulting in his possession, the feel of him, the musky heat of his body, her own, as her heartbeat slowed to a normal rhythm.

A single tear hung suspended at the edge of her jaw, then fell, and she heard his soft oath, felt the tips of his fingers trace her cheeks, discover the wet rivulets.

Then he drew her down against him and cushioned her head into the curve of his shoulder.

She felt his lips brush her forehead, felt him pull the bedcovers up over them both and felt a hand settle at her nape while the other soothed a path along her spine.

What they'd shared, she reflected tremulously, had been all about her.

Her pleasure, her climax.

'Go to sleep.'

Sure. As if that would happen any time soon.

Except she did slip into blissful oblivion, eventually, long after his breathing steadied.

CHAPTER FOUR

KAYLA stretched languidly, felt the pull of unused muscles, the lingering sensation of fairly vigorous sex and closed her eyes against the flood of memories filling her mind.

Dammit, she could still *feel* him inside her. His imprint, the touch of his mouth, his hands.

The sexual heat, the witching, incredibly sensuous *sex*.

For that was all it had been. A physical coupling of two people sexually in tune with each other.

Sure. Who was she trying to kid?

Rise and shine, shower, dress and face the day, she commanded silently as she slid quickly from the bed and made for the *en suite*.

Cargo pants, a cotton singlet top, heeled sandals, her hair caught in a low pony-tail, she made her way down to the breakfast room…and discovered Duardo had already left for the city.

'Shopping,' Spence informed as he entered the room just as she finished her coffee.

'You're kidding. Again?'

He inclined his head. 'Duardo's instructions.'

Well, then…who was she to argue? 'And visit Jacob,' she added as she rose to her feet.

'We need to be home no later than three. The ceremony is scheduled at five.'

The *wedding*.

Dear heaven. By the end of the day she'd be Kayla Antonia *Alvarez*.

For the second time.

'Of course.' Was that her voice? It sounded calm, when inside she was rapidly becoming a nervous wreck.

Something which didn't diminish as the day progressed.

If anything, it became worse…so much so, she could barely eat, as each morsel seemed to stick in her throat.

It didn't help that Jacob was heavily sedated with pain management, and kept lapsing into drug-induced silence.

All day she'd alternated between running off at the mouth with seemingly inane conversation, and lapsing into silence.

She needed support. Yet there was no one to call on. Not even the man who was soon to become her husband.

Their wedding wasn't sufficiently important for him to make any concession other than to indicate, via Spence, to expect him home earlier than usual.

She'd never felt so alone in her life.

Everything was laid out on the bed in readiness, and she thanked Maria for her kind attention.

'I've put everything away, except this.' The housekeeper picked up a large envelope. 'It was in one of the bags. It has your name on it.'

A slight frown creased Kayla's forehead an instant before comprehension hit.

The legal paperwork Duardo's lawyer had been instructed to hand her…documenting proof of the takeover bid.

Kayla slit open the flap and extracted the document.

Dates. She didn't need to read the legalese. Nevertheless, she skimmed it just the same.

And felt her stomach execute a slow somersault as it became shockingly aware Benjamin had lied to her.

She closed her eyes, then opened them again.

If her father had lied about this…what other lies had he fed her?

How could he? To have gone to these lengths… Her mind whirled at the implications.

Dear heaven.

Somehow she had to gather her shattered thoughts, for in a little more than an hour she was due to get married. And she needed to shower, fix her hair, apply make-up…and dress.

It was almost four-thirty when she stepped into the cream beaded dress, and reached for the zip fastening.

'Let me help with that,' Duardo drawled, and his fingers brushed hers as he slid the fastener home.

He had the tread of a cat, for she hadn't heard him enter the room.

He turned her around to face him, and his eyes narrowed at the sight of her pale features, the large sapphire-blue pools' dilation depicted some of her inner stress.

Don't…offer platitudes, or touch me, she silently begged, feeling utterly fragile. If he did either, she'd splinter into a thousand pieces at his feet.

'Give me twenty minutes to shower, shave and dress, then we'll go downstairs together.'

There was never going to be a right time…but she needed to say the words. 'I owe you an apology.'

He stilled, and she rushed into speech. 'The takeover bid. Dates. My father lied.' Oh, God, she was a trembling mess. 'I'm sorry.'

'Apology accepted,' he said quietly, then shrugged out of his jacket, dispensed with his shoes and disappeared into his *en suite*.

He made it in nineteen…sheer nervousness ensured she'd checked almost every passing minute.

Spence, Maria and Josef, together with the Celebrant, were waiting for them in the formal lounge. A small linen-covered table was set with a beautiful display of roses, and a candle sat waiting to be lit.

Introductions complete, the Celebrant intoned the necessary words that legally bound Kayla and Duardo together as husband and wife.

The exchange of rings completed the ceremony, and she felt the breath catch in her throat as he slid the wide diamond-encrusted band on her finger, for it was the original ring he'd gifted her to seal their first marriage. So, too, was the wide gold diamond-studded band she was handed to slip onto his finger.

He'd kept them?

Why?

Duardo lowered his head and lightly brushed his lips against her own. In that instant her eyes fused with his, their expression naked for a few timeless seconds in the intense desire to glimpse anything in his expression that would give hint their spoken vows held meaning. That the passion they'd shared through the night was more than just…very good sex.

Even now, she still carried the sensual awareness of sexual possession. The instinctive flare of arousal as the mind provided a tellingly vivid image.

He knew. She could tell by the slumberous gleam in those dark eyes, so close to her own.

Was it male satisfaction at reclaiming her as his wife? Or

the culmination of revenge? Sadly, she suspected it was both.

Together they lit the candle, signed the marriage certificate and thanked the Celebrant.

Spence presented a bottle of Cristal champagne, filled crystal flutes and made a toast, while Maria produced a tray of canapés.

Within what seemed to be a fairly short space of time the Celebrant took her leave, Maria and Josef made a discreet exit, followed by Spence.

'I've made a booking for dinner at seven.' Duardo took the empty flute from her fingers and placed it with his own on a nearby chiffonier.

Dinner? They were eating out? Again?

'A personal celebration.'

It was certainly personal. But hardly a celebration, she determined as she ascended the stairs to freshen up.

Although, on second thoughts, she preferred being in the company of others to an intimate meal *á deux* at home.

There was a matching evening purse that came with the dress, and she quickly popped in lipstick, tissues and a folded note.

Money, darling, she could almost hear her late mother's words in musing wisdom. *Never go anywhere without it. Especially in the company of a man.*

Mad money. Taxi money, Kayla reflected as she retreated downstairs.

The Aston Martin was Duardo's chosen method of transport for the night, their destination the exclusive Ritz Carlton at Double Bay, whose exemplary restaurant was high on the list of *places to be seen*.

Was that his intention?

The *maître d'* led them to a secluded table, Duardo

conferred with the drinks steward and, after perusing the menu, they placed their order.

Exquisite food, artistically presented, accompanied by a fine wine…

Beautiful, elegantly attired patrons willing to pay the price to portray a given façade.

Somehow it was difficult to see Duardo buying into it. Yet to him it was a game, an ongoing challenge, to be perceived as the man he had become. Proof that wealth could conquer almost anything.

Yet the core of the youth he had been in the tough streets of New York remained buried deep beneath the acquired sophisticated image.

It was evident in the hardness of his eyes, the leashed savagery apparent in the frightening stillness of his body.

She'd witnessed it three years ago when she'd chosen family and handed back his ring.

Control…he had it. But the hidden threat remained.

'Have I suddenly grown horns?'

Duardo's drawl held faint mockery, and she met his steady gaze with equanimity. 'The jury is still out.'

His soft chuckle curled round her nerve-ends and tugged a little. 'And not about to reach a decision any time soon.'

'No.'

There was no sense of elation at re-entering the social scene, even as Duardo's wife. The prospect of needing to play *pretend* didn't thrill her at all, for the knowledge that the smiles, the bonhomie, were as fake as their marriage would merely serve as proof almost everything about her life was based on falsehood.

'Nevertheless, I suggest you practice a smile.'

'You have a reason?'

'A photographer scouting for a newsworthy shot.'

Oh, hell. 'Charming.'

'Play nice, hmm?'

'I wouldn't dream of doing otherwise,' she assured, adding, 'in public.'

Then it was photo time, and when the photographer's sidekick noticed both wedding rings there were voiced congratulations and much scribbling on a notepad.

By tomorrow, news of their remarriage would be recorded in the social pages of the city's major newspapers.

Kayla waited until the team was out of earshot. 'A deliberate orchestration, Duardo?'

'No.'

Could she believe him? Did it matter?

'It's timely,' he continued with thinly veiled mockery. 'Given we're due to appear together at a charity fundraiser tomorrow evening.'

They were?

The thought of being launched onto the social scene after a long hiatus was a trifle daunting.

'Advance information to feed or minimize the gossip-mill?'

He replaced his flatware onto the plate before choosing to respond. 'I imagine it will achieve both.'

Without doubt. A ready smile curved her lips, but her eyes lacked humour. '*Wonderful.*'

'You'll cope.'

Yes, she would. But she retained vivid memories of her father's slide on the social scale. Dinners postponed, then cancelled, and invitations dwindling down to none. Long-time friends who no longer wanted to be associated with Benjamin Enright-Smythe or his daughter or son.

The experience had made her very aware that life was all about survival of self in a world where reality ruled.

Kayla took a sip of wine, and replaced the stemmed goblet with a steady hand.

A charity fund-raiser attracted the city's social echelon, where the female guests vied to outdo each other in evening gowns, jewellery, and spent the entire day in personal preparation for each event.

'I have yet to add an evening gown to my purchases.'

Duardo sank back in his chair and viewed her with veiled scrutiny. 'I suggest you take care of it tomorrow.'

'Acquiring a trophy wife could prove expensive.'

His eyes narrowed fractionally. 'If I had wanted a trophy wife, you wouldn't be here.'

The implications sent ice scudding through her veins as a mental picture flashed through her mind...new town, new identity for herself and Jacob and living in constant fear of when the loan-shark thugs would find them.

Kayla pushed her plate to one side, her appetite gone. There was nothing cognizant she could offer in response, and it was a relief when the waiter delivered coffee prior to Duardo settling the bill.

It wasn't late when they exited the restaurant, and as the car whispered almost soundlessly through the streets it was impossible not to recall her first wedding night. A meal where they had fed each other morsels of food and were oblivious to everything and everyone. How they'd walked barefoot along the white sands at Waikiki Beach, savouring each moment until they returned to their suite to make love all through the night.

Magic. The distant lap of an incoming tide, the soft sound of background music from the resident band.

She'd gifted him her body, her soul...*love*. And believed it to be reciprocated.

Nothing else had mattered then.

Until reality intervened, and she'd made the wrong choice.

Had there been any *right* choice?

Now she was back with the man who'd succeeded in stealing her heart. Except everything had changed. This time round, revenge was his motive, not love.

And *you*? a mental voice intruded. Is survival your only motive?

Are you *insane*?

Don't answer that.

Lights sprang on along the curved driveway as Duardo used the remote to open the electronic gates guarding the entrance to his home, and sensor-activated illumination lit the portico and selected interior lighting.

'Champagne? Coffee?'

Kayla's steps didn't falter as she crossed the foyer and made for the stairs. 'Neither, thanks.'

He could follow, or not. It hardly made any difference, and she didn't look back to check as she entered the master suite.

On the night of their first marriage he'd swept an arm beneath her knees and carried her into their hotel suite, fed her sweet strawberries tipped with chocolate and dipped in champagne, then slowly, with infinite care, divested her of her clothes, his own, and gently tutored her in the art of lovemaking.

Now she slipped off her stilettos, carefully removed her dress then padded into the *en suite*. It took only minutes to complete the nightly ritual, undress and slip on her robe.

When she emerged the bedroom was empty, and she crossed to the alcove, opened the television and flicked through a few channels until she found an interesting pro-gramme, then sank down into a chair to watch it.

There was little awareness of the passage of time as she became engrossed in the documentary.

'Unable to sleep?'

She gave a startled gasp and turned to face him, unaware he'd entered the room or exchanged clothes for his robe. 'How long have you been here?'

'Only minutes.' He scooped her into his arms in one fluid movement, then sank down in the chair with her on his lap.

'What do you think you're doing?' She attempted to struggle free, and failed miserably.

He curved a hand over her shoulder and edged her close in against his chest. 'You need me to answer that?'

She felt the warmth of his palm as it slid beneath her robe, cupped her breast and rested there.

Her heartbeat picked up, and she silently damned the effect he roused in her. Worse, that he couldn't fail to be aware of it.

How easy would it be to lift her face to his and nuzzle her lips to his throat, then seek his mouth with her own? To indulge each other with an exploratory tasting…

Fool.

The past and the present didn't mesh. First time round, love had had everything to do with it. Now it didn't form part of the equation.

To sit here quiescent was impossible, and she caught hold of his wrist in an attempt to pull free. Without success.

'Let me up.'

'Uncomfortable?'

Brilliant blue eyes stormed his. 'Don't play me.'

'You think this is a game?'

The anger intensified. 'Yes!' And she added a silent *damn you.*

He caught hold of her chin and tilted it, then his mouth captured her own in a kiss that plundered with devastating effect and stilled any protest she tried to voice.

Kayla balled one hand into a fist and aimed a wild punch that found no purchase.

His mouth lifted briefly, then resettled to conduct a frankly sensual invasion…tormenting, caressing without surcease until she gave in with an almost inaudible groan and began to respond.

It wasn't until she felt the mattress beneath her back that she realized he'd moved to the bed, and she stilled for a few timeless seconds before giving in to the heat, the passion, exulting in his touch and her own rapturous response.

The desire to test his control and have him lose it was impossible to resist, and she waited until he was on the edge of sleep before initiating an evocative exploration of her own.

With fingers as light as a butterfly's touch she traced the compacted muscles above his stomach, felt the reactive flex, then trailed to one male nipple and gently rolled it between thumb and forefinger before scraping it lightly with a lacquered nail.

She found the indentation of his navel, teased its outline and delved into its centre before trailing a slow path to sink fingers into the pubic hair couching his penis. Caught his faint intake of breath and felt his erection.

A fascinating part of the male anatomy…such strength and flexibility. An instrument able to bestow such pleasure. Sensitive to the slightest touch.

A secret smile curved her lips, only to freeze as strong fingers closed over her wrist. 'I suggest you stop right there.'

Revenge, such as it was, felt so darned *good*. '*Darling*.' The word slipped from her tongue with droll mockery, in deliberate payback. 'I've barely begun.' She paused almost imperceptibly. 'Too much for you to handle?'

A faint sound emerged from his throat…a subdued groan, or stifled laughter?

She told herself she didn't care.

He released her hand. 'Be aware it can have only one end.'

It became an endurance test…his, as she teased and tantalized, with her hands, the edge of her tongue, the gentle nip of her teeth. A delicate salutation that caused male fingers tracing the length of her spine to dig in as if in silent warning.

An action that had her cup his scrotum and squeeze a little, before tracing the swollen, distended length of his erection with the tip of her finger, circle its head, then tease with unrelenting fervour.

'Enough.'

Duardo reversed their positions and surged deep inside her with one powerful thrust, unleashing an erotic, primeval coupling that became wild as they drove each other to the limit, suspended themselves there, then sent each other spiralling in a glorious free fall.

Had she cried out? There was no recollection of anything other than the witching sorcery of incredible sex and its aftermath.

The long, slow slide of his hand traced the contours of her body, and she felt the brush of his lips to her temple.

She didn't want to move. Didn't think she *could*.

A husky protest escaped her lips as strong arms slid beneath her body, carried her into the *en suite* and joined her in a spa bath filled with warm scented water.

She didn't bother opening her eyes. 'This is a dream, right?'

'Uh-huh.'

The water felt good, so, too, the leisurely ministrations, the soft towel blotting moisture from her body, the comfortable mattress, the bedcovers.

And the arms that held her as she slept.

'Rise and shine. It's after ten.'

Kayla heard the words, and burrowed her head beneath the pillow. Only to groan out loud as the pillow was removed.

'Doesn't rhyme,' she muttered. 'Should be nine.'

'Ten,' a familiar male voice corrected, and she rolled over to face her nemesis. Only to close her eyes and open them again.

He looked too rested, too relaxed and too darn *male*.

'Breakfast,' Duardo drawled. 'Followed by some retail therapy.'

She lifted a hand and smoothed back a fall of hair from her cheek. 'I'm all shopped out.'

'Tonight. Charity fund-raiser. Evening gown.'

'Oh, *hell*.'

'Just so. Except the charity is a very worthy cause, and the event is one I'm expected to attend.' He leant down and placed a hand on the bedcovers. 'Spence is waiting for you.'

So he was, she determined as she finished off a healthy breakfast and two cups of black coffee.

They visited Jacob, who appeared in good spirits, and his congratulatory hug and good wishes held genuine warmth. It was a relief to have his assurance the pain factor was manageable, and the orthopaedist pleased with his progress.

'This is becoming a habit,' Kayla imparted as Spence hit Double Bay and they entered the first of several boutiques.

By early afternoon Spence had a number of glossy carrier-bags in his possession, and there was a sense of relief they were done.

'Home,' Kayla declared as he stowed everything in the Lexus.

'Not quite.'

She looked at him in silent askance, then voiced, 'Why do I get the feeling there's *more*?'

'Lunch.'

'That's it?'

'Jewellery.' He named an exclusive boutique. 'Duardo suggests you choose from a few pieces he instructed be put aside.'

She almost refused to comply. Except she recognized the purpose. As Duardo Alvarez's wife there were certain expectations to uphold. It was everything to do with image.

An hour later she stood with Spence in locked seclusion as she examined exquisite diamonds in various settings. After some deliberation and adherence to quality, she selected a pair of ear-studs, a slender necklace and a matching bracelet. A dress watch was added, its sapphire diamond-studded face classifying it as an item of jewellery rather than a conventional timepiece.

'Mr Alvarez instructed me to present you with this.' The jeweller withdrew a rectangular velvet case and released the catch with the slight flourish of one about to display a magnificent surprise.

Kayla looked at the sapphires…the beautiful drop pendant, matching ear-studs, bracelet…and felt her stomach plummet.

'Where did you get these?' Was that her voice? It sounded incredibly hushed.

'Mr Alvarez acquired them a few years ago at an estate auction, I believe.' He passed a reverent finger over the stones. 'They were recently handed into my care to ensure the settings are intact.'

They had once belonged to her mother. A birthday gift in the days when Benjamin had been on top of his game.

The jeweller appeared to sense her disquiet. 'You do not like them?'

'They're beautiful.' Indeed they were, and had numbered high among Blanche's most loved pieces of jewellery. The question was why they were in Duardo's possession.

She stood in silence as the jeweller carefully packaged everything, provided valuation certificates and handed the glossy bag into Spence's safekeeping.

It was almost five when she entered the house, and on determining Duardo's whereabouts she made for his home office.

He glanced up from examining graphs and figures on his laptop, saved the data then swivelled in his chair to face her, noting her air of determination, the deep brilliance in her eyes…and waited for the fall-out.

'A successful day?'

The mildness of his voice merely strengthened her resolve. 'I want to thank you.' She paused almost imperceptibly. 'The diamonds. The watch.' She sounded incredibly polite, even to her own ears. 'They're fitting gifts to showcase the wife of a billionaire.'

He leant back in his chair and regarded her steadily. 'You've developed an aversion to jewellery?'

The brilliance intensified. 'No.'

'Then I don't see the problem.'

'It doesn't concern you that I do?'

'Not in the least.'

She wanted to hit him. Instead she stood her ground and aimed for controlled politeness, despite her inwardly seething anger. 'You bought Blanche's sapphires.'

His eyes sharpened, then became slightly hooded. 'I bid for them successfully. Yes.'

'Why?'

He uncoiled his body with lithe ease and moved around to lean one hip against the desk. 'Is the *why* of it so important?'

'Yes, dammit!' She eyed a paperweight on his desk and mentally weighed throwing it at him.

'Don't.' The silky warning held a lethal quality.

A host of conflicting thoughts clouded her features, and he defined each and every one of them.

'You deserve to have something that belonged to your mother.'

She didn't believe him. Couldn't.

'Then.' She struggled with the knowledge. 'Even *then* you were planning our remarriage?'

His eyes hardened and became bleak. 'It was never in doubt.'

Her chin tilted. 'And Benjamin?' She couldn't help herself. 'Did you plot his downfall?'

'Your father managed that of his own accord.'

So much fine anger seething beneath the surface. He had a mind to take and tame it into something else.

With one easy movement he tunnelled his hand through her hair and cupped the back of her head, while the other hand slid down to her waist and drew her close.

She didn't have time to utter a word as his mouth closed

over hers, then angled in possession as he plundered at will, using his tongue, the edges of his teeth to subdue and seduce until he sensed her capitulation, caught the faint groan of despair deep in her throat…and coaxed her response.

It was a while before he lifted his head, and he viewed the deep, slumberous quality evident in her eyes, the slightly parted swollen mouth…and resisted the temptation to take it to another level.

Kayla almost swayed beneath his probing gaze, and she fought against the shimmering tension, aware one wrong move, a castigating word would unleash an emotion she didn't want to deal with.

Instead she stood her ground and aimed for controlled politeness. 'If you'll tell me how long before we need to leave.'

He checked his watch. 'An hour and a quarter.'

'I'll ensure I'm ready on time.'

It wasn't the best exit line, but it would do.

CHAPTER FIVE

'DUARDO, *darling*.'

Kayla watched as the society matron did the air-kiss thing and followed it with a coquettish chuckle.

'And this is your wife.' She turned towards Kayla. 'How lovely to meet you, my dear.' The smile was a little too bright. 'The newsprint photograph didn't do you justice.'

The restaurant, the photographer.

The media hadn't failed to produce caption, photograph and an interesting piece for the morning's newspapers.

Tonight was indisputably *showtime*.

Hence the gown, the jewellery.

She'd chosen taffeta in a rich midnight-blue, with a fitted bodice and slender full-length skirt. Matching stilettos added height, and the colour highlighted the creamy texture of her skin, accented the smooth lines of her blonde upswept hair. The newly purchased jewellery provided a perfect finishing touch.

'Thank you.'

'Duardo has kept you a well-guarded secret.'

Act. A stunning smile curved her lips. 'Yes, hasn't he?'

Duardo caught hold of her hand and lifted it to brush

his lips to her palm. 'With good reason.' His eyes held hers, darkly captivating and infinitely seductive.

Hell, he was good.

'We shall expect you both at the Leukaemia Foundation dinner.'

He released her hand and gave the society doyenne his attention. 'Of course.'

'Overkill,' Kayla commented quietly when the woman moved out of earshot.

'You think?' He sounded mildly amused, and she offered a sweet smile.

'Definitely.'

'Ah, but there are certain…expectations, wouldn't you agree?'

'We get to play pretend.'

'Will it be so difficult?'

'I shall give it my best,' she assured with mock solemnity.

He looked incredible in a black evening suit, white dress shirt and black bow tie. Fine tailoring…Armani or Zegna? Together with handcrafted Italian shoes, gold cufflinks, an elegant watch and a touch of very expensive cologne.

It wasn't his clothing which drew attention, but the man who wore it. There was something dark and untamed beneath the sophisticated surface…a wary primitiveness apparent in the depths of his eyes that had the potential to both frighten and fascinate.

Undoubtedly for some women, it was a powerful aphrodisiac.

As it had been for her, at first. Except she'd caught a glimpse of the child he had been, the boy hardened by street-life and the need to stay one step ahead of the law in order to survive.

'You certainly know how to spring a surprise.'

The male voice held a degree of mockery, and Kayla slowly turned to face its owner. Not someone she knew, and, if first impressions were any indication, not a man she'd trust.

'Congratulations are in order.'

He made it sound like a condemnation instead of a compliment.

'Max.' Duardo's acknowledgment held cool politeness.

An eyebrow arched in silent query. 'No introduction, Duardo?'

There was something apparent, barely hidden beneath the surface, which she couldn't quite pinpoint.

'My wife, Kayla.' He paused almost imperceptibly. 'Maximillian Stein. The actress Marlena's husband.'

Max bowed. 'Marlena is indisposed. She sends her regrets, and her congratulations on your very recent marriage.' His smile held pseudo-pleasantness. 'Née Enright-Smythe, and your ex. Interesting.'

His expressionless gaze speared hers as he extended a hand, which she took out of politeness, hating the deliberate way his fingers curled over her own before she could pull them free. 'A rescue mission, or revenge?'

Kayla spared Duardo an adoring look. 'Shall I tell him, darling? Or will you?'

She lifted a hand to his cheek, felt the smooth warmth of his skin and managed not to blink when he covered her hand with his own.

'By all means share, *querida*.'

She turned towards Max. 'Romance,' she revealed sweetly. 'True love.'

Max's gaze narrowed, and she kept her voice light, sweet. 'Perhaps you've yet to experience it.'

He executed a slightly mocking bow. 'I'm so pleased for you.'

'Thank you.' Her tone was the model of decorum, and she waited until he moved away before meeting Duardo's steady gaze.

'You don't like him.'

Duardo's expression remained unchanged. 'I have reason not to trust him.'

'He's an associate?'

'From the days of my youth in New York.'

'I see.'

His mouth formed a wry twist. 'I doubt you do.'

'You share a rivalry.'

It was more than that. Whereas he had cleaned up years ago and only dealt legitimately...Max ran with wolves of another creed beneath the carefully constructed cover of respectability.

If it hadn't been for Marlena's father, he'd have severed all ties long ago. Except he owed a debt, one he'd promised to honour. And he had. Fostering Marlena's career, helping making her the *name* she was today.

'Isn't this fun?'

Duardo cast Kayla a look that held musing humour, and she offered him a beauteous smile before letting her gaze skim over the room.

A strange prickling sensation hit the back of her neck, and she turned slightly to find herself the object of Max Stein's studied appraisal.

It was more than interest, and strangely indefinable. Worse, it made her feel uncomfortable...almost afraid.

Soon the ballroom doors would open with the request everyone be seated at their designated tables.

In the past she'd attended many such events, as her parents had been strong supporters of various charities.

Another lifetime, she mused wryly, when she'd taken her father's wealth and social standing for granted.

Now she had no such illusions about life…or love. And she was back on the social scene as Duardo's wife.

Would the knives be out, and, if so, who would hold them?

Duardo Alvarez was a powerful man. Few would dare risk crossing him. Yet there were those who might not have the same reservations about his wife, given the speculation surrounding her background circumstances.

'Congratulations, darlings.'

Kayla turned to see a stunning brunette whose features were vaguely familiar.

'Elyse,' Duardo greeted warmly.

Of course. Model, tall, impossibly slender, with curves in all the right places, and utterly gorgeous. Known as *the face* of a major cosmetics company.

Elyse sent Kayla a sparkling glance. 'I was beginning to despair of him.'

'Really?' What else could she say?

'Companion of many, but lover of few.'

There were times when words were superfluous, and she settled for a musing smile.

'Catch you later.' With a waft of exotic perfume Elyse faded into the crowd.

'Was that meant to be reassurance, do you think?' Kayla arched sweetly, and caught the slight humour evident in those dark eyes.

'The ballroom doors have just opened.' He placed a hand at the back of her waist. 'Shall we go in?'

The table they were directed to held prominent position,

and Kayla's stomach sank a little as she saw one of the city's social doyennes already seated there.

Marjorie Markham and her husband. Tom? Or was it Tim? Hostess *par excellence*, with a dangerous tongue, the woman was a purveyor of gossip and known to take fact and embellish it with fiction.

Oh, *joy.*

Benito and Samara Torres appeared, and following an affectionate greeting, Samara took a seat next to Duardo.

The remaining six seats were soon filled by a judge and his wife, one of the city's scions and his partner and a mother and daughter.

An eclectic mix guaranteed to evoke interesting conversation based on superficial politeness, Kayla perceived a trifle wryly, aware nuances and practised manipulation formed part of the social game people played.

Drinks waiters circled the tables, pouring complimentary wine and accepting orders, followed by the charity's chairperson, who took the podium to provide an introduction, a list of past achievements together with a projection of future aims before wishing the guests an enjoyable evening.

'I doubted you'd show tonight. No honeymoon, darling?' Samara arched as waiters began serving the entrée. 'If I recall correctly, you didn't manage one the first time round.' She lifted her goblet of wine and gestured a toast. 'To the bride and groom.'

Oh, my. This had all the makings of being a *fun* evening.

'Hawaii,' Marjorie Markham announced with the satisfaction of remembered knowledge. 'You originally married there.'

'Indeed.' Duardo's accented drawl was pure silk. A silent warning the subject was off-limits, and one only the foolhardy would ignore.

Fortunately the waiters provided a diversion, and the focus shifted to food.

Kayla was supremely conscious of Duardo's close proximity, the occasional touch of his hand, his warm smile—purely for appearance's sake—and her own in reciprocation.

Playing the game, she perceived a trifle wryly.

Yet there was awareness beneath the surface, a heightened sense of the sensual magic he seemed to exude with effortless ease. Each time she looked at him, she had no difficulty imagining how his mouth felt on her own…as it trailed her body to tease sensitive pleasure pulses.

Oh, for heaven's sake! It's just sex…albeit mind-blowing, but just *sex* none the less.

So…*enjoy*, why don't you? To imagine there might be more was crazy. To *want* more…let's not go there! She dared not, for fear it might be more truth than she could bear.

At that moment Duardo turned towards her, his dark eyes inscrutable for several time-spinning seconds, then his mouth curved into a faint smile…almost as if he'd read her mind.

To compound it, he brushed his fingers down her cheek. And watched her melt a little.

It's only an act, she assured, and did some acting of her own by sending him a sparkling *sensual* smile, silently challenging him with a deliberate *two can play this game* look.

'Really, darling, get a room, why don't you?' Samara suggested, and her pouting moue reflected a degree of mocking humour which didn't reach her eyes.

'The preliminary teasing is part of the fun, don't you agree?' Kayla responded without missing a beat.

It was doubtful anyone other than Duardo could hear their conversation against the background noise, although retreat was probably a wise option.

Entertainment was provided between courses, and first up was the obligatory fashion parade, with waif-thin models displaying the latest in overseas designer wear bearing exorbitant price tags, and vied for by the social set's fashionistas.

The mother and daughter team made notes on their programmes; so, too, did Samara.

'That particular gown is *mine*.'

Benito Torres offered an indulgent smile at his wife's determined proclamation, at the exquisite sapphire silk chiffon with its multi-layered skirt, while the mother and daughter shot Samara a glittering *in your dreams* look that was quickly masked.

Kayla tamped down a mental image of all three women making a concerted dash in a bid to be first to secure the designer original.

'A gown I've reserved as a gift for my wife.' Duardo's indolent drawl earned him the unsolicited attention of all four women.

'Really?' Samara was the first to recover as she turned towards Kayla. 'Congratulations. I would have killed for it.' And she shot Benito a telling glare, while the mother uttered, 'Unfair,' to her daughter.

'How generous, darling,' Kayla managed sweetly, inwardly hating the public spectacle that seemingly emphasized her position as Duardo's trophy wife.

'My pleasure.' His answering smile left no one in any doubt as to what form that pleasure would take.

Oh, my. What a way to make enemies. If looks from those three women could kill, she'd be dead.

A comedian took the podium between the main and dessert courses, and a popular vocalist performed two numbers while the waiters served coffee.

With the evening's planned events at a close, it left guests the option to catch up with friends seated elsewhere in the ballroom.

Kayla barely held back her relief when Duardo indicated they should leave, although their passage from the ballroom was interrupted at frequent intervals by several fellow guests offering their congratulations.

'Nothing to say?' he queried with faint mockery as the Aston Martin purred through the city streets.

She spared him a sober look. 'I'm all talked out.' Smiled out, too. And she had the beginnings of a headache.

The evening, her first among guests as Duardo's wife, was over. She'd held her own with a degree of dignity. Except it was only the first of many, and it would be a while before their marriage ceased being the current topic of thinly veiled speculation.

'Please tell me I'm not in line to beard the lion's den again any time soon.'

'That bad, huh?'

Not really. Just that she was out of practice. 'It's been a long hiatus between social appearances,' she informed dryly, and glimpsed his mouth curve in the dim interior of the car. She felt compelled to add, 'Women home in on you like bees seeking a honeypot.'

'That bothers you?'

Big-time. Except she had no intention of telling him so. 'Should it?'

He brought the car to a halt inside the garage and cut the engine.

'I couldn't fault you.'

'A compliment, Duardo?'

'You find it difficult to accept I might gift you one?'

She offered him a startlingly direct look. 'Yes.' She reached for the door clasp with one hand and released her seat belt with the other.

He let her go, mirroring her actions with his own as he accompanied her into the house and watched as she made straight for the staircase.

Duardo reset the security alarm, minimized the main interior lighting system and followed her at a leisurely pace.

'Problem?'

Kayla heard the smooth silkiness in his voice as she made a third attempt at releasing the safety catch on her necklace, and offered, 'Nothing I can't handle.'

For heaven's sake, the catch had been easy to close …why was it so difficult to release?

'Allow me.'

His fingers touched hers, and she reacted as if she'd been burnt by a flame. To stand quiescent almost robbed the breath from her throat.

Fool. She'd been in his company for the past several hours. Why now was it any different?

Because they were alone in the bedroom. He was standing far too close for comfort. And she had no illusions as to how the night would end.

Worse, she wanted what he could give her. The stirring of her emotions…dammit, the *passion*. To lose herself in the sensual nirvana only he could provide.

To believe, if only for a while, that what they shared was real…as it had once been.

Except you could never go back. There was only *now*.

Was it her imagination, or did his fingers linger at her nape as he freed the catch?

She heard the faint chink as he placed the necklace down onto the bedside pedestal, then he caught hold of her shoulders and turned her round to face him.

He'd discarded his jacket, removed his bow tie and freed the top few buttons of his shirt.

Kayla met the darkness in his eyes with fearless regard, and barely quelled the faint hitch in her breath as he reached for the zip fastening on her gown.

'I can undress myself.' Her voice sounded stiff, and she glimpsed the way the corners of his mouth curved in humour.

'And deprive me of the pleasure?'

'As long as you don't expect me to reciprocate.'

The zip slid free, and she didn't move as it slithered down onto the carpet in a heap of silk.

All that separated her from total nudity was a slender thong brief, and her hands automatically lifted to shield her breasts in a gesture of modesty.

Unnecessary, given he knew their weight, texture, the sensitive peaks, how they tasted…and her reaction to his touch.

He lifted a hand and traced the curve of her waist, felt the slight quiver of her flesh beneath his touch and felt momentary satisfaction. 'Why so shy?'

Faint colour tinged her cheeks and her eyes deepened and became stormy. 'Don't *play* me.'

'Is that what you think I'm doing?'

'Aren't you?' she demanded, sorely tried, as his fingers brushed her navel, then slid slowly down to trace the seam of her thong.

The silent scream for him to desist remained locked in her throat as his finger hooked beneath the narrow seam and slid it down with practised ease.

His eyes held hers as he released the remaining buttons on his shirt, then pulled it free and tossed it over the valet frame. In seeming slow motion he toed off his shoes, his socks then he undid and removed his trousers.

'I don't want to do this.' The words left her lips in a shaky undertone.

Liar. Every nerve-end in her body was alive and vibrating with need. Worse, sensation spiralled deep within, making a mockery of the emotions she strove so hard to suppress.

His arousal was a potent force beneath the black silk barely sheathing its powerful rigidity, and she felt her insides clench in anticipation of his possession.

'No?'

He sounded almost amused, damn him, and her eyes flashed blue fire as he cupped her face, then fastened his mouth over her own.

His tongue traced the firm line of her lips, angling a little as she held back in a senseless stubborn gesture that had him nibbling the soft lower lip with the edges of his teeth, followed seconds later by a painful nip.

Her mouth parted in silent protest and his tongue swept hers, teasing in an evocative dance that was all persuasive mastery.

She didn't stand a chance.

Although the knowledge didn't stop her initial resistance, and she balled her hands into fists as she aimed for his shoulders, his back, anywhere she could connect with.

Only to give in with a stifled groan of despair as he cupped her bottom and lifted her against him, parting her thighs so the highly sensitized clitoris nestled against his erection.

Dear heaven.

Sensation arrowed deep within, radiating with pulsing intensity as he slowly slid her against him, creating an unbelievable friction that swept her to the brink…and he held her as she shattered.

'You don't play fair.' Her voice was little more than a husky whisper as his lips nuzzled the sensitive curve of her neck.

'Did you expect me to?'

He adjusted her slightly as he discarded his briefs, and she cried out at the skin-on-skin contact, the deep, pulsing need as he positioned her to accept his length…the long slow slide as she sank down on him.

The slick heat, the slight stretch of silken tissues as he reached the hilt…and began to move, slowly at first, until she caught his rhythm and their desire became rawly primitive, wild.

Almost beyond reason as he carried her to the bed and assaulted her senses until she lost all reason, every concept of where or who she was…except *his*.

His woman.

Only his.

CHAPTER SIX

THERE had to be a reason for each day, Kayla reflected as she folded the morning's newspaper and finished her coffee.

It didn't seem so long ago she'd wished for time to spare, not to have to rush from one job to the next, eating on the run, with one day seemingly merging into another.

Conferring with Maria was a token exercise, for the housekeeper and her husband maintained a well-established routine that needed no guidance or interference.

Retail therapy for the sake of it didn't hold much appeal. Besides, recent shopping expeditions had done much to provide her with clothes, shoes and lingerie for every occasion.

Establishing a social diary was something she'd prefer to forestall as long as possible. Invitations were beginning to appear to one social luncheon or another under various guises…some genuine, others merely a reason for the wives of wealthy city men to play dress-up and congregate together.

She'd been there, done that…taking time off at her father's instigation to ensure her face, her name made the social pages as the daughter of Benjamin Enright-Smythe.

Fêted…until life had taken a downward turn, so-called friends became elusive and invitations ceased.

Now the thought of filling her days with regular visits to the manicurist, hairdresser, beauty therapist in search of self-beautification held little appeal

The insistent burr of her cellphone interrupted her thoughts, and she picked up.

'Spence. Enquiring if you need my services this morning?'

Kayla made a split-second decision. 'Would you mind dropping me into the city?' She checked her watch. 'In about forty minutes?'

'I'll have the car waiting out front.'

It didn't take long to change into a smart business suit. Black, straight skirt, beautifully cut jacket. Tights, stilettos, minimum jewellery, skilfully applied make-up, her hair swept into a smooth knot.

Her CV bore her maiden name…Smythe, minus the hyphened Enright.

Personal presentation mattered in her bid to canvass a few employment agencies, and she bade Spence a bright 'Thanks' as she slid out from the car onto the busy city street. 'I'll get a taxi home.'

He shook his head. 'We've already done this. Duardo's instructions. Phone when you're ready and I'll swing by to collect you.'

The concept of having Spence at her beck and call seemed ridiculous. She could drive, she had a licence…she really needed a car of her own!

'This afternoon?' Kayla hazarded. 'After I've visited Jacob in hospital.'

'You haven't forgotten the foreign-film festival begins this evening?'

She closed her eyes, then opened them again as she recalled the agenda.

A premiere, filmed in Madrid with Spanish actors, subtitled in English, and attended by members of the Spanish Consulate, various dignitaries and society mavens.

'Got it. Cinema at seven, cocktails, socialize, seated at seven forty-five for an eight o'clock start.'

Note to self…purchase diary, check the week's upcoming social events and write them down.

Kayla did a swift mental calculation. Hawking her CV, lunch, hospital… 'Four o'clock outside the main hospital entrance? If there's any change, I'll phone you.'

'Take care.'

Was it her imagination, or did his words hold a hidden meaning?

Oh, for heaven's sake, get a grip, she silently castigated as the Lexus pulled out into traffic and moved swiftly from her line of vision.

The first agency went through the motions and politely insisted Kayla make an early-afternoon interview appointment. The second agency requested she return in an hour.

Time to sip a latte, call Jacob and browse through one of the city's major department stores.

Lunch was something light at a boutique café, and she entered Jacob's hospital room with a sense of satisfaction that both interviews had gone well; one particularly had sounded very positive, with a follow-up call promised the next day.

'Hi,' Kayla greeted with affection. 'You're looking great.'

'The orthopaedist is pleased, physiotherapist ditto.' He indicated the suite with a sweeping gesture. 'Great room, service, friendly nurses, pain management…' He offered her a teasing grin. 'The opportunity to flirt a little…What's not to like?'

'I've brought you a few things.' Books, the latest sports magazine, some personal clothing.

'Are you OK?'

Oh, heavens. 'What makes you think I might not be?'

His expression sobered, and his eyes held affectionate concern. 'Duardo. You. Marriage.'

He was too perceptive by far. 'It all worked out.' She summoned a smile and kept it in place.

'I'd like to think it has. For you.' He caught hold of her hand and threaded his fingers through her own. 'Thanks.'

Keep it light. There was no way she'd let him guess she was caught in a trap…an empty marriage, with no indication of how long it might last.

'For saving some of your skin?' She indicated his leg, the slowly fading bruises. 'You haven't exactly had an easy ride.'

'Nor you.'

'Hey,' she managed gently. 'We're a team.'

'Bro and sis for ever, huh?'

'Got it in one.'

They talked until visiting hours concluded, and a casual glance at the time had her reaching for her cellphone.

A few minutes later she cut the connection and stood to her feet.

'Spence is on his way.' She leant forward and brushed her lips to his cheek. 'Don't go climbing any cliffs.'

'As if.'

It was almost five when she entered the house, and she raced upstairs to shower, wash and dry her hair. Only to come to a halt at the sight of a large, glossy box resting on the bed.

The sapphire silk chiffon gown from the charity event,

neatly folded beneath layers of tissue paper. So he hadn't been joking. It was exquisite, and the exact shade of her mother's sapphires.

The comparison didn't escape her as she hung it carefully in her walk-in wardrobe. Had this been the reason behind Duardo's choice?

When she emerged into the bedroom Duardo was in the process of loosening his tie with one hand while freeing shirt buttons with the other.

The sight of him did strange things to her equilibrium. Olive skin, superb musculature…he emanated power from every pore of his body.

'Hi.' Good manners rose to the surface. 'The gown was delivered while I was out. It's beautiful. Thank you.'

He inclined his head, and his dark eyes swept her features and lingered a little. 'How was your day?'

Was she being super-sensitive in imagining his query was not as innocuous as it seemed?

'Fine.' Did Spence report her every move? Kayla pulled on casual clothes. 'I spent time in the city, had lunch, then visited Jacob.' It was the truth, with a few omissions.

Duardo released the belt at his waist and undid his trousers. 'Maria is serving dinner in fifteen minutes.'

Time to select what she intended to wear, pop a few essentials into an evening purse then do something with her hair.

The form-fitting red silk, she determined, with its scooped neckline, spaghetti straps and fitted evening jacket in matching red silk. Stilettos, minimum jewellery.

Maria had prepared a seafood paella, and Kayla merely picked at it, settled for salad and declined wine in favour of iced water.

'Not hungry?'

She replaced her cutlery, and met his dark gaze with equanimity. 'Is that a problem?'

'Should it be?'

'If you'll excuse me, I'll go change and do the make-up thing.'

'I'll be up in five minutes.'

All he had to do was add a tie and shrug into his suit jacket, whereas she required ten minutes minimum.

She was almost done when he entered the bedroom, and she checked her mirrored image, added lip-gloss, another sweep with the mascara wand then she crossed to the bed, collected her evening purse and turned to face him.

The butterflies in her stomach executed a dangerous flip, and she forced them to settle.

Three years on, and she was as susceptible to him as she had been from very first sight.

There was something about him, some intrinsic magic she'd yet to define that stirred her senses and sent them spiralling out of control.

He had the power to possess her…mind, body and soul, and she continually fought a losing battle to retain a semblance of sensual sanity.

It was crazy. *Love* wasn't part of the equation. Yet she was drawn to him like a helpless moth to a flame.

Would she survive…or burn and die?

Survive, a silent voice attested. It was the only answer.

'Shall we leave?' Her voice was cool, her smile practised, and she glimpsed something shift in those dark eyes as he crossed to her side.

The theatre foyer was crowded when they entered it, and Kayla felt the customary warmth as Duardo laid his arm along the back of her waist.

Proprietorial possession, protection…or *display*?

She told herself she didn't care as she slipped into an adopted part, lifting her face towards his and projecting a stunning smile.

'This promises to be a stimulating evening, darling.'

His mouth curved a little. 'Indeed.'

'Challenging,' she continued quietly, 'considering my knowledge of the Spanish language is severely limited.'

His fingers moved against the edge of her waist. 'I'm sure you recall a few important words.'

His voice was infinitely sensual, and a familiar, shivery sensation shook her slender frame.

Damn him. He was playing a deliberate game, evoking emotions…memories she tried so hard to suppress.

'Spoken with practised ease in the heat of the moment?'

He wanted to shake her…and almost did. 'Careful,' he warned quietly. 'At the end of the evening I get to take you home.'

She was playing with fire, and knew it. Yet her smile deepened. 'Is that a threat or a promise?'

'Your choice.'

'Duardo. Kayla,' a bright feminine voice intruded. 'How wonderful to see you.'

The both turned slightly to face one of the city's most prominent society matrons. Although *matron* was a misnomer, for Ashley Baines-Simmons was in her thirties and the wife of a man some twenty years her senior. A rare love match that had nothing to do with chronological age. Five years ago their marriage had caused a stir among the social set, with the usual slurs cast in aspersion. Yet Ashley had held her head high and sailed through it all with her integrity intact.

Sadly there was one very important difference.

Ashley had the unconditional love and support of her husband.

Kayla, on the other hand, suffered no illusions regarding Duardo's motivation.

'I can't begin to tell you how delighted I am to see you two back together again.'

Ashley brushed her lips to Kayla's cheek, then copied the action to Duardo.

'Our delight mirrors your own.' Duardo's response held practised warmth, and Kayla silently applauded his acting ability.

'We must get together,' Ashley declared. 'I'll be in touch.'

A waiter bearing a tray of canapés wove his way in their direction, followed by a waitress with a tray filled with flutes of champagne.

Kayla selected champagne, and took an appreciative sip, enjoying the slightly sharp taste, the faint bubbles.

'Duardo.'

Another sycophant? She turned slightly and instantly revised such a thought.

This woman was beautiful. Different. Dear heaven…breathtaking.

Actress? Model? *Former lover*?

'Jennifer,' Duardo acknowledged warmly and leaned forward to brush his mouth to her cheek.

Lover…definitely. Hopefully *former*. But not, Kayla perceived, too far distant, given the blatant message briefly evident and quickly hidden in the woman's liquid dark eyes.

OK, so you didn't expect him to remain celibate for three years, surely? Divorce gave him every moral right to bed any woman he chose.

It was *she* who hadn't been able to bear the thought of intimacy with anyone else.

'My wife, Kayla.'

The sound of Duardo's voice brought her sharply into the present, and with it…indecision.

Should she offer a smile? Handshake? Resort to the air-kiss thing? *Hell*, what was the protocol for the husband's wife and his ex-lover?

Jennifer made the first move by extending her hand. 'I'm so pleased to meet you.'

You are? Compliment, or contradiction?

Kayla took the woman's hand and played polite with a degree of genuine sympathy for any woman who'd loved and lost the man whose name she bore.

Duardo Alvarez was something else. Assuredly almost without equal. In bed and out of it.

Hadn't she hungered for his touch, wept for the loss of it? And now, experienced an emotional maelstrom as a result of the return of it?

Life, she determined a trifle grimly, held a certain irony.

'Enjoy the evening,' she evinced quietly.

'Thank you. I hope we'll have the opportunity to spend time with each other.'

Oh, my. With a view to what? Sharing coffee and confidences? Discussing Duardo?

Somehow she doubted the ex-lover and the current wife could ever be friends.

Jennifer melted into the crowd, and Kayla sent Duardo a mocking look in silent askance.

'Her husband was killed last year piloting a small plane in hazardous conditions during a snowstorm.'

'How noble of you to console the grieving widow.'

His eyes darkened. 'He was a friend. It was the least I could do.'

Where was her compassion? 'I'm sorry.'

One eyebrow lifted. 'For mistaking friendship for something else?'

There had been something else…on Jennifer's part, if not his. She was willing to swear to it. No woman looked at a man quite like that without being emotionally involved…even if it didn't lead to intimacy.

It was a relief when Duardo's attention was taken by one of the Spanish Embassy's dignitaries, and a personal introduction to the Spanish Ambassador.

Formality and politeness ruled, together with a degree of awe. Afterwards Kayla could barely recall a thing she'd said.

'You'd already met,' she managed quietly minutes later.

'Yes.' Duardo's acknowledgment held faint amusement. 'In New York.'

'Should I find that interesting?'

'Perhaps.'

'Although you've no intention of disclosing just *how* interesting.'

'No.'

It was a relief when the electronic buzzer sounded, summoning everyone to enter the theatre auditorium.

Relief that was short-lived when Samara Torres encouraged Benito towards the two vacant seats at Duardo's side.

Kayla leaned in close as the lights began to dim. 'Three conquests in one evening, *darling*? Perhaps you should give me a list.'

He took possession of her hand and threaded his fingers through her own. She dug the tips of her nails into his palm, and felt his grasp tighten in silent warning.

She bore his name, wore his ring and lived in his beautiful home.

Once she'd had his heart…something she doubted he'd gift her again.

The music began, the curtains parted electronically and the screen filled with Technicolor images.

Pathos, humour and temperament. Lost love, angst and misunderstanding, closing with found love and resolution.

The film had won plaudits at the Cannes Film Festival, the director was lauded for his interpretation and Kayla enjoyed the concept despite the captions in English making for slightly disjointed viewing.

Coffee was served in the foyer, and a number of the guests lingered, while others took their leave.

'Would you care to join Benito and I for coffee?' Samara named an upmarket coffee boutique in Double Bay.

'Thank you,' Duardo responded. 'Perhaps another time? I have an early-morning flight.'

Samara offered a disappointed pout that held overtones of petulance, and Kayla likened her image to a playful kitten...with claws.

'Say "goodnight", *querida*,' Benito instructed with thinly veiled mockery. 'We'll browse the café scene and find someone to amuse you.'

Were they for real, or simply game-playing?

'Benito likes to indulge her,' Duardo drawled as they walked to where their car was parked.

'How...generous of him.'

'She fulfils his needs.'

Now that was a comment open to interpretation, if ever there was one! 'Too much information,' she managed with an edge of mockery.

They reached the Aston Martin and he released the security mechanism, saw her seated then crossed round to slip in behind the wheel.

Soft, misty drizzle clouded the windscreen as he drew into the flow of traffic, and she watched the silent swish of wipers, the strong beams of light from oncoming cars.

Idle conversation for the sake of it escaped her, and she leaned back against the head-rest and closed her eyes.

He'd mentioned an early-morning flight. Where was he going, and how long would he be away?

Did it matter?

She told herself she didn't care...and knew she was kidding herself.

It was after eleven when they entered the house, and Kayla reached the main bedroom bare minutes ahead of him. Somehow she'd expected he'd check emails, stock options, graphs...whatever, before coming to bed.

She slipped off her shoes, removed jewellery, dispensed with her evening suit then crossed to the *en suite* to undress and deal with her make-up.

When she was done, she donned a towelling robe and emerged into the bedroom to discover Duardo in the process of discarding his shirt.

'Don't you have something you should tell me?'

Her eyes flew wide as he crossed to stand in front of her. Not good, for his close proximity had an effect on the tenure of her breathing.

'I can't think of a thing.'

He caught hold of her chin between thumb and forefinger, and tilted it so she had to look at him.

'Let me refresh your memory.' His drawled voice was pure silk. 'You had interviews with two city employment agencies today.'

Consternation jolted through her body, and she barely controlled her expression. 'You know this *because*...?'

'Our recent remarriage gained local and national news,' he reminded her wryly. 'How long did you imagine you'd remain incognito as Kayla *Smythe*?'

'Long enough to get a job on my own merit.'

Duardo shot her a measured look. 'You have no need to seek employment.'

'Don't you get it?' Her eyes assumed a fiery sparkle. 'I *want* to work.' She took a deep breath. 'To do something constructive with each day. Dammit, I'm not asking for your approval.'

'Good. Because you don't have it.'

She curled her hands into fists, and barely refrained from hitting him.

'Are you implying you'll blacklist me with every employment agency in town?'

He had the power to do it...and could, all too easily. 'Don't put words in my mouth.'

'You should have married a yes-woman who'd revel in the role of social butterfly,' she fired with unaccustomed vehemence.

'Instead, I have a pocket spitfire.'

His voice held silky amusement, and she lashed out at him. Only to find her wrist caught in a painful grip.

'You want to fight?'

She couldn't hope to win. He had the strength to outmatch her, and would, easily, without compunction. 'Yes, damn you!'

His expression remained unchanged, with the exception of his eyes. Dark, still and faintly hooded, they held something in their depths that sent chills scudding down the length of her spine.

She had no idea how long she stood there. Seconds...minutes. It was as if time stood still, the tension between them electric, volatile, where a word, a sudden move could unleash the unknown.

There was so much *more* at stake than the issue at hand. She hated that she owed him. Resented the balance of power was so heavily weighted against her.

Most of all, she hated herself for the compelling need he aroused in her…for him, only *him*.

It wasn't fair. None of it was fair.

Duardo watched the fleeting emotions chase her expressive features, and defined each and every one of them.

He could reach out and pull her in against him…make her his in a way that would dispel all thought, except the primitive joy of very good sex.

And he would…soon.

'It is so important you work?'

Kayla waited a beat. 'Yes.'

No reason, no qualification. 'You want to do this on your own?'

'I need to,' she managed simply.

It was impossible to determine anything from his silent scrutiny.

'If I were to offer you a position with one of my companies—'

Kayla didn't wait for him to finish. 'I'd refuse.'

'You intend arguing with me?'

'It's inevitable.' Kayla effected a light shrug and met his narrowed gaze. 'We have opposing viewpoints.'

One eyebrow slanted. 'Indeed.'

It would be all too easy to accept Duardo's offer. Stipulate flexi-hours, employment without pressure…

She struggled with her conscience, and won.

'I had the token employment in a prime office for a large salary with my father…and lived with the accusation of nepotism, the snide, behind-my-back innuendos from his associates and fellow staff.'

He recognized the challenge, the need to succeed, and silently applauded it…and her. For no other woman of his acquaintance would choose to take the more difficult path, given similar circumstances.

'What about setting up a business of your own?'

Kayla searched his expression for a degree of cynicism, and found none. 'You can't be serious?' She hardly dared breathe.

Something to put her heart and soul into creating, then completing with her own individual flair.

A pie-in-the-sky idea that had teased her mind for some time. Only to be discarded as not only unrealistic, but also impossible due to lack of funds and massive debts.

Now she had no problem recalling her vision of an upmarket bathroom-accessory boutique, with the finest towels…face, hand and bath towels, embroidered, lace borders, the finest Egyptian cottons. Luxurious soaps, bath oils, candles. Elegant cut-crystal bottles and jars, of the finest quality. Catering to the wealthy and lovers of beautiful wares.

Duardo felt something tug his gut as he watched her expressive features. Had she any idea how easy he found it to read her? The luminous quality apparent in her eyes, the softly parted mouth?

'Run it by me.'

He wouldn't go for it. Besides, she couldn't finance such a venture.

A tiny hysterical bubble of laughter rose and died in her throat. What was she *thinking?*

She gave a negligible shrug. 'I doubt it'll fly.'

He stroked his thumb over the fullness of her lower lip, and felt it tremble. 'Why not?'

Kayla just looked at him. 'Money.'

'I'm not averse to becoming a silent partner in a viable business proposition.'

She dared not get her hopes up. Yet it was impossible to still the excitement fizzing through her veins.

Oh, hell, what did she have to lose?

The words spilled out, tentatively at first, as she described the format, style, preferred location.

'Set everything on paper, get quotes, find suppliers and present me with a proposal.'

Just like that? She was almost speechless. 'You're kidding, right?'

'You'll need an office. I'll have Spence refurbish a room downstairs with the necessary equipment.'

She needed the venture to be hers. Something she strove and worked for. 'There's just one thing.' Her eyes speared his. 'If this works out, I insist everything you invest is in the form of a legitimate loan for which I'm responsible.'

'I'll see to it.'

'Thank you.'

'Are we done?'

'For now.'

'Good.' He lowered his head and covered her mouth with his own. One hand slid to cup her buttocks as he drew her close, and she leaned in, savouring his touch.

Here, like this, she could lose herself in him and pretend for a while that what they shared was *real*. More than just very good sex…the sensual magic of two people completely in tune with each other on every level.

As it had been when they'd made love for the first time. Before displaced family loyalty had intervened and her life began its downward spiral into an ever-deepening pit.

From which she'd been rescued…at a price.

The question was not whether the price was too high, but if she could survive with her pride and integrity intact.

The moment held a certain bitter sweetness.

Later, as she lay sated in his arms and dreamy in the post-coital aftermath, she told herself she didn't care.

There was time in the cool light of day for reality to surface, and the doubts and resentment to creep in.

But for now, on the edge of sleep, nothing else seemed to matter.

CHAPTER SEVEN

KAYLA woke to find she was alone in the large bed, and she hastily checked the time, groaned then hit the shower.

Duardo would be at the airport about to board his flight to Melbourne, where he'd be in meetings all day, and therefore incommunicado, emergencies notwithstanding.

Requesting his approved list of contractors didn't fall into the emergency category, she decided as she pulled on jeans, added a cotton top then twisted her hair into a careless knot atop her head.

Breakfast comprised fresh fruit, yoghurt, toast and coffee eaten on the terrace, and she had just poured her second coffee when Spence joined her, carrying a folder.

'Duardo suggested you might like to check through these.'

These were a comprehensive sheaf of papers detailing various contractors, shop-fitters, tradesmen. Another outlining real estate owned by the Alvarez consortium, together with properties up for tender in a few of the city's upmarket suburbs.

Kayla indicated a chair. 'Join me in a coffee.'

She skimmed through the paperwork with a sense of mounting disbelief. 'We only discussed this idea last night.'

'It was just a matter of accessing the computer and downloading the appropriate file.' He spooned sugar into his cup, then took an appreciative sip of coffee. 'This morning we'll check out locations, then we'll discuss your plans with an architect and designer to obtain an overview of what you require.'

'Today?'

'You sound surprised.'

She offered a rueful smile. 'I didn't expect such fast action.'

'Duardo has a certain reputation for getting things done.'

Without doubt. 'When do we hit the road?'

'As soon as you're ready.'

'Not the inner city,' Kayla specified as Spence swung the Lexus onto New South Head Road. 'Too much competition from the major stores.'

'Agreed. There are two possible locations, one in Double Bay that Duardo has recently added to his investment portfolio.'

If she could name the ideal location, Double Bay would top the list. She almost held her breath in the silent hope the property might be one of several old cottages converted and refurbished into boutiques. Tucked close side-by-side, they lined both sides of a street frequented by the city's social set in the heart of one of the city's most prestigious upmarket suburbs.

'You're kidding me,' she said with undisguised delight as Spence turned into the street and indicated one of the cottages.

'It's exactly *right* in every way.' She hardly realised she was voicing her thoughts. 'I had imagined a shop, one room. But this…' She spread her hands, lost for words.

The cottages were built very close together on pocket-handkerchief-sized land, each cottage small with no hallway, just each room opening onto the room immediately behind it.

'The lease has run out, the cottage forms part of a deceased estate and the family decided to sell.'

For a phenomenal figure. Had to be, given the location.

Spence found a parking space. 'Let's go look, shall we?'

Wooden floors, rich Oriental rugs, select apparel tastefully displayed. Spence presented the *vendeuse* with a card.

'Yes, of course. I've been notified to expect you.'

Two rooms, which could easily be opened up into one large room, if need be. With the requisite kitchen-utility room at the rear, followed by an antique bathroom.

It was perfect. Kayla tamped down her enthusiasm and summoned a degree of caution.

This was a major venture, involving major money.

Duardo's money.

What if her vision didn't succeed? What if a bathroom-accessory boutique in this area simply didn't fit the market?

Running a business wasn't for the faint-hearted. Clientele could prove remarkably fickle.

Spence spared her a discerning look as they reached the pavement. 'You have doubts?'

How could she explain? Or confide in him?

'It's an ideal position.'

'Prime.' He pulled out his cellphone. 'You want to check out the alternative location? Otherwise I'll contact the interior designer and tell him we're on our way.'

Nothing could beat this. 'Measurements, floor plan—'

'I have them. At this point you need to explain your ideas, what you envisage for the end result. He'll work from there, and send in sketches to scale for you to examine, amend and ultimately choose.'

She attempted to tone down her amazement. 'Just like that?'

'Just like that,' Spence reiterated with a flash of musing humour. 'He's worked with Duardo on a number of projects.'

It became a day like no other day, for the speed with which things were achieved and set in motion made her head spin.

'The existing tenant vacates the cottage at the end of the week,' Spence informed her as he headed the Lexus for home. 'If you decide any structural changes are required, the plans will be submitted to Council, and once they're approved the contractors will move in.'

Spence's cellphone rang and he picked up, listened, said, 'Yes, I'll tell her.' And cut the connection.

'Duardo. Unresolved issues. He'll stay overnight and continue negotiations tomorrow.'

The prospect of losing Duardo's disturbing presence for one night didn't faze her in the least. She wanted to double-check paperwork, set up her own sketches, determine the interior layout, stock agents.

At least she wasn't going into this blind. She *knew* what she wanted, how she needed the cottage to be set up.

There had been action at home, Kayla discovered at Josef's bidding, with a room next to Duardo's home office cleared and set up with a desk, cabinets, state-of-the-art laptop, printer, phone station.

Spence set the folder down on the desk. 'All yours,' he indicated smoothly. 'There's a wireless router, which allows you to access the internet from anywhere in the house.'

It was almost too much. 'Thank you. For everything you've done today,' she added.

He was, she knew, just following Duardo's instructions. They'd achieved far more than she had ever imagined possible in a day. Oh, go with honesty! She'd have been ecstatic if it had taken a week!

'You're welcome.'

He left, and Kayla wandered the room, touching the desk, the cabinets, then she examined the laptop, noted it was already set up with all the necessary software, and sank into a chair.

It was little wonder Duardo Alvarez had achieved billionaire status if this was an indication of his *modus operandi*.

Yet why was she so surprised?

Hadn't he moved on her with equal speed? Initially sweeping her off her feet to Hawaii and marriage?

What about *now*?

A hollow feeling encompassed her heart, her mind.

Had he stood by, deliberately waiting for the figurative axe to fall so she had no recourse but to turn to him?

Was remarriage a form of revenge?

She'd been convinced of it from the onset. So *sure*.

Yet—

The in-house phone rang, and she picked up.

'I can serve dinner in fifteen minutes, if it suits you.'

'That's fine, Maria. Thanks.'

Time to shower and change, then she'd seclude herself in the office and check out suppliers on the 'net.

It was almost seven when she re-entered the office, and she set to work with organised diligence. She knew the products she wanted: Excellent-quality milled soaps, exotic oils, beautiful packaging.

At some stage her cellphone rang, and she picked up, voiced an automatic 'hello', then heard Duardo's familiar drawl in response.

'You sound distracted.'

'Make that *overwhelmed*.'

His faint chuckle curled round her nerve-ends, and tugged a little.

'The day has gone according to plan?'

'Exceeded it, in spades.' She waited a beat. 'Thank you.'

'You can thank me when I get home.'

An erotic image came immediately to mind. One she was unsuccessfully able to dismiss. 'I think I can manage to do that.'

'Imagining *how* is liable to keep me awake and uncomfortable all night.'

'There's a remedy for it. Although I believe it's rumoured to send you blind.'

'Indeed?'

'I can't indulge in phone sex. I have work to do,' she managed primly, and heard his soft laughter.

'Now, there's an interesting concept.'

'Work?' It was fun to tease him from a distance.

'Goodnight, *querida*. Sleep well.' He cut the connection before she had a chance to respond.

It was late when she closed the laptop and ascended the stairs to bed.

Her mind was in overdrive, making it difficult to covet sleep, and when she did finally slip into somnolence she was consumed by dreams…harrowing episodes of the past, when she worked every waking hour and there was insufficient money to pay essential bills.

Kayla woke in the early hours, unaware in those brief

few seconds of where she was, the images so vivid in her head she could almost believe she was back in the tiny flat she'd shared with Jacob.

With shaky fingers she switched on the bedside lamp and experienced relief at the visual proof of *this* bedroom, Duardo's home…even if the large bed was lacking his presence.

Auto-suggestion, she reasoned as she dragged weary fingers through her hair.

New business. Money. Fear of failure.

She checked the time, saw it was almost dawn and knew she'd never settle back to sleep.

If Duardo were here, he'd reach for her…and channel her wakefulness into leisurely sex.

Thinking of their shared intimacy resulted in a languorous sigh, and she rolled over and thumped her pillow with a frustrated groan.

OK, so she'd dress, pad downstairs, make coffee, take it into her office…and work.

Breakfast was something she took a ten-minute break for, and she chose to eat lunch at her desk.

By late afternoon she'd refined a list of suppliers and narrowed it down to two. Luxury proved to be expensive, but the items were way above what could be found in department stores and speciality shops.

The designer had faxed through preliminary sketches, from which she took copies to play around with, pencilling in an old-fashioned bathtub on one side of the room and a hip-bath in the other. Towels, meticulously folded in stacks, featuring an artistic bath-sheet spilling from the top to enable the clientele to feel the superb texture without disturbing the stacks…in the same colour, multi-colours forming a glorious rainbow.

Shelving with cut-crystal jars in all shapes and sizes containing exotic bath salts, bath oils, scents.

She could see it, almost embrace the vision and delight in the subtle scents.

Scrubs, sponges, long-handled luxury brushes. Apothecary jars holding multi-coloured cotton balls…beautiful shower-caps. A skilful blend of old and modern.

Candles. Gorgeously scented in delicately coloured wax.

Kayla felt like a child as she took a box of pencils and shaded in the colours, watching the sketch come alive before her eyes.

Dinner became an intrusion, although she bowed to Maria's voiced wisdom in the need of food and offered praise for the dish the housekeeper had prepared.

Then she took her coffee back to the office and worked on the costings, profit margins. She needed to factor in lease payments, utilities, and consider the possibility of hiring part-time staff.

She'd also need her own transport. It was ridiculous to continue relying on Spence.

It was relatively easy to create graphs, projections, a tentative profit and loss account, tax expenditure…

It was there Duardo found her, fingers flying over the laptop keyboard, while stacks of paperwork sat neatly on the desk.

She was so totally absorbed she didn't realise he'd entered the room, and he stood observing the fierce look of concentration creasing her features, saw the tip of her tongue edge out, and noticed the way she caught her lower lip with her teeth.

Her hair looked as if she'd raked her fingers through it, and the once secure knot on top of her head looked in danger of total collapse.

Word had it she'd been sequestered in this room since dawn, with time out only for meals.

Enough, he decided, was enough, and at that moment she looked up, offered a startled smile and followed it with a huskily voiced, 'Hi, you're home.'

He crossed to her side, skimmed the screen and ran a light hand over her shoulders. 'Press the *save* button, and close it down for the night.'

'I'm almost done.'

'It'll keep.'

'Two minutes.'

'One,' he allowed, and watched her fingers fly.

Then she closed out of the programme, shut down the screen…and gave a sigh of pleasure as he began kneading the kinks from her shoulders, her neck.

Her eyelids fluttered down and she rolled her head, then simply enjoyed his ministrations.

It felt so good, and she commended him. 'Thank you.' He deserved more. She indicated the room. 'For all this,' she said simply. 'The Double Bay location is perfect.' His hands stilled and curved over her shoulders. 'Everything is happening so fast.' She broke off as he lifted her from the chair. 'What are you doing?'

'Taking you to bed.'

Kayla linked her hands at his nape as he moved from the room. 'I've worked longer hours than this,' she protested. Every day, for the past few years.

'I'm not doubting your stamina or strength of will.'

'Put me down,' she insisted as he ascended the stairs.

'Soon.'

He entered the bedroom, closed the door, slid her down then he cupped her face and kissed her…thoroughly.

She was too weary to think, or hesitate. Instead she

allowed her instincts to rule as she moved in close and kissed him back, exulting in his touch, the feel of him. His taste, the faint muskiness that was *his*...all male, a faint edge of cologne.

Dear heaven, this was good. So good.

She wanted more, much more, and her fingers sought the buttons on his shirt, freed them and savoured the feel of his skin, barely aware he'd unsnapped her jeans and was in the process of removing her top.

Her bra followed, and a helpless groan emerged from her throat as he cupped her breasts and began easing his thumbs back and forth over their burgeoning peaks.

Sensation spiralled through her body, heating it to fever-pitch, and she cried out as he buried his mouth against the sensitive curve at the edge of her neck.

His hands slid down and edged beneath her jeans to cup her bottom, and she reached for his belt, released it and freed the zip fastening of his trousers.

The size and force of his erection almost undid her, and she stroked it gently, heard his faint primitive growl and she gasped as he lifted her high to attach his mouth to one sensitive breast.

Kayla curved her legs over his hips and held on.

Their clothes became a hindrance, and were soon dispensed with, then his mouth possessed hers in a kiss that shattered her completely.

'Share my shower.'

It wasn't an invitation, but a statement of intent, and she didn't think...didn't *want* to think as he carried her into the large shower stall and set the water temperature gauge.

Skin soon became slick with soap and water as they took pleasure in cleansing each other, playful, daring and incredibly sensual until it wasn't enough.

In one easy movement Duardo lifted her high and she wrapped her legs around his waist, then sank onto him, loving the erotic sensation as she took all of him, then held on as they caught a rhythm…long, slow strokes that nearly drove her wild, until she took the initiative and sent him to the edge.

And exulted in the sense of power as he lost control.

It was a while before they turned off the water, caught up towels then, dry, slid between the sheets.

'My turn, hmm?' Duardo moved over her and trailed kisses down her throat, savoured the soft swell of her breasts and teased each tender peak with the edges of his teeth before moving to her waist, caressing her abdomen. Then he sought the aroused clitoris and bestowed the most intimate kiss of all…holding her hips as his tongue, the delicate nip of his teeth, became more than she could bear.

Let go, a silent voice encouraged, and she held back until she shattered, splintering into a thousand pieces, sobbing uncontrollably with an emotion so intense she lost all sense of who or where she was.

He held her close, his lips caressing her cheek as his hands soothed a pattern up and down her spine. He murmured words she didn't understand, and kissed her so gently she was unable to stem the slow trickle of tears.

Magic. Evocative. Libidinous. Myriad sensations defying adequate description.

Once, she'd called it *love*. Convinced her primitive hunger for this man and how he made her feel could only be that ultimately prized emotion.

Dear God, what an innocent she'd been.

CHAPTER EIGHT

A PRIVATE dinner party…her first as Duardo's wife, where impressions and image vied with the importance of the invitation.

Kayla selected classic black in a fitted design whose lines hugged her slender curves. The wide scooped neckline displayed her cream-textured skin, and she added the diamond pendant Duardo had gifted her, then fixed the matching ear-studs.

Hair was swept into a smooth twist and held in place with a glittery comb, while her make-up was understated with subtle emphasis on her eyes, the curve of her mouth.

The dress came with a matching fitted jacket, and she slipped it on, cast her mirrored image a brief overall glance then collected her evening purse and crossed to Duardo's side.

He looked magnificent, as always. Faultless tailoring, crisp cotton shirt, silk tie. A flash of gold at his wrist. Freshly shaven, gorgeous…and hers.

She bore his name, occupied his bed and in the dark night hours it was almost possible to believe there was no past…only the present, and a glimpse of what the future might hold.

The doubts, the insecurities, came with the daylight, when she unconsciously searched his expression, examined his mood, every word…and attempted to analyse each nuance for any hidden meaning. Only to silently castigate herself for wanting the impossible.

'Whenever you're ready to leave.'

His smile was swift and held an edge of mockery. 'And face the social jungle?'

'Ah, you're familiar with the terrain,' Kayla offered lightly and saw one eyebrow slant.

'And the cats?'

She rolled her eyes 'I gather we're not talking the domestic variety?'

Duardo placed a hand at the edge of her waist. 'Behave.'

'Always.'

The venue was a gracious stately home in suburban Vaucluse, high on the hill with panoramic views over the harbour.

Several luxury cars lined the driveway, and Kayla steeled herself for the evening ahead as Duardo brought the Aston Martin to a halt.

Their hosts were a charming couple…an associate of Duardo's and his wife. Plus ten guests, six of whom Kayla recognized from previous social occasions attended as Benjamin's daughter. An actress and her much older producer husband, Max, a noted author and his PA made up the other four, with introductions completed.

The beautiful people, Kayla silently accorded without rancour, each one of whom was groomed, trained from birth to play a certain part. The right schools, holidays abroad, command of at least one other language, the requisite gap year overseas.

She had been one of them, once. Until her circumstances changed and she discovered the hard way that so-called friends were notoriously fickle.

Now, as Duardo's wife, she was being welcomed back into the fold with open arms and voiced delight.

Genuine or superficial? She wasn't sure she wanted to do the maths.

How long would it take for someone to ask the predictable query about her remarriage?

Perhaps politeness would reign, and curiosity would remain unvoiced.

Did piglets fly?

Flutes of champagne and social conversation. She could do that. She'd had plenty of practice, and she summoned sufficient warm charm as she circulated at Duardo's side.

It was interesting to engage the writer in conversation, to laud his success in the marketplace and enquire about his work-in-progress.

'I have a valid reason not to discuss it.'

She inclined her head in silent acknowledgement. 'While it's between you and the computer screen, it remains sacrosanct?'

His eyes took on a musing gleam. 'You comprehend the creative process.'

Her smile was genuine. 'Perhaps refine that to believing discussing it too much could jinx the end result?'

'Ah, *touché*.' He arched an eyebrow. 'Might one assume you have a creative endeavour in mind?' He gave a soft chuckle and touched a telling finger to the side of his nose. 'Enough said.'

'What, darling, is *this* all about?' His PA copied his action as she moved to join them, and the look the woman cast him was tellingly intimate.

Intriguing, Kayla determined as a fellow guest engaged Duardo in conversation.

She began moving towards their hostess, only to be forestalled by the actress.

'Marlena,' Kayla acknowledged, and controlled the faint sinking feeling in her mid-section at the thinly disguised disregard evident.

'Duardo has tickets for my opening night.'

The stage? She'd have to brush up on what and who was currently in vogue, and a name. 'We'll look forward to your performance.'

'He's never missed an opening night since he left you.'

She longed to correct the actress that it was *she* who had walked away. Instead, she summoned a polite smile. 'Really?'

'Duardo is one of my most ardent fans.'

Marlena wanted her to believe it was more than that, Kayla deduced. Why?

Oh, for heaven's sake, she dismissed in self-denigration. As if you don't know!

'*Querida*,' a familiar voice drawled close by, and Kayla turned towards Duardo with a brilliant smile, ensuring it didn't falter as he threaded his fingers through her own and brought their joined hands to his lips.

It bore every evidence of loving devotion. Except, only she glimpsed the darkness in his eyes, the silent probing query she chose to dismiss.

He turned towards the woman at her side. 'Marlena.'

The actress's smile alone could have won her plaudits. 'Darling, I was just telling Kayla you're one of my most ardent fans.'

'Indeed?'

A suitably innocuous response, if ever there was one.

'You'll excuse us?' Duardo continued.

'Just when it was becoming interesting,' Kayla declared quietly as he led her towards two fellow guests.

'Marlena enjoys—' His pause provided the opportunity for her to intercept.

'You?'

'Creating drama, for the sake of it,' he concluded, and she inclined her head in all seriousness.

'Ah, living the soap opera, huh?'

'Remind me to take you to task when we're alone.'

She offered a stunning smile. 'Oh, *darling*, why wait?'

He didn't, and she cursed herself for issuing the challenge as his mouth closed over hers in an erotic kiss that brought soft colour to her cheeks and left her feeling vaguely mortified.

It took every effort to summon a misty smile and lay her palm against his cheek in a seemingly intimate gesture.

A gesture he compounded by moving his head slightly to press his lips to her palm.

It was all she could do not to utter 'you win'. Except that would have spoilt the display.

Now, there's the thing…if he was intent on making a silent statement, who was it aimed at? Marlena?

Dinner comprised an elaborate collection of small courses…ten in all. Each a superb compliment to the catering firm their hosts had hired for the evening.

Having served restaurant tables, Kayla could only wonder at the number of matching dinner sets used, the constant replacement of exquisite Cristofle flatware.

Entertaining was an art form, and one at which their hosts excelled. The planning alone would have taken days, involving consultations over the choice of dishes, wine, even the blend of coffee.

It had been something her mother had taken pride in during the days when Benjamin's business boomed and money was no object.

How things changed, Kayla reflected, glad her mother hadn't had to witness Benjamin's downfall. It would have killed her to be cast aside by the very people she considered to be her friends. To have to downgrade from her magnificent harbour-front home.

'We are always in need of valuable members of the community to give their time to help raise funds for the sick and the needy. Would you be interested in helping out, my dear?'

Kayla replaced her goblet of water, and gave their hostess her attention.

'I'll need to confer with Duardo. We've yet to define my daytime role.'

'Darling,' Marlena offered with pseudo-sweetness, 'no one could be in any doubt as to your night-time role.'

It was almost possible to hear the collective indrawn breath of their fellow guests.

Oh, my. Marlena wanted to fight dirty? In public?

'You would insult me?' Kayla responded quietly.

Marlena chose not to answer, and the author's PA sought to defuse the situation with a change of subject.

It wasn't over. Not by any stretch of the imagination. Unless she was mistaken, it was important for Marlena to score…and she hadn't.

Coffee was served in the lounge, and it was almost a relief when Duardo indicated they would leave.

'No recriminations?' she posed when he eased the car towards Point Piper.

'Why would you think I might offer any?'

'For a few minutes it wasn't pretty in there.'

He cast her a dark glance as he paused at a set of traffic lights. 'You gave as good as you got.'

Yes, she had. Except there was no satisfaction to it. And unless she was mistaken, she'd made an enemy. One who'd feel compelled to strike back.

Kayla chose silence during the long minutes it took to reach Point Piper, and indoors she made straight for the stairs, uncaring whether he followed or not.

'I'll be up soon.'

His voice held an element of something she didn't care to define. 'Don't rush. I need to prepare for my night-time role.' Stupid, foolish words that held an edge she hadn't intended as they spilled from her lips without thought.

'Kayla.' A single word, yet it held infinite warning.

She didn't pause or turn towards him, and seconds later she cried out in shocked surprise as strong hands gripped her waist and lifted her bodily over one masculine shoulder.

'Put me down!'

Duardo kept on walking, and she balled a hand into a fist and hit him *hard*...with no effect whatsoever.

'You fiend! What do you think you're doing?'

He reached their bedroom and closed the door so quietly, she could almost wish he'd slammed it. Then he released her down onto her feet.

She'd lost one stiletto, and she slid out of the other...bad move, for she lost valuable inches.

'Let's get one thing clear.' His voice was quiet, too silky, and she could see him almost visibly reining in his anger.

'You made me your wife, not your whore?' She arched with undue solemnity. 'And for that I should be grateful?'

She had to be mad, *insane*...and for one terrible

moment his eyes took on a frightening darkness, then became faintly hooded as he caught both of her hands in one of his.

'You want I should show you the difference?'

He reached out and flicked open the buttons of her evening jacket.

'Don't.' Defiance brought a flood of pink to her cheeks, and she attempted to pull her hands free without success.

The evening jacket came off, he reached for the zip fastening on her dress, slid it down and the garment slithered in a heap to the carpet.

Only her bra and briefs remained, and her eyes beseeched his as he undid the clasp, then stripped the briefs from her body.

'Duardo.' It was a plea, overlaid with instinctive fear.

His own clothes followed, first the jacket, his tie, then he freed his shirt buttons and shrugged the shirt off one shoulder, then the other, before tossing it onto the floor.

He loosened the belt on his trousers, undid the zip then toed off his shoes, his socks then stepped out of his trousers and tore the silk briefs free.

'You can't mean to do this,' she whispered as he pulled her close.

Then his mouth was on hers…hard, possessive, voracious and destructive as he plundered the soft inner tissues without care, using his tongue, his teeth to devastating effect.

It was like nothing she'd experienced…and never wanted to again. Ever.

If only that was all. Except it wasn't. She could see it in his eyes, the taut facial muscles assembling over bone, the grim line of his mouth.

It was then she began to fight in earnest, kicking out

with her feet, aiming to fasten her teeth on any part of his anatomy she could reach.

With no success whatsoever.

Her chest heaved from the exertion, and her breath came in gasps as he held her at arm's length.

Dear heaven. He couldn't…*wouldn't*. Surely?

For a long time he simply looked at her, and she stood mesmerized, unable to move in those few timeless minutes.

She could feel the tears begin to well behind her eyes and she blinked them back, willing them not to fall, for it would be the ultimate humiliation.

'Go to bed.' His voice was harsh. 'Before I do something regrettable.'

He released her and caught up his briefs, stepped into them then pulled on his trousers and tugged on his shirt.

Work. He needed to lose himself in graphs, figures, projections. Check emails, make calls.

Anything to remove his mind from the scene that had just taken place.

He turned and left the room, closing the door with an almost silent click, and went downstairs to seclude himself in front of a bank of computers. He brought up the screens and began checking data.

It was late when he closed everything down and quietly retraced his steps.

The bedroom was lit by one dimmed lamp on low, sufficient for him to see the large bed was empty. He scanned the room, saw clothes had been picked up.

He checked the *en suite*, then he turned down the bed, discarded his clothes, pulled on a robe and began checking the upstairs rooms.

Kayla wasn't in any one of them.

A faint chill settled deep in his gut. She hadn't left the house…the security alarm hadn't beeped an alert that any of the external doors had been opened.

Duardo descended the stairs and checked the kitchen, dining room, lounge, her home office. Dammit, the garage, each car.

There was only the media room remaining, and he crossed to it, saw the large screen was blank, the sound system off.

Where was she?

He was on the verge of leaving the room when something caught his eye. A faint movement, the slight swish of a tail.

And then he saw her. Curled up in a chair, her feet tucked beneath her, with the kitchen cat Maria usually kept in the laundry overnight comfortably settled on her lap.

Bright cat's eyes blinked at the intrusion, watching warily as he approached, and he soothed gentle fingers over its fur, lingered, then caught the animal's soft purr of appreciation.

'Sorry, little fellow,' Duardo murmured as he carefully dislodged and returned the soft ball of fur to its laundry bed.

He returned to the media room and stood looking down at her for what seemed an age. Then with infinite care he collected her into his arms and carried her upstairs to bed.

It was there, in the soft, muted lamplight, that he glimpsed the faint tracks of dried tears where they'd run unchecked on the edge of sleep.

The sight of them almost undid him, and he closed his eyes in silent self-castigation. A soft imprecation whispered from his lips as he laid her down between the sheets…and watched her body curl into a protective ball.

Por Dios.

He'd brought her to this? By his own hand, over a few wayward words tossed in anger?

Mierda.

With extreme care he slid down beside her and gently gathered her in. Felt her instinctive recoil as she came awake.

His lips teased her temple, then slipped down to settle at the edge of her mouth. 'Trust me, *querida*. And *feel*. Just…feel.'

He explored her lips, slipping in to soothe the swollen tissues with such incredible gentleness she almost wanted to cry.

His hands traced the delicate contours of her face, then slid to caress her shoulders, savoured the lingering perfume of the body lotion she favoured, then dipped low over her breast to take its sensitized peak into his mouth.

Something tore inside him as he felt her unbidden response, and he used his hands to cup her, shape the indentation of her waist, trace a path over her stomach. He felt it quiver beneath his touch, then he sought the heart of her femininity, gifting her the most intimate kiss of all.

Kayla closed her eyes and let her mind detach from her body, feeling it float to a place where she could examine the sensations he aroused, analyze and separate them from her heart.

She could feel the burgeoning sensuality, and she attempted to contain it…only to fail dismally as the familiar heat of orgasm coursed high, spiralling out of control as her body arched beneath his touch, bowed in exquisite suspension as she held on.

Then, after seemingly endless seconds, she gave in to the tactile nirvana he created, aware she had no choice as he sent her high again and again until she cried out her release and his mouth covered hers in a kiss that melted her bones.

There was the need for more. To feel him inside her, the long, slow thrust of his possession, and the silken fit as her inner muscles enclosed him.

He knew...how could he not?

A helpless groan emerged from her throat as he carefully positioned himself and slid slowly in to the hilt, paused there, then began to move, creating an age-old rhythm that brought them to the brink, held them there, then tipped them over in a glorious sensual free fall to a place where nothing else mattered.

Except them, and the emotion they shared.

If he wanted to impress the power he commanded over her, then he'd succeeded. In spades.

But that was all it was.

Sexual expertise.

The love they'd once shared no longer existed.

Survival meant accepting her life with Duardo *now*. Taking forward steps. Not looking backwards.

It was better for her health, welfare and state of mind.

Anything else was sheer folly.

Kayla slept, caught close against him, his lips buried at the edge of her temple.

CHAPTER NINE

It wasn't a big deal, Kayla silently assured herself as she entered the theatre foyer at Duardo's side.

Marlena in the lead role on stage posed no threat. And if by chance they mingled with selected guests backstage after the performance, there would be others present to defuse the tension.

Although Marlena was likely to be charm personified, providing an award-worthy act pretending friendship with the wife of one of her former consorts…*lover*, had yet to be determined.

It hardly mattered. There was no reason for it to hold any importance.

Yet it did. And Kayla was reluctant to explore *why*.

Mingling with fellow theatre-goers, indulging in social pleasantries provided a welcome distraction, and she was conscious of Duardo's close proximity, the sensual heat beneath the superb tailoring, the lurking sexuality that was his alone.

He had the power to affect her as no other man ever had…or ever would. Pheromones? Basic sexual chemistry, or something incredibly more profound?

There had to be a reason why two people were drawn

together, forsaking all others…because no one else could arouse quite the heightened degree of sensual magic that made it uniquely theirs.

The electronic buzzer summoned everyone to seek their reserved seating, and Kayla welcomed the dimmed lighting, the emergence of the orchestra, the curtain lifting to display the first scene, Act One.

The mastery of Shakespeare, the prose, sonnets…on occasion the subtle darkness in the hands of the costumed actors provided enjoyable entertainment. More, if one shared the cadence and expertise of the delivered word.

Kayla viewed the performance as a pleasant way in which to spend an evening. She was well aware to a Shakespearean buff it was whether the actor was worthy of the part, in comparison to the greats noted for their portrayals on some of the world's finest stages.

Was that the reason for Duardo's fascination?

Sadly she didn't know. There hadn't been the time or the opportunity to share such things.

Marlena, she had to admit, commanded a certain presence in the lead part. The actress's ability to *become* the character was truly an awesome transition, for during her time on stage she was so utterly convincing that no one, not even her worst enemy, could fault her.

Was it her acting prowess which drew Duardo's attention? Or did his fascination extend to her ability to portray any part a man might request in private…from the chaste virgin to the coquette, the innocent to the tart?

Certainly Marlena appeared to enjoy her role. So much so that, when the actress beseeched the audience, it appeared it was Duardo she directed her attention to.

A trick of the actress in the role of her character's

plight? Or a deliberate attempt to appear to be playing to Duardo alone?

Kayla told herself it hardly mattered...but it did. The thought Marlena might have been one of his intimates almost tore her apart.

Not only the actress, she decided shakily. *Any* woman.

She closed her eyes, then opened them again.

Give it a break. Reflecting on the past served little purpose, and changed nothing.

Focus on the stage production.

Sure, an inner voice derided. *That's easy when the lead actress's very presence is in your face.*

So...get over it.

It was something of a relief when the curtain closed at the end of the first act, and she met Duardo's slightly musing look as the lights came on during the short intermission.

'Marlena is very good in the part,' Kayla declared quietly, and saw his mouth curve a little.

'You sound almost surprised.'

She shot him a look of mild reproof. 'I'm attempting a sincere compliment.'

'Regarding her talent?'

'On the stage,' she qualified, and glimpsed the humour apparent in those dark eyes.

'Of course.'

He read her too well.

Did he know how often she fought with her emotions? The past vying constantly with the present? How in the darkness of night the line between love and hate was becoming increasingly hazy?

She wanted to be in control. Yet each day, each night it became more of a struggle for her to maintain a sense of distance.

Sharing good sex didn't equate to *love*.

And she couldn't afford to love him.

It was as well the lights began to dim, the orchestra resumed and the curtain lifted on the next act.

The ensuring hour and a half proved fascinating, and there was almost a sense of disappointment when the curtain fell on the final act.

Audience applause ensured the players took another bow, followed by a general exodus from the theatre.

'Marlena has invited a few friends to meet backstage.'

A refusal was impossible. Besides, she wouldn't give the actress the satisfaction of a no-show.

Smile-time, Kayla silently accorded, grateful she'd had plenty of practice in the social art.

There were security people, managers...who skilfully sorted bona fide guests from those hopeful of slipping through the security net undetected.

With Max in the background. His facial expression belying the cold stillness in those hard grey eyes. He resembled a predator, waiting, watching...for what?

Unbidden, a chill slithered down her spine.

Accolades were given, floral tributes delivered and the actress basked in the attention.

Not that any of it was undeserved, Kayla accorded silently. There were the congratulatory kisses...the light touch of lips to Marlena's cheek, the smiles, the laughter.

Including Duardo's salutation, for which the actress turned her head so his lips briefly touched her own.

Not such an innocent move, Kayla determined, noting the satisfied gleam evident in Marlena's eyes before it was quickly masked...and she was totally unprepared for the shaft of jealous pain lancing through her body.

To feel such a degree of anguish meant she had to care.

The knowledge hurt unbearably, for a one-sided love was no love at all.

With a tinkling laugh and a wave of her hand, the actress retreated into her dressing room to change.

Security staff began dispersing the crowd, with discreet invitations being given to selected guests to accompany the actress and some of the cast at an after-theatre party.

'Shall we join them?'

Kayla heard Duardo's drawled query, and sent him a steady look. 'Why not?'

Wisdom had nothing to do with her response. If she had a care for her emotional health or a modicum of common sense she'd have uttered a resounding *no*.

The venue was an upmarket inner-city restaurant lounge bar, where Marlena's people checked out the invited guests and provided a security escort to a private room.

Champagne flowed in abundance, finger-food was offered by uniformed waiters, background music filtered through speakers…and a selection of the city's theatre artistes mingled.

Marlena made the grand entrance half an hour later, exquisitely gowned, freshly made-up with not a hair out of place.

Her husband, obviously well-versed in his wife's *modus operandi*, quickly stepped aside to let Marlena take the limelight.

No matter there were other cast members present, Marlena was the *star*. In true diva form, she commanded attention and milked it for all it was worth. Each coquettish smile, the fluttering eyelashes, the expressive hand gestures…essentially performance-worthy, and geared towards the men present.

One man in particular.

Duardo Alvarez.

It was a game. One Marlena played for her own amusement, Kayla perceived. To provide an edge of excitement, mystery. A mischief-maker *par excellence*.

No doubt the actress saw Duardo's recently acquired wife as a challenge. The intrigue element already existed. Maybe if Marlena threw a few balls in the air, they might land where least expected.

The actress had already attempted one minor skirmish. Was she deliberately setting up the next one?

Kayla didn't have to wait too long to find out, and afterwards she had to examine whether she didn't unintentionally precipitate it by seeking the powder room.

There was a queue…isn't there always? The number of stalls allocated in such establishments were usually inadequate, and after taking her turn she crossed to the wide expanse of basins, used the soap and water then pulled down a paper towel.

'I was beginning to think you were joined to Duardo's hip.'

A quick glance in the mirror was all it took to see Marlena standing close by.

The actress's sultry purr set Kayla's teeth on edge.

'Perhaps he's joined to mine.'

'Oh, darling, don't delude yourself.'

She met the malevolent gleam in Marlena's eyes. 'Presumably you have a purpose?' Nothing like cutting to the chase.

'Duardo is—' the actress paused deliberately '—very important to me.'

'You imagine it's reciprocal?'

Marlena took a moment to examine her beautifully lacquered nails. 'He's a very *sexual* animal.' She glanced up and shot Kayla a vitriolic look. 'I doubt you're—'

'Enough for him?'

'Precisely, darling.'

'And you're more than willing to take up the slack?'

'Any time.'

The cat-like purr was back in evidence.

'Wouldn't your husband object?'

'We have an arrangement.'

'How—' it was her turn to use an effective pause '—interesting.'

'Darling, Max is gay. Where have you been?' The strange glitter was back in Marlena's eyes. 'Oh, of course. Working nine to five and waiting tables every night…for how long? Three years? Duardo's revenge must be very sweet, given he plotted your father's downfall and then chose to stand by and watch as you slipped deeper into poverty.' She sharpened figurative claws and homed in for the kill. 'Divine justice, darling, to have you abandon pride and grovel at his feet.'

Supposition was a dangerous thing… Hadn't Kayla been guilty of the same, only to discover she'd misjudged him?

There were occasions when silence was golden, and a dignified retreat even more effective.

Unfortunately, this wasn't one of them.

Kayla lifted her chin a little. 'Perhaps I *do* grovel well.' Her eyes sparked blue fire. 'But why *wife* when mistress would have sufficed?'

'Duardo's desire for an heir?'

Damn, she fell right into that one!

'As part of the perceived deal?' she countered with a deliberate lift of her eyebrows. 'Wrong, Marlena.'

Cut, and leave. *Now.*

For a moment she thought the actress might strike her, and she mentally reeled from the bitter acrimony evident in those dark eyes before Marlena turned away and made a flouncing exit from the powder room.

Dear heaven. It was possible to cut the tension with a knife.

She needed a few seconds to gather herself together before going back to the party. Lipstick, a few deep breaths, a practised smile and she emerged into the vestibule.

The temptation to keep walking and hail a cab home was difficult to resist. And she almost did. Except such an action would be a cop-out, and she was done with taking the easy route.

A hysterical bubble of laughter rose and died in her throat. *Easy?* She had money for the cab…but not the modem to free the front gates, the garage doors. Dammit, a key to any of the house doors. Nor did she have a clue how to disarm the security alarm.

It was past midnight. Maria and Josef would be in bed, ditto Spence.

'Are you OK?'

She didn't know whether to laugh or cry at the sound of that familiar drawl and the man who owned it…owned *her.*

'I'm perfectly fine.'

One eyebrow rose slightly. 'Uh-huh.' He touched a finger to the fast-beating pulse at the hollow beneath her throat. 'Cool, calm and collected.'

'I think I hate you.'

Duardo curled a hand round her chin and lifted it. 'Only *think?*'

Hot, angry tears threatened to cloud her vision, and she blinked rapidly to disperse them. 'Don't *play* me.' She couldn't fall apart. Not now, not here. Not ever, she decided fiercely.

He traced the edge of his thumb over her lower lip, felt it tremble and cupped her face. Her eyes were dark, so dark he could almost drown in them.

'Let's go. Home,' he added.

Kayla didn't offer so much as a word as the Aston Martin purred through the city streets, nor when Duardo garaged the car. Indoors, she made straight for the stairs, uncaring whether he followed her or not.

She wanted solitude. Preferably to sleep alone. In another bed, another room.

And she would, she determined as she entered their bedroom and crossed to her *en suite*.

The stilettos were the first to go, then the red silk chiffon evening gown with its fitted bodice and exquisite diagonally cut skirt.

Make-up removal took only minutes, and she released the pins from her hair, brushed its length and caught it into a loose pony-tail before pulling on a robe.

Duardo was in the process of undressing when she re-entered the bedroom, and she barely glanced at him as she moved towards the door.

'Where do you think you're going?'

She kept walking. 'Any room except this one.'

'You don't want sex…that's your prerogative. But we share the same room, the same bed.'

'You wish.'

He wanted to haul her in and kiss her senseless. Except it wouldn't solve a thing. 'Marlena. The powder room.'

'Brilliant deduction.'

He could imagine how it had gone. The very reason he'd gone looking for her when she was absent too long.

Kayla turned to face him, her expression tense, her eyes a shattering mix of blue fire and ice. 'I was going to walk out and get a cab. Except this…house—' she was darned if she'd refer to it as *home* '—is locked up like Fort Knox, and I don't have a key.' She drew in a deep breath and released it slowly. 'Marlena I can handle.'

'She's a temperamental diva. A very talented one who is contracted to a theatrical company in which I retain a financial interest.'

She got it. 'So it's in your best interests to play *nice*.'

'We share a professional relationship. That's all.'

The ice began to melt, but the blue fire remained. 'Perhaps you should tell her that.'

'I already did. Up front before she signed her first contract with me.'

'Well, there's the thing,' Kayla managed sweetly. 'Marlena doesn't appear to understand the boundaries.' She met the darkness in his eyes with silent mockery. 'Next you'll tell me she's a raving nymphomaniac who regards you as an ongoing challenge in between relationships.'

'That's a fairly accurate assumption.'

'Life should be so tough.' She turned back towards the door and pulled it open.

'The bedroom arrangement stays.'

'No.'

'You want to fight me?' His voice was a silky drawl that sent shivers scudding down her spine.

'Physically I could never win.' Even so, it wouldn't stop her from trying.

Duardo let her walk. She'd tire before he did, and while she slept he'd gather her up and bring her back where she belonged.

It was the early pre-dawn hours when he went searching for her, although she'd made no attempt to hide, as the room she'd chosen was only two removed from their own.

She looked so peaceful in the dim light reflected from the hallway, curled into a small, protective ball, her head burrowed against the pillow, hands tucked close to her chin.

For a moment he almost left her there. Except he wanted her with him, *there* beside him where he could reach for her. To place a possessive hand at her waist, a slender thigh, and bury his lips in the sweetness of her hair.

If he was careful she wouldn't stir. And if she did...he'd deal with it.

Kayla was lost in a dream, one where everything was good...so good she didn't want to leave it. Except a distracting shadow intruded where it had no place, and she murmured in protest as she fought off the return to reality.

Strong arms held her, and she could feel the heavy thud of a human heartbeat close to her cheek. Seconds later there was a shift in position, and she came sharply awake with the instant recognition of where she was and with whom.

'You don't play fair.' She balled a hand into a fist and threw a punch at his shoulder as he settled onto the bed and drew the covers over them both.

'Go to sleep.'

'You ruined my dream.' Her voice sounded faintly petulant even to her own ears.

He drew her in and settled her head against his chest. 'I can always provide you with another.'

'Emotional blackmail.'

'Sleep, *querida*.'

Amazingly, she did, and when she woke Duardo had already left for the city.

CHAPTER TEN

A NEW day inevitably held promise, and Kayla dressed in jeans, a singlet top, added a shirt and made it downstairs for a late breakfast.

It was a beautiful, clear day, the sun shone and there was barely a drift of cloud in an azure sky.

Spence appeared as she drained the last of her coffee.

'Ready whenever you are.'

'Five minutes.' She needed to collect her bag, laptop, cellphone, notes, suppliers' quotes…and apply lipstick.

'I'll bring the car around.'

She made it in six, and she checked her list as he headed towards Double Bay. The cottage should be cleared of stock, and she wanted to physically *see* the bare rooms, the better to visualize the designer's plans for fixtures and fittings. She also needed to confer with him on site, estimate refurbishment time, check stock arrival and placement, advertising and think about plans for the grand opening.

It made for a very busy morning, and it was Spence who called a halt for lunch.

Kayla picked up her cellphone and punched in a series of digits.

'I'll go grab something. Sandwiches? Any preference?'

'Chicken and salad. Bottled water. Thanks.'

He was back in ten minutes, and she took another ten as a break before reaching for her cellphone.

The designer arrived at three, and together they made a few minor adjustments to the plan. A sample box of votive candles, soaps and aromatherapy oils was delivered by courier, and at four Spence insisted on closing down for the day.

'I can manage another hour.' And still have time to shower, change and be ready for dinner.

'We have an appointment.'

A puzzled frown furrowed her forehead. 'Not that I recall.'

'Duardo's instructions. Collect what you need, I'll lock up and bring the rest.'

Everything. Swatches, samples, catalogues. Laptop.

'Where are we going?' The question seemed reasonable as Spence turned towards the city, instead of in the direction of Point Piper.

'We're almost there.'

A Porsche car dealership where a top-of-the-range silver four-wheel-drive stood waiting for her to claim.

'You're kidding me.'

Spence grinned at her disbelief. 'Yours. Unless you'd prefer another colour.'

Colour? The colour was just fine. 'I get to drive it home?'

'Perhaps a test run first?'

They did that, and it handled beautifully in spite of the fact she hadn't driven a vehicle for some time.

'You want to head out first, or shall I?'

'I'll follow you.'

It purred beneath her touch, all leashed power and class as she handled it through traffic and brought it to a smooth halt inside the garage.

Spence drew the Lexus in alongside, and handed her two modems together with two sets of keys.

'You'll need these.'

He collected samples, her laptop, and indicated he'd deposit everything in her office.

'Thanks for your help today. Everything. I really appreciate it.' She wrinkled her nose at him. 'And don't say you were just doing your job.'

She moved quickly upstairs, hit the shower then, towelled dry, she pulled on a robe. When she emerged into the bedroom Duardo was there in the process of discarding his clothes.

Her heartbeat immediately went into overdrive, visible in the pulse in the hollow of her throat, and she lifted a hand in an instinctive need to hide her body's wayward reaction to him.

'How was your day?' He emptied his pockets and placed his wallet and spare change on the valet frame.

'Busy. We achieved a lot.' Her eyes met his. 'Thank you for the wheels.'

'So…thank me.' His voice held a degree of musing mockery.

'I don't think we have time. Before dinner. I mean—' Oh, hell, she was digging herself into a deeper hole with every word! Worse, she could almost sense his silent amusement.

'Maybe a simple kiss will tide me over?'

'OK.' All she had to do was walk over to him, cup his face and bring it down to her own, then place her mouth on his.

Easy. *Simple.*

She should have known better.

The tentative kiss she offered didn't cut it, and she reached up on tiptoe, leaned in close then slid her tongue around his and drew it into her mouth. Savoured, explored and angled her head to gain better purchase.

Strong hands cupped her bottom as he lifted her against his hard-muscled frame, wrapped her legs around him and she held on, exulting in the feel of his arousal against the most sensitive part of her anatomy.

Its potent power robbed her of breath, and she groaned deep in her throat as his fingers sought the intimate heart of her, probed the highly sensitized clitoris and skilfully brought her to orgasm.

He plundered her mouth, swallowed her scream as she shattered and held her close as the intensity subsided.

'That wasn't fair,' she managed shakily.

His lips brushed her forehead and came to rest against her temple. 'How so?'

'All me, and not you.'

Kayla sensed his lips part a little, and imagined his smile.

'You want to miss dinner?'

It was a teasing game. Nothing more. And she entered into the spirit of it with a light laugh.

'And have Maria's efforts go to waste?' She pressed her lips to his, then drew back to regard him with mock severity. 'Besides, I'm hungry. For food.' Her eyes danced with wicked humour. 'Here's the plan. We'll go eat, indulge in polite conversation and you can anticipate what the night will bring.'

'In that case, go put on some clothes before I change your mind.'

He could, all too easily. He slid her down to her feet, saw the momentary indecision evident in those vivid blue eyes and pressed a light kiss to her lips.

'Go.'

Three years ago she would have given a seductive

laugh, caught hold of his hand and gone willingly into the shower with him. And they would have missed dinner without a second's thought, made love far into the night, snacked on food at some ungodly hour, then…

Don't go there. The words screeched silently inside head.

Love. Then it was love.

Now…it's just sex.

Was it too much to want him to shatter as she did and lose all sense of time and place…so there was only *her*? The one woman above all others who could take hold of his emotional heart and call it her own.

Kayla sought control, partially succeeding as she moved out of his arms and crossed to her walk-in wardrobe, selected clothes at random and began pulling them on.

Dinner was a convivial meal eaten out on the terrace overlooking the harbour. As they sampled Maria's fine cuisine the dusk began to shroud the landscape, turning colour to muted shades of silver and grey.

Streetlights flared and bright neon signs seemed more vivid against the night-time sky. Lit ferries glided through dark waters between the city and the northern suburbs, and the constant flow of traffic highlighted main arterial roads leading to and from the city.

It became a fairy wonderland Kayla would never tire of admiring.

But for how long? Duardo hadn't put a time limit on the length of their marriage. Her initial demand had elicited *as long as it takes*. Nor had he asked her to have his child.

Neither of which boded well for *ever after*.

It shocked her to acknowledge she wanted it all. His

love, fidelity…the gift beyond price mutually exchanged at their first wedding.

She'd meant it then, upheld it in her heart, her soul.

The question was…did he?

The knowledge that he might have disregarded it hurt unbearably, and she reiterated a silent vow to take each day, each night as it came, rather than agonise over the future and what it might hold. To do otherwise was madness.

'I distinctly recall you mentioned polite conversation.' Duardo's voice held indolent amusement, and she summoned a brilliant smile.

'Shall we begin with the mundane?'

'Work?' He sank back in his chair and regarded her thoughtfully. 'Meetings, phone calls, negotiations, mediating.' His shoulders lifted in a careless shrug. 'The usual.'

Kayla liked him like this. At ease, having exchanged a formal business suit for chinos and a chambray shirt. Relaxing at the end of the day over fine food and a glass of wine, with nothing more mentally taxing than sharing time with his wife on a beautiful early summer's night.

Yet even in relaxed mode, he bore the lithe strength of a warrior, the waiting, watchful quality of a man who'd seen much and weathered more in places no respectable person would frequent…where survival was the only game in town.

'You've reached a compromise with the shop fittings?'

Her features became animated as she replaced flatware and sank back in her chair. 'Just a few minor adjustments. It's all happening so fast. When the shop's done, maybe you'll come look it over?'

'Naturally.'

A faint smile teased her mouth as an idea came to mind. 'Maybe you'll let me test some of the samples on you?'

'You plan stocking supplies for men as well as women?'

'Select toiletries, oils.'

'This personal demonstration,' Duardo drawled. 'When do you envisage it taking place?'

She tilted her head a little. 'Tonight? If you're up to it, of course.' A mischievous gleam deepened her eyes. 'Shall we say nine-thirty? Your *en suite*?'

He rose to his feet. 'Done.'

An hour and a half later he entered the master suite to soft lighting, muted baroque music and the faint aroma of incense.

The bed was stripped to a covering sheet and layered with thick bath towels. A tray containing exotic shaped bottles was set on a bed pedestal, and Kayla stood wrapped in a towelling robe...waiting.

The door to his *en suite* was open, and steam drifted from the large bathtub.

'You get to remove your clothes.'

Duardo slanted an eyebrow. 'Does this personal demonstration allow you to remove them for me?'

'Definitely not.'

'Pity.' This was her game, and he'd play by her rules...for now.

Getting naked didn't take long, although he deliberately didn't hurry, and he turned towards her with a faintly quizzical smile. 'What next?'

'Please lie face down on the bed.'

He complied, with an animal-like grace that was uncontrived, and Kayla silently let out the breath she'd unconsciously been holding.

She knew every inch of his masculine body, each muscle flex, the strong bone structure. The small tattoo on one shoulder...the jagged keloid scar low on one hip flank.

The aromatic oil sample she chose held woodsy tones

and an element of musk, and she warmed it in her hands, then carefully massaged it in over his powerful shoulders, his arms, travelling towards his waist, hips, the tight curve of his butt, the muscular thighs.

He possessed a masculine beauty in size and muscular symmetry, honed by physical fitness, but not overstated or pumped. Just…lithe, powerful and all male.

She loved the feel of his body beneath her hands, its strength, and unbidden her hands slowed and lightly caressed…for how long? Surely only mere seconds?

Dear heaven, what was the matter with her? This wasn't meant to be seduction.

Dammit…what in hell are you *doing*?

The silent castigation never left her lips, and she forced her voice to sound normal.

'You can turn over now.'

Oh, my. The breath caught in her throat at the sight of his erection, and she almost chickened out. Except for a determined persistence to finish what she'd begun.

Start with his chest, and work your way down…way down, with scant attention to the part of his anatomy between his waist and the tops of his thighs.

Which was fine until she reached his waist, lingered over one hip, then the other, and heard the faint hiss of his breath as her hands slipped over the springy male hair couching the base of his penis and scrotum.

The temptation to tease and tantalize was paramount, but it would have only one end…and she wasn't done. Not yet. His arms and legs remained, followed by the bath.

The whole deal, not part of it.

His eyes remained closed, and when she had finished she capped the bottle of aromatic oil, then used a towel to wipe the excess oil from her hands.

'You can get up now.'

Kayla gasped in startled surprise as Duardo's hand encircled her wrist and tugged her close.

'If you ever use your hands quite like that on anyone else,' he intoned with dangerous silkiness, 'I can promise you'll live to regret it.'

His voice was a husky growl, and sensation arrowed through her body as she caught the dark intensity in his eyes, the flex of muscle and sinew as he sought control.

The tension was electric, and for a moment she couldn't move. Dared not, in case she invoked something she wouldn't be able to handle.

Her eyes remained locked with his, caught spellbound by an emotion she didn't want to define.

'There's the bath.' Her voice didn't even sound like her own. For the love of heaven, get a grip! 'Candles.' She was suddenly having trouble getting the words out. 'I need to light them.'

He released her hand, and she moved into the *en suite*, retrieved a taper with shaky fingers, lit and touched it to each wick in turn.

A delicate scent rose in the air, and she switched off the electric light, then turned to see Duardo standing in the aperture.

A lump rose in her throat, and she attempted to swallow it without visible effort. 'It's meant to be a total sensual experience.'

'For two, surely?'

'That's how it'll be promoted. I—merely want your reaction.' She was dying here. 'Opinion,' she corrected.

'Which won't be accurate if I bathe alone.' He moved in close and released the belt fastening her robe.

'I don't think—' She clutched the edges without success, and she cried out as he placed an arm beneath her knees and stepped into the bath.

The warm scented water closed over her as he turned her to face him.

He was too close, much too close, and her eyes widened as he picked up the sponge and placed it in her hand.

'This wasn't part of the plan,' Kayla began helplessly in a bid to wrest back some control.

'But you agree it can be adapted any which way?'

How difficult could it be?

Sure, a silent voice mentally derided. And who do you think you're kidding? Mere minutes ago *he* was the only one naked.

Now they both were.

So…soap the sponge, smooth the oil from his body…and leave.

She didn't linger, deliberately choosing not to meet his gaze as she dispensed the oil.

'It won't matter if there's some residue,' Kayla managed quietly. 'It's very good for your skin.' She replaced the sponge and began rising to her feet, except Duardo's hands curved over her shoulders, stilling her progress.

'Where do you think you're going?' His voice was dangerously soft, and her eyes widened as she sank down. 'My turn, hmm?'

The oil matched the scented candles, creating an ambience that was infinitely sensual, and she watched the steady flumes with a sense of fascination as he eased the soapy sponge over her silken skin.

It was sinfully erotic, the warm water, the scent, the candles. Being here with him.

His touch was slow, lingering at her breasts, shaping

and testing their weight as he brushed each tender peak with the edges of his thumbs.

They beaded beneath his touch, and her eyes dilated as piercing sweetness flooded the intimate heart of her. Myriad sensations coursed through her body, heating it with primitive hunger…for him, only him.

She wanted to cry out, but no sound emerged from her lips as he lifted her high…and held her as he used his mouth, his tongue, in an erotic tasting that had her clinging on to him as he took his fill. Urging her to the brink, until she shattered into a thousand splintering shards.

Then he positioned her carefully onto his rigid penis and eased into her, watching her body coalesce as she took him in to the hilt, briefly resting there before he began to move.

A heartfelt groan left her lips as she held on to him and enjoyed the ride, only to cry out as his mouth took possession of her own in a kiss that was so incredibly tactile she felt as if she'd lapse into serious meltdown.

Afterwards he tucked her head into the curve of his neck and held her, gently tracing the length of her spine in a soothing gesture.

Her hair was in disarray, and he thread his fingers through its silken length, easing it back behind each ear.

Like this, she could almost believe everything was right between them, and the past three years were a bad dream that had never happened.

If only.

In another lifetime…the one they should have had…there might have been a child by now. Surely that was what would have eventuated, even though the possibility had never been discussed?

Did a child form part of Duardo's agenda? A reason to

tie her to him in a loveless marriage? A legitimate successor to inherit his fortune and take it into another generation?

What if she was to share with him the fact that she'd accidentally missed taking a contraceptive pill?

A faint shiver shook her slim frame, and he moved, lifting her from him as he rose to his feet and stepped out from the bath with her in his arms, then he let her slide down to her feet and caught up a bath towel, wrapping it round her slim form before filching another for himself.

'On a scale of one to ten, the products deserve a ten.' He lowered his head to hers and captured her mouth in a brief, hard kiss. 'You,' he emphasised, 'were off the scale.'

'Thank you. I think.'

His lips formed a devilish curve. 'We could always arrange a repeat performance.'

Kayla swallowed compulsively. 'Not tonight.' Her emotions couldn't take it.

'When I return from New York.'

Her eyes searched his. 'When do you leave?'

'Tomorrow. Early. I'll be away a week.'

She wanted to ask to go with him. Except there was the boutique to organise, stock...

'I'll miss you.' The words slipped out, words she hadn't meant to say, and she felt the lick of heat course through her veins beneath the warmth of his smile.

Fool, she derided silently as she began extinguishing the candles and emptying the bath.

He finished with the towel, plucked hers and let both fall to the tiled floor. Then he curved a hand round hers and led her into the bedroom.

'Now for the soporific aftermath.'

A relaxed slide into somnolence.

She didn't think it would happen, for she didn't feel in the least tired.

Yet she drifted asleep within minutes of her head touching the pillow, oblivious to the man who lay quietly at her side.

CHAPTER ELEVEN

EACH day seemed more hectic as boxes of supplies were delivered and stacked in the back room of the boutique. Boxes Kayla quickly opened, checked the contents of against the stock-list, then quickly re-sealed to prevent fine builder's dust from infiltrating the packaging.

Carpenters worked widening the aperture between two distinct rooms, so they resembled one large, partially divided room. Then painters moved in, followed by the floor and wall tilers. When they finished, the shop-fitters delivered and fixed all the fittings in place.

Spence was there, overseeing operations, as he called it, and acting as go-for whenever needed.

Consequently Kayla rose early and drove to Double Bay each morning in time to allow the various tradesmen access into the cottage.

An hour's break around midday to catch up with Jacob, and she rarely arrived home much before dark. A shower, dinner, time on her laptop, late to bed…only to do it all over again the following day.

Duardo rang or sent an SMS each day in between meetings and negotiations…usually brief, given the time difference and their conflicting schedules.

The night hours were the worst, for it was then she'd turn over, reach for him in sleep… and discover an empty space in the bed.

She missed being held, his body's warm strength. Dammit, she missed *him*.

It was the reason she stuck to generalities and kept her voice light whenever they spoke on the phone. Glad he had no idea how the sound of his accented drawl curled round her heartstrings and tugged a little.

More than anything she wanted to sink into his arms and gift him her heart, her soul.

Except she didn't possess the courage.

Better to accept what he offered, and not wish for the unattainable.

Plans for the grand opening of the bathroom boutique were almost complete, the advertising organized. Invitations issued to browse were ready to be mailed, and tomorrow she'd put the general stock on display, create the special displays.

There were gift samples to assemble, and she decided each package would comprise a quality towelling washer, soap, a delicately fashioned bottle of aromatherapy oil and a small pouch of exquisite pot-pourri.

Tomorrow she'd purchase the sheer silk chiffon pouches, ribbons and tend to the gift samples.

Everything was falling into place, on schedule, and the excitement, the anticipation built with each passing day.

The boutique *had* to be a success. For many reasons, but uppermost was the need to prove her worth, to be able to repay Duardo the funds he'd supplied to set her up in business. It was a matter of pride, a measure of her integrity, and she determined not to fail.

Wednesday began as any other day, with an early breakfast, after which Kayla drove to the boutique and set to work on the special displays.

The stock she'd unpacked looked good on the shelves. Better than good, and the colours were beautifully co-ordinated.

She had a mental image of how the displays would look, and sketches to back them up.

It was midday when she broke for lunch, locked the cottage, grabbed a sandwich at a local deli. Then she went in search of pouches and ribbons needed for the gift samples.

Spence would check in around two, and with luck she'd manage to finish the special displays as well as package a number of samples by day's end.

'Soon,' Kayla promised as Spence tapped his watch and declared *time*. 'You go on ahead. I'll call in to see Jacob, and be home by eight.'

'I'll stay.'

'Why? There's no need.'

His pleasant features assumed a serious expression. 'Duardo—'

'I'll be behind locked doors, my car is parked round the corner, I carry a personal alarm, and—' she paused for effect '—you're forgetting I walked from the railway station to my flat late at night *every* night for more than two years.' She gestured with her hands. 'I'll be fine.'

'Call me when you're ready to leave the hospital.'

'Promise. Now go.'

She locked the door behind him, pulled down the new shade and set to work. Another hour, and she'd be well ahead. What was more, she'd call Jacob, put the cellphone on loud-speaker and chat for a while in lieu of stopping by.

Kayla hadn't long cut the call to Jacob when her cellphone rang and she picked up, heard Duardo's voice, felt the warmth pool deep within and leant against the new counter. 'Hi.'

'How is the cottage shaping up?'

Business. OK, she could do that. 'Really well.' She relayed the current rundown in brief. 'What about things on your end?'

'Tense.'

His negotiation skills were legendary. 'You're playing hardball.'

His soft laugh played havoc with her nerve-ends. 'Tactics.'

The sudden blast of a car-horn street-side provided a momentary intrusion.

'You're not driving?'

His query was sharp, and she was quick to assure, 'It's outside.'

'Outside *where*?' His voice was quiet…almost too quiet.

'The cottage.'

'Put Spence on.'

Oh, hell. 'He left ahead of me.'

'On your instructions?'

There was no point denying it. 'Yes.'

'Lock up and leave.'

Her fingers tightened on the cellphone. 'Excuse me?'

'Do it.'

'You're being unreasonable.'

She could almost hear him reining in his anger. 'Kayla—'

'OK. Consider it done.' She didn't wait for his response, and cut the connection.

Damn his arrogance. She was almost inclined to ignore his dictum by remaining another half-hour, just for the hell of it.

Except she wouldn't put it past him to call Spence, and no way was it fair he should take any of the blame.

However, she picked up a silk pouch, added a potpourri sample, towelling washer, soap and aromatherapy oil. Then she looked at the five assembled piles comprising her quota for the day, and assembled a few more. Tomorrow would see them done, then she could begin with the ribbons.

Just then her cellphone rang, and she checked caller ID, swore softly and picked up. 'I'm on my way. Seriously,' she assured Spence, and reluctantly collected her bag, checked the external doors, set the alarm and locked the main door behind her.

The early-evening café society crowd was beginning to fill the pavement tables, and she resisted the temptation to order a latte and sit awhile. Instead, she ordered a latte to go.

Summer daylight-saving was in force, and it was good to feel the sun's warm rays on her skin as she walked to where the Porsche was parked.

Once darkness fell it would become cool, but for now the promise of summer was in the air, the azure sky clear and there was a feeling of satisfaction she'd put in a productive day's work.

Someone bumped into her, and she almost lost her footing, then he was gone.

Definitely a *he*, and young by the fluidity of his gait, although it was impossible to tell for sure, with the hood of his jacket covering the back of his head.

Kayla shrugged her shoulders and crossed to the Porsche, delved into her bag for the key and alarm modem…and felt something warm trickle down her arm.

Blood?

From where?

When she looked, her singlet top bore a long slice across a lower rib. Blood welled and seeped into the cotton from a nasty-looking gash. It was then she felt the sting of pain.

What on earth? That silly idiot had slashed her with a knife. He hadn't tried to snatch her bag. So...*why*?

She grabbed a handkerchief from her bag and held it against the wound in an effort to stem the flow of blood.

At that moment Spence drew alongside in the Lexus and leapt out from behind the wheel.

'The cavalry has arrived.'

'Not before time.' He took one look, then whipped out a handkerchief of his own and compressed it against the wound. 'It needs sutures.' He took the keys and modem from her hand, checked the Porsche then led her to the passenger side of the Lexus. 'In you get.'

He took her to a private hospital, sat with her while the doctor sutured the wound then he phoned in a report to the police, made a second call, talked quietly and handed Kayla the cellphone.

'Duardo.'

Charming. Just what she needed...the third degree. 'I'm fine,' she said without preamble.

'Debatable.' His voice was icily calm, and brought goose-pimples to her skin. 'The medic will prescribe pain-killers and something to help you sleep. Take them, *querida*.' He paused fractionally. 'Spence will fill you in on the rest.'

'He can't *do* this,' Kayla vented an hour later as she pushed a plate of partly eaten food to one side, her appetite gone.

'It's as good as done,' Spence assured quietly. 'Notices will be printed, ready to be mailed out late tomorrow.

Posters will be fixed to both cottage windows and affixed to the door announcing a two-week delay in opening.'

'But—'

'No *buts*.'

'He's being ridiculous.'

'Protective.'

Kayla's eyes sparked with blue fire. 'Ridiculous.'

'You can tell him so tomorrow.'

'What do you mean...*tomorrow*? He's not due back until Sunday.'

Spence checked his watch. 'He's boarding a flight around now.'

'Whereupon his arrival will cause the shit to hit the fan,' she deduced, and glimpsed the faint humour evident in his gaze.

'Inelegantly put, but an accurate assumption.'

'It was merely a random action,' she opined with a careless shrug. 'Could have happened to anyone any-where.'

'Except you're the wife of an extremely wealthy man, familiar to many via recent media coverage,' Spence re-layed quietly. 'Therefore more vulnerable than most. Hence the reason certain protective measures are in place.'

Which she'd chosen to ignore. He couldn't, wouldn't alarm her with the rest. Investigative suspicions were due for confirmation any day soon.

Her eyes clouded. 'You think the attack was deliber-ate?'

'There are those who know Duardo is out of the coun-try.'

'And he has enemies?'

Stupid question.

Any man who'd hauled himself off the streets as a

youth and made a fortune had to have engineered some high-risk deals. Envy and jealousy had the power to become volatile in the minds of some. Men who'd felt wronged…women slighted.

Spence appeared to choose his words. 'Shall we say his absence provides a window of opportunity to get to him through you?'

You're wrong, she managed silently. I'm merely someone he's sought to avenge for wronging *him*. He doesn't *care*.

What she needed, Kayla decided, was a long, commiserating chat with someone who *did* care. 'I'll go call Jacob, take a shower then hit the bed.'

Spence retrieved a small packet and placed it in her hand. 'A measured dose of painkillers and a sleeping pill. Take them when you're ready to go to sleep.'

The shower helped ease some of the tension, and she lingered far longer than necessary, enjoying the warm, pulsing water, the scented body-wash. Then, dry, she pulled on a towelling robe, collected her cellphone and propped herself up in bed.

Jacob answered on the third ring, recognised something in her voice and demanded, 'What's wrong?'

Kayla relayed minimum facts, offered reassurance and slid straight into active listening mode.

'Why do you think Duardo is already on his way home?'

'To bawl me out in person,' Kayla offered, and heard her brother's 'tsk tsk' in response.

'Do you ever wonder why he married you?'

Every day. 'Because he could call the shots.'

'Not that he might never have stopped caring?'

'Oh, sure. Like that's a possibility.' And it snowed in summertime!

'Any fool could see you shared something special.'

It felt as if something tore inside her heart. 'Maybe. *Then.*'

'Our father was a pompous ass.'

'Hey,' she chastised. 'Don't speak ill of the dead.'

'He wanted to keep us to himself. I wasn't old enough for it to matter. But you were. And he ruined your life.' There was a pause for breath. 'Then he pulled the plug on his own, and left you to pick up the pieces.'

'That's harsh judgement.'

'But true.'

She hesitated, then offered slowly, 'I pegged Duardo's motivation as revenge.'

'Maybe you're wrong.'

'I don't see how I can be.'

'Because he waited for you to approach him?' She didn't answer, and Jacob went on, 'There was every chance he'd turn you away. But he didn't.'

Yet he stipulated conditions. And put Spence on my tail.

'He's given back everything you had.'

Except his love.

'He's postponed the shop opening,' she protested.

'Sensible, given you'll need to provide police statements and recuperate. Not to mention allow for the aftershock element.'

'Oh, for heaven's sake,' Kayla extrapolated. 'Don't you get on the "fragile flower" bandwagon, too!'

'It's good to know you're being well taken care of.'

She was, but that didn't make it any easier.

'Get some sleep, sis,' Jacob bade gently. 'And don't *think* too much. Ring me in the morning. Promise?'

'OK. Goodnight.'

Kayla checked the time, saw it was just after ten, and she filled a glass with water and swallowed down the pills Spence had given her.

The pain wasn't too bad, but her mind was too active for easy sleep.

How long before the pills took effect?

Maybe if she read for a while…

She picked up a book and read two pages, and that was the last thing she remembered until she woke the next morning, stretched then gasped in pain.

Wound. Sutures. Images flooded her brain in a flash, and she slid carefully from the bed, crossed to the *en suite* then began pulling on clothes.

Breakfast, then more painkillers, and she'd be ready to face whatever the day would bring.

Maria fussed over her like a mother hen, Josef enquired about her health and Spence was so solicitous it almost made her weep.

Kayla chose to eat on the terrace, and called Jacob while she sipped a second cup of coffee. The police arrived at nine, asked numerous questions, took her statement and left more than an hour later.

Lunch came and went, and she waved aside any suggestion she should rest. What she needed, she decided, was something to do.

Time spent in her home office would suffice. She could double-check stock, anticipate sales and precipitate new orders. She also needed to check the time margin between order and delivery…if she should prepare for any hiccups. She didn't want to run short of anything. When it came to luxury items, clients tended to want them at once…not have to wait for orders to come in.

It was there Duardo found her, and he stood drinking in the sight of her as she sat head bent over the laptop screen.

Conflicting emotions tore at him, and he controlled them with effort.

She *looked* fine. A little pale, and he hoped she'd slept better than he had during the long flight home. He'd caught a cab from the airport and spent the entire time on his cellphone, checking with Spence re his investigative process. Then he made a few calls to certain unlisted numbers and called in a few favours.

If his suspicions were correct… It would take time, but the unravelling process had begun within minutes of Spence taking Kayla to hospital.

The faint click of the door closing caught her attention, and she looked up, met his dark gaze and held it as he crossed to her desk.

'What do you think you're doing?'

His presence was a formidable force, and she sensed the tension emanating from his powerful frame.

'Hello to you, too.'

'Close the programme down and shut the laptop.'

'Bite me.'

He didn't move, but she felt the lethal intent barely held in restraint. 'You have no idea how close I am to doing just that.'

All day she'd anticipated this moment, and she'd become increasingly wound up with each passing hour. 'There was no need for you to rush back. I'm fine. Really.'

'Sure you are. Those dark circles beneath your eyes are simply a figment of my imagination.'

'Maybe you should take a look at your own.'

A muscle bunched at the edge of his jaw. 'Shall we start over?'

'Aim for polite neutrality?'

Duardo moved round the desk, leant forward, pressed the *save* key on the laptop then closed the screen.

'Don't—'

'I just did.'

He was too close, too male…too *much*. If he touched her, she'd fall to pieces.

For a long moment she bore his appraisal, refusing to bow beneath it, then her eyes flew wide as he cupped her face and lowered his mouth to hers in a slow, gentle kiss that almost tore her apart.

When he lifted his head she could only look at him with tear-drenched eyes, and she veiled them, afraid of what he might see.

With care he drew her to her feet, caught her hand in his and led her from the room.

'Duardo—'

'I need a shower and a change of clothes.'

'And that involves me…how?'

'For a start, you can hush that sassy mouth.'

He crossed into the foyer and made for the stairs. When he reached their suite he drew her inside and closed the door.

Kayla watched as he discarded his jacket, dispensed with his tie and the rest of his outer clothing.

'Five minutes, hmm?' With that he crossed to his *en suite*. Seconds later she heard the hiss of water, glimpsed the escaping steam…and knew she shouldn't stay.

To remain quiescent, *waiting,* seemed the height of folly. Except her limbs didn't want to obey the dictates of her brain.

Fool. If you leave, he'll only come after you, and that won't help at all.

She crossed to the splendid antique dresser and moved the baccarat crystal ornament, looked at it with an analytical eye then slid it back to its original position.

Her stomach felt as if a dozen butterflies had invaded it and were desperate to escape.

You and me, both!

Go. Stay. What a mess of contradiction. So go look at the view outside the window. Anything. But *do* something.

She moved restlessly to the wall of glass, heard the shower cease and endeavoured to focus on the clean-cut symmetry of the lawn, the garden borders alive with flowers and the small, carefully pruned shrubbery.

The water in the tiled pool shimmered beneath the sun's rays, and she watched a bright-plumed parrot coast in to perch on the edge of the bird-bath, drink from the water, look around then spread its wings and fly to settle high in the branches of a large tree.

She sensed rather than heard Duardo cross the room and stand behind her, then his hands curved over her shoulders.

His warm breath teased tendrils of hair close to her temple, and heat coursed through her veins as his lips settled against the curve of her neck.

'Come lie with me, hmm?'

'It's the afternoon,' Kayla protested.

'What's that got to do with anything?'

'You should sleep.'

'I will. Soon.' He turned her round to face him, and she couldn't read anything from his expression. The towelling robe moulded his muscular shoulders, the broad chest, and accented his narrow waist.

'But first,' he began as he reached for the buttons on her blouse. 'I need to see—' He freed the last button and pushed the fine cotton edges aside. A sterile gauze pad covered the wound, and he carefully eased the lower tapes free.

It wasn't deep, but the blade's tip had sliced sinew and touched bone at her ribs.

She knew what it looked like. Betadine, sutures, slightly swollen, puckered skin. The wound would heal, the swelling subside, and in time a fine white line would be all that remained.

His eyes blazed with a primitive dark savagery, and he said something vicious beneath his breath before carefully pressing the tapes back in place.

'You have to know I'll tear everything apart until I find who did this.'

Kayla felt the breath catch in her throat, and the beat of her heart went into overdrive.

She could almost feel sorry for the culprit. It was on the tip of her tongue to say it could have been worse. Except one glance was all it took to realise he was already three steps ahead of her, that having endured long hours on the flight had done little to ease his rage.

As she would have been, if the situation had been reversed.

For a few timeless seconds she stood frozen, unable to move if her life depended on it.

No one could feel quite this degree of anger…if they didn't *care*.

Could Jacob possibly have it right? The mere thought made her head spin.

Whoa. Going there wasn't good for her peace of mind.

Dammit, Duardo hadn't *said* anything.

But then, neither had she.

A hand cupped her chin and tilted it. 'Want to talk about it?'

About *what*? How much I love you? How I never really stopped? And…*do you love me*?

Like that was going to help!

'You didn't have to cut short your trip.' That was safe, ordinary.

'Yes,' he said quietly. 'I did.' His hands slid over her face and buried themselves in her hair. His head descended and his mouth captured her own, angled and went in deep with such exquisite gentleness she sank in against him and let him feast.

He began lightening the kiss, felt her soundless moan and gradually lifted his head. With infinite care he eased her blouse free, then undid the clasp of her bra before moving to the snap on her jeans.

'Please—'

'Patience, *querida*.' He traced a finger along the waistline of her jeans, felt her stomach quiver then lowered the zip fastening.

Dear lord. She was going up in flames, and he'd hardly touched her.

He eased the jeans down over her hips, let her step out of them, dispensed with her briefs then led her towards the bed.

With one fluid movement he tossed back the covers and drew her down onto the sheets, shrugged out of his robe and joined her.

Kayla searched for something flip to say, but the words didn't find voice as he brushed his lips to her shoulder.

'Indulge me, *querida*. I so badly need to do this.'

He began tracing a path to her breast, savoured its peak, teased its twin then trailed down to caress the indentation at her navel.

She thread her fingers through his hair and held on as he travelled low, seeking the moist labia, tracing the folds with the tip of his tongue before unerringly finding the sensitized clitoris.

Involuntarily she arched against him and he held her hips, laving the warm moistness until she cried out and begged for release...then soothed her as she came.

Earth-shattering, explosive…more, so much *more* than she'd ever experienced as he recaptured her heart, her soul.

Emotional tears welled and spilled to run in slow rivulets down each cheek as she lay there bare…so utterly bare, and wholly *his*.

As she had always been. Always would be.

Did he know?

Dear God, how could he *not* know?

Her body shook slightly as he trailed light kisses over her stomach, then traced a slow path to the hollow at the base of her throat before settling over her mouth in a slow, evocative kiss.

She shaped his face with her hands, and kissed him back, loving him with her mind, the touch of her lips…until he reluctantly lifted his head and reached for the bedcovers.

'Stay with me, *querida*.'

He drifted into sleep within minutes, and she lay at his side until the sun's light faded and dusk became dark.

CHAPTER TWELVE

IT WAS a beautiful morning, the sun's warmth already evident as they lingered over coffee on the terrace.

Kayla poured a second coffee, then she sank back in her chair and viewed the man seated opposite.

Duardo looked refreshed and incredibly vital after a good night's sleep, and sharing breakfast with him on a weekday was a bonus. Somehow she'd expected him to follow his usual pattern and leave early for the city. But he was here, apparently not in any hurry…and it was nice.

Another concession to her knife attack?

Last night had been something else. Just thinking about his intimate supplication brought a flood of heat pooling deep inside, and she involuntarily shifted a little to contain the involuntary spasm spiralling through her body.

He had to know how he affected her…how could he not?

She spared him a glance, and almost died at the brooding passion evident in those dark eyes…then it was gone.

'Finish your coffee,' he indicated with indolent ease. 'You need to pack. Spence is driving us to the airport in an hour.'

She looked at him in disbelief. 'You're joking, right?'

'We're taking a late-morning flight to Brisbane, then driving to Noosa.'

'There's a reason?' She paused deliberately, then offered, 'Other than the obvious one?'

Duardo lifted an eyebrow. 'Meaning?'

'Moving me out of town.'

'You object to spending the next few days in my company?'

'Queensland? *Noosa*? Sunshine, sandy beaches, top restaurants…what's not to like?'

'That wasn't the question.'

'I guess having you along won't be a hardship,' she conceded and witnessed his mocking smile.

'*Gracias.*'

Her eyes gleamed with wicked humour. 'Don't mention it.'

'An hour, Kayla,' he reminded as he ascended the stairs at her side.

'We're talking beachwear, something suitable to wear to dinner?'

'Casual.'

OK, she could do that.

Kayla made it with a few minutes to spare, and she slid into the Lexus as Spence deposited both bags in the rear compartment.

The flight to Brisbane was uneventful, and on arrival Duardo organised a hire car.

It was years since she'd last visited the Sunshine Coast, and the changes were many, with numerous resorts, apartment buildings and boutiques.

Magical, and she said so as they rode the lift to the penthouse apartment in one of the very modern buildings overlooking the ocean on Hastings Street.

Exquisitely furnished, it was a multi-million-dollar dream with two bedrooms, each with an *en suite*, a study, lounge and ultra-modern kitchen, offering magnificent ocean views.

'It's beautiful,' she complimented with utter sincerity.

'Thank you.'

'Another of your acquisitions?'

He inclined his head. 'The building has only recently been completed, and now seemed a good opportunity for a personal inspection.'

Why should she be surprised? His entrepreneurial skills were well-known.

'So we get to unpack, change into casual clothes, wander Hastings Street, find a restaurant and eat dinner?'

'Sounds like a plan.'

They began with a stroll along the boardwalk fronting the beach, chose *Sails* restaurant, nestled at the far end where the boardwalk finished and the side-street began.

Lovely ambience, great food and fine wine completed a relaxed evening, and Kayla said as much as they returned to the penthouse.

It would have been so easy to say 'I love you' as Duardo undressed her and took her to bed. Except the words remained locked in her heart, unable to find voice.

One day melded into another as they rose when they felt like it, took breakfast at a different restaurant each morning, explored the shops, the boutiques, spent a day driving to the Glasshouse Mountain, Montville, Maleny…beautiful country, lush green hills and quaint villages with numerous craft shops.

There were times in the apartment when Duardo plugged in the laptop and she settled herself in a comfortable chair, leafed through a magazine, read or watched television.

The nights were something else. Nights she didn't want to end, or the loving to change.

It was almost as if the past three years didn't exist, and Kayla experienced a sense of reluctance as Sunday dawned and they took the late-afternoon flight home.

Tomorrow Duardo would return to the city, and she felt strangely restless, wanting, *needing* to do something constructive.

The bathroom boutique was an addictive lure, and she wanted so badly to go check it out.

'Just for an hour or two,' Kayla pleaded as Duardo drank the last of his coffee over breakfast next morning.

'No.'

'I'll ensure Spence stays with me.'

'That's a given, wherever you go.'

'Bodyguard duty?'

His eyes speared hers. 'Until whoever is responsible for injuring you is behind bars.' His voice was hard, inflexible…dangerous.

He rose to his feet, shrugged into his suit jacket, crossed round the table and settled his mouth on hers in a possessive kiss, then he collected his briefcase and laptop. 'Take care.'

OK, so she'd spend an hour or two in her home office, call on Jacob and have Spence deliver her home in time to shower and change for dinner.

'This is definite overkill,' Kayla evinced as Spence negotiated the Lexus through heavy late-afternoon peak-hour traffic.

'One slip was bad enough. There won't be another.'

She had to ask, 'Any development in the investigation?'

'A lead. Duardo has access to contacts—'

'The police can't or won't use,' she concluded in shrewd summation.

'You could say that.'

Dinner was a pleasant meal, in that Maria served one of Kayla's favoured dishes, followed by an exquisite dessert. The caring thought touched her tender heart, and she made the impulsive decision to gift the housekeeper a complete bathroom package from the boutique.

Duardo took his coffee into his home office, and Kayla settled comfortably into a chair in the media room and slotted in a DVD. When the credits rolled, she closed the set and went to bed, read for a while then fell asleep.

It was an hour later when Duardo entered the room, and he took in her peaceful features—the cream-textured skin, the soft mouth—and felt his body tighten with need.

She was beautiful. Inside, where it mattered most, with a strength of character. Values...and pride.

So much pride, there were times when he wanted to wring her slender neck.

Yet he identified with it...admired, even as he cursed the quality. For it was a quality he also possessed.

A tenacity to succeed against all odds.

He banked down a surge of anger that anyone would choose to harm her...for whatever reason. Soon, very soon, he'd have the answers. And when he did, the person responsible would be consigned to their own private hell.

It took only seconds to discard his clothes and slide into bed beside her. She didn't stir, and he closed the bedside lamp, then settled down to sleep.

The insistent peal of a cellphone intruded on Kayla's subconscious, and she slid up against the pillows as Duardo activated the call.

It was late. Really late. Who on earth could be ringing at this hour?

'Yes.' Duardo's voice was deep, clipped. 'Of course. I'm on my way.'

'What's wrong?'

It was inevitable she'd ask, and he slid out of bed, walked naked across the room and hurriedly pulled on briefs, jeans and a T-shirt.

'I'll be gone awhile. Go back to sleep.'

'Sure. And I can do that easily, not knowing where you're going or why.'

She'd discover the truth soon enough, and better she heard it from him.

'That was the police. There's been a fire.'

Her face paled and her eyes widened into huge dark sapphire pools. 'Not the boutique?'

He stepped into trainers and fixed the laces. 'Yes.'

'I'm coming with you.'

She was already out of bed and pulling on underwear.

'The hell you are.'

She reached for jeans, pulled on a T-shirt and raked fingers through her hair. 'Try and stop me. I'm with you, or following you. Choose.'

'Kayla—'

She slid her feet into trainers, then filched the keys to the Porsche from a drawer. 'Choose, dammit!'

Duardo caught hold of her wrist. 'Give them to me. I'll drive.'

The acrid smell of smoke was in the air as they reached Double Bay, and she saw the revolving red lights atop two fire-trucks as they turned into the street. Two police cars, blue and red lights flashing, were positioned to provide a traffic block.

'Stay here.'

'No way in hell.' She was out of the seat the instant he cut the engine.

'Move one inch from my side, and I'll haul your sweet ass into the car and lock it.'

'My ass?'

'The car.'

Kayla shot him a dark look. 'Got it.'

He caught her hand in his, and she didn't think to remove it.

One glance was enough to determine the firefighters had the blaze under control. Long, thick hoses snaked across the road, and there was water everywhere.

Voices rang out in the night air, the words mostly indistinguishable, and uniformed police conferred with whoever was in command of the fire.

Duardo identified himself, *her*, and listened as a detective reported an update on the incident.

'The twenty-four-hour security you posted on the building paid off. A youth was caught running away from the scene. We have him in custody.'

Kayla tuned out, and did her best to check the damage from her vantage point.

It didn't look good beneath the floodlights illuminating the scene. The cottage windows were black from smoke, half the roof appeared to have fallen in and she could have wept at the state of the stock…what, if anything, was left of it.

Everything took on a blur-like quality as statements were given, information supplied and Duardo conferred with his private security.

Yellow crime-scene tape was placed around the cottage, one fire-truck pulled away, closely followed by a police car.

'Let's go.'

Duardo led her to where he'd parked the Porsche, and she climbed into the passenger seat, fixed the seat belt in place then looked at him in silent askance as he captured her face and fastened his mouth over her own in a kiss that was many things.

Possessive, frankly sensual and hopelessly flagrant.

'What was that for?' Kayla demanded helplessly when he lifted his head.

'Distraction.'

'It didn't work.'

He clipped his belt in place, ignited the engine and headed home.

She looked sightlessly out the windscreen. 'Who would do such a thing?'

'If the youth in custody is also responsible for injuring you, it won't take long to get him to name whoever paid him.' He'd make sure of it. And if the lead he already had was proven…

She felt numb with shocked emotion.

So much vengeance. Aimed at *her*. Why? Because Duardo had made her his wife? It didn't make sense. But then the actions of someone possessed of an unstable mind rarely made sense…except to those trained in psychiatry.

There was nothing she could think of to say, and she sat in silence during the short drive home.

Duardo took one look at her strained features as they entered the bedroom and swore softly beneath his breath.

'*Querida*. Bed, hmm?'

Her dark eyes were dilated with delayed shock as she turned towards him. 'I needed to see it for myself.'

He caught hold of her hand and brought it to his lips.

'Bricks and mortar, timber. Stock. It can be replaced. All of it.'

'But it was my stock.' My dream. The work, the magic…gone.

He undressed her, discarded his own clothes, slid into bed and gathered her in, then held her until she slept.

CHAPTER THIRTEEN

KAYLA swore softly beneath her breath when her cellphone rang, and she automatically picked up and identified herself.

Two days had passed since the cottage fire…days she'd spent secluded in her home office, accessing data for insurance purposes, tending to police procedure, redrawing plans. It was too soon to gain building quotes, as no one was allowed on site.

The paperwork kept her busy, occupied her mind and helped prevent her *thinking* too much.

'Kayla?'

The sound of her name brought her sharply into the present.

'Spence will bring you into my office.'

Duardo, sounding incredibly *formal*. Why?

'Now?'

'Yes, now.'

She heard the soft click as he cut the connection.

Well. No hello, no goodbye… She had half a mind to call him back and tell him to go jump.

In fact, she was about to hit speed-dial when there was a knock at her office door.

Maria? Josef? Spence?

She crossed the room and pulled open the door.

Spence.

'I have the Lexus out front.'

'Just like that? No questions asked, no answers given?'

'Duardo intimated the matter is urgent.'

'So I gather.' She threw him an exasperated look. 'I'll go grab my bag.' It took only minutes before she slid into the front seat beside him. 'This had better be good.'

They made the city without hitting too many traffic snarls, and Spence swung the Lexus down into the underground car park beneath Duardo's office building, parked then accompanied her in the lift to the high floor housing Duardo's suite of offices.

Whereupon there was instant recognition from the girl on Reception, followed by the appearance of Duardo's PA.

'They're waiting for you.'

They?

A minute later they were ushered into Duardo's office, and Kayla's eyes dilated at the sight of the woman seated opposite him.

Marlena.

Kayla watched as Duardo rose to his feet and crossed the room to her side, lowered his head and brushed his mouth against her own.

In silent apology for his brusque summons?

Spence remained standing just inside the closed door. The entire scenario was seriously weird.

'Really, *Duardo*,' the actress said in reproof. 'Our business affairs hardly need the presence of your—' she paused deliberately '—wife. Or your major-domo.'

He caught hold of Kayla's hand, linked his fingers

through her own and brought them to his lips. 'But they do,' he offered smoothly.

'I wish you'd move it along, darling. You've kept me waiting almost half an hour. I've read the new contract, it's fine. Why don't I sign it, your PA can witness my signature and I'll leave?'

'Because I'm withdrawing the contract, and declaring it null and void.'

'I beg your pardon?'

He turned slightly and filched duplicate copies of a thick document from his desk, released Kayla's hand and tore the pages in half, then in half again and tossed them into the waste-paper bin.

'Have you gone mad?'

Very much in *diva* mode, Kayla noted with interest as Duardo took hold of her hand again.

What in hell was going on here?

'Maybe I can jog your memory,' Duardo declared with dangerous silkiness. 'Bryan McIntyre. Two thousand dollars. Your instructions to harm my wife.'

She had to hand it to Marlena...the actress didn't so much as blink.

'I have no idea what you're talking about.'

'Five thousand dollars. The deliberately lit fire in my wife's boutique in the dead of night.'

'For heaven's sake. You can't possibly believe—' She pressed a hand to her heart in horror. 'We're *friends*. More than friends. I couldn't—'

'But Max did.'

'He may have meddled—' A hand fluttered eloquently. 'He enjoys a little mystery.'

'It was Max who let Jacob's debt at the casino ride and accumulate.' Duardo's voice held a lethal silkiness. 'Max who orchestrated Jacob's beating with instructions to break his leg.' Each word fell with damning truth. 'Kayla's attack. The fire.'

'Max wouldn't do that!'

'The police have him in custody.'

'*No*. I'll sue—'

'My line, I think. Bryan McIntyre was found at the scene of the fire and taken into custody. He's been singing like a canary in an effort to protect his own skin.'

Marlena rose to her feet. 'I don't believe you.' She turned towards the door. 'I'm leaving. You'll never hear from me again.'

Spence didn't move, and Kayla watched as the actress turned to face Duardo.

'Tell your *henchman* to step aside.'

He wasn't done.

'Max's bank and telephone records have been accessed. Bryan McIntyre's prints were found on a tin of flammable liquid discarded at the scene of the fire. His confession is sufficient to convict you.'

'You can't do this!'

'I can. And I have.'

'Max did it for me!'

'Except this time he took the game too far.'

'I wanted you,' the actress voiced with explanatory despair. 'We have a history. We would have been good together!'

'There were no strings, Marlena.' Duardo's voice held a quality Kayla had never heard before. 'I was indebted to your father. I made him a promise. Which I kept.'

The actress burst into tears.

'No one,' he intoned with dangerous silkiness, '*no one*

attempts to harm the woman I love…and gets away with it without answering to me. Understood?'

He inclined his head, Spence opened the door and two uniformed policemen entered the room.

'What are you doing?' Marlena shrieked as they stood either side of her, caught her hands together and snapped on a pair of handcuffs.

'Arresting you, ma'am. I suggest you accompany us quietly.' They each took hold of her arms. 'It won't help if you make a scene.'

Kayla watched with a sense of stunned disbelief as the trio left, followed by Spence, who quietly closed the door behind him.

For a moment she simply stood there, then she turned slowly to face Duardo.

'What did you say?' Her voice sounded impossibly husky even to her own ears.

'You heard.'

She swallowed the sudden lump that rose in her throat. 'I think you should say it again.'

He didn't pretend to misunderstand. 'The woman I love,' he said gently, and watched as she struggled to find the words. He wanted to take her in his arms and kiss her senseless…until all the doubts and insecurities no longer existed. And he would…soon.

But first, there were things he needed to say.

'Marlena and I shared a professional relationship. Nothing more, in spite of what she liked to imply.'

He was drowning in those beautiful blue eyes, the soft, trembling mouth. *Por Dios*…all of her.

'I admired her talent as an actress. But not the games she chose to play off-stage.'

Realisation provided clarity. 'Max procured men for her.'

'Yes.'

'Except you were the unattainable prize,' she deduced slowly.

'Yes.'

He saw her moisten her lips, and the action almost undid him.

'I had you. Back in my life...my bed. No one was going to take you away from me again.'

Kayla felt the tears well behind her eyes, and she blinked them back. This was the time for truth, honesty. Not platitudes.

'I was a fool. I made the biggest mistake of my life in letting you walk away.'

'Benjamin—'

'Was a selfish, pompous ass.' She lifted a hand, then let it drop again. 'Jacob's words.'

An apt description, but one Duardo chose not to verbally endorse.

She had to ask. 'Did you deliberately seek revenge?'

'By watching you sink further into a debt you could never hope to cope with?'

'Yes.'

'Would you have accepted my help if I'd offered it?'

Stubborn pride would have forced her to refuse. Honesty made her admit it. 'No.'

'You could have asked at any time, and it would have been yours.'

Except she hadn't. Instead she'd struggled hopelessly, working harder, longer hours in order to eke out a living. Until there was no way out.

He saw the shimmer of moisture well in those vivid blue eyes, and felt his heart turn over. 'Come here.'

His gentleness undid her, and one tear escaped to roll

slowly down her cheek as she moved towards him. 'I love you. So much. I don't think I ever stopped. Even when I hated you.'

Duardo smiled at the contradiction, and caught hold of her chin between thumb and forefinger so he could tilt it towards him.

'You're the love of my life,' he vowed quietly. 'My heart, my soul. The very air that I breathe.' He brushed his lips to the tip of her nose, then slid to hover over her mouth. 'Everything. Always.'

He felt her smile as his lips settled over her own in a gentle, evocative possession that heated her body and invaded her soul.

One hand cupped her bottom as he pulled her in against the rigidity of his erection, and he threaded fingers through her hair, holding fast her nape as he went in deep.

So deep she needed to come up for air.

One look in those dark, slumberous eyes was sufficient to know mere kissing wasn't enough…for either of them.

'Any chance you can leave early?'

His smile was to die for. 'You mean you have reservations at clearing my desk and allowing me to ravish you on top of it?'

'And risk your PA witnessing her boss's complete lack of control?' She ran the tip of her tongue along his lower lip and gently nipped it. 'It would ruin your reputation.'

Duardo reached behind him and depressed a button on the inter-office communication system. 'Cancel whatever I have for the rest of the day, and transfer any important calls to my cellphone. I'll check them later.'

Much later.

He collected his laptop, his briefcase and caught her hand in his.

She waited until they were in the car and he was negotiating traffic. 'There's just one thing.'

He spared her a brief glance, caught sight of her impish
smile…and waited.

'How do you feel about babies?'

The thought of her swollen with his child almost
brought him undone.

Duardo changed lanes and swept to a halt at the kerb.

A soft laugh lilted from her lips. 'What are you doing?'

'This.'

He captured her face and closed his mouth over hers in
a kiss that was so incredibly evocative it melted her bones.

'I take it that's a *yes*?'

The expression in those dark eyes would live with her
for ever.

'Let's go home.'

The Marriage Deal

HELEN BIANCHIN

CHAPTER ONE

'Cut,' the director called. 'That's a wrap.'

They were the sweetest words she'd heard all day, Sandrine decided as she lifted a hand to ease the weight of her elaborate wig.

Period costume was not the most comfortable wearing apparel, nor was the boned, tightly laced corselet worn to achieve an eighteen-inch waist and push her breasts impossibly high and bare them almost to the point of indecent exposure.

Add the heat of the studio lights, a lead actor who had an inflated ego and delusions of grandeur, the director from hell, and the axiom, 'One should suffer in the name of one's art', had never been more pertinent.

'A word, sweetheart.'

From Tony's lips, *sweetheart* was not a term of endearment, and she froze, then she turned slowly to face the aging director whose talent was legend, but whose manner on occasion belonged in a backstreet of Naples.

'Dinner tonight, my place. Seven.' Hard dark eyes speared hers. 'Be there.' He turned his head and swept an arm to encompass five of her fellow actors. 'Everyone.'

Sandrine stifled a faint groan. All she wanted to do was to change, shower, put on her own clothes and drive to the waterfront villa she called home for the duration of filming, catch a snack and read through her lines for tomorrow.

'Do we get to ask *why*?' the lead actor queried petulantly.

'Money. The film needs it. My guest has it,' the director declared succinctly. 'If his request to meet the cast will clinch an essential injection of funds, so be it.'

'Tonight?' Sandrine reiterated, and suffered the dark lance of his gaze.

'Do you have a problem with that?'

If she did, voicing it would do no good at all, and she affected an eloquent shrug in resignation. 'I guess not.'

He swung an eagle eye over the rest of the cast. 'Anyone else?'

'You could have given us more notice,' the lead actor complained, and earned an earthy oath for his temerity.

'Difficult, when the man only arrived in the country yesterday.'

'Okay, okay, I get the picture.'

'Pleased to hear it,' was the cryptic response. 'Continuity,' he commanded, and Sandrine gave a heartfelt sigh.

Fifteen minutes later she was done with wardrobe, and she crossed the car park and slid in behind the wheel of her hire-car. Dressed in casual shorts and top, her long sable hair wound into a careless knot atop her head made for comfort in the intense afternoon heat.

Sandrine activated the air-conditioning the instant the engine purred into life, and minutes later she gained the main southern highway.

Her leased accommodation was a two-level villa overlooking water at Sanctuary Cove, a prestigious suburb on Queensland's Gold Coast, only a ten-minute drive from the Coomera film studios.

She activated the CD player as she took the Hope Island–Sanctuary Cove exit ramp and let the funky beat ease the kinks of a rough day.

A tree-lined river wound its way towards a man-made canal system, a nest of beautiful homes and the lush grounds of a popular golf course.

A view that exuded peace and tranquillity, she conceded as she veered towards Sanctuary Cove, then, clear of the security gate guarding the entrance to one of several residential areas, she took the gently curved road leading to the clutch of two-level villas hugging the waterfront.

Cement-rendered brick, painted pale blue with white trim, pebbled gardens adorned with decorative urns provided a pleasant, refreshing facade, Sandrine acknowledged as she used a remote control to open the garage door.

Inside, there was an abundance of cool marble floors, sleek lacquered furniture, soft leather sofas and chairs, and the kitchen was a gourmand's delight with a wealth of modern appliances. The open-plan design was pleasing, encompassing a wide curved staircase at the far end of the foyer leading to a gallery circling the upper floor, where three large bedrooms, each with an en suite, reposed.

Wide, sliding glass doors opened from the lounge and dining room onto a paved terrace that led to a private swimming pool. There was also a boat ramp.

Sandrine discarded her bag, changed into a bikini and spent precious minutes exercising by swimming a few laps of the pool. She needed the physical release, the coolness of the water, in a bid to rid herself of the persistent edge of tension.

A shower did much to restore her energy level, and she towelled her hair, then used a hand-held dryer to complete the process before crossing to the large walk-in robe.

Basic black, she decided as she riffled through her limited wardrobe. A social existence hadn't been uppermost in her mind when she'd hurriedly packed for this particular sojourn, and most of her clothes were divided between three luxurious homes far distant from this temporary residence.

Don't even *think* about those homes or the man she'd shared them with, she determined as she cast a designer gown onto the bed, then extracted stiletto-heeled pumps and an evening bag in matching black.

Yet the image invaded her mind, his broad, sculpted features with their angles and planes hauntingly vivid. Slate-grey eyes seemed to pierce right through to her soul, and she shivered at the memory of his mouth, its sensual curves and the devastating skill of its touch.

Michel Lanier. Mid-thirties, and ten years her senior. Successful entrepreneur, patron of the arts, dark-haired, dark-eyed, with the features of a Renaissance prince and the skilled mentality of a street warrior. Born of French parents in Paris, he'd begun his education in France and completed it in America.

Husband, *lover*. A man who'd swept her into his arms, his heart, and made her his wife.

They'd met at the party of a mutual friend in New York. Sandrine had just completed a modelling assignment during a seasonal break and was due to return to Sydney the following week to resume the filming of a long-running Australian-based television series.

Sandrine flew in with Michel at her side, and within a week she'd introduced him to her family, announced her engagement and had the script writers rewrite her part in the series. As soon as the chilling episodes filming her character's accident and demise were completed, she accompanied Michel back to New York.

Two months later they were married quietly in a very private ceremony among immediate family, and divided their time between New York and Paris. Michel bought a luxury apartment in Sydney's prestigious Double Bay with magnificent views out over the harbour. Their Australian base, he explained.

For six months everything was perfect. Too perfect, Sandrine reflected as she selected black underwear and donned it, then pulled on filmy black hose before crossing to the mirror to begin applying make-up.

The problem had begun three months ago when they spent two weeks in Sydney and a friend gave her a script to read. The story was good, better than good, and she felt an immediate affinity with the supporting character. A vision of how the part should be played filled her head and refused to leave.

Sandrine had known the production time frame wouldn't fit in with Michel's European schedule. She told herself there was no way he'd agree to her spending four weeks in Australia without him.

On a whim she decided to audition, aware her chance of success was next to nil, and she'd almost dismissed it from her mind when, days later, they returned to New York.

Her agent's call confirming she had the part brought a mixture of excitement and trepidation. Production was due to begin in a month at the Coomera studios in Queensland.

She signed the contract when it arrived but delayed telling Michel, all too aware what his reaction would be. Each day that passed had made the telling more difficult, until there were too few days left.

A hundred times she'd rehearsed the words in her mind, yet none of them came out sounding right, and what began as a discussion rapidly digressed into an argument of such magnitude she'd simply thrown some clothes into a bag in the early hours of the morning and booked into a hotel until it was time to take her scheduled flight to Brisbane.

Sandrine had qualified that four weeks wasn't a lifetime, yet with every passing day the physical and spiritual distance between then widened to a point where she feared it might never be repaired.

Worse, Murphy's Law descended, and production had suffered one delay after another. An estimated four weeks extended to five, then six. Budget was shot to pieces as they went into their seventh week. The subtropical midsummer heat was a killer, and tempers frequently ran short as professionalism was pushed to the limit.

Sandrine stood back from the mirror, secured the last pin in the simple knot of hair atop her head, then slid her feet into the elegant black pumps, collected her evening bag and made her way downstairs.

The day's high temperatures had gone down a notch or two, and there was a slight sea breeze teasing the early evening air as Sandrine crossed the paved apron to the entrance of Tony's Main Beach apartment building.

Minutes later she rode the lift to a designated floor and joined the group of fellow thespians enjoying a cool drink on the wide, curved balcony overlooking the ocean.

A portable barbecue had been set up, and a hired chef was organising a selection of seafood, prawns and kebabs ready for grilling.

Sandrine accepted a wine spritzer and sipped it slowly as she cast the guests an idle glance. All present and accounted for, with the exception of the guest of honour, she perceived, and pondered his identity.

'Smile, darling. It's almost ''show time'' and we're expected to shine,' a husky male voice intoned close to her ear.

She turned slowly to face the lead actor, whose birth

name had been changed by deed poll to Gregor Anders. He was handsome in a rugged, rakish way and took his studio-generated image far too seriously, acquiring so many layers during his professional career it was almost impossible to detect the real man beneath the projected persona.

'Gregor,' Sandrine greeted coolly, and summoned a smile to lessen the sting of her words. 'I'm sure you'll shine sufficiently for both of us.'

It was easy to admire his ability as an actor. Not so easy to condone were the subtle games he played for his own amusement. Yet his name was a drawcard. Women adored his looks, his physique, his sex appeal.

'Now, now, darling,' he chided with a wolfish smile. 'We're supposed to share a rapport, *n'est-ce pas*?' One eyebrow slanted in mocking query.

'On screen, *darling*,' she reminded sweetly, and remained perfectly still as he lifted a hand and traced his forefinger down the length of her arm.

'But it is so much easier to extend the emotions beyond the screen for the duration of filming, don't you agree?'

Her eyes locked with his. 'No.'

'You should loosen up a little,' he cajoled, exerting innate charm.

'I play *before* the camera. Off the set, I suffer no illusions.'

'Strong words,' Gregor murmured. 'I could ensure you regret them.'

'Oh, *please*,' Sandrine protested. 'Go play Mr

Macho with one of the sweet young things who'll simply *swoon* at the thought of receiving your attention.'

'While you've never swooned over a man in your life?'

You're wrong, she almost contradicted, but held her tongue. Gossip ran rife and, in these circles, quickly became embellished until only a grain of recognisable truth remained.

'If you'll excuse me?' She lifted her empty glass a few inches aloft, then turned and crossed to the bar.

Within minutes she was taking a refreshing sip of orange juice. A waiter paused beside her and proffered a tray of hors d'oeuvres. She smiled automatically, selected one, then took a delicate bite. It was delicious and brought an onset of hunger. A sandwich at lunch, followed by an apple and mineral water wasn't much in the way of sustenance.

Sandrine took a mini vol-au-vent and popped it into her mouth.

'Where *is* the guest of honour?' a feminine voice asked in bored tones, and she turned towards the attractive young lead actress.

'Bent on making a grand entrance, perhaps?'

'That's a woman's prerogative, sweetheart.'

The smile was a little too artificial, the voice a fraction too contrived. Cait Lynden had acquired *star* status and wasn't about to let anyone forget it. Especially a fellow actress playing a minor part, Sandrine decided silently.

'No one seems to know who he is,' Cait mused. 'A successful entrepreneur is all Tony will reveal.' An acquisitive gleam darkened her beautiful blue eyes. 'Obviously rich. As long as he's presentable and under sixty, it could prove to be an interesting encounter.'

'And single?' Sandrine posed, only to hear the other's musical laugh.

'*Darling*, who cares?'

Not Cait, obviously.

Minutes later Sandrine detected a change in the buzz of conversation, a shift in tone definition that caused her to lift her head.

So he had finally arrived. Almost a half-hour late.

Some sixth sense alerted her attention, followed by a quick stab of apprehension.

'*Mine*,' Cait uttered, sotto voce.

Even as Sandrine turned slowly to conduct a sweeping appraisal of the room, a telltale prickle of awareness slithered down the length of her spine.

There was only one man who could generate this effect. One man whose soul was so closely attuned to her own they were almost twin halves of a whole.

Sandrine caught sight of a tall male frame, felt the familiar tug on her senses as she recognised the broad-boned, chiselled profile, the dark, conventionally groomed hair, which seven weeks ago had lain longer at his nape, adding a refined, untamed quality that was equally as dangerous as the man himself.

She'd adored threading her fingers through the silky thickness, the purchase it lent when she held fast his head and simply clung during the slow, exquisite torture of his lovemaking, the dazzling heat of their passion.

Those had been the wild, sweet days when there had been only love to guide them, she reflected. A time when she'd given him everything without thought of denial.

Now she watched Michel while he paused in conversation to lift his head as if he, too, sensed her presence. Dark grey eyes locked with hers, probing, intense, and totally lacking in any humour or warmth.

Time stood still as everything and everyone in the room faded to the periphery of her vision.

There was only Michel. The man, the moment, the exigent chemistry evident. She could sense it, *feel* its powerful pull as she became caught up in the magical spell of something so intensely primitive she felt raw, exposed and acutely vulnerable.

Then he smiled, and for an instant she was transported back to the time they first met. Almost a duplicate situation to this, where they'd caught sight of each other at the same time across a crowded room.

Except the past had little place in the present. She could see it in the sudden flare in those beautiful slate-grey eyes and sense it in his stance.

Body language. She'd studied it as part of her craft and she could successfully determine each movement, every gesture.

Did anyone else recognise the cool ruthlessness or define the latent anger that lurked beneath the surface of his control? They lent his features a dark, brooding quality and gave hint to a refined savagery, which unleashed could prove lethal.

He was a man who held no illusions and whose

youthful passage had moulded him, shaping a destiny many of his peers could only envy.

Sandrine watched in mesmerised fascination as he murmured an excuse to their host, then crossed the room and stepped out onto the terrace.

Fine Armani tailoring sheathed an awesome muscle definition in that powerful frame, and every movement held the lithe, flowing grace of a superb jungle animal.

Her heart thudded and quickened to a faster beat. Each separate nerve end became highly sensitised as he moved towards her, and she couldn't think of one sensible word to say in greeting. Considering the carelessly flung words they'd hurled at each other all those weeks ago, a simple hello seemed incredibly banal.

She didn't get the chance, for he captured her shoulders, slid one hand to hold fast her head, then his mouth took possession of hers in a kiss that sent her emotions spinning out of control.

It was claim-staking, she acknowledged dimly when she was able to breathe. Flagrant, seductive and hungry.

Worse was her own reaction as, after the initial shock, she relinquished a hold on sanity and opened her mouth to him.

She savoured the taste and feel of his tongue as it created a swirling, possessive dance with hers and lured her into an emotional vortex where time and place had no meaning.

When he lifted his head, she couldn't move. Gradually she became aware of the sound of background music, the indistinct buzz of conversation, as the room and its occupants filtered into her vision.

Dear heaven. How long had they remained locked in that passionate embrace? Thirty seconds, sixty? More?

All he had to do was touch her and she went up in flames. In seven weeks the passionate intensity hadn't lessened.

What did you expect? a tiny voice taunted. He's haunted your dreams every night since you left him and invaded your thought processes almost to the detriment of your work.

The emotional intensity shimmered between them, exigent, electric and mesmeric. Yet there was also anger, not forgotten nor forgiven.

'What are you doing here?'

Was that her voice? It sounded so cool, so calm, when inside she was a seething mass of conflicting tensions.

'I concluded my business in Europe.'

Important meetings where his presence was paramount. No opportunity for delegation there, she reasoned. What excuse had he given explaining her absence to family in Paris? To his elder brother Raoul, his *grand-mère*?

She experienced a moment's regret and banked down the edge of remorse she felt for the elderly matriarch who ruled with a fist of iron, yet had the heart of a pussycat and of whom she'd become very fond.

'And discovered I wasn't waiting in the New York apartment,' Sandrine voiced evenly. Her chin lifted fractionally and the topaz flecks in her eyes shone deep gold. 'Subdued and contrite at having thwarted you?'

'Difficult,' he acknowledged with wry cynicism. 'When a delayed filming schedule kept you here.'

Sandrine opened her mouth to refute that was something he couldn't have known, then she closed it again. All he had to do was lift the phone and instruct someone to report her every move. It angered her unbearably that he had.

'What's your purpose, Michel?' she launched with polite heat. If they were alone, she would have hit him. Or made every effort to try.

'You didn't answer any of the several messages I left on your message bank.'

She'd let every call go to voice mail and become selective in whose messages she returned. 'What was the point when we'd said it all?'

'Nothing is resolved in anger.'

So he'd let her go, sure in the knowledge that, given time, she'd come to her senses and run back to him? How many nights had she lain awake fighting against the need to do just that? Except pride and determined resolve had kept her firmly where she was. As well as loyalty to a project and a legally binding contract.

She looked at him carefully, noting the fine lines that fanned from the outer corners of his eyes, the faint shadows beneath. Unless it was her imagination, the faint vertical crease slashing each cheek seemed deeper.

Once, those dark grey eyes had gleamed with naked

passion...for her. Only her. She'd looked into their depths and melted.

Now there was only darkness and a hard quality that chilled her bones.

'You haven't explained why you're an invited guest in Tony's apartment,' Sandrine managed evenly, and saw one eyebrow arch.

'You mean you haven't guessed?'

There was soft mockery evident in his tone, an underlying hint of steel that tore the breath from her throat.

'Your sojourn in Europe is over and you've come to haul me home?'

Her facetiousness didn't escape him, and his mouth assumed a cynical slant. 'Try again.'

Anger overlaid fear. 'You want a divorce.'

His expression didn't change, but something in his eyes shifted, hardened. 'There hasn't been a divorce in the Lanier family for three hundred years.'

'You mean women have suffered the overbearing, arrogant, autocratic will of Lanier men for *centuries* without offering a word in complaint?'

'I imagine any complaints were soon—' he paused, the emphasis significant '—satisfactorily dealt with.'

She took his meaning and rode with it. 'Sex isn't the answer to everything.'

'Lovemaking.'

There was a difference. Dear heaven, such a difference. Even *thinking* about Michel's powerful body joining with hers brought a surge of warmth that raced through her veins, heating her body to fever pitch.

He saw the reaction in the subtle shading of her skin, the faint convulsive movement of her throat, the sudden, too rapid sweep of eyelashes as she sought to veil her response. And he experienced satisfaction.

'You haven't answered my question.'

'Which particular question is that?'

Her lashes flew wide, and the intensity of those deep brown, gold-flecked eyes held a brilliance that danced close to anger.

'What you're doing here, *tonight*?'

His gaze was direct, probing, and held a degree of cynical humour. 'Why, *chérie*, I am the guest of honour at this soiree.'

'The guest of honour touted to inject sufficient funds to rescue the film?'

Michel confirmed it with the faint inclination of his head. 'For a price,' he conceded with chilling softness.

Something inside her stomach curled into a painful knot. 'And that is?'

'A reconciliation.' Succinct, blatant and chillingly inflexible.

Dear God. Pious salutation had nothing to do with the words that remained locked in her throat.

From somewhere she dredged up the courage to confront him. 'A marriage certificate doesn't transform me into a chattel you own.'

Michel took in her pale features, the dark eyes that seemed too large for her face, the loss of a few essential kilos, and barely restrained himself from wringing her slender neck.

Sandrine became aware of the circumspect glances,

the ripple of curiosity Michel's action had generated. Cait Lynden's expression was composed, although her brilliant blue eyes were icy.

Their marriage hadn't been written up in any of the international society pages. It was doubtful anyone in this room knew the guest of honour's identity, much less his connection with a little-known supporting actress.

'This is hardly the time or place.'

Michel's smile was a mere facsimile and bore not the slightest degree of humour. 'No discussion, no negotiation. Just a simple yes or no.'

Simple? How could he deem something so complicated as *simple*? 'You can't demand conditions.'

'Watch me.'

'Blackmail, Michel?'

He gave an imperceptible shrug. 'Label it what you will.'

'And if I refuse?' Sandrine queried bravely.

Something moved in those dark eyes, making them appear incredibly dangerous. 'I walk out of here.'

And out of her life? As she'd walked out of his? Temporarily, she amended.

So why did she have the feeling she was poised on the edge of a precipice? One false move and she'd fall to unknown depths?

She could see the grim purpose etched in his features and she felt her stomach muscles clench in pain. 'You don't play fair.'

His expression didn't change. 'This isn't a game.'

No, it wasn't. Yet she hated him for employing manipulative tactics.

'Yes or no,' Michel reiterated with deadly quietness.

CHAPTER TWO

SANDRINE looked at Michel carefully, her eyes steady, her composure seemingly intact. Only she knew what effort it cost to present such a calm facade.

'I'm sure Tony has other sources available from which to raise the necessary money.'

'He has exhausted all of them.'

'How can you know that?' It didn't warrant an answer, she acknowledged wryly. The Lanier family consortium held immense holdings, and Michel was extremely wealthy in his own right. As such, he had contacts and access to otherwise privileged information.

Without the injection of funds, the film wouldn't be completed or make it into the cinemas, and the resulting financial loss would be disastrous.

The knowledge she held the film's fate in her hands didn't sit well. Nor did the fact that Michel had very skilfully planned it this way.

'With the possible exception of Gregor Anders, the film doesn't have the big-name leads to attract a runaway box office success,' Michel relayed with damning accuracy. 'The director and producer are both scrambling to resurrect their ailing careers with a period piece currently out of vogue.'

Add to that, she knew the film's financial backers

had set a limited budget that made little allowance for countless takes in a quest for perfection, delays, escalating expenses, and the result was a high-risk venture no sensible investor would touch.

Sandrine cast him a level look. 'That's your opinion.'

Michel's gaze remained steady, obdurate. 'Not only mine.'

'If that's true, why are you prepared to invest?'

His expression didn't change, and for several seconds she didn't think he was going to answer. 'Honesty, Sandrine?' he mocked lightly. 'You.'

Her eyes widened, then narrowed slightly.

'What did you think I would do, ultimately?' Michel demanded silkily. 'Just let you *walk*?'

She gritted her teeth, counted to five. 'I didn't *walk*,' she denied vehemently. 'I was committed to a signed contract. If I hadn't checked into the studio on the designated date, I could have been sued.'

'A contract you chose not to tell me you'd signed.'

'*You* were locked into meetings in Europe.'

'Aren't you going to introduce me, darling?'

Damn. Sandrine barely swallowed the vengeful curse as Cait placed an arm along the back of her waist in a gesture that indicated they were the closest of friends.

'Michel Lanier,' Michel interposed smoothly.

'Cait Lynden.' The smile, the voice, the actions, combined to provide maximum impact. 'So, you're our knight in shining armour.'

Sandrine watched an exquisitely lacquered nail trace

a provocative pattern down his suit sleeve and was overwhelmed by the desire to sweep it aside.

'And Sandrine's husband.'

Ouch. She felt Cait's slight intake of breath, glimpsed the coy smile and felt the faint increase of pressure as fingers bit into the back of her waist.

'Well,' Cait acknowledged as she turned to shoot Sandrine an icy glare, 'aren't you the secretive one.'

Michel took hold of Sandrine's hand and lifted it to his lips, then he spared Cait a level glance.

'If you'll excuse us? We were in the middle of a private discussion.'

Oh, my. He didn't pull any punches. She watched as the lead actress proffered a sizzling smile, then turned and walked away with a blatant sway of her hips.

'Another conquest,' Sandrine commented lightly.

'Let's focus on the immediate issue, shall we?'

The master manipulator. Dammit, why did she want to crack his cool facade when she knew what lay beneath the surface of his control?

His skill with words in the midst of her volatile diatribe had been chilling. Hell, he hadn't even raised his voice. *She* had been the one who'd lost it.

Now he was using that skill to employ invidious blackmail, cleverly positioning her between a rock and a hard place. She was the price, the film her prize.

'You leave me little choice,' she said with deliberate coolness, then waited a beat and added, 'For now.'

He reached out and brushed the back of his fingers down her cheek. 'No conditions.'

She felt her body's betraying response to his touch, the heated sensation that invaded her bones and melted them to molten wax.

Sandrine's eyes deepened, and her mouth shook a little. With anger, resentment and a need to swing into verbal attack mode. Except this wasn't the time or place if she wanted to retain any sense of dignity.

As it was, speculation undoubtedly ran rife among the cast members and fellow guests. Did Tony know that Sandrine Arnette was Michel Lanier's *wife*?

Michel watched as she fought to keep her conflicting emotions under wraps, and defined each and every one of them. With a degree of dispassionate anticipation, he was aware the fight between them had scarcely begun. He intended to win.

'I need a drink,' she admitted, watching as Michel's lips curved to form a musing smile.

He lifted a hand, and in an instant a waitress appeared at his side. Michel had that effect on women. All women, of any age. It was an inherent charm, one he used quite ruthlessly on occasion.

He lifted two flutes of champagne from the tray and handed one to Sandrine.

'*Salut.*' He touched the rim of her flute with his own.

She ignored the temptation to drain the contents in one long swallow and deliberately sipped the chilled aerated wine, savoured the taste, then let the liquid slide down her throat.

'Shall we join our host?'

Sandrine's eyes clashed momentarily with his, then

she veiled their expression. There would be an opportunity later to unleash the verbal diatribe seething beneath the surface. Round one might be his, but she had every intention the next would be hers.

She summoned a slow smile, her acting ability prominent as she tucked a hand into the curve of his elbow.

'Having provided the guests with an unexpected floor show, don't you think introductions are somewhat overdue?'

Minutes later Michel moved easily at Tony's side, displaying an interest in each guest's professional background as he posed questions with practised charm.

Working the room, Sandrine recognized with cynicism. A retentive and photographic memory ensured he was never at a loss in the business arena or among the social set.

'As secrets go, yours is a doozey.'

She turned slightly and encountered a slender young woman whose name temporarily escaped her.

'Stephanie Sommers, marketing.'

'Yes, of course,' Sandrine responded, warming to Stephanie's faintly wicked smile.

'I can understand you keeping him under wraps. Where did you find him?'

'New York. We married in Paris.'

'Ah, the universal city for lovers.'

Sandrine felt a shiver slither its way over the surface of her skin as she experienced instant recall of the city, the ambience. The magic. Paris in the spring, when the grey skies cleared and everything came alive. As her heart had when she first met Michel.

An ache centred in the region of her diaphragm, intensifying as memories surfaced. Memories that had held such promise, so much love, she'd imagined their lives together were inviolate and forever entwined.

The stuff of which fantasies are made, she reflected wryly. With little basis in reality.

'Tony is on his best behaviour.'

Sandrine summoned a quick smile. Something that was becoming a habit as the evening progressed. 'The future of the film is at stake.'

'Is it?'

The query bore a certain quizzical humour as if Stephanie had already concluded the injection of essential finance was a done deal.

It was, although Sandrine wondered what the marketing manager's reaction would be if she discovered the reason for Michel's investment.

'Okay. So the rest of us get to sweat it out a little longer.'

Sandrine looked suitably enigmatic until Stephanie gave a low, throaty chuckle.

'You can't say I didn't try.' The attractive blonde spared a glance at her watch. 'I'm going to have to leave soon.'

'A date?'

'With a baby-sitter who can only stay until ten,' the marketing manager replied with a touch of cynicism.

'Divided loyalties?'

'No contest. My daughter wins out every time.' She

quickly scanned the room, then lowered her voice to a confidential tone. 'Your husband has escaped from Tony and is heading this way. Impressive beast, isn't he?'

Beast was an apt description. Although not in the context Stephanie implied. 'Tony, or Michel?'

She met Stephanie's direct look with equanimity, glimpsed the momentary speculation before it was quickly masked and cast her a wicked smile.

'Surely you jest?'

Sandrine refrained from responding as Michel loomed close.

She felt her body stiffen in anticipation of his touch and she unconsciously held her breath, only releasing it when he made no attempt at physical contact.

'Michel, you've met Stephanie?' she managed smoothly.

'Yes. We shared an interesting discussion on marketing techniques.'

'Albeit that it was brief.'

'Something we will correct, *n'est-ce pas*?'

Oh, my, he was good. The right amount of interest, the desired element of charm, with hard business acumen just visible beneath the surface.

'It will be a pleasure,' Stephanie accorded, then she excused herself, and Sandrine watched as she talked briefly to Tony before exiting the room.

'She is a friend?'

The mildness of Michel's voice didn't deceive her. 'Actors have little to do with the business heads.'

'Am I to assume, then, that tonight is the first time you've met?'

She cast him a mocking glance. 'Would you like me to give you a run-down on everyone at this soiree? Whom I speak to, touch?' She paused a beat. 'Kiss?'

'Careful,' Michel warned silkily. 'You're treading dangerous ground.'

'In the name of one's craft, of course,' she added, and derived a degree of personal satisfaction at the way his eyes narrowed.

'If I thought otherwise,' he drawled, 'I'd carry you kicking and screaming onto the first plane out of here.'

'Neanderthal tactics belong to a distant civilisation.'

'Neanderthal and civilised do not mesh, *chérie*. Persist in baiting me, and I'll show you just how uncivilised I can be.'

Her chin lifted, and her eyes remained remarkably steady as they clashed with his. 'Too late, *mon amant*. I've already been there, remember?'

'I retain a vivid memory of a little wildcat who threw a few objects at me in temper.'

Expensive Waterford crystal. An inkwell, a paperweight and a small clock decorating the antique desk in his study.

At the time she'd been too angry to care, but afterwards she'd experienced a pang of regret for the exquisite crystal items that formed part of a desk set. And the panelled wall they'd collided with before falling to the marble floor to shatter in glittering shards when Michel deftly moved out of the line of fire.

Now, as she reviewed her explosive reaction, she

felt ashamed for having displayed such a lack of control.

'You provoked me.'

'It was reciprocal.'

Words. His, cool and controlled, whereas hers had been the antithesis of calm. Yet equally hurtful, uttered in frustrated anger.

'Space and time, Michel?' Sandrine queried with a trace of bitterness. 'In which to cool down and pretend it never happened?'

'I imagined we'd already resolved the situation.'

The gold flecks in her eyes became more pronounced as she held on to her anger. Twin flags of colour highlighted her cheekbones as the memory of the very physical sex they'd shared immediately afterwards came vividly to mind. On top of his magnificent antique desk. Hard, no-holds-barred sex, libidinous, barbaric and totally wild. Afterwards he'd cradled her close and carried her upstairs, bathed and gently towelled her dry, then he'd taken her to bed where he made exquisite love long into the night.

She'd waited until he'd fallen asleep, then she'd dressed, thrown clothes into a suitcase, penned a hastily scrawled note and left as the new day's dawn was lightening a shadowed grey sky.

'No.' The single negation emerged with quiet dignity. Sex...even very good sex, she amended, didn't resolve anything.

He had never felt so frustrated in his life when he discovered she'd left. If he could have, he'd have boarded the next Australia-bound flight and followed her. Except Raoul was in America, and Sebastian, youngest of the three Lanier brothers, was honeymooning overseas. He'd had no option but to attend scheduled meetings in various European cities, then conclude them with a brief family visit with his *grandmère* in Paris.

'An empty space in bed, a brief note, and a wife on the other side of the world who refused to take any of my calls.' For that, he could have shaken her senseless.

'If you're through with the interrogation,' Sandrine said stiffly, 'I'd like to leave. I have an early call in the morning.'

His features hardened and his eyelids lowered slightly, successfully masking his expression. 'Then let's find our host and thank him for his hospitality.' He took hold of her arm, only to have her wrench it out of his grasp.

'I'm not going anywhere with you.'

One eyebrow arched in a deliberately cynical gesture. 'Are you forgetting our bargain so soon?'

'Not at all,' Sandrine declared bravely. 'But I'm damned if I'll allow you to share a house with me!'

His smile bore no humour at all. 'Separate residences aren't part of the deal.'

'Go to hell,' she vented, sorely tried.

'I've been there,' Michel said with dangerous softness. 'I don't intend a return trip.'

'I think,' she declared with controlled civility, 'we should save any further discussion until later.'

'I haven't even begun,' he stated with deliberate

emphasis. 'And the guests are free to speculate as they like.' He curved an arm around her waist and anchored her firmly to his side. 'Place one foot in front of the other and smile as we bid Tony goodnight.'

'*Or else*?' Sandrine countered with controlled anger.

'It's a matter of dignity. Yours,' Michel declared in a silky smooth tone. 'You can walk out of here or you can exit this apartment hoisted over my shoulder. Choose.'

Her stomach turned a slow somersault. One glance at his set features was sufficient to determine it wouldn't be wise to oppose him.

Her eyes held a chill that rivalled an arctic floe. 'I prefer the first option,' she said with icy politeness.

It took ten minutes to exchange pleasantries and have Michel confirm a business meeting with Tony the following morning. Sandrine didn't miss the slight tightness of Tony's smile or the fleeting hardness evident in his eyes.

'He's sweating on your decision,' she inferred as they rode the lift down to the ground floor. 'A calculated strategy, Michel?'

He sent a dark, assessing look in her direction, and she glimpsed a faint edge of mockery beneath the seemingly inscrutable veneer.

The query didn't require a verbal affirmation. The three Lanier brothers, Raoul, Michel and Sebastian, controlled a billion-dollar corporation spearheaded by their father, Henri, who had ensured each of his three sons' education encompassed every financial aspect of business.

The lift slid to a smooth halt, and they crossed the foyer to the main external entrance.

Sandrine extracted her cell phone and flipped it open. 'I'll call you a taxi.'

The streetlight nearby provided a luminous glow, the shadows highlighting the strong planes of his face.

'I have a hire-car,' Michel informed her silkily. 'I'll follow you.'

'You can move in tomorrow—' She broke off as the connection engaged. 'Could you send a cab to—'

Michel ended the call by the simple expediency of removing the small unit from her hand.

'How *dare* you?' The words spilled out in spluttered rage, and she made a valiant attempt to snatch the cell phone from him, failing miserably as he held it beyond her reach. 'Give it to me!'

One eyebrow arched in silent cynicism as she stamped her foot in wordless rage.

'Where are you parked?'

She glared at him balefully, incensed that much of her visual anger was diminished by the dark evening shadows. 'Aren't you booked in somewhere?'

She had tenacity, temper and *tendresse*. The latter had never been so noticeably absent. A faint twinge of humour tugged at the edge of his mouth. 'I checked out this morning.'

Damn, *damn* him, she silently vented. 'My car is the white Honda hatchback,' she told him in stilted tones. She turned away, only to have his hand snag her arm, and she whirled back to face him in vengeful fury. 'What now?'

'Your cell phone,' Michel said mildly as he held it out to her. She snatched it from him as if his fingers represented white-hot flame.

She would, she determined angrily as she slid in behind the wheel and engaged the engine, drive as fast as she dared and hope to lose him. Fat chance, Sandrine silently mocked minutes later as she ran an amber light and saw, via the rear-vision mirror, his car follow.

Knowing Michel's attention to detail, it wouldn't surprise her if he had already discovered her address and was therefore quite capable of reaching it with the aid of a street map. It was a sobering thought and one that relegated her actions to a foolish level.

No more taking risks with the traffic lights, she determined as she settled down to the twenty-minute drive and tried to ignore the twin set of headlights following several metres to the rear of her car.

Sandrine switched on the radio, selected a station at random and turned up the sound. Heavy rock music filled the interior, and she tried to lose herself in the beat, hoping it would distract her attention from Michel.

It didn't work, and after several minutes she turned down the sound and concentrated on negotiating a series of traffic roundabouts preceding the Sanctuary Cove turn-off.

A security gate guarded the entrance to the road leading to her waterfront villa, and she activated it, passed through, then followed the curving ribbon of bricked road past a clutch of low-rise apartment buildings until she reached her own.

After raising the garage door by remote control, she eased the car to a halt as Michel slid a sleek late-model sedan alongside her own.

The garage door closed, and Sandrine emerged from behind the wheel to see Michel pop the boot of his car and remove a set of luggage. She wanted to ignore him, but Michel Lanier wasn't a man you could successfully ignore.

Something twisted painfully in the pit of her stomach as she unlocked the door leading from the garage into the villa.

Pausing, she turned back towards him. 'There are three bedrooms upstairs,' she informed in a tone resembling that of a hostess instructing a guest. 'Choose one. There's spare linen in the cupboard.'

He didn't answer, and the silence was enervating. Without a further word, she stepped through to the hallway and made her way towards the kitchen.

The villa's interior was light and modern, with high ceilings and huge glass floor-to-ceiling windows. Large urns painted to blend with the muted peach-and-green colour scheme held a variety of artificial flowers and greenery, adding a tropical ambience to the expanse of marble-tiled floors.

The only sound was the staccato click of her stiletto heels as she crossed into the kitchen, and within minutes the coffee machine exuded an exotic aroma of freshly dripped brew.

Sandrine extracted two cups and saucers, sugar,

milk, placed them on the counter, then she filled one cup and took an appreciative sip.

It was quiet, far too quiet, and she crossed into the lounge and activated the television, switching channels until she found something of interest. The images danced, her vision unfocused as her mind wandered to the man who had invaded her home.

Temporary home, she corrected, aware that filming would wrap up within a week or two. Less for her, as she was only required in a few more scenes. Then what? Where would she go? There were a few options, and she mentally ticked them off. One, return to Sydney. Two, find modelling work. Three... No, she didn't want to think about the third option. A marriage should be about equality, sharing and understanding each other's needs. Domination of one partner by another was something she found unacceptable.

Sandrine finished her coffee, rinsed her cup, checked her watch, then released a heavy sigh. It was late, she was tired, and, she decided, she was damned if she'd wait any longer for Michel to put in an appearance. *She* was going to bed.

The silence seemed uncanny, and she found herself consciously listening for the slightest sound as she ascended the stairs. But there was none.

If Michel had showered, unpacked and made up a bed, he'd achieved it in a very short time.

The curved staircase led onto a semicircular, balustraded gallery. Three bedrooms, each with an en suite, were positioned along it, while the double doors at the head of the stairs opened to a spacious sitting room.

Sandrine turned right when she reached the top and entered the bedroom she'd chosen to use as her own. Soft lighting provided illumination, and her nostrils flared at the scent of freshly used soap and the lingering sharpness of male toiletries even as her eyes swivelled towards the large bed.

The elegant silk spread had been thrown back, and a long male frame lay clearly outlined beneath the light covering.

Michel. His dark head was nestled comfortably on the pillow, his eyes closed, his breathing slow and even.

Dammit, he was in *her* bed! Asleep!

Well, that would soon change, she decided furiously as she marched across the room. Without hesitation she picked up a spare pillow and thumped it down onto the mattress mere inches from his chest.

'Wake up,' she vented between clenched teeth. 'Damn you, wake up!' She lifted the pillow and brought it down for the second time. 'You're not staying in my room!'

He didn't move, and in a gesture of sheer frustration she pounded the pillow onto his chest.

A hand snaked out as she made to lift the pillow for another body blow, and she gasped as his fingers mercilessly closed over her forearm. Dark eyes seared hers.

'This is my room, my bed. And you're not occupying either.'

'You want a separate room, a separate bed?' His eyes seemed to shrivel her very soul. 'Go choose one.'

'You're doing this deliberately, aren't you?' she demanded, sorely tried. Pain focused behind each temple, and she lifted her hands to soothe the ache with her fingers. 'I'm not sleeping with you.'

'*Sleep* is the operative word,' Michel drawled.

She controlled the urge to hit him...by the skin of her teeth. 'You expect me to *believe* that?'

He looked...magnificent, and dangerous as hell. The brooding sexuality he exuded sent warning flares of heat racing through her veins.

Sandrine shifted her attention to his face and settled fleetingly on his mouth. Her lips quivered in vivid memory of how they'd moved beneath his own only a few hours ago. A traitorous warmth invaded her body, and she almost waived controlling it. *Almost*.

'Afraid to share the bed with me, Sandrine?'

Yes, she longed to cry. Because all it will take is the accidental brush of skin against skin in the night when I'm wrapped in sleep to forget for a few essential seconds, and then it'll be too late.

'Sex isn't going to make what's wrong between us right.'

'I don't recall suggesting that it would.'

'Then perhaps you'd care to explain why you've chosen my room, my *bed*?' she sputtered, indicating the bed, *him*. She drew in a deep breath, then released it slowly. 'If you had any gentlemanly instincts, you would have found another room!'

'I have never pretended to be a gentleman.'

Sandrine glared at him. 'No,' she agreed. 'Barbarian is more appropriate!'

'Careful, *chérie*,' Michel warned silkily.

A small decorative cushion lay within easy reach, and she swept it up in one hand and hurled it at him. 'I hate you.'

Two seconds later she lay pinned to the mattress as Michel loomed close above her. 'Let us put this *hate* to the test, hmm?'

She fought him, vainly twisting her body beneath his own as she attempted to wrench her hands free. 'Don't do this.'

It was a statement, not a plea, and he noted all her fine anger, her fearless tenacity and her passion. All it would take was subtle persuasion and sensual skill to have her become pliant in his arms.

'Then you should have thought before you pounded me with a pillow.'

'If you bait me, expect a reaction,' she launched in pithy response.

His expression didn't change although she could have sworn she glimpsed a glimmer of amusement.

'So...do you want to continue with this game of one-upmanship, or shall we bring it to a halt? Your call, Sandrine.'

She wanted to yell *Fight to the death*, and be damned. Except it would be *her* death. Emotionally, mentally, physically. And she didn't want to offer him that power.

'If you'll *move* yourself,' she suggested with expressive intonation, 'I'll go change and shower.'

'*Oui*, but first…' He took her mouth in a fleeting soft kiss, lingered at the edge, then swept his tongue into the silky interior to wreak brief and devastating havoc before easing his lengthy frame back onto the mattress. '*Bonne nuit, mignonne.*'

He rolled onto his side, pulled the covering to his waist and closed his eyes.

Sandrine lay frozen for a few seconds as she savoured the taste of him. Warm, musky and wickedly erotic. Damn him, she swore silently. He might have allowed her to call the tune, but he'd managed to have the last word.

With extreme care, she slid off the bed and crossed to the en suite, undressed, then took a leisurely shower, allowing the hot spray to ease the tension tightening her neck and shoulder muscles. Then she closed the dial, reefed a towel and, minutes later, donned a cotton nightshirt.

It seemed ironic and, she perceived wryly, probably owed something to her rebellious streak that she possessed complete sets of exquisite satin-and-lace French lingerie, yet alone she chose to wear something plain and functional to bed.

Michel lay still, his breathing deep and even as she crossed the room to snap off the light.

Afraid to share the bed with me? His words whispered in an unspoken challenge, taunting her.

Maybe she should turn the tables on him and do the unexpected. He'd sleep for hours, and although she wouldn't be there to witness it, she'd give almost anything to glimpse the look on his face when he woke and saw she'd occupied the other half of the bed.

A secret smile curved her lips as she slipped under the covers. He wanted to play games, huh? Well, let the games begin!

It gave her satisfaction to devise one scheme after another until sleep claimed her and tipped her into a world of dreams where Michel was alternately lover and devil, the location changed from one side of the world to another and became a film set where she was centre stage without any recollection of her lines.

CHAPTER THREE

SANDRINE came sharply awake to the shrilling sound of her digital alarm and automatically reached out a hand to turn it off. Except she was on the wrong side of the bed, and her fingers came into contact with a hard, warm male shoulder.

Michel. She tore her hand away as he uttered a muffled Gallic curse and reared into a sitting position.

'My alarm,' she explained sweetly as she slipped out of bed and crossed round to still the strident sound. The illuminated numerals registered four-thirty. 'Sorry if it woke you.'

She wasn't sorry at all. It was payback time for last night, and victory was sweet.

Drapes covered the wall of glass, filtering the early dawn light. This was Queensland, and the height of summer when the sun rose soon after four in the morning.

Sandrine crossed to the walk-in robe, selected jeans and a sleeveless ribbed top, then she collected fresh underwear and stepped into the adjoining en suite.

Ten minutes later she emerged, dressed, her face completely devoid of any make-up and her hair twisted into a loose knot at her nape.

She didn't give the bed or its occupant a single glance as she caught up her bag and exited the room.

In the kitchen she extracted fresh orange juice, drank it, then picked up a banana and made her way through to the garage.

Fifteen minutes later she was in make-up, mentally going over her lines while the wizard in cosmetic artistry began transforming her for the camera.

On reflection, it was not a happy day. Everyone was edgy, tempers flared as the temperature rose, and professionalism was strained to the limit.

It hadn't helped when Michel put in an appearance on the set after the lunch break. He stood in the background, his presence unquestioned given his possible investment, an apparently interested observer of the film-making process as the actors went through their paces...again and again as Tony sought perfection in his quest to impress.

No matter how hard Sandrine tried to ignore her indomitable husband, he was *there*, a constant on the edge of her peripheral vision, ensuring that her total focus was shot to hell.

'What are you doing here?' she demanded sotto voce during a break from filming.

Michel leant forward and brushed his lips to her temple. '*Chérie*, is that any way to greet your husband?'

'Please. Go away.'

She caught a glimpse of humour lurking at the edge of his mouth and bit back the need to scream.

'If I'm going to invest a considerable amount of money in order to salvage this venture,' he drawled, 'I think I should check out the action.'

'This is supposed to be a closed set.'

'I'm here at Tony's invitation.'

'Very cleverly baited, I imagine, so that our esteemed director took the hook?'

His smile didn't reach his eyes. 'You know me so well.'

No, she wanted to refute. I thought I did, but now I feel I hardly know you at all.

'How long do you intend to stay?'

'On the set? Until you finish for the day.' He lifted a hand and brushed gentle fingers across one cheek. 'Why? Does my presence bother you?'

She sharpened her verbal claws. 'Isn't that your purpose?'

'Shouldn't you read through your lines?' Michel countered, watching as she turned without a word and crossed to pick up her copy of the script.

It didn't help any that Cait Lynden chose that moment to exert her considerable feminine charm or that Michel appeared responsive, albeit politely so.

A ploy to make her jealous? It's working, isn't it? a wretched little imp taunted.

She watched them surreptitiously beneath veiled lashes and had to admit the blood simmered in her veins as Cait flirted outrageously with the deliberate touch of her hand on his sleeve, the wickedly sensual smile, the brazen *knowledge* evident in those glittering blue eyes.

Sandrine felt the knot in her stomach tighten as she sightlessly scanned the upcoming scene in her copy of the script.

Damn Michel. For every darn thing. And especially for invading her professional turf.

'Okay, everyone. Places, please.'

Thank heavens for small mercies, Sandrine accorded as she mentally prepared herself to be in character and silently rehearsed her few lines.

It was late afternoon before Sandrine was dismissed from the set with the news she wouldn't be required until Tuesday. The person responsible for continuity took the requisite Polaroid, and Sandrine went through the process of discarding the elegant costume and wig with help from the wardrobe assistant, then she removed her make-up and shook her hair free from the confining hairnet.

The comparison between screen actress in character and the modern jean-clad girl was remarkable. So remarkable, she decided ruefully, that it was unlikely anyone would recognise her as being one and the same person.

It was after five when she emerged into the parking lot, and she filched keys from her carry-bag as she walked towards her car.

'Hoping to slip away undetected?'

Michel fell into step beside her, and she quickened her pace, choosing not to answer him.

A minute later she slipped the key into the lock and opened the door, then slid in behind the wheel and fired the engine.

A great exit line would have been *Eat my dust*, except the moment was dramatically reduced as her tyres squealed faintly on smooth bitumen, and she was forced to adhere to the low speed limit.

However, once she hit the highway she put her foot down and let the speedometer needle soar as far as she dared without risk to life or limb or threat of a speeding ticket. It provided some release for the build-up of tension.

Sandrine reached Sanctuary Cove in record time, and inside the villa she ran lightly upstairs, changed into a maillot, grabbed a towel, retraced her steps and went out to the pool.

The water was refreshingly cool, and she stroked several lengths of the pool before turning onto her back and lazily allowing the buoyancy of the water to keep her afloat.

It was all too easy to allow her thoughts to wander and reflect on the day's events.

And Michel.

She hadn't slept well and had spent much of her waking hours wondering at her sanity in sharing the same bed. It was madness, an act that amounted to masochism. For to lie so close, yet be so far from him, attacked her emotional foundation and tore it to shreds.

What would he have done if she'd reached out and touched him? If he'd ignored her, she'd have died. Yet if he'd responded, how could she hope to handle the aftermath?

Such an act could only amount to sexual gratification and achieve nothing except provide mutual satisfaction. Akin to scratching an itch.

The attuning of heart, mind and soul would be missing, and somehow just *sex* wasn't enough.

She was mad. Insane, she added mentally. Any other woman would catch hold of Michel's coat-tails, exult in all that his wealth and social prestige could provide and hang in there for the ride.

And what a ride! Even the thought of it sent warmth flooding through her body. Each separate nerve end quivered in anticipation, and sensation wreaked havoc with her equilibrium.

It had been bad enough when they were oceans apart. Now that he was here, it was a thousand times worse.

Magic, she thought. Highly sensitised, sensual sorcery of a kind that defied valid description. Transmuted in the touch, the look, the promise...and the anticipation.

To part after a long night of loving and count each hour until they could be together again. To counter and feed that need with a phone call, a softly spoken promise. The delivery of a single red rose. That special look lovers exchange in a room filled with people. And the waiting, the wanting.

Was it love? The to-die-for, till-death-us-do-part kind of loving? Or was it sexual satiation, a sensual nirvana?

She'd thought it was both until their first serious argument. Now she wasn't so sure.

'Pleasant thoughts, I trust?'

The faintly inflected drawl caused her to jackknife

and turn towards the tall male figure standing close to the pool's edge.

Michel had discarded his jacket and tie and loosened the top two buttons of his shirt. His hair looked slightly ruffled, as if he'd dragged impatient fingers through its groomed length.

'How long have you been standing there?' she demanded.

'Does it matter?'

Watching her unobserved almost amounted to an invasion of privacy, and she didn't like it one bit.

A few strokes brought her to the side of the pool, and she levered herself easily to sit on its edge. Her towel lay out of reach on a lounger, and she rose to her feet, then caught it up in one quick movement.

His faint amusement didn't go unnoticed, and she determinedly blotted the excess moisture from her body before tending to her hair.

'I've booked a table for dinner at the Hyatt.'

Sandrine heard the words but momentarily chose to ignore them.

'I'm sure you'll enjoy the meal,' she managed calmly. 'I've heard the chef has an excellent reputation.'

'For two,' Michel informed her. 'At seven.'

'I shan't wait up.'

'You have an hour to shower and get ready.'

She looked at him steadily. 'I'm not going anywhere with you.'

'Damn, you try my patience!'

'And you try mine!'

'Is it unacceptable to want to share a meal with my wife in pleasant surroundings?'

'No,' Sandrine said sweetly. 'Providing your wife is willing. And in this instance, she's not!'

'Sandrine—'

'Don't threaten me, Michel.' She tried for quiet dignity but didn't quite make it. Her eyes speared his, dark and intense with emotion. 'I refuse to fall in with every suggestion you make.'

'You prefer to eat here?'

'Don't you get it? I don't want to share a meal with you. *Anywhere*.' A faint tremor shook her body, and she tightened her grip on the towel.

His eyes narrowed. 'You're shivering.'

'How perceptive,' she mocked. 'If you'll excuse me, I'll go take a hot shower.' As she moved past him, she endeavoured to ignore the sheer magnetism of the man. And her body's traitorous reaction.

Two more weeks, she reasoned as she ran lightly upstairs. Maybe less. And filming would be over. At least, her participation would finish. Could she go the distance, living in the same villa, sharing the same bed as the man who was bent on using any advantage he could gain?

Sandrine reached her bedroom and crossed into the adjoining en suite. A swift turn of the dial and warm water cascaded onto the tiled floor of the shower.

It took only seconds to strip the wet Lycra from her body, and she stepped into the large cubicle, reached for the bottle of shampoo, then began the task of lathering it through her hair.

Ten minutes later she emerged into the bedroom and came to a sudden halt at the sight of Michel in the process of discarding his clothes.

'Finished?'

Sandrine's left hand flew to the towel carelessly caught in a knot between her breasts, and with her right she steadied the towel wound high on her head.

'There are two other bathrooms on this level,' she pointed out in a slightly strangled voice.

'You object to sharing?'

Oh, my, he was good. Reasonable, faintly teasing beneath the edge of cynicism.

'Yes,' she returned, regaining her equilibrium as she crossed the room to collect fresh underwear. 'Considering your main purpose is to unsettle me.'

'An admission I'm succeeding, Sandrine?'

She'd fallen straight into that one, hadn't she? 'Not at all,' she responded calmly, and knew she lied. Her entire nervous system jangled at the very thought of him.

Watching Michel as he crossed the room to the bathroom created a havoc all of its own as she took in his broad frame, the muscular set of his shoulders, superb pectorals, the hard-packed diaphragm and firm waist.

She controlled a faint shiver at the thought of what it felt like to be held close, to feel the strength in those arms as he enfolded her firmly within them.

It was almost possible to breathe in the musky aroma of his skin, the clean freshness of the soap he used, the male cologne. Sense the way he tasted when her mouth joined with his, the faintly abrasive and moist slide as their tongues caressed and explored in an erotic mating dance.

The essence of his sex, the degree of power she experienced in taking him to the brink of his control, the way that large male body shook as he tumbled over the edge. Man at his most vulnerable.

Sandrine tried to restrain the way heat flared through her body, but she failed as the image of his lovemaking rose to taunt her.

He had the look, the touch, the power to drive a woman wild. And much to her chagrin, there was a part of her that wanted him badly. Without question or recrimination.

She heard the faint buzz of his electric razor, followed minutes later by the fall of water in the shower stall.

She immediately visualised Michel's naked form, his potent masculinity, the impressive power sheathed at the apex of his thighs.

Focus, concentrate, *remember* the accusations they'd exchanged seven weeks ago, she silently raged as she discarded the towel and stepped into briefs, then fastened her bra before pulling on a pair of jeans and a cotton top.

That fateful night she had looked at Michel... someone she'd loved with all her heart, in whom she had implicit trust, and believed their lives, their love, were forever entwined...and now it was like looking at a stranger.

With an irritated gesture, Sandrine unwound the

towel from her head and shook out hair that fell in a cloud of sable silk onto her shoulders.

How did the axiom go? *Marry in haste, repent at leisure?*

She reached for the hair dryer, plugged it in, then began combing the warm air through her hair.

What would have happened if she'd stayed? If she'd cancelled her flight and risked a breach of contract? Would they have resolved anything? Or had her abrupt departure merely precipitated their separation?

Seven weeks. Weeks that could be viewed as a brief respite, or a lifetime, depending on the interpretation.

'You intend wearing casual gear to dinner?'

Sandrine reached forward and switched off the hair dryer. Via mirrored reflection, she saw him discard the towel, step into briefs, then pull on tailored trousers before crossing to the wardrobe and extracting a shirt.

'I hadn't planned on dressing up.' She caught her hair and began winding it into a knot.

'Leave it loose.'

Her hands didn't falter as she fastened the knot with pins. 'It's cooler if I wear it up.'

Michel buttoned his shirt, fastened his trousers, then pulled on socks and shoes.

'No make-up?'

'Why?' Sandrine countered. 'I'm not planning on going anywhere.'

His expression didn't change, but his eyes hardened. 'I leave in five minutes, Sandrine. With, or without you. Your choice.'

She turned to face him. 'You could always ring

Cait. She'd just *die* to share anything with you.'
Without a further word, she walked from the room and
made her way downstairs to the kitchen.

A tin of salmon and a tossed salad were poor sub-
stitutes for the appetiser, main course, fruit and cheese
board Michel would no doubt enjoy with table service,
a fine wine, subdued lighting and soft background music. She told herself she didn't care as she heard him
exit the house, followed by the start of a car engine.

Half an hour later she rinsed the few plates she'd
used, placed them in the dishwasher, then filled a glass
with bottled water and crossed into the lounge to
watch television.

At ten she dimmed the lights and went upstairs to
bed. For a few minutes she dithered over *which* bed,
rationalising that the main bedroom was *hers*, and if
Michel was determined to make it *his*, then he could
damn well *suffer* because she didn't intend to move.

Yet sharing the bed was akin to playing with fire,
and no way did she want to get burned. To slip into
the convenience of pleasurable sex wasn't on her
agenda.

With that thought in mind she collected linen and
made up the bed in a room farthest from the one
Michel had designated his own. Then she moved a few
essentials in clothes and toiletries and determinedly
slid between cool percale sheets, then turned out the
light.

Moonlight shone through in between the painted
wooden shutters, and after what seemed an intermi-

nable length of time spent tossing and turning, she padded across to the window to adjust them.

Sleep was never more distant, and she did the yoga thing, counted sheep and endeavoured to think pleasant, relaxing thoughts. Except the image that rose to taunt her belonged to Michel, and she rolled onto her stomach and punched the pillow.

Her room faced the water and was therefore at the opposite end of the house to the garage. Was he home yet? She hadn't heard so much as a sound to indicate he'd returned.

Maybe some gorgeous female had insisted on sharing his table and right this minute they were caught up in a web of harmless seduction. Or would it be harmless? Michel was a practised raconteur, and charm personified. He also possessed an indefinable sensual aura that had most women conjuring up every ploy in the book to attract his attention.

Sandrine played numerous different scenarios in her mind, damning Michel in every one of them until her subconscious mind took her deeper into vivid dreams that seemed no less real.

It was after eleven when the powerful car whispered to a halt in the garage. Michel entered the house and turned out lights as he gained the upper floor.

The empty bed gave him a bad moment, then he systematically conducted a quiet search of the remaining rooms and experienced an enormous degree of relief when he discovered his wife's recumbent form caught in a tangled twist of sheets.

He stood in the open doorway for several long minutes, then crossed to the bed.

She was beautiful. So fiercely independent and possessed of so much spirit. He wanted to smooth the hair back from her forehead and brush his lips across her temple.

Damn. He wanted more, so much more than a gesture of tenderness. He craved what they'd once shared. The mesmeric magical heat that culminated in shameless passion and encapsulated them as twin halves of a whole. Complete, inviolate, *one* on every level... spiritually, mentally, emotionally.

Another curse whispered from his lips, one that would have scorched the ears of anyone who chanced to overhear it. Directed entirely at himself for allowing the strictures of business to take precedence over love for his wife.

Instead of taking the next flight in pursuit, he'd thrown himself into resolving extremely delicate financial negotiations in a takeover bid integral to the family's overflowing coffers. And ensured Sandrine's safety by employing a pair of highly reputable professionals to watch over her twenty-four hours a day.

His manipulative skill in the business arena was highly regarded among his peers. Women actively pursued him for his wealth and social position. They pandered to his ego, made all the right practised moves in an existence that he'd come to consider artificial. Experience had made him both cynical and wary.

Until Sandrine.

Sandrine, with her lack of guile and artifice, whose

laughter was both infectious and earthy. Her smile could light up her whole body so that her skin glowed and her eyes gleamed with a reflected warmth that came straight from the heart.

He'd wanted her from that first moment, not just in the biblical sense. Instinct warned it would be more than that. Much more.

She was his most precious possession, and from the beginning he'd wanted to shield and protect her.

There was no way he could sanction her flying off to the other side of the world without him. Or staying there alone. The timing, given his professional responsibility, couldn't have been worse.

A wry smile twisted his mouth. Financial wizardry was his speciality, and fate had been on his side. He could rescue a movie on the brink of foundering and employ emotional blackmail to salvage his marriage. What was it they said? *Kill two birds with one stone.*

The movie didn't present a problem. Sandrine, on the other hand, would be no easy victory.

It was a challenge. The most important of his life, and one he was determined to win.

A slight sound caught his attention, and he watched as she turned restlessly onto her back.

She looked defenceless in sleep, he mused. Her skin smooth and translucent in the reflected hall light. Her eyelashes impossibly long, and her mouth soft and lushly curved.

His emotions stirred into life, and he determinedly tamped them down as he gathered her into his arms and carried her back to the room they'd shared the previous night.

She stirred slightly as he lowered her into bed, then she settled, and he removed his clothes and slid in beside her to lie silent and unmoving in the darkness until sleep finally claimed him long after the witching hour of midnight.

CHAPTER FOUR

SANDRINE woke slowly as gradual awareness dispensed one layer of unconsciousness after another, bringing with it the reality of a new day.

Sunday, she determined with a restful sigh. No early-morning call, no studio.

Then she remembered, and with memory came the realisation that she wasn't in the bed or the room she'd retreated to last night.

What's more, she wasn't alone.

A masculine arm held her anchored closely against a very male frame. A very aroused male.

Michel's hand splayed over her stomach, and she could feel his steady, rhythmic heartbeat against her shoulder.

Dear God.

Seeking help from the Deity didn't work. Nor did the fervent but faint hope she might be dreaming, for no one dreamed with their eyes open.

Her thoughts reflected a kaleidoscope of conflicting emotions as she rationalised what action she should take.

If she kept her breathing even and she moved slowly, an inch at a time, maybe Michel wouldn't notice, and eventually she'd be able to slip free from his grasp and the bed.

A ridiculous strategy, she silently castigated herself seconds later when the slightest movement resulted in an involuntary tightening of his hold.

What now? Jab her elbow into his ribs? Thump a fist against his forearm? Maybe both? Yes, that might work.

'Planning your method of attack?' a deep voice drawled far too close to one ear.

'You got it in one,' she responded thickly, aiming a vicious jab with her elbow...and missed as he successfully deflected the manoeuvre. Kicking her heel against his shins didn't make an impression at all, and she uttered a growl in rage. 'Let me go!'

'*S'il vous plaît*?' he queried musingly.

'Go to hell.'

'If you want to play...'

'You're enjoying this, aren't you?' she retorted vengefully as she twisted helplessly to free herself.

'Not particularly. I prefer a woman to be pliant and willing in my arms.'

'Fat chance!'

'You would like me to prove how easily I can change your mind?'

Sandrine lay very still as she attempted to control the sudden hitch in her breathing. All too easily, she agreed silently, much to her chagrin.

He buried his mouth in the soft curve of her neck, then trailed a path to her temple. His hand moved up to cup her breast, and her stomach muscles tightened against the onslaught of sensation.

'Is this where you insist I fulfil my part of the bargain?'

With one easy movement he rolled onto his back and carried her with him to straddle his waist. His features were dark, accentuated by the visible evidence of a night's growth of beard. His eyes held a watchful quality, assessing and vaguely analytical.

This, *this*, she qualified shakily, could prove highly dangerous.

He resembled a lazy tiger, supine, visually content, but exuding a primitive degree of power. One wrong word or move on her part and she entertained no doubt his indolent facade would swiftly vanish.

Her position was extremely tenuous, to say the least.

He lifted a hand and brushed the back of his fingers down her cheek, then slid them forward to cup her chin. 'Your definition, not mine.'

He pressed his thumb against the centre of her lower lip, and acute sensation quivered through her body. 'I moved into another room by choice.'

'And I brought you back here.'

'Because you don't like sleeping alone?' she queried with deliberate sarcasm.

'Sex isn't necessarily a prerequisite to sharing the nuptial bed.'

'You expect me to believe that? Of *you*?'

He was silent for several telling seconds, and when he spoke his voice was so silky it sent shivers scudding down the length of her spine. 'I have a vivid memory of the long nights we shared, *chérie*.'

So did she. Nights when she became a willing wanton in his arms as she embraced a sensual feast so erotic there were times when she wept from the joy of it.

'That was then,' Sandrine said slowly, and glimpsed his wry smile.

'And this is now, hmm?'

'Yes.'

'In that case, let's get dressed and go downstairs for breakfast.' In one smooth movement he lifted her to stand on the floor, then he swept aside the covers and slid to his feet.

Clothes, bathroom, she decided, in that order, gathering jeans and a stretch rib-knit top. Seconds later she was safely ensconced behind a closed door with, she hoped, total privacy.

There were no locks on the internal doors, and she took a quick shower, dressed, then emerged to find the bedroom empty.

Sandrine descended the stairs and followed the aroma of freshly brewed coffee to the kitchen, where Michel looked completely at ease breaking eggs into a bowl while a skillet heated on the stove top. Dressed in black designer jeans and a white polo-neck knit shirt, he looked indecently male.

His actions reminded her of the breakfasts they'd shared and their easy camaraderie. Then, she would have teased him mercilessly, applauded his skill and uttered a husky laugh as he carried her back to the bedroom.

Now, she silently filled two glasses with orange

juice, poured the coffee and transferred everything onto the table.

Michel placed one plate with a steaming omelette before her, then settled in the seat opposite.

Her stomach felt as if it were tied in knots, and it irked her considerably that his appetite didn't appear in the least affected.

Sandrine forked a few morsels into her mouth, bit off a segment of toast, then sipped the strong black coffee.

Michel refilled his cup, added sugar, then pushed his empty plate to one side and sank back in his chair. 'We have the day. What do you suggest we do with it?'

She replaced her cup on its saucer and met his steady gaze with equanimity. 'I plan to go shopping.'

'Specifically?'

'Food,' she answered succinctly. 'Staples such as bread, milk, eggs, fruit.'

'And then?'

'Take the car and explore a little.'

Michel rose to his feet and began clearing the table. 'I'll drive. You can play navigator.'

'Excuse me?'

He cast her a musing glance that held a hint of patient forbearance. 'We'll take in the supermarket, then explore.'

'Since when did *I* become *we*?'

His silence was telling, his expression equally so, and she was the one to break his gaze as she gathered up a few spreads and carried them to the refrigerator.

'What if I'd prefer to be alone?'

'Don't push it, Sandrine.'

It took only minutes to rinse and stack the few plates in the dishwasher, then Sandrine collected her shoulder-bag, slid sunglasses atop her head and walked through to the garage, uncaring whether Michel followed or not.

Sanctuary Cove village comprised a wide variety of up-market stores and trendy boutiques, numerous cafés and restaurants and was accessed via two bricked lanes whose median strip held immaculately trimmed palm trees. The adjoining grounds fringed a lush green golf course, which seasonally hosted international competitions.

The few grocery staples required to boost supplies could have been selected in five minutes, but Sandrine deliberated over the choice of fruit, the varieties of lettuce, and opted to visit the local bakery rather than select packaged sliced bread.

Michel added a few selections of his own and appeared mildly amused when she rejected more than one.

Half an hour later they retreated to the villa, stored their purchases and returned to the car.

'Where to?'

'There are mountains, beaches, theme parks,' Sandrine responded as Michel eased the car through the security gate. 'Your choice.'

'Noosa.'

She cast him a startled glance. 'That's more than a two-hour drive north.'

He gave a slight shrug. 'Is that a problem?'

'No, I guess not.'

He reached a large roundabout and circled it. 'Navigate, Sandrine.'

She directed him onto the multilane highway where they joined the swift flow of traffic travelling north, and after an hour they took the Sunshine Coast bypass.

Soon they were driving through farmland devoted to sugarcane, avocados, pineapples, strawberries and a variety of fruit trees. Small country towns reflected a slower-paced lifestyle, old-style buildings mingling with modern, and in the distance lay the brooding range of bush-clad hills, a deep blue-green against the azure skyline.

'The Glasshouse Mountains,' Sandrine revealed, studying the tour-guide booklet. 'Montville, Maleny. Craft ware, quaint teashops, picturesque.'

'We'll go there tomorrow.'

She frowned and cast him a quick glance. It was difficult to determine anything from his expression for his eyes were shaded by dark sunglasses and his focus was on the road ahead.

'What do you mean...*tomorrow*?' she demanded.

'We'll detour through on the way back to the Coast,' Michel explained patiently.

'You intend for us to stay overnight in Noosa?'

'Is that a problem?'

'You're darn right it's a problem. I don't have a change of clothes for a start,' she said heatedly.

'It's a tourist strip. The shops will be open. We'll buy what we need.'

She turned on him with ill-concealed anger. 'Did you plan this?'

'It seems foolish to travel back to the Coast tonight, only to turn around and return again tomorrow,' he said reasonably.

'You could have asked me!'

'And given you the opportunity to refuse?'

She shot him a fulminating glare. 'I dislike being hijacked.'

'Look on it as an adventure.'

Some adventure! If she managed to get through the next thirty-six hours without hitting him, it would be a miracle.

'If I'd known you had this in mind, I'd have brought along the script. It might have escaped your attention, but I'm due on the set Tuesday and I need to study my lines!'

'I have it on good authority the lines are few, and unless the scene needs to be reshot, you should be done by midday.'

'I hate you.'

'Hate is a strong emotion and, as such, better than indifference.'

'You just missed the turn-off.'

'Caused by a navigational distraction?' he mocked as he decelerated, then swung the car into a wide turn.

Her lips tightened, and she refrained from uttering a further word except for curt, explicit instructions.

Michel chose the most up-market hotel resort on the main Hastings Street strip, relinquished the vehicle for valet parking, then led her into the main foyer to register.

It would serve him right if the hotel was fully booked, she reflected vengefully. Luck wasn't on her side as Michel completed the necessary paperwork and accepted a card folder with their room security tags.

Their suite overlooked the river towards a bank of riverfront mansions, Sandrine discovered on crossing to the window. The tranquil vista exuded a different ambience from that of the Gold Coast.

'Lunch,' Michel declared. 'Let's go find a place to eat.'

Sandrine turned towards him. 'I don't want to be part of a game you've chosen to play.'

'Specifically?'

'You're a superb tactician, Michel,' she acknowledged dryly.

'Is that a compliment, or a condemnation?'

'Both.'

'*Merci*,' he returned with wry humour. 'What game is it you imagine I'm playing?'

'One of revenge.'

He didn't pretend to misunderstand. 'Choosing to keep you in suspense as to when I begin collecting on our deal?'

'Yes.'

He wanted to cross the room and shake her until she pleaded for mercy. Instead, he thrust a hand into his trouser pocket and controlled the timbre of his voice. 'What if I said *tonight*?'

Something inside her stomach curled into a hard, painful ball. 'Why wait? Why not now?'

She reached for the buttons on her blouse and slowly undid one, then the other, forcing her fingers to remain steady until all the buttons were freed.

'Do you have any specific requirements?' Dear heaven, how could she sound so calm when inside she was shaking like a leaf?

'Enlighten me.'

'You're the one calling the shots.' She slid the blouse off one shoulder, then the other, and draped it carelessly over a nearby chair. As her fingers went to the snap fastening on her jeans, she looked over at him. 'Aren't you going to get out of your clothes?'

How far would she go? 'When you're done,' Michel drawled, calling her bluff, 'you can undress me.'

Pain arrowed through her body, so acute it almost made her wince. *Act*, a tiny voice prompted. You're good at it.

Sandrine managed a faint shrug. 'If that's what turns you on.' She slid the zip down on her jeans and slowly eased the denim over her hips. She slipped off her joggers, lifted one leg free, then the other, and tossed the jeans on top of the blouse.

He wasn't going to let her go through with this, was he?

She stood in briefs and bra, and although they covered her more adequately than a bikini, she felt vulnerable and exposed.

He stood perfectly still, his gaze steady and unblinking as she looked at him.

Damn him, he wasn't going to help her out.

With slow, sure steps she crossed to where he stood. His shirt was short-sleeved with three buttons at the neck. She caught hold of the knit fabric on either side of his rib cage and pulled it free from his waistband. Then she tugged upwards with little success until he obligingly raised his arms and lowered his head to accommodate the shirt's easy removal.

Too much. He really was much too much, she muttered silently. The spread of his shoulders, the breadth of chest, the strong musculature that rippled and bunched with every movement.

She threw the shirt in the path of her blouse and jeans, then turned back and reached for the snap on his jeans, pulled it open, then stifled a soft curse.

Buttons. No zip for easy unfastening.

Each one presented a fresh torture. Her fingers fumbled, and she felt totally inadequate for the task. It didn't help any that the denim was stretched tight against a hard male arousal.

She could, she reasoned, literally throw up her hands and tell him to complete the task himself. Except she was darned if she'd allow him the satisfaction of winning a challenge. She could almost hear his musing drawl, see the faint mockery in those dark eyes as he finished discarding his clothes.

As he would, if only to witness her discomfort, she determined as she dealt with another button.

How things had changed, she reflected wryly. In the not-too-distant past she'd have laughed and delighted in the task, taking pleasure in teasing him outrageously and exulting in his reaction.

Now, he had control while she slipped into such a state of nerves she couldn't even manage something as simple as undoing a series of buttons!

Just do it, the tiny voice urged. Slip into pretend mode and imagine he's someone who means nothing to you.

There, it was done. Stretch fashion jeans possessed one inescapable flaw. They were the very devil for someone else to remove! Tailored trousers wouldn't have presented any problem, but jeans were a different story, she decided, gritting her teeth as she tugged the fabric down over powerful thighs.

The action brought her face close to a vulnerable part of his anatomy, and she entertained the brief vindictive thought that with one quick movement she could cause him considerable pain. The consequences, however, wouldn't be worth it.

In a few swift movements he slid off his joggers, then stepped out of his jeans and kicked them to one side. Fine black silk skimmed his hips and couched his manhood, emphasising olive skin roughened by hair and a male frame in superb physical shape.

Sandrine momentarily closed her eyes, then opened them again. Michel wasn't an unknown lover. Why hesitate?

There was a part of her that longed for the feel of his mouth, the tactile skill of those clever hands as they created havoc with each separate pleasure zone. She wanted to lose herself in the wealth of emotional and spiritual sensations, to go to that special place where there was only *him*...and the unique alchemy they shared.

It had been good. Better than good, she amended.

A hand caught hold of her chin, lifted it so she had to look at him. His thumb traced the edge of her jaw, lingered there, then slid slowly down the column of her throat.

Sandrine swallowed compulsively, wanting to move away but held mesmerised by the darkness of those deep grey eyes as he forced her to hold his gaze.

Then he lowered his head and angled his mouth over hers in a kiss that was hard and mercilessly plundering as he took what she wouldn't willingly give.

Just as she thought her jaw would break, the pressure eased, and his tongue caressed and cajoled in a teasing dance that almost made her weep.

Not content, he savoured the taste of her lips, their soft, swollen contours throbbing beneath his touch. He nipped the full centre with the edge of his teeth, caught her indrawn breath, then angled his mouth to hers in a kiss that tore at the very threads of her soul.

With considerable ease his lips trailed a path down her neck, lingered as he explored the hollows at the edge of her throat, then travelled to the soft fullness of her breast.

In one easy movement he freed the twin hooks of her bra and dispensed with it before returning his attention to the rounded curve.

A soft flick from the tip of his tongue brought a

surge of sensation, and she arched her neck, allowing him access.

Her whole body began to melt as heat flowed through her veins, warming her body until she was on fire with a passion so strong, so tumultuous, there was only the man and the aching, wanting *need*.

His hand slid down to her waist, then splayed low over her stomach, his fingers slipping beneath the satin and lace of her briefs, seeking, probing, *teasing*, until she scaled the heights, clung, then descended in a free-falling spiral.

He caught her as she fell, held her, then took her on a return journey that was even more devastating than the first.

This time she was unable to still the soft, throaty cries or stop the flow of tears as they trickled slowly down her cheeks.

Michel brushed a thumb against each rivulet in turn, dispensing the dampness with a tenderness that brought a lump to her throat. His lips settled at the corner of her mouth, caressing the soft fullness of her lower lip with the edge of his tongue.

He paused to nibble the moist inner tissue, then conducted a seductive foray, tracing her tongue with his own, before taking possession with claim-staking action.

Sandrine was barely conscious of her hands creeping up to link together at his nape as he folded her close, and she kissed him back, giving, taking, in what became a storm of sensual exploration.

It wasn't enough. Not nearly enough, and she

moved against him, instinctively seeking more. Her hands shifted to his shoulders, then slid down over his back, urging him closer as she unconsciously raked her nails over muscled flesh to emphasise her need.

Without missing a beat, Michel swung an arm beneath her thighs and swept her into his arms, then tumbled with her down onto the bed. In one easy movement he rolled her beneath him, caging her body as he tore his briefs free.

It was as if every pore of her skin became highly sensitised to his touch, and an exigent sexual chemistry was apparent—vital, electric, lethal—for it melted her mental resistance, leaving only the craving for physical release.

Now, she urged, unaware whether the word left her lips or not. She was burning up inside, on fire with a primal heat so intense she lost sight of who and where she was in the need to have him deep inside her, matching each primeval movement until that deep, rhythmic possession transported them both simultaneously to exquisite sensual sensation.

Sandrine almost cried out loud when his mouth left hers and began a slow, tortuous descent, pausing to savour delicate hollows at the base of her throat before trailing a path to her breast, suckling first one acutely sensitised peak before delivering a similar assault on its twin.

Her stomach tensed as he explored the delicate indentation of her navel, and she gasped as he moved low to caress the most sensitive pleasure spot of all.

Her body arched as she became consumed by a

wicked ecstasy so acute she began to plead, muted guttural sounds she didn't recognise as being her own voice.

She reached for his head, seeking purchase on his hair, and she pulled it mercilessly in a bid to have him desist. Only to have him catch hold of her wrists and effortlessly clamp them to her sides.

'Michel.' His name emerged endless minutes later, accompanied by a mindless, tortured sob. 'Please.'

Seconds later he slowly raised his head and gave her a long, impassioned look. His eyes were so incredibly dark they were almost black.

Her breath came in ragged gasps, and her pulse seemed to beat so fast it was almost out of control. Her eyes felt too big for her face, their expression wild, dilated with an emotion she didn't care to define.

When his head lowered, she gave an anguished cry and felt her flesh quiver uncontrollably as he began bestowing an agonisingly slow trail of soft, openmouthed kisses to her navel, the soft slope of her breasts, their tender aureoles, the slender column of her neck, before taking possession of her mouth.

Timeless minutes later he freed her hands, and the breath stilled in her throat as he entered her with one powerful thrust.

She could feel herself stretching to accommodate his length, the tightness as she enclosed and held him, followed by the primitive rhythm that he kept erotically slow at first, so measured and deep she was aware of every muscle contraction.

She was almost falling apart when he quickened the

pace to a heavy, pulsating action that took her so high she became wild with the force and strength of it.

Her body felt as if it were a finely tuned instrument played by a virtuoso until it was wooed to such a fine crescendo that the only possible climax was to fracture and splinter into a thousand pieces in the accompanying electric silence.

He remained buried deep inside her as he cradled her face and kissed the teardrops trickling slowly down each cheek, trailing their path to the edge of her lips.

How was it possible to weep with such a combination of acute pleasure and sadness? Sadness, she rationalised, for an awareness that the pleasure had been all hers.

Michel supported his weight, then bestowed a series of butterfly kisses to the contours of her mouth before lifting his head to gaze down at her.

'Okay?' he queried gently.

What could she say? There wasn't one adequate word that came readily to mind. 'Speechless,' she managed at last.

'I meant *you*,' he qualified slowly.

'Fine.' You lie, the tiny voice chastised. Your body still vibrates from the feel of him, and you ache with a hurt that has little to do with physical pain.

Michel saw the faint clouding evident in those beautifully luminous brown eyes and glimpsed the rapid pulse beat at the base of her throat.

He leant forward and placed his lips to that frenetically beating hollow, felt her tremor and gently tucked a stray swath of hair from her cheek.

Sandrine wanted to close her eyes and block out the sight of him, but that wasn't an option. Instead, she wrinkled her nose at him in silent, mocking remonstrance.

'Lunch,' she declared. 'I'm hungry.' In one easy movement she slid off the bed and crossed the room to the en suite.

Michel followed and merely arched an eyebrow when she lifted a hand in mute denial that he share her shower.

'Modesty is inappropriate,' he drawled as he stepped in beside her, caught up the soap and began lathering it over her body.

'Give it to me,' she said in a strangled voice as she attempted to take the soap from his hand.

'No.'

She didn't want to fight. Dammit, she didn't possess the energy or the inclination right at this moment to do more than submit to his ministrations.

When he finished, she let the fine needle spray rinse the soap from her body, then she slid open the glass door and reached for a towel. By the time Michel emerged she was dressed, her hair was swept into a knot on top of her head, and she was applying colour to her lips.

He pulled on his clothes, ran his fingers through his dampened hair, then he inclined his head in bemused mockery and swept an arm towards the door. 'After you.'

CHAPTER FIVE

THEY selected a small intimate restaurant with an appealing blackboard menu, chose an outdoor table shaded by a large umbrella, ordered seafood pasta, *focaccia* and white wine, and were impressed by the quality of the food and the service.

Sandrine declined anything to follow and settled for strong black coffee.

'You enjoyed the food?'

She looked at the man seated opposite and fought against an enveloping wave of sensation.

How was it that he had this cataclysmic effect on her? He exuded an unfair share of sensuality, an inherent quality that was both mesmeric and magical.

'Yes, thank you.'

His mouth curved into a faint smile. 'So polite. More coffee?'

She shook her head, then watched as he gestured to the waiter to bring the bill.

'Shall we leave?' Michel queried minutes later, and Sandrine rose to her feet in acquiescence.

Together they strolled along the main street, pausing every now and then to examine a shop window display. Sandrine purchased a few postcards, added moisturiser and sun-screen cream, insisting on paying for them herself. Use of her credit card took care of a bikini and sarong wrap in glorious turquoise.

'The resort pool or the ocean?' Michel asked as they deposited an assortment of carry bags in their hotel suite.

She didn't hesitate for a second. 'Ocean.'

It took only minutes to change, collect a towel and cross the street to the beach.

A number of people inhabited the clean white sand; children laughed and squealed as they played while adults were bent on improving their tans or relaxing beneath large beach umbrellas.

The sea looked peaceful, with the gentle waves of an incoming tide encroaching on the foreshore. The curved bay was picturesque with its outcrop of rocks, a steep, bush-clad hill that led to a Natural Reserve.

There were many such beaches, coves and bays along the eastern coast, but Noosa held a reputation all its own.

Bliss, Sandrine silently reflected as she spread her towel beneath the beach umbrella Michel had erected. First, she'd sunbathe, then she'd swim.

Applying sun-screen cream was a sensible precaution, given the strength of the summer sun, and it took only minutes to cover her legs, arms and midriff.

'What do you think you're doing?' she demanded as Michel extracted the plastic bottle and squeezed a generous portion onto his cupped fingers.

'Applying cream to your back.'

Her mouth pursed at the amusement apparent as he

began smoothing the protective cream onto her shoulders.

He was thorough. A little too thorough, she decided as he ensured every centimetre of exposed skin was covered. He even went to the extent of loosening the clip of her bikini top, then refastening it. And his fingers caused havoc with her nervous system as they conducted a firm, circling massage across her back, over her waist and down to the line of her bikini briefs. Controlling her breathing became an effort, and she was grateful her expression was hidden behind dark glasses.

'Thanks.' Her voice was husky, almost indistinct.

'You can return the favour,' Michel instructed her indolently, handing her the bottle.

His request was deliberate, she was sure of it. Part of a strategy to test the effect such an action would have on her. Well, she'd show him just how easy it was to touch him. It wouldn't trouble her at all.

Ten seconds in and she knew she lied. He could have done the macho thing and flexed every muscle. Instead, he simply sat with his knees raised, his back to her, and his breathing didn't alter a fraction as she completed the application in record time.

Sandrine didn't want to think about the way her pulse raced into overdrive or how every nerve end uncurled in sensitive anticipation. An ache began deep inside, radiating from her central core until it encompassed her whole body.

'All done,' she managed evenly as she recapped the

bottle, mirroring his movements as he stretched out, face down, on the towel.

Twenty minutes later she strode across the sand to the water's edge, took a few steps, then dived into the cool blue-green sea, emerging to the surface to cleave the waves with leisurely strokes parallel to the shore.

There was something infinitely tranquil about the unlimited expanse of an ocean and the sensation of being at one with nature. Quite different from using a swimming pool, she mused as she trod water and admired the exotic landscape with its many brightly painted, low-rise apartment buildings and houses dotting the foreshore.

It was—how long since she'd last holidayed in Noosa? Years, she perceived wryly. A midyear school break with her parents in the days before divorce had torn the family in two, introduced bitterness and a division of loyalties with the advent of step-parents and step-siblings.

Exclusive boarding schools had effectively ensured a safe haven when she no longer fitted easily into one family or the other. There had always been love and welcome whenever she visited. But there had also been an awareness she was a reminder of another life, another time. An awkwardness, she reflected, that had resulted from her own sensitivity. Something that could have had a detrimental effect.

Instead, she had learnt to be self-sufficient, to strive and succeed on her own merits. And she had, utilising her talent with speech and drama by channelling it into acting, initially in school plays. Part-time modelling with an agency resulted in her appearance in a television commercial, and the rest, as they say, became the substance of dreams when she was offered a character role in a long-running Australian television series.

A modelling assignment in New York during a seasonal filming hiatus had garnered an invitation to a party where Michel numbered one of several guests. Two linked events that had changed her life.

'Intent on solitude?'

Sandrine's eyes widened at the sound of that familiar drawl, and she turned to see Michel within touching distance. Wet hair and water streaking his face did nothing to detract from the chiselled perfection of his features or lessen the degree of power he managed to exude without any effort at all.

'No.'

'Care to try your hand at something more adventurous?'

She was unable to read anything from his expression, and his eyes were too intently watchful for her peace of mind. 'Such as?'

'Hang-gliding, parasailing, jet-skiing?'

'Surely you jest?'

'Hiring a boat and exploring the waterways?' Michel continued as if she hadn't spoken, and she scooped up a handful of water and splashed him with it. 'I could retaliate,' he warned.

'I'm trembling.'

His lips formed a musing smile. 'It can wait.'

It wasn't the words but the implication that sent a

shivery sensation feathering the surface of her skin. His eyes held a warm, purposeful gleam that did much to melt through a layer of her resolve.

Her eyes remaining locked with his, she was aware of him to a degree that was vaguely frightening. Magnetic sensuality. She didn't want to be held in its thrall, for it clouded logic and decimated any rationale.

Michel divined her ambivalence, successfully attributed its cause and chose to cut her a little slack. 'Race you in to shore.'

He even held back, matching his strokes to meet hers, and they emerged from the water together. On reaching their shaded location, he caught up his towel, blotted off the excess moisture, then wound and secured the towel low on his hips.

'Feel like a drink?'

'After a shower and I've changed into something a little more respectable,' Sandrine parried as she copied his actions.

Michel pulled the beach umbrella from the sand and returned it to the hire stand en route to their hotel. 'Go on up,' he directed when they reached the entrance. 'I'll be there in ten minutes.'

She inclined her head, then crossed to Reception to collect their room card. Inside their suite, she made straight for the shower and emerged into the bedroom to discover Michel in the process of discarding several glossy signature carry bags onto the bed.

'You've been shopping.'

'Something to wear to dinner,' he declared as he divided and emptied the bags. 'Here.' He picked up a tissue-wrapped package and tossed it onto the pillow. 'This is for you.'

This, she discovered, was a pair of black silk evening trousers, together with a silk camisole in soft antique gold. There was also a pair of exquisite, lacy black briefs.

'Thanks,' she murmured appreciatively, watching as he shook free a pair of black slacks and a deep blue, short-sleeved silk shirt.

If only he'd relayed his intention to stay overnight, she could have packed a few clothes and he'd have saved some money. Although money was hardly an issue, she decided as she discarded the towel and quickly donned underwear.

The evening trousers and camisole were a perfect fit, and she was in the process of applying make-up when Michel re-entered the room.

Sandrine glanced away from the mirror and met his gleaming gaze. 'They're lovely,' she complimented.

'*Merci*,' he acknowledged with mocking amusement as he discarded the towel.

She returned her attention to applying eye shadow, willing her fingers to be steady as she brushed a soft gold to one upper lid.

The mirror proved her worst enemy, for it reflected heavily muscled thighs, smooth hips and buttocks and a fleeting glimpse of male genitalia as he stepped into briefs. The action involved in pulling on the pair of dark trousers emphasised an impressive display of honed muscle and sinew, and she was unable to glance away as he shrugged into his shirt and tended to the buttons.

Get over it, she derided in silent chastisement, and determinedly focused her attention on completing her make-up. It was something of a relief to enter the en suite minutes later, and she activated the hair dryer, opting to leave her hair to fall loose onto her shoulders.

'Beautiful,' Michel complimented when she re-entered the bedroom. 'But there's something missing.'

She felt on edge, jittery in a way that could only be attributed to acute sensitivity to this particular man. All her fine body hairs seemed to stand on end, quivering like miniature antennae, and her stomach didn't belong to her at all.

This was madness. Why did she feel as if she were being stalked by a prowling predator waiting for the right moment to pounce?

'What is that?' she managed lightly, and felt her body tremble slightly as he moved towards her.

'These.' He took hold of her left hand and slid first her wedding ring, then the magnificent pear-shaped diamond onto the appropriate finger.

Sandrine looked down at her hand, saw the symbols of his possession and didn't know whether to laugh or cry. 'Michel—'

Anything further she might have uttered was stilled as he pressed a finger to her lips. 'Let's go have that drink, shall we?'

The hotel lounge held a mix of patrons, and Michel quirked an eyebrow when she insisted on orange juice.

'The need for a clear head?'

'Definitely!'

'Afraid, Sandrine?'

Of you? 'No,' she responded evenly. Her reaction to him was something different entirely.

His husky chuckle was almost her undoing, and she could have hit him when he raised his glass in a silent, mocking gesture.

'How is your grandmother?' A safe subject, surely, she considered as she took a sip of the refreshing juice.

Michel's eyes held hers as he settled back in his chair. 'She expressed regret that you were unable to join me.'

Not so safe, she mentally corrected. 'She's an incredible lady.'

'Who regards you with affection.'

What could she say to that? After a few seconds she settled with 'How kind.'

'I promised we'd visit her after our return to New York.'

She didn't want to think that far ahead. It was enough just to get through each day.

'Would you like another drink?'

Sandrine shook her head, then watched as he set his empty glass down on the table. 'Shall we go have dinner?'

They chose Italian, the best restaurant, they were assured, in town. Michel ordered a smooth vintage Lambrusco to accompany a gnocchi starter, and they both settled for veal scallopini as a main, with an exquisite lemon tart for dessert.

The ambience was definitely European, the waiters

were Italian, and the food...*perfetto*. Sandrine expressed her pleasure as the waiter served them with a liqueur coffee.

'I don't think I'll eat a thing until at least midday tomorrow,' she declared as they walked out onto the street.

One shoestring strap slipped down over her shoulder and she absently slid it back in place. It had been a great few hours, reminding her far too vividly of previous evenings they'd shared over good food and fine wine.

'That was nice,' she said, offering him a warm smile. 'Thank you.'

His expression was equally warm, and those brilliant grey eyes bore a gleam she didn't care to define. 'My pleasure.'

'Let's walk,' she suggested on impulse. Hastings Street ran parallel to the foreshore, and it wasn't late. A number of tourists were enjoying the evening air, walking, drinking coffee at pavement tables adjoining numerous cafés and restaurants.

Michel caught her hand loosely in his, and she didn't pull free.

Did they look like lovers? Somehow she didn't think so. Their body language wasn't right.

He traced an idle pattern across the delicate veins at her wrist and felt the sudden surge in her pulse as it leapt to a faster beat.

When she attempted to tug her hand free, he forestalled the action by lifting her hand to his lips and kissing each finger in turn, aware of the slight tremor that shook her slender frame.

Sandrine lifted her head and met his steady gaze. 'Are you trying to seduce me?'

'Am I succeeding?'

Only too well.

'Resorting to the neutrality of silence, *mignonne*?'

She offered him a stunning smile. 'Of course.'

'On the grounds that anything verbal might give me a swelled head?'

'Something like that.'

They strolled along one side of the street, pausing every now and then when something in a shop window caught their attention, then they crossed over and wandered back to their hotel.

It was after eleven when she preceded him into their suite, and she automatically stepped out of her shoes, then reached for the waistband of her evening trousers.

Only to discover he'd already beaten her to it. She stood perfectly still as he slid the garment down past her thighs and she didn't move when he slipped the camisole over her head.

It was difficult to retain much dignity clad only in lacy black briefs, and she retreated into the en suite as Michel began divesting his clothes.

The lack of a nightgown caused her a moment's consternation, then she plucked a towel free and wound it sarongwise round her slim form. She might have little option but to sleep nude, but she was darned if she'd walk naked into the bedroom!

Misplaced modesty, she decided ruefully as she met

the dark, gleaming gaze of the man settled comfortably against a nest of pillows. The expanse of sun-kissed olive skin covering honed muscle and sinew was impossible to ignore, so she didn't even try.

His faintly quirked brow didn't help any, nor did his slow, teasing smile as she slid between the sheets before discarding the towel.

'It's a little late to play shy, *chérie*.'

'Perhaps I don't feel comfortable parading nude.'

'Do you?'

A slight frown creased her forehead. 'Do I—what?'

'Feel uncomfortable with me,' Michel pursued patiently as he rolled towards her and supported his head with a propped elbow.

He was too close, and much too dangerous. She became conscious of her breathing and monitoring every breath she took. The beat of her heart seemed loud in her chest, and she was willing to swear the pulse at the base of her throat was visible and far too fast.

'*I* feel uncomfortable with me when I'm around you,' Sandrine admitted with husky honesty, and her eyes widened as he lifted a hand and stroked a forefinger lightly down the length of her nose.

'And that's bad?' He pressed the pad of his thumb against her lower lip, then slowly traced its curve.

Heat suffused her body and pooled between the apex of her thighs. Sensation flared deep within, and her fingers clenched in an effort to control the aching need that made her want to reach for him.

'You're doing this deliberately, aren't you?' Sandrine queried in a slightly strangled voice.

'What am I doing, *mignonne*?'

'Seducing me.'

His head lowered and his lips brushed against her own. 'Mmm,' he teased, his breath warm as it mingled with her own. 'Want me to stop?'

She nearly said *yes*. Then his mouth was on hers, gentle at first, then the pressure increased as he took her deep.

Unbidden, her arms lifted as she linked hands at his nape, and she held on during the sensual storm that followed, giving, taking, in a manner that left her weak-willed and malleable. *His*.

It was a long time before they lay spent, and curled in each other's arms they drifted easily into a blissful sleep from which they stirred in the early dawn hours to shower, then make exquisitely slow love until the waiter delivered their breakfast.

'What to you want to do with the day?' Michel queried as he drank the last of his orange juice, then poured strong black coffee.

Sandrine spooned muesli and fruit, added milk into a bowl, then looked enviously at the plate of bacon, eggs and fried tomato. She was famished. And filled with a languid warmth that owed everything to sensual and sexual satiation.

'Maleny, Montville, the Glasshouse Mountains.'

'I was afraid you would suggest that.'

'Why?' she asked, feigning innocence. 'What else did you have in mind?'

'We could stay here, order a late lunch, then drive back to the Coast.'

The thought of spending several more hours in bed with him would weaken her defences, and they couldn't afford to be weakened further! 'It's a new day,' she proffered solemnly. 'Let's make good use of it.'

'My intention precisely.'

'Let's not go for overkill. We scratched an itch, and it was great.' Better than great. There weren't the words to even begin a satisfactory description for what they'd shared.

His gaze sharpened. 'That's all it was for you? Scratching an itch?'

Sandrine lifted her cup, sipped the dark, sweet brew, then replaced it on the saucer. 'You want to conduct an analysis, Michel? Should I determine a points system and rate you accordingly?'

He wanted to drag her to her feet, sweep her back into the bedroom and change that tepid warmth into blazing heat.

She'd been with him every inch of the way, through the night and in the morning. He was prepared to stake his life on it. He'd felt the tremors shake her body, the sweet tug of her muscles as she took and held him in a fit so snug he grew hard at the very thought of it.

She was slipping into self-protection mode in the clear light of day. He could cope with that as long as he had the nights.

'I don't recall your confiding too many comparisons,' he drawled. 'And as we never did indulge in the Was-it-as-good-for-you-as-it-was-for-me? scenario, I see no reason to begin now.'

'Confidence is a fine thing.'

'Knowledge,' Michel corrected with a tinge of mockery. 'Of you.'

Oh, yes, he had that, she admitted wryly. He knew precisely which buttons to push, and where and when. It gave him an unfair advantage.

They finished breakfast in silence, then showered and dressed before checking out of the resort and collecting the car.

It was a beautiful day, the sky a clear azure with only a few wispy clouds in sight. Warm sunshine promised high summer temperatures as they left Noosa and headed towards the mountains.

Soon there were roadside stalls selling a variety of fruit and vegetables, and as they ascended, the ground undulated with acre upon acre in a patchwork of green pasture. It was a visual vista Sandrine found relaxing.

Not so relaxing were the events of last night. It was all too easy to reflect on the heaven of being in Michel's arms, savouring his taste, his touch, exulting in the sheer sensation of two lovers in perfect accord.

Even now, her body ached in places, and all it took was one glance, a vivid memory, and the heat began to simmer deep inside, flaring acutely until Michel became her total focus. Intense sexual chemistry, and ruinous to her peace of mind.

It brought a lump to her throat for a few long seconds and made swallowing difficult.

Dear heaven, think of something else! There, in the

paddocks, were cattle, and overhead a helicopter swung east. On a rescue mission, perhaps?

The car braked suddenly and an arm shot out in front of her, providing a barrier as she was flung forward against her seat belt simultaneously with Michel's muffled oath.

'What on earth?' Sandrine queried in startled surprise as the car came to a screeching halt, only to see the answer for herself as a small dog streaked from the road into the opposite paddock.

'Idiot animal. It could have been killed,' Michel muttered angrily as he directed her an encompassing glance. 'Okay?' She nodded wordlessly, and his gaze sharpened. 'Sure?'

He caught hold of her chin between thumb and forefinger and turned her head towards him, subjecting her to a sweeping appraisal.

'Yes.' It would never do for him to guess her shaken composure was due to *him*, and not the near accident.

She lifted a hand to her throat to hide the fast-beating pulse thudding in the hollow there, and she breathed a silent sigh of relief when he released her and turned his attention back to the road.

It was almost midday when they reached Montville, and Sandrine was captivated by the quaint buildings, the cafés and tearooms, the abundance of craft shops.

Together they browsed in a few of the shops, and she selected a few gifts for her step-siblings, then they enjoyed a delicious lunch in a café overlooking the valley before heading back to the Gold Coast.

It had been a pleasant break, and she said so as they entered the Sanctuary Cove villa just after six.

'All of it?' Michel drawled with a distinctly wicked smile.

'Most of it,' Sandrine qualified, and heard his faint laugh.

'Let's change and eat out.'

'I could make something,' she prevaricated, mentally assessing the contents of the refrigerator. It held steak, sufficient greens to make a salad, and fresh fruit.

'I'll book a table at the Hyatt,' Michel determined firmly.

'I have lines to study,' Sandrine warned as he placed the heel of his hand at the back of her waist and propelled her towards the stairs.

'We'll be home by nine. You can curl up in a chair and go through them then.'

Sandrine chose a casually elegant cream pant suit, dressed it up with gold, stiletto-heeled sandals, then fixed a long, matching cream fringed scarf at her neck so that half its length trailed down her back.

The Hyatt was well patronised, and the maître d' escorted them to a table close to a window with a pleasant view out over the river.

Michel ordered wine, then they selected their starter and main course, but deferred dessert.

Sandrine was enjoying her prawn starter when she heard a familiar light voice exude an affectionate greeting, and there was Cait Lynden, a veritable feminine siren dressed in black, looking like a model who'd just stepped out of *Vogue*, hair and make-up the picture of perfection. With Gregor at her side.

'*Darling*,' Cait effused, proffering an air kiss to one cheek. 'Fancy seeing you here.'

Sandrine spared Gregor a quick glance, glimpsed the slight roll of his eyes and deduced that Cait was on a mission. A mission named 'snaring Michel'.

'The long arm of coincidence,' Sandrine agreed, and sent Michel a mocking glance beneath partly veiled eyelashes.

'You won't mind if we join you?' Cait slipped into a chair without waiting for an answer.

Oh, *great*. This held the promise of turning into quite an evening.

'I'll order another bottle of wine,' Gregor insisted as the wine steward and the waiter hovered attentively while Cait and Gregor perused the menu and gave their order.

Cait turned towards Sandrine. 'Are you not feeling well, darling?' False concern coloured her voice, and Sandrine silently applauded Cait's acting ability. 'You look a little pale.'

Sandrine summoned a sweet smile. 'Do you think so?'

'Gregor is hosting a party Saturday night. You must both come.'

'Unfortunately we'll be in Sydney,' Michel drawled, and lifted his glass to take an appreciative sip.

Really? Sandrine queried silently. She certainly intended to visit her family there, but she hadn't given a thought to whether Michel would join her.

Cait hid her disappointment well. 'What a shame.'

The waiter removed their plates and returned in minutes with Cait's and Gregor's starters.

'It should be an interesting shoot tomorrow.' Sandrine could almost sense Cait's sharpening figurative claws as she sought to scratch. 'Sandrine has this intimate scene.' She paused, then went for the kill. 'Knowing she's with other men must be difficult for you to handle.'

'I don't have a problem with it.' Michel's smile was deadly, his voice dangerously soft. 'Considering I'm the one who gets to take her to bed.'

Sandrine watched with fascination as Cait fluttered her lashes. 'I adore a proprietorial male.'

'Really, darling?' Gregor interposed. 'You surprise me. I had you pegged as calling the shots in a relationship.'

If looks could kill, Gregor would be dead and Cait would be up on a murder charge, Sandrine mused.

Well versed in the subtle games some women felt compelled to play, on one level she found Cait's behaviour amusing. On another, she wanted to scratch her eyes out! Jealousy, she reflected wryly, was not an enviable trait.

She spared Michel a quick glance and caught the faint gleam evident in those grey eyes. Was she that transparent? He had acquired the ability to read her mind with remarkable accuracy almost from the beginning, whereas his was mostly a closed book. As a poker player, he would be superb.

The waiter appeared with Cait's and Gregor's main dishes, and Sandrine concentrated on doing her salmon justice.

'How long will you stay in Sydney?'

Sandrine had to hand it to Cait…she was persistent. 'I'm—' not sure, she was going to add, except Michel intercepted.

'Until the film wraps up and the publicity is done.'

'And afterwards?' Cait persisted with light coquetry.

Michel proffered a polite smile. 'New York. Then Paris.' He turned towards Sandrine, caught hold of her hand and lifted it to his lips.

Careful, Sandrine silently warned. This is definitely overkill.

Except there was nothing she could do to still the tide of warmth sweeping through her body. It was as if his slightest touch activated a switch, leaving her with little or no control over her emotions. Something she found difficult to bear, given the state of their relationship.

'French is such a romantic language,' Cait said with an envious sigh. 'To have a lover so lost to passion in my arms he lapses into his native tongue…it drives me wild.'

'There have been so many,' Gregor drawled. 'One imagines you must be multilingual.'

'Beast.'

'Just telling the truth as I know it, darling.'

Cait transferred her attention to Sandrine. 'I've auditioned for the lead in a new Lucas film. I think I'll get it.' She smoothed a hand over her hair. 'Do you have anything in mind?'

Sandrine replaced her cutlery and sipped the contents of her glass. 'Congratulations.'

'You didn't answer my question.'

She was conscious of Michel's intent interest in her response and deliberated for several seconds. 'I don't have any immediate plans.'

'Coffee, *chérie*?' Michel queried smoothly, and he summoned the waiter as she shook her head. 'You'll excuse us if we leave.' He made it a statement. 'I need to check some computer data, and Sandrine has to study her lines.' He signed the credit slip, then rose to his feet. 'Good night.'

They reached the main entrance and within minutes the concierge had summoned their car. Sandrine slid into the passenger seat and laid her head against the cushioned rest.

'No comment?'

She turned her head slightly as Michel eased the car onto the bricked roadway and negotiated the roundabout. 'None whatsoever,' she offered wryly, and heard his low, husky laugh.

Within minutes Michel activated the security gate leading to the waterfront villas, and in no time at all he drew the car to a halt inside the garage.

'Where would you prefer to study?' he asked as they entered the lounge.

'Here.' She wanted to kick off her shoes and curl up in one of the cushioned chairs.

'I'll set my laptop up on the dining-room table.' He shrugged off his jacket and hooked it over one shoulder. 'Will you make coffee, or shall I?'

'You,' she delegated. 'I'm going upstairs to change.'

Michel was still bent over the laptop when she re-entered the bedroom a few minutes before midnight, and she fell asleep within minutes of her head hitting the pillow.

She didn't hear him slip into bed beside her, nor was she aware of his arm drawing her close.

CHAPTER SIX

SANDRINE breathed a sigh of relief. Seven takes wasn't bad. The scene had come together, no one had fluffed their lines, and the electric intensity had been achieved at a level even Tony could applaud.

She was tired, hot, and the boned corselet pulling her waist into an impossibly small measurement was killing her. The heavy make-up felt as if it was a mask of greasepaint about to slide off her face, and if she didn't get rid of the elaborately coiffed wig *soon*, she'd scream.

Added to which, it was late, and she was impossibly thirsty and hungry. The instant she discarded the heavy period costume, she intended to drink half a litre of water, follow it with a powdered protein drink, then sink her teeth into a fresh, crisp apple.

'You look fragile, darling,' Gregor murmured. 'Too many late nights catching up on time lost between the sheets?'

'Yes.' She was in no mood to participate in his game of verbal thrust and parry.

'Lucky you.'

She offered him a stunning smile. 'Aren't I just?'

'Our esteemed investor looks immensely *physical*. Tires you out, does he?'

'Wrong, Gregor,' she responded sweetly.

His eyes gleamed. 'Mmm, hidden talents, darling?'

She merely smiled and crossed to join the wardrobe assistant.

Twenty minutes later she felt considerably better, dressed in jeans and a T-shirt, her feet encased in heeled sandals, her hair twisted into a careless knot at her nape. All she had to do was check what time she had to report on the set the next day, then she was free to go home.

Seven was an improvement on the early hour of five, and she turned towards the exit, caught sight of Michel deep in conversation with a man whose tall frame seemed familiar.

Both men glanced up at the same time, and Sandrine's eyes widened in surprise at his identity. What on earth was Michel's elder brother doing here? She'd last seen Raoul Lanier three months ago in Paris. Then, he'd regarded her with warmth and affection.

Sandrine was aware of his veiled scrutiny as she crossed to where they stood.

'Finished for the day?' Michel queried.

'I was just checking tomorrow's filming schedule.' She turned towards the man at his side. 'Raoul,' she greeted evenly. 'How are you?'

'Well. And you?' he returned smoothly.

'Fine.' Such polite formality. Her smile was over-bright. 'When did you arrive?'

'This morning.'

Ask a direct question and she might get a direct answer. 'A social visit?'

'Not entirely.'

'Raoul is joining me in meetings with marketing,' Michel informed her in a voice that held a faint sardonic edge. 'Then he's due in Sydney to initiate negotiations on another matter.'

'Taking care of business,' Sandrine mocked lightly, aware of Raoul's level scrutiny.

'Yes.'

'I didn't ask Michel to inject finance to rescue the film.'

'I'm aware of that.'

'You mean to ensure he's not making a foolish investment.' It was a statement, not a query.

'Michel makes his own decisions.'

'Obviously.'

Raoul's gaze didn't falter. 'I understand you've reconciled?'

'We're working on it,' Michel drawled.

'And you, Sandrine,' Raoul posed. 'Are you working on your marriage to my brother?'

'Michel is sharing my villa, and my bed.' She'd wanted to shock him, but there wasn't a flicker of emotion evident on those chiselled features.

'That doesn't answer my question.'

'It's as much as you're going to get.' She turned on her heel and walked away. One Lanier brother was enough. Two was one too many!

Sandrine was halfway to Sanctuary Cove when her mobile phone rang, and she automatically engaged it.

'Raoul is meeting Stephanie Sommers, the film's

marketing representative, for dinner,' Michel informed her. 'He has invited us to join them.'

'No.'

'I'll be home in an hour.'

'*No*, Michel.' The stressed negative went unheard for he'd already ended the call.

She depressed the button and tossed the phone onto the passenger seat. Damn him. She cursed him again as she garaged the car and ran lightly upstairs.

An hour later she had showered, dressed, and was applying the finishing touches to her make-up when Michel walked into the bedroom.

He gave her a long, considered look, then quirked one eyebrow. 'Dressed to do battle?'

Black did things for her. It highlighted the texture of her skin, accented the burnished sheen of her sable-coloured hair and emphasised her luminous brown eyes.

Sandrine capped the mascara wand and tossed it into her make-up bag. 'You could say that.' She turned towards him. 'What time and where is this momentous dinner taking place?'

'At the Mirage Hotel, in an hour.'

She tossed a lipstick into her evening purse and snapped it shut. 'It'll take twenty minutes to reach Main Beach.' She slid the long chain strap over one shoulder and walked to the door. 'I'll be in the lounge catching the evening news.'

She descended the stairs and moved into the lounge, switched on the television and prowled the room, too restless to sit.

Mindful that she'd eaten very little all day, she filled a glass with water and drank it, then she splashed a small quantity of excellent Chardonnay into a crystal goblet.

It was half an hour before Michel entered the lounge, and the sight of him adorned in black evening suit, crisp white shirt and dark tie made the breath catch in her throat.

He possessed an exigent sexual chemistry that melted her bones. Dear heaven. How was it possible to want something so badly with your heart, yet conversely deny it with the dictates of your brain?

With a faintly mocking gesture she lifted the goblet in a silent salute, then raised it to her lips and took a small sip. 'This is solely for Stephanie's benefit.'

'The wine, or your attendance at dinner?'

A slow smile curved her generous mouth. 'Dinner. It isn't fair to pitch her alone among the wolves.'

'*Wolves*, Sandrine?' he queried with ill-concealed mockery. 'Isn't that a little extreme?'

'No.'

His voice held a certain dryness. 'I'm sure Stephanie can take care of herself.'

'Against Raoul? Are you kidding?'

It would be interesting to see how Stephanie reacted to the elder Lanier brother. A single mother raising a child alone had to have more than her share of courage and perspicacity.

'I'm sure you'll enjoy playing the role of her protector,' Michel mused as he crossed the room.

With one hand he extracted the goblet from her fingers and placed it on a nearby side table. At the same time he slid his other hand to cup her nape, drawing her close as his mouth fastened over her own in a kiss that tore at the restraints of his control.

He felt a slight tremor slither through her slim frame and he deepened the kiss to something that resembled possession.

It was several minutes before he slowly lessened the intensity, trailing the soft, swollen curve of her lower lip with a touch as light as a butterfly's wing.

'We'd better leave or we'll be late,' Michel murmured as he eased her to arm's length.

Sandrine stood motionless for a few seconds, her eyes wide in a face that was pale beneath its cosmetic enhancement. Then she extracted a lip pencil from her evening purse and crossed to the ornate mirror to effect repairs to a mouth devoid of colour.

Her fingers shook slightly, and she cursed beneath her breath at the level of emotional helplessness Michel was able to achieve.

When she was done, she replaced the lip pencil in her purse and preceded him through to the garage, slipping into the passenger seat as he slid in behind the wheel.

The Sheraton Mirage resort was built on a narrow peninsula, a luxury low-rise facing the ocean. It was renowned for its innovative design, extensive use of marble, an elegant waterfall and tranquil views out over a wide pool with its island bar to the ocean beyond.

Michel relinquished the car to the valet to park, and

Sandrine entered the magnificent foyer at his side. Raoul rose to his feet from one of the large cushioned sofas and moved forward to meet them. Of Stephanie there was no sign.

'Punctuality appears not to be Ms Sommers's forte,' Raoul indicated dryly. 'Shall we go into the lounge for a drink while we wait?'

'Maybe she's caught up in traffic.'

'Or the baby-sitter didn't show or the child was sick,' Raoul added with thinly veiled mockery.

So he'd had Stephanie investigated. Undoubtedly initiated before he left Paris as part of the Lanier modus operandi, Sandrine concluded cynically.

'I imagine if Stephanie is going to be delayed for any length of time, she'll call,' she felt impelled to defend.

At that moment a cell phone rang, and Raoul extracted a slim compact model from inside his dinner jacket. Two minutes and two curt words later, he cut the connection.

'It appears Ms Sommers has been held up with a flat tyre. She'll be another ten minutes.'

Stephanie entered the lounge one minute ahead of time, and Sandrine had to admire her cool unruffled demeanour as she crossed to where they sat.

'I must apologise. I hope there wasn't a problem holding the booking?' She glanced from one man to the other and offered Sandrine a warm smile. 'Shall we go in?'

Sandrine silently applauded Stephanie's style. The

young marketing executive had panache. What's more, she wasn't averse to taking control.

Something Michel would soon alter in his favour, Sandrine perceived as the maître d' seated them at their table and beckoned the drinks waiter. To whom Stephanie made it clear *she* was hostess.

Michel's features were inscrutable, while Raoul opted for chilling politeness.

Perusing the menu and selecting a starter and main required deliberation, and when their orders were placed Michel eased back in his chair and regarded the attractive strawberry blonde seated opposite with studied ease.

'Perhaps you'd care to relay your marketing strategy, Ms Sommers.' He paused a beat. 'For this film in particular.'

'Stephanie,' the marketing executive corrected with a faint smile. 'When we receive the finished film from the studio, it will be viewed in a private cinema by about thirty people. We'll then arrange meetings to discuss the target market and determine to what age group the film will have most appeal.'

Sandrine watched as Stephanie paused to lift her glass and take a measured sip of chilled water. Her hand was steady, her actions carefully controlled, and she displayed admirable poise as she replaced the glass and subjected both men to a level gaze.

'Further discussions will follow on which segments should be selected for the trailer, the shots to appear in press releases overseas and locally, and which of these will be released to the television stations and other media, including the entertainment pages in newspapers and magazines.'

'Worldwide?' Michel queried, and Stephanie inclined her head in silent acquiescence.

'Of course,' she confirmed. 'We'll also push to heighten public awareness of the film by organising a fashion shoot with one of the prestige fashion magazines to ensure coverage in the major national weekly magazines.'

'In which only the lead actors appear?' Raoul posed.

'Not always,' Stephanie qualified, and Sandrine successfully hid a faint smile at the other woman's ability to cover all the angles. 'We can arrange to include focused shots of local actors to draw their attention to their involvement in the film. Press shots of Michel and Sandrine at a social gala would draw public attention and highlight the film.'

'Sandrine's involvement in professional modelling would also be of interest, would it not?'

The waiter arrived with their starters, and there was a pause as the wine steward made a production of opening a bottle of wine, which he mistakenly proffered to Raoul for tasting.

Sandrine watched with interest as Raoul deferred the sampling to Stephanie and she could only admire her very skilled acceptance. For a moment she even thought she caught a glimpse of amusement in Raoul's gaze, only to decide it was her imagination.

'We organise press interviews in the star's hotel,' Stephanie elaborated, 'or if they've stipulated private leasing, we arrange a mutually agreeable venue for the interview.'

'Simultaneously?'

'In an intense push to raise public awareness.'

'Impressive,' Michel commented, and began on his starter.

'It's my job to impress.'

'Tell me,' Raoul interjected in a deceptive drawl. 'Don't you have family obligations that might interfere with total dedication to optimum marketing of this film?'

Sandrine wanted to kick his shin *hard* beneath the table. What game was he playing, for heaven's sake?

'I'm sure you're already aware I'm a single mother with a three-year-old daughter,' Stephanie responded smoothly. 'Should there be a crisis, I'd deal with it in the best way possible.' She fixed Raoul with a penetrating look. 'And my daughter would always take precedence.' Her chin lifted fractionally. 'Does that answer your question?'

Oh, my, Sandrine breathed. It was possible to cut the air with a knife!

'Yes.'

'Good.'

Michel cast his brother a brief, considering glance, then returned his attention to his starter.

'Were you able to get a baby-sitter for tonight without difficulty?' Sandrine posed conversationally.

'Given that I had very short notice, yes.'

'The Lanier brothers expect instant action in response to their slightest whim.' She was conscious of Michel's swift glance but ignored it.

'Really?' Stephanie's voice was dry. 'And you married one of them?'

'I thought it was a good idea at the time.'

'Total bewitchment, followed by a reality check?'

'Something like that,' Sandrine said with a wicked smile. She was beginning to enjoy herself!

'More wine, Ms Sommers?' Raoul queried silkily.

'Stephanie,' the marketing executive corrected with equal smoothness. 'And no, thank you. I get to drive home after this.'

'Pity.'

'For declining the wine?'

Sandrine watched as Raoul leant back in his chair. She seriously doubted any woman of his acquaintance had challenged him on any count.

'For endeavouring to treat this as other than a business meeting.'

'That's unfair,' Sandrine protested quickly.

'And unjustified,' Stephanie added, folding her napkin and placing it beside her plate. 'You insisted on meeting tonight.' She picked up her evening purse and focused her attention on Michel. 'I've already relayed our marketing strategy. Therefore my presence here is no longer necessary. Enjoy the rest of your meal.'

Sandrine watched the attractive blonde turn from the table and step quickly towards the main desk, pause briefly as she presented a credit card, then disappear through the door.

'A slight case of overkill, Raoul?' Michel mocked,

raising one eyebrow at his brother's narrowed gaze, then added thoughtfully, 'Are you going to let her get away?'

Raoul shifted his napkin onto the table and rose to his feet. 'No, I don't believe I am.'

'That was extremely—'

'Inappropriate,' Michel completed with dry cynicism.

'Yes, it was.'

'I hope he catches her.'

'Even if he does, I doubt it'll do him any good,' Sandrine opined, annoyed at Raoul's inexplicable behaviour and Michel's subsequent amusement.

'You don't think Raoul will be able to mend fences?' He lifted his glass and took an appreciative sip of the excellent wine.

'Not easily.'

His eyes gleamed with humour as they swept her expressive features. 'You don't think my brother would benefit from the love of a good woman?'

'Whatever happened to the reverse side of the coin?' Sandrine parried. 'Shouldn't a woman benefit from the love of a good man?'

'Of course.'

'It's unfortunate the Lanier men have their thinking locked into another century.'

Michel's gaze narrowed fractionally. 'Specifically?'

The waiter removed their plates and summoned the wine steward to replenish their glasses.

'You're amused by Raoul's reaction to Stephanie. What if it progressed into something serious?' She lifted a hand in an expressive gesture. 'Do you imagine Raoul would countenance Stephanie's continuing with her career?'

He subjected her to an unwavering appraisal as he leant back in his chair with indolent ease. 'As you are determined to do?' he riposted with deceptive mildness.

'You don't get it, do you?'

'Get what, precisely?'

'It's not about a *career* as such.' She should have a script, dammit! She'd carefully thought out everything she wanted to say. Hell, she'd had enough time! Where were all those fine words now? Out the window, along with her sanity.

She took a slow, calming breath. 'It's about seizing an opportunity and striving to achieve the best possible result. Not for fame and fortune, but to satisfy a creative need.' She waited a few seconds before adding, 'Because there's a depth, an inner feeling so in tune with the part that you feel *you* are meant to be the medium to convey the written words, actions and emotions on film for the audiences to appreciate the true depth of the character.'

Michel remained silent. The silence stretched into minutes as the waiter brought their main course and made a production out of flourishing a gigantic pepper-mill, explaining the intricacies of the chef's skill before bidding them *bon appétit* in appalling French.

Michel picked up his fork and speared an artistically carved carrot rosette. 'You didn't pause to consider that if you got the part, it would involve your being in Australia at a time when I was locked into important business meetings in Paris?'

'Do you know how many actresses auditioned for that part?' she demanded. 'My chances of succeeding were as hopeful as a snowflake surviving in hell.'

He was calm, his movements controlled, but she sensed leashed anger beneath the surface. 'Yet you did succeed,' he reminded her with deceptive mildness. 'You also signed a contract, confirmed flight arrangements and waited to tell me coincidentally two days prior to my being due in Paris.'

He pressed his fork into a baby potato, slid it into the small pool of hollandaise sauce and sampled it with evident enjoyment, then he lifted his head and his gaze pierced hers, steady and unblinking. 'You expected me to say, ''That's fine, darling. Call me. See you next month''?'

The nerves in her stomach tightened and curled into a painful knot. 'The timing was wrong. So was the film location.' She ran the tip of a fingernail along the hemmed edge of her napkin. 'I knew you'd protest, but I hoped you'd understand.'

'Enough to agree to your being apart from me for a considerable length of time?'

'It was only a few weeks.'

'At a time when I couldn't delegate in order to join you,' he reminded her. 'If you remember, we opted against an open relationship for the commitment and permanency of marriage, determining to arrange our lives so we could be together.'

'Are you implying I placed more importance on an acting part than *you*?'

'Deny your actions confirmed it.'

'You reacted as if I were a *possession*, someone who should be available whenever you happened to snap your fingers!' Sandrine accused, and saw his eyebrow lift in silent mockery. 'I wasn't referring to the bedroom!'

'I'm relieved to hear it,' Michel drawled.

'Am I interrupting something?'

Sandrine turned towards the owner of the faintly accented voice and summoned a wry smile. 'Only a current battle in the continuing war.'

Raoul slid into his seat. 'Want me to play mediator?'

'No,' she responded sweetly.

'Michel?'

'It'll keep.'

A devilish imp prompted the words that slipped easily from her tongue. 'We have a capricious airhead opposing a dictatorial tyrant.'

'A moment ago I was labelled possessive,' Michel relayed with marked cynicism, flicking his brother a dark glance. 'You caught up with Stephanie?'

'Yes.'

'I assume you offered an apology.'

'Which she refused to accept,' Raoul indicated dryly, and Sandrine proffered a musing grin.

'Verbally flayed you, did she?'

'You could say that.'

'So, when do you intend seeing her again?' Michel asked archly.

'Not at all, if she has anything to do with it.'

'Let me guess,' Sandrine posed. 'Tomorrow? On what grounds?'

Raoul lifted one eyebrow. 'Do I require any?'

No, of course he didn't, she dismissed. All he had to do was exert a measure of innate charm and women fell at his feet. Stephanie, she perceived, could prove to be an exception.

The waiter came with his main course and appeared affronted when Raoul dismissed his spiel before he even had the chance to begin with it.

'How long will it take to wrap up filming?' Raoul queried as he sliced into a succulent fillet of beef.

'I have another day scheduled. Maybe two at the most,' Sandrine told him. 'Tony is hopeful two weeks will do it.'

'I understand you have to remain on call for the possibility of retakes, publicity, promotion?'

'Yes.'

Raoul turned towards Michel. 'You intend remaining on the Coast?'

'Sydney,' Sandrine interjected. 'I have family there. If the studio calls me in, I can take the next flight out and be here the next day.'

'Aren't you forgetting something, *chérie*?' Michel queried silkily.

'You?' Her smile was a little too wide and too bright.

'So brave,' he mocked lightly.

Foolish, she amended silently, for thinking she could best him. Verbally, physically, or mentally.

'Dessert?'

'Coffee,' she said firmly, aware of the need to be decisive. 'Liqueur. Kahlua.'

Michel beckoned the waiter, conferred with Raoul, indicated their order, then requested the bill.

'The account has been settled, *m'sieur*.'

'I think you're mistaken.'

'No, *m'sieur*. The lady who was dining with you instructed the account be billed to her credit card.'

Sandrine hid a smile. Stephanie had managed to score on two counts. She'd walked out on Raoul Lanier and she'd added insult to injury by taking care of the bill.

'It appears Ms Sommers is a young woman to be reckoned with,' Michel commented dryly.

'Indeed.'

She detected mockery in Raoul's drawled response and was unable to suppress a grin. 'I'm with Stephanie.'

Both men sent her a level glance.

'Take her home,' Raoul instructed as he rose to his feet. 'And hush her mouth.'

Michel's eyes gleamed with humour. 'I intend to,' he said, suppressing a laugh.

Raoul accompanied them through the foyer to the main entrance and stood while the concierge summoned their car.

'Sweet dreams,' Sandrine teased as she bade Raoul goodnight, then slid into the passenger seat.

His expression was unreadable, and she gave a soft chuckle as Michel eased the car down to street level. Unless she was mistaken, Raoul had met his match, and she, for one, was going to enjoy watching the game!

CHAPTER SEVEN

SANDRINE focused her attention on the scene beyond the windscreen as the car entered the flow of north-bound traffic.

The night was clear, the air sharp, and the lighted windows of various high-rise apartment buildings vied with far distant stars in an indigo sky.

'Shall we continue where we left off?'

She cast Michel a steady glance, aware that the night's shadows were highlighting the angles and planes of his face.

Her voice assumed unaccustomed cynicism. 'It won't change the fact that we had a major fight over my decision to fulfil an acting contract.'

He smote a clenched fist against the steering wheel, and she looked at him in startled disbelief.

'*Mon Dieu*. This is not about you pursuing a career.' He paused at a roundabout, waiting for two cars to circle and exit. 'It's about us being together. Not me being forced to spend time in one city while you're on the other side of the world in another. *Comprends*?'

'It was unavoidable.'

'It need not have been if you'd enlightened me about the audition at the time,' Michel enunciated with restraint. 'Thus giving me the opportunity to implement a contingency plan.' He directed her a dark look that spoke volumes before returning his attention to the road. 'I won't allow it to happen again.'

She drew in a deep breath and released it slowly. 'Excuse me? You won't *allow* it?'

'No,' he reiterated hardily. 'In future there will be no misunderstandings, no assumptions. We communicate and leave nothing in doubt.'

'I'm not sure we have a future,' she countered wretchedly, and could have bitten her tongue for uttering the foolish words.

'Oh, yes, we do, *mignonne*.' His voice was deadly soft.

'How can you say that?'

'Easily.'

'What about unresolved issues?'

'Name them,' Michel challenged.

'*You*,' Sandrine began, crossing each of his sins off on her fingers. 'Keeping tabs on me, investigating everyone to do with the film, conspiring to come up with a financial rescue package and making *me* a condition. Blackmail,' she asserted finally, 'is a criminal offense.'

'You're the wife of a wealthy man whose access to a family fortune makes anyone associated with me a prime target. Ransom, extortion, kidnapping. Of course I had someone watch over you.'

'You could have told me! How do you think I'd have reacted if I saw someone following me?'

'You refused to take or answer any of my calls, remember?' he retorted. 'And I pay for the best. Not some amateur who'd frighten you by being visible.'

'What did he do?' she demanded, immeasurably

hurt. 'Report whom I spoke to, where I went, what I did…every minute of every day?'

'It wasn't about my lack of trust in you,' he bit out angrily. 'It was about protection. *Yours.*'

'It was an invasion of privacy. *Mine.*' She was on a roll and couldn't seem to stop. 'I hate you for it.'

'So hate me, *mignonne*. At least I knew you were safe.'

'I guess the film running overtime and over budget played right into your hands. It gave you a lever, a figurative gun to hold to my head. *Do what I say, or else.*' She directed him a fulminating glare. 'I'll never forgive you for that.'

'"Never" is a long time.'

'It's as long as my lifetime.'

'Tell me,' Michel drawled. 'What did you intend to do when filming was completed?'

'Visit my family.'

'And afterwards?'

That was in the hazy future and something she'd deliberately not given much thought.

'I don't know,' she admitted honestly, and grimaced at the husky oath that rent the air.

'*You don't know.*' He raised both hands off the wheel, then gripped it hard. 'Next you'll tell me you intended contacting me through a lawyer.'

'I suppose it was a possibility.'

'Not telephoned me? Or caught a flight home?'

'Where *is* home, Michel?' she queried wryly. 'You have a residential base in several cities. I'd have had to have your secretary check on your whereabouts at the time.'

'*Sacré bleu*. You have my personal cell phone number where you can reach me anywhere at any time!'

'Maybe I wouldn't have wanted to!'

'Did it not occur to you that I might have taken all that into consideration and put, as you so cynically called it, "a figurative gun" to your head?'

The car slowed almost to a halt, and Sandrine was startled to see Michel activate the security gate permitting access to the Sanctuary Cove residential suburb. Seconds later the gate slid open and they drove through.

'Believe me, I would have used any weapon I had.'

'Blackmail, Michel?'

'You wouldn't answer my calls. If I arrived on your doorstep, would you have let me in?'

'Probably not.' At least, not at first. Her initial instinct would have been to slam the door in his face. The next…call the police? No, she refuted silently. She wouldn't have gone that far.

Was he right insisting on an enforced reconciliation? Putting them in the same residence, giving her no choice in the matter?

Within minutes they reached the villa, and once inside she crossed to the stairs and made her way up to the main bedroom.

For weeks she'd been so angry with Michel, herself, the circumstances that had caused the dissent between them. Now there was a degree of self-doubt, a measure of regret…and pain.

In the bedroom she slipped off her shoes and crossed to the floor-to-ceiling window. She made no attempt to draw the drapes as she looked out across the bay to the brightly lit restaurant cantilevered over the water.

Within a few days she'd leave here and probably not return. Sydney beckoned, and family. Her mother would be pleased to see her, likewise her father. But on separate occasions at different venues. She'd visit, take gifts, greet each of her step-siblings, and pretend she belonged.

She closed her eyes and tried to ignore the loneliness deep inside. An ache behind her eyelids culminated in tears that escaped and slid slowly down each cheek.

A faint sound, a slight movement, alerted her to Michel's presence, and she prayed he wouldn't turn on the light.

Sandrine sensed rather than heard him cross to stand behind her, then his hands closed over her shoulders as he drew her back against him.

'We made a deal, remember?'

'What deal are you referring to?'

'Never to spend a night apart. Except in circumstances beyond our control.'

So they had. And somehow taking a bit part in a movie being shot on the other side of the world didn't come close in the qualifying stakes of circumstances beyond our control.

'Where do we go from here?' she queried quietly, and he didn't pretend to misunderstand.

'Let's just take it one day at a time, hmm?'

For several minutes he didn't move, then his hands slid down her arms and linked together at her waist. She felt his lips brush against her ear, then trail slowly down the sensitive cord of her neck to nuzzle the soft hollow there.

It was heaven to lean her head into the curve of his shoulder and just *be*. To absorb the warmth of that large pulsing body, to take comfort in the shelter it afforded her, and to luxuriate in the touch of his hands, his lips.

He didn't offer a word, nor did she. They didn't move, just stood there for what seemed an age.

Then Michel gently turned her to face him, and she lifted her arms to encircle his neck as he lowered his head down to hers.

His mouth explored the soft lower curve of her own, grazing it with the edge of his teeth before sweeping his tongue to test the delicate tissues and tease the sensitised ridges in an erotic tasting that made her want more than this gentle supplication.

He'd removed his jacket and tie, but his shirt was an impossible barrier she sought to remove. She needed to touch his skin, to feel the heavy pulse of his heart beneath his rib cage and to explore the very essence of him.

By tacit agreement, they divested each other's clothes in a leisurely, evocative fashion, the slither of silk over skin arousing and heightening the senses to fever pitch.

Now. She wanted him *now*. Hard and fast. She needed to feel his strength, his unfettered passion.

Her mouth met his hungrily as he tumbled her down onto the bed, and she was aware of uttering small sounds of encouragement as he explored her, then she groaned out loud with pleasure as he entered her in one long thrust, stilling for timeless seconds as she absorbed him.

He withdrew and she lifted her hips as he plunged deep inside. She clung to him, urging him harder, closer, until pleasurable sensation reached an almost unbearable intensity.

Sandrine cried out, beseeching him with a litany of pleas as she became helpless beneath an emotion so treacherous it almost succeeded in destroying her.

Afterwards she could only lie there and attempt to regain control of her ragged breathing. And her sanity.

His eyes never left hers, and she felt as if she were drowning as he traced a finger over the soft curve of her mouth, probing the inner skin with erotic sensitivity.

Not content, he trailed a path down the length of her throat, then lowered his head to her mouth to create fresh havoc with her senses as he kissed her, thoroughly, mindlessly, then feathered his lips to the sensitive hollows beneath her throat, her breasts, savouring each peak in turn with devastating eroticism.

As he travelled lower, her body quivered, then tautened against an invasion so blatantly intimate she began to burn with the intoxicating heat of his touch.

After play merged into foreplay as passion reignited, and she was driven by a hunger so intense she became a willing wanton in his arms, taking intimate liberties that had him groaning beneath her as they both became lost in mesmeric rapture.

They took the late-morning flight out of Coolangatta airport, approaching the outskirts of Sydney just over an hour later.

The jet banked towards the ocean, providing a panoramic view of the harbour and city. Tall skyscrapers vied with elegant homes dotting numerous coves and inlets. Scenic landmarks such as the Sydney Harbour Bridge and the Opera House were distinctive from this height, and Sandrine felt the familiarity of home as they began their descent.

This was where she'd been born, raised and educated. Her family, her friends were here. For a while she could relax, visit family, meet friends and indulge a penchant for shopping.

The benefit of travelling first class was the speed of disembarking, and in no time at all Michel had collected their bags from the luggage carousel and organised a taxi.

It was a bright sunny day, with hardly a cloud in the sky. In some ways it seemed an age since she'd left Sydney; in others it was as if it were only yesterday.

Nothing had changed, she noted as the taxi took the customary route from the airport. Industrial areas gave way to semi-industrial, then residential. The terrace houses looked the same, although a few had received a fresh coat of paint. Traffic hurtled along the busy road at maximum speed, accompanied by the hydraulic hiss of heavily laden trucks, the occasional squeal of hastily applied brakes as a driver attempted a risky switch of lanes and miscalculated.

A turn-off led towards wide, tree-leafed roads, older-style homes, most lovingly restored and some still standing in palatial grounds.

Double Bay housed an eclectic mix of homes and apartment buildings. It was an inner suburb where old-money status sat next to new, where Porsches, Bentleys and BMWs parked nose to tail with Ferraris, Audis and Rolls-Royces. It housed one of the city's most exclusive shopping centres where trendy cafés nestled between designer boutiques, classy restaurants and a ritzy hotel.

Michel's apartment was situated atop a three-level, spacious old home that had been gutted and architecturally designed to resemble the original homestead. Pale lemon stucco with a white trim and black-painted, iron-lace railings provided a gracious exterior. Each floor housed a separate apartment, reached by a lift instead of the original staircase, and modern materials had been crafted to resemble the old, thereby retaining a sense of timeless grandeur that was complemented by exquisite antique furniture.

Sandrine had fallen in love with it at first sight, and now she crossed the spacious lounge to wide glass doors guarding the entrance to a long veranda that offered panoramic views over Port Jackson Harbour.

'Penny for them,' Michel teased with measured indolence as he joined her. He linked his arms around her waist and drew her back against him.

'Nothing in particular,' she said reflectively. 'Just a feeling of satisfaction at being home again.'

'You'll want to ring your family and make arrangements to meet them.'

'Yes,' she agreed. But not collectively. There was definitely a *yours* and *mine* definition apparent, and she'd learnt from an early age not to shift the line between the two!

'Lunch or dinner, whatever suits,' Michel offered. 'As long as I can put in a few hours on the laptop each day.'

She watched a ferry glide across the harbour and glimpsed a freighter on the horizon. 'You want to work this afternoon?'

'Unless you have a better idea.'

The temptation to tease him was irresistible. 'Well, it's ages since I had a manicure, my hair could do with a trim, and I need to replenish some make-up.'

'I work, you shop,' he quipped with a musing drawl.

'Are you sure you don't mind?'

His hands slipped up to cover her breasts, the touch light, tantalising, and she caught her breath at the sensual promise evident as his lips settled in the sensitive curve of her neck.

'Go, *chérie*. Be back by six, and we'll eat out.'

Unpacking could wait until later, and with a light laugh she slipped from his arms, caught up her shoulder-bag, then blew him a cheeky kiss before heading for the front door.

Sandrine enjoyed a wonderful few hours. The manicure proved to be no problem, and the hair salon readily fitted her in between appointments. Tempted by a trendy café, she ordered a cappuccino, a salad and sandwich, then she browsed among several boutiques lining a narrow street of converted old-fashioned cottages.

An arcade in the Ritz-Carlton Hotel housed several exclusive shops, and in one she discovered a perfect pair of shoes.

It was almost six when the taxi pulled into the kerb adjacent to the apartment, and she cleared security, then rode the lift to the top floor.

Michel was seated at an antique desk in one corner of the lounge, and he glanced up from the laptop as she entered the room. He'd changed out of his suit and wore dark chinos and an ivory chambray shirt.

He caught sight of the brightly coloured carry bags, glimpsed the beautifully styled hair and offered her a warm smile as he closed down the computer.

Sandrine deposited the bags on a nearby chair. 'I bought shoes.' She wrinkled her nose at him. 'Very expensive shoes.'

A husky laugh escaped his throat as he crossed to her side. 'Hmm, new perfume?'

'You noticed.'

'I notice everything about you.'

Just as she'd developed a keen sixth sense about him. The clean male smell of his soap and cologne, freshly laundered clothes and a masculine scent that was his alone.

'What time did you book the restaurant?'

'Seven.'

'Then I'd better go unpack, shower and dress.'

He slid a hand beneath her hair and cupped her nape as he lowered his head down to hers. The kiss held passion and promise, and she felt vaguely regretful as he let her go.

It was a warm summer's evening, and she selected black silk evening trousers, a jewelled singlet top, then added a sheer black evening blouse. Stiletto-heeled pumps, a matching jewelled evening bag completed the outfit. Make-up was understated, with emphasis on her eyes.

Michel had chosen a restaurant specialising in sea-food, and they each selected a prawn starter and ordered grilled fish to follow. The wine steward presented a bottle of Dom Pérignon champagne.

'Did you get in touch with your parents?'

She felt guilty that she hadn't. 'I'll ring them both in the morning.'

He lifted his flute and placed the rim against her own. '*Salut.*'

Their starter arrived, and she bit into a succulent prawn and savoured the taste. Heaven. The sauce was perfect.

'With both you and Raoul in Australia, who is minding—'

'The store?'

'Figuratively speaking.'

'Henri heads a very capable team in our absence.'

'When is Raoul returning to Paris?'

His smile held a faint wryness. 'Twenty questions, Sandrine?'

She gave a slight shrug. 'Curiosity, I guess.'

'His plans are less flexible than mine.'

'And you, Michel?' she queried fearlessly. 'How long will you stay in Australia?'

His gaze was direct, unwavering. 'As long as it takes.'

She didn't pretend to misunderstand. Something curled inside her stomach and tightened into a painful ball. 'I might be called back to the Gold Coast studios to reshoot a scene. Then there's the publicity promotion…'

'I've been working, myself, every day since I arrived in Australia.'

The laptop. In this electronic age it was possible to access and transmit data at the touch of a button.

'It isn't necessary for—'

'Yes,' Michel interrupted. 'It is.'

The waiter removed their plates, and the wine steward refilled their flutes with champagne.

'Michel…' She trailed to a halt, and although her eyes searched his, she was unable to gain much from his expression.

'We promised to take each day as it comes, remember?'

Yes, so they had. But with every day that passed she realised how hard it would be to have to live without him. And she knew she didn't want to. It should be so simple to mend an emotional bridge. You just said the words, and everything was fixed.

Except they had to be the right words, and it had to be the right time and the right place.

When they made love, she freely gave him her body, her soul, and prayed he knew what he meant to her. But she was a wordless lover, and ''I love you'' hadn't passed her lips since the night before she left New York.

The waiter presented their main dish, and Sandrine looked at the succulent barramundi, the artistically arranged salad and discovered her appetite had fled.

So, too, had her conversational skills. For how did

you talk banalities with someone you'd soon share sexual intimacy?

She had only to look at him, and in her mind she could feel the touch of his hands, his lips, *know* the reaction of her traitorous body as he led her towards sensual fulfilment. Just as she knew *he* was equally as aware.

It was akin to a silent game they played. Except there was no deliberation, no premeditation. Intense sensual chemistry sizzled between them, ready to ignite as easily as dry tinder at the toss of a lighted match.

It had always been the same. Had she confused sexual attraction with love? *And what is love?*

If you took away sexual desire, what was left? A solid friendship? She would have said yes, until he forbade her to take the movie role. A friend would have been pleased she'd auditioned successfully.

Still, although friendship was important in marriage, a legal union was about commitment, honesty and trust. Because if you love, you want to commit, and there needed to be trust and honesty for the union to succeed.

When it came to honesty, she'd shifted the boundaries, signed a contract without his knowledge and against his wishes, confronted him at the eleventh hour, taken the flight, the job, regardless.

At the time she'd been so angry over his inflexibility she hadn't really given anything else coherent thought. There was a part of her that cherished the sanctity of marriage. And her feelings for Michel weren't in question.

Yet she was an independent young woman. She'd

owned her own apartment, her own car; she had not one, but two great jobs she loved, and for the past seven years she'd been a free spirit, answerable only to herself.

Why had she imagined marriage to Michel wouldn't change that?

Be honest, a small voice taunted. *Love* was the prime moving force in this union. She'd been so caught up in the wonder and magic of it all that she hadn't focused too much on the future.

Carpe diem. Seize the day. And she had, only too willing to allow Michel to sweep her off her feet, exultant with joy at the thought of sharing her life with this man, and confident love would conquer all.

In a world where women had fought and won equality with men in the business arena, she'd taken it for granted she would combine her career with marriage. Michel hadn't objected to her participating in a few modelling assignments. Why should he object to her taking a part in a film?

Yet he had. Warning irrevocably that he didn't view marriage as two partners pursuing separate careers and leading separate lives.

'The fish isn't to your liking?'

Sandrine glanced up quickly. 'No. I mean, yes.' She gave a helpless shrug. 'I'm not that hungry.' She forked a mouthful of salad, alternated it with the succulent fish, then took another sip of champagne in the hope it would renew her appetite.

'I've managed to get tickets for *Les Misérables*,' Michel remarked, and she offered him a smile.

'That's great.' She'd seen two different productions and loved both. 'When?'

'Tomorrow night.'

There was also a popular movie she wanted to see, and she mentioned it. 'Perhaps we could ask Angelina to join us?' she posed, aware how much pleasure it would give her stepsister. In which case she'd have to even things out by issuing a similar invitation to her stepbrother.

'Of course. But first, ascertain which night suits your mother and your father for dinner. As our guests.'

Step-family politics, she mused, required delicate handling.

It was almost ten when they left the restaurant, and within minutes Michel hailed a taxi to take them home.

Sandrine felt pleasantly tired as they entered the apartment, and she slid off her shoes and hooked the sling-back straps over one finger.

'Coffee?'

'I'll make it,' Michel offered as he shrugged out of his jacket. 'I need to go on-line and check some data.'

'Okay.' She tried to stem a feeling of disappointment. A part of her wanted to curl up in his arms and enjoy a leisurely lovemaking. Maybe she wouldn't be asleep when he came to bed, or if she was, he'd wake her. 'I'll go to bed and read.'

Except she only managed one chapter before the book slipped from her fingers and hit the carpeted floor, and she didn't stir when Michel slid quietly in beside her two hours later.

CHAPTER EIGHT

SANDRINE took the cordless phone into the bedroom after breakfast and rang her mother, had the call diverted to a mobile number and interrupted Chantal at the manicurist.

'Dinner, darling? Love to. How long are you in town?'

'A week, at least.'

'The weekend is out. Thursday?'

'Thursday's fine,' she agreed.

'Cristal. Seven o'clock? We'll meet you there.'

Her father was in a business meeting, but Lucas took the call, his conversation equally as brief as that of her mother.

'Friday,' Sandrine wrote in her diary planner.

That left Angelina and Ivan, step-siblings and arch-rivals for her attention. They were both in school and couldn't be contacted until late afternoon.

There were a few close friends she wanted to communicate with and she spent the next hour glued to the phone.

Michel was seated at the desk in the lounge when she emerged. The laptop was open, and he was speaking rapid French into his cell phone.

Sandrine wandered into the kitchen, poured herself

some fresh orange juice, then sat down at the dining-room table and leafed through the daily newspaper.

'What do you want to do with the day?' Michel queried when he finished his call.

'Me as in *me*?' she posed with a faint smile. 'Or me as in *you and me*?'

'You and me,' he drawled, reaching across to catch hold of her chin.

'Too much togetherness might not be wise.'

'You have me at your mercy. Choose.'

She pretended to consider as she ticked off each option on her fingers. 'The beach, a movie, shopping, wander around Darling Harbour, the Rocks, visit the Chinese Gardens, visit a few art galleries, the museum. Hmm,' she deliberated, then added without changing her voice, 'Or I could tie you to the bed and have my wicked way with you.' She sent him a stunning smile. 'Darling Harbour, I think. I'll go get changed.'

He tilted her chin and settled his mouth on hers in an all-too-brief evocative kiss. 'I'll take a raincheck.'

'On Darling Harbour?'

His eyes gleamed with latent humour. 'The bed.'

She slipped from his grasp. 'You did say I get to choose.'

It was a lovely day, with just enough of a breeze to take the edge off the summer's heat. Together they strolled along the boardwalk stretching the length of the Darling Harbour complex, enjoyed an excellent lunch at a waterfront restaurant, then browsed through the shops and crossed the pedestrian bridge. On impulse they took in a two-hour harbour cruise, then caught the monorail into the city.

It was almost six when they re-entered the apartment, and after a quick shower they each changed into elegant evening wear and took a taxi into the city.

There wasn't time for a leisurely meal, so they skipped the starter, settled for the main and forewent coffee in order to take their seats in time for the first act of *Les Misérables*.

It was a magnificent production, and Sandrine was lavish with her praise as they emerged into the foyer after the final act.

They chose a trendy café in which to have coffee, then hailed a taxi to the apartment.

Michel curved an arm round her waist as they stepped into the lift, and Sandrine rested her head against his shoulder. It had been a pleasant day, followed by a lovely evening, and she told him so.

'Thank you,' she added simply as they entered the lounge.

'For what, *chérie*? Spending a day with my wife?'

'For taking the time.'

He pulled her into his arms and kissed her, gently at first, then with increasing passion as she lifted her arms and wrapped them round his neck.

It was a while before he released her, and she stood there, his arms linked loosely around her hips. 'You're not going to check the laptop for messages?'

'There's nothing that can't wait until morning.'

She crossed to the wide hallway and made her way to the main bedroom, where she removed her shoes, the slim-fitting black gown and the beautifully crafted sequined jacket, then she reached to take the pins from her hair and encountered Michel's hand in the process of undoing the elegant French pleat.

When he was done, she helped him remove his jacket, the dress shirt, then the trousers. His eyes held hers as he slipped out of his shoes and peeled off his socks.

All that remained between him and total nudity was a pair of black hipster briefs, and she let her hand slide over his chest, teasing one male nipple, then the other, before skimming her fingers down to his waist.

She didn't tie him to the bed, but she did tease and tantalise him in a wicked exploration that tested the limit of his control. With her lips, the soft feather-light stroke of her fingers, the brush of her skin against his.

Sandrine lost track of time as she played the role of seductress, and just as he reached for her, she sank onto him and took his length in one exultant movement that shattered both of them.

What followed became a sweet, savage lovemaking that broke through the barriers of ecstasy and took them to a place where sensation ruled the mind, body and soul.

They went to sleep in each other's arms, and the last thing Sandrine remembered was the touch of Michel's lips against her temple, the deep, heavy tempo of his heart as it beat strongly in his chest.

Dinner with her mother, stepfather and Angelina carried undertones she was loath to pin down. Chantal

was so incredibly vivacious it hurt, Roberto overdid
the charm, and Angelina barely touched her food.
Consequently the evening became something of a
strain.

A call to her mother the next day brought an assurance Sandrine didn't buy for a second. It would do no
good to question her father, and she didn't even bring
up Chantal's name during dinner the following evening.

A shopping expedition on Saturday with Angelina
brought forth a confidence that settled the question.

'Mum and Dad are getting a divorce,' Angelina
blurted out as they shared lunch.

Sandrine experienced a gamut of emotions but managed to school most of them as she took in her stepsister's pinched features and lacklustre expression.
'How do you feel about it?' she queried gently.

'I hate it.'

I'm not that rapt, either, she echoed silently.
Roberto may not be the ideal husband, but he was a
caring father.

'She's seeing someone else,' Angelina informed her
morosely.

'*She's* the cat's mother,' Sandrine corrected absently.

'*Mother*,' her stepsister declared with mocking emphasis, 'has a toy boy. I doubt he's thirty.'

Hell, that put a slightly different complexion on
things. 'Maybe she's just—'

'Using him for sex?'

'Taking time out,' she continued, and wondered
why she was trying to play down Chantal's behaviour

to a sixteen-year-old who was more au fait with the situation.

'He drives a Ferrari, has oodles of money and looks like he stepped out of *GQ* wearing a Versace suit.'

Some contrast, when Roberto was on the wrong side of fifty, three stone overweight and losing his hair.

'And you hate him,' she deduced, and saw the younger girl work herself into a hissy fit.

'I hate *her*. What does she think she's *doing*? Dad practically lives at work, and I may as well not have sat my exams, the marks were so bad.'

Sandrine finished her *latte*. 'How long has this been going on?'

'Six months.'

'Okay.' She rose to her feet. 'Let's go.'

'Let's go? *That's it*?'

'Shopping.' She cast Angelina a purposeful smile. 'When the going gets tough, women go shopping.' She made a beckoning gesture. 'On your feet, girl. I'm about to indulge your wildest fantasy.'

Her stepsister's face was a study in conflicting emotions. 'You are?'

'Indeed.'

Sandrine was as good as her word, and when she had the taxi drop Angelina home early that evening, her stepsister was weighed down with a wide assortment of emblazoned carry bags.

'Thanks, Sandrine.' Angelina planted a kiss on her cheek before sliding out from the taxi. 'You're the best.'

No, Sandrine silently denied as the taxi swung back

into the flow of traffic. I merely trod the same path when Chantal and *my* father broke up, and I'd have given anything to have someone understand my pain.

She'd rung Michel from her cell phone to say she'd be late, and it was almost seven when she entered the apartment.

Michel met her at the door, saw her apparent tenseness and immediately cancelled plans he'd made for the evening. Instead, he brushed his lips across her forehead, then pushed her lightly in the direction of their bedroom.

'Go change, and I'll order in.'

Sandrine shot him a grateful glance. 'Pizza?'

'Okay.'

She kept walking, and in the bedroom she went into the en suite, took a leisurely shower, then she slipped on a short silk robe and pinned up her hair.

Michel sat sprawled on one of several sofas in the lounge, and he patted the seat beside him as she crossed the room. 'Come here.'

It would be heaven to receive some comfort, and she slid down onto the seat and curled her feet beneath her as he pulled her into the curve of his body.

'Want to tell me what's bothering you?'

Was she that transparent? Or was it because this man was so attuned to her that very little escaped him?

She told him briefly, wondering how anyone who hadn't shared a similar experience could possibly understand the breakdown of the family unit.

'You're concerned for Angelina.'

'The emotional upheaval has a far-reaching effect,'

Sandrine said slowly. 'It made me very aware of my own survival. I became very independent and self-contained. I guess I built up a protective shell.'

Yes, Michel agreed silently. She had at that, removing it for him, only to raise the barrier again at the first sign of discord. Self-survival... He was no stranger to it himself.

The intercom buzzed, and Michel answered it, releasing security for the pizza-delivery guy, and afterwards they bit into succulent segments covered with anchovies, olives, capsicum, mushrooms and cheese, washing them down with an excellent red wine while watching a romantic comedy on video.

The days that followed held a similar pattern. Michel divided the first half of each day to business via his laptop and cell phone, while Sandrine caught up with friends over coffee. Most evenings they dined out, took in a show or visited the cinema.

Sandrine's stepbrother, Ivan, chose the premiere screening of the latest *Star Wars* episode, and they indulged his preference for burgers and Coke.

Pinning down Chantal for a mother-and-daughter chat proved the most difficult to organise, with two lunch postponements. Third time lucky, Sandrine hoped as she ordered another mineral water from the waitress and half expected a call on her cell phone announcing Chantal's delay.

Fifteen minutes later Chantal slid into the chair opposite with a murmured apology about the difficulty of city parking and an express order for champagne.

'Celebrating, Chantal?' She hadn't called Chantal *Mother* since her early teens.

'You could say that, darling.'

'A new life?'

'Angelina told you,' Chantal said without concern, and Sandrine inclined her head.

'The news disturbed me.'

'It's my life to lead as I choose.'

'With a man several years younger than yourself?'

Chantal gave the waitress her order, then she leant back in her chair and took a long sip of champagne. 'I thought I was meeting my elder daughter for a chat over lunch.'

'I think I deserve some answers.'

'Why? It doesn't affect you in any way.'

That stung. 'It affects Angelina.' Just as your break-up with Lucas affected me.

'She'll get over it,' Chantal said carelessly. 'You did.'

Yes, but at what cost? It had succeeded in instilling such a degree of self-sufficiency that she thought only of herself, her needs and wants. And such a level of self-containment had almost cost her her marriage.

A slight shiver shook her slim frame. She didn't want to be like Chantal, moving from one man to another when she was no longer able to live life on her own terms. That wasn't love. It was self-absorption at its most dangerous level.

'This new man is—how old? Thirty?'

'Thirty-two.'

'Which means when you're sixty, he'll only be forty-four.'

'Don't go down that path, Sandrine,' Chantal warned.

'Why? Because you refuse to think that far ahead?'

'Because I only care about *now*.'

I don't, she noted with silent certainty. I care enough about the future to want to take care of every day that leads towards it. And I care about Michel enough to *want* a future with him. Desperately.

It was as if everything fell into place. And because it did, she chose not to pursue Chantal's indiscretions. Instead, she asked a string of the meaningless questions Chantal excelled in answering as they ate a starter and a main, then lingered over coffee.

They left the restaurant at three, promising to be in touch *soon*, and Sandrine took a page out of her own advice to Angelina. She went shopping. Nothing extravagant. A silk tie for Michel, despite the fact he owned sufficient in number to be able to wear a different one each day for several months. But she liked it and paid for it with a credit card linked to her own account and not the prestigious platinum card Michel had given her following their wedding.

'For you,' she said, presenting it to him within minutes of entering the apartment.

'*Merci, chérie.*'

'It's nothing much.'

His smile held a warmth that sent the blood coursing through her veins. 'The thought, *mignonne*, has more value than the gift itself.'

He pulled her into his arms and kissed her with such slow eroticism she almost groaned out loud when he released her.

'A call came through this afternoon. Tony wants you back on the set to reshoot a scene.'

Damn. Having to reshoot was something she'd been hoping to avoid. 'When?'

'Tomorrow. I've booked an early flight and accommodation at the Sanctuary Cove Hyatt.'

For the next few days the pace would be frenetic, she perceived. After the film wrapped, the publicity promotion would follow.

'Go change,' Michel bade her. 'We'll eat out, then get an early night.'

They chose an intimate French restaurant that served exquisite nouvelle cuisine, then afterwards they strolled along the street, pausing now and then to admire a shop window display. Michel threaded his fingers through her own, and with daylight-saving providing a late-evening dusk, the magic of pavement cafés and ornamental street lighting provided an illusory ambience.

Darkness fell, breaking the spell, and Michel hailed a cruising taxi to take them home.

CHAPTER NINE

IT HAD been a fraught day, Sandrine reflected as she garaged the car. Her final scene had to be shot again and again, and instead of being able to leave the set around midday, it was now almost seven.

She was tired, she had a headache, she was past hungry, and all she wanted to do was sink into a hot spa bath, slip on headphones and let the pulsing jets and music soothe her soul. For an hour.

Heaven, she breathed, entering the villa.

'I was just about to embark on a rescue mission,' Michel drawled as he strolled towards her. He took in her pale features, darkened eyes, the slight droop of her shoulders, and withheld an imprecation. 'Bad day?' he queried lightly. His hands curved over her shoulders as he drew her close. His mouth touched hers, lightly, briefly, and emotion stirred as she turned her face into the curve of his neck.

'Tony insisted the scene be shot so many times. I lost count after fifteen.' He smelt so good, *felt* so good, she could have stayed resting against him for ages. After a few timeless minutes she lifted her head and moved out of his arms. 'I'm going to soak in the tub.'

Warm water, scented oil, an Andrea Bocelli CD on the Walkman. Sandrine closed her eyes and let the tension gradually seep out of her bones.

She didn't hear Michel enter the bathroom, nor did she see him step into the tub, and the first indication she had was the light brush of fingers down her cheek.

Her eyelids flew wide and her mouth parted in unvoiced surprise as Michel positioned her in front of him.

She lifted a hand to remove the headphones only to have his hand close over hers holding them in place, then both hands settled on her shoulders and his fingers bit deep in a skilful massage that went a long way to easing the knots and kinks out of tense muscles.

She sighed blissfully as Michel handed her a flute of champagne, and she took a generous sip of the light golden liquid.

A slow warmth crept through her body, and with each subsequent sip she began to relax. Even her head felt light. Probably, she decided hazily, because she hadn't eaten a thing since lunch.

Sandrine had no idea how long she stayed in the gently pulsating water. It seemed ages, and she uttered a mild protest when the jets were turned off.

Michel lifted her from the tub, then caught up a large fluffy towel and dried the excess moisture from her body.

'You didn't have any champagne,' she murmured as he swept her into his arms and carried her into the bedroom.

'How do you feel?'

'Relaxed.'

He switched on the bedside lamp, hauled back the

bed covers and deposited her onto the sheeted mattress, then joined her.

All she wanted to do was curl into his arms, rest her head against his chest and absorb the strength and comfort he could offer her.

She felt his lips brush her own and she whispered his name in a semiprotest.

'Just close your eyes,' he bade huskily, 'and I'll do all the work.' His mouth grazed the edge of her jaw, then slipped down the slope of her throat.

What followed was a supplication of the senses as he embraced her scented skin with a touch as light as a butterfly's wing. With his lips, the pads of his fingers, he trailed a path from one sensory pleasure spot to another, lingering, savouring, until the warmth invading her body changed to slow-burning heat.

He lifted her hand and kissed each finger in turn, stroking the tip with his tongue, then when he was done he buried his mouth in her palm.

It was an evocative gesture that brought her response, only to have her touch denied as he completed a sensual feast that drove her wild.

He entered her slowly, and she groaned out loud as he initiated a long, sweet loving that was exquisite, magical. It left her weak-limbed and filled with languorous warmth.

Afterwards he folded her close into the curve of his body and held her as she slept. Her hair, loosened from its confining pins, spilled a river of silk over his pillow.

Michel waited a while, then carefully eased out of

bed, showered, dressed in jeans and a cotton shirt, then went downstairs to the kitchen and began organising the evening meal. He'd give her an hour, then wake her.

When he returned to the bedroom, she lay precisely as he'd left her, and he stood quietly at the foot of the bed for several minutes watching as she slept.

She possessed a fierce spirit, an independence that was laudable. It had been those very qualities that had drawn him to her, as well as her inherent honesty. His wealth didn't awe her, any more than *he* did. It was a rare quality to be liked for the man he was and not the Lanier family fortune.

Was she aware just how much she meant to him? She was the very air that he breathed, the daytime sun, the midnight moon.

Yet love alone wasn't enough, and he wasn't sufficiently foolish to imagine a ring and a marriage certificate were a guarantee of lifelong happiness.

Sandrine stirred, opened her eyes, focused on the man standing at the foot of the bed and offered him a slow, sweet smile.

'You shouldn't have let me sleep,' she protested huskily. 'What time is it?'

'Almost ten. Hungry?'

She didn't have to think about it. 'Ravenous.'

'I've made dinner.'

Surprise widened her eyes. 'You have?' She pushed herself into a sitting position and drew the sheet over her chest, then grinned at his teasing smile. 'Give me five minutes.'

She made it in seven, after the quickest shower on record, and slipped on a silky robe rather than dress.

'Oh, my,' Sandrine mused with pleasure as she sat down at the table. 'You do have hidden talent.'

'Singular?' Michel queried mockingly.

'Plural. Definitely plural,' she applauded as she sampled a sip of wine with a sigh of appreciation.

Filet mignon, delectable salad greens, a crusty baguette, and an excellent red wine, with a selection of fresh fruit.

Sandrine ate with pleasurable enjoyment, finishing every morsel on her plate, and she watched Michel cross to the stereo and insert a CD. Then he moved towards her and drew her up from the chair.

'What are you doing?' she queried with a faint laugh as he led her to the centre of the room and pulled her close.

The music was slow, the lyrics poignant, vocalized in the husky tones of a popular male singer.

Mmm, this was good, so good, she silently breathed as he cradled her body against his own. His hands stroked a sensuous pattern down her spine, then he cupped her bottom as she lifted her arms and linked her hands together at his nape.

The warmth of his body seemed to penetrate her own, and she melted into him as they drifted as one to the seductive tempo.

His lips settled at her temple, then slid down to the edge of her mouth, and she angled her head, inviting his possession in a kiss that was slow and so incredibly sweet she never wanted it to cease.

Sandrine gave a soundless gasp as he swept an arm beneath her knees and lifted her into his arms, then held on tight as he carried her through to the bedroom.

'Move, darling. Just a little closer now. Smile.'

If the photographer said *smile* one more time, she'd scream!

It was the end of what had been a very long day. Newspaper interviews and photographs from nine until eleven this morning, followed by a fashion shoot for the Australian edition of a top fashion magazine. Then an appearance at a high-profile charity luncheon held at the Sheraton Mirage, with a brief turn on the catwalk.

There had been photographs at *Movieworld*. One of the prime television channels was videotaping coverage for a spot on the evening news.

Tonight was the gala black-tie event to publicise the movie. Dignitaries would be present, and the city's wealthy socialites would have paid handsomely to mix and mingle with the producer, director and actors.

It was all a planned marketing strategy to provide maximum impact in the publicity stakes. Gregor and Cait had given interviews in their hotel, and advertising trailers would run on television and in the cinemas.

Sandrine didn't have star status in the film, but as a home-grown talent in acting and modelling, she gained attention. As Michel Lanier's wife, she was guaranteed media coverage.

'Pretend, darling,' Cait murmured with a mocking edge. 'You're supposed to be an actress, so act.'

'As you do, *darling*?' she responded sweetly.

'She really is a barrel of laughs,' Gregor muttered to Sandrine sotto voce. 'Desperate, dateless and deadly.'

'I can have any man I want,' Cait ventured disdainfully.

'No,' he denied smoothly. 'Most, darling. But not all.'

'Go get stuffed.'

'I don't participate in anatomically impossible feats.'

'You could always try.'

'We'll move it over there,' the photographer called, indicating the marina and one luxury cruiser in particular, whose owner had generously lent it for publicity purposes.

How much longer before she could escape? Surely they didn't require her much longer?

'Okay, Sandrine, you can go. Cait, Gregor, I want a few inside shots.'

Thank heavens. She'd almost kill for a long, icy cold drink with just a dash of alcohol to soothe the day's rough edges.

'Lucky you,' Cait voiced cynically. 'You're off the hook.'

For now. She stepped off the cruiser and quickly cleared the marina. The adjoining luxury condominiums of the Palazzo Versace were spectacular in design, resembling a precious jewel set in a sparkling sapphire-blue sea.

Their hotel was reached via an overhead footbridge

from the shopping complex, and Sandrine went directly to their suite.

Michel was seated at the small desk, his shirt sleeves turned back, studying the screen on his laptop as she entered. He glanced at her, then raised an eyebrow as she moved straight to the bar fridge, extracted a bottle of sparkling fruit spritzer and rummaged through the assortment of miniature bottles in the minibar.

'That bad?' he queried as he rose to his feet and crossed to her side.

'Oh, yes.' She broke the seal on the gin, added a splash, then filled the glass with spritzer and took a long sip. 'And tonight will be worse.' She felt his hands on her shoulders and sighed as he skilfully worked the tense muscles there. 'Remind me we're flying out of here tomorrow.'

She heard his husky chuckle and leaned back against him. He felt so good she just wanted to close her eyes, absorb his strength and have the immediate world go away.

'Two days in Sydney,' he drawled, and brushed his lips to her temple. 'Then we fly home.'

Home had a nice ring to it. She pictured their New York apartment overlooking Central Park and sighed again, feeling some of the tension subside.

'I have a few things to tie up there, which will take a week, maybe longer, then we'll spend some time in Paris.'

'I think I love you,' Sandrine said fervently.

'Only *think, chérie*?'

She opened her mouth to protest, then closed it again. 'I was being facetious.'

'So one would hope.'

She turned slowly to face him, saw the gleam of humour evident in those dark eyes and aimed a loosely clenched fist at his chest. The next instant she cried out as he removed the glass from her fingers and hoisted her over one shoulder.

'What are you *doing*?'

He walked towards the adjoining en suite, released her down onto the tiled floor, then began removing her clothes, followed by his own.

'Michel?'

'Taking a shower.'

She glimpsed the slumberous passion evident and shook her head. 'We don't have time for this.'

He reached into the glassed shower cubicle and turned on the water, adjusted the temperature dial, then stepped inside and drew her with him. 'Yes, we do.'

The water beat down on her head, and she heard his husky chuckle as she cursed him. Then she stilled as he caught up the soap and ran it over her slim curves.

He was very thorough. Too thorough, Sandrine decided as heat flared through her body at his intimate touch, and she moaned out loud as his mouth closed over hers in an erotic tasting that almost sent her over the edge.

When he raised his head, she looked at him in dazed disbelief as he handed her the soap and encouraged her to return the favour.

She did, with such sensuous, lingering skill he lifted her high against him and plunged deep inside, again and again while she clung to him.

Afterwards he caught up the plastic bottle of shampoo and washed her hair, then rinsed it before shutting the water and reaching for both towels.

Dry, he pulled her close and kissed her with unabated passion, then put her firmly at arm's length.

Sandrine looked at him with musing suspicion. 'You planned that.' It was a statement, not a query.

'Guilty.'

She pulled the hair dryer from its wall attachment and switched it on. 'We'll be late.'

'No, we won't.'

Five minutes didn't count, Sandrine acknowledged less than an hour later as they entered the large downstairs foyer.

Michel looked striking in full evening dress, and she felt confident in encrusted ivory silk organza with a scooped neckline. Elegant evening pumps in matching ivory completed the outfit, and she'd swept her hair high in a smooth French pleat.

The function-room doors were open and guests were beginning to enter. The Gold Coast's social glitterati were evident in force, Sandrine perceived, noting the elegant gowns, expensive jewellery, exquisitely made-up and coiffed women present. Without exception, the men were in full evening dress and bow tie.

Sandrine sighted Stephanie, who returned her smile and joined them within seconds.

'I've seated you with Cait Lynden, Gregor Anders,

the charity's chairwoman and her husband, and myself. The mayor and his wife are at Tony's table immediately adjoining yours. There'll be two tables seating the studio heads and various representatives from
the marketing team.'

Sandrine saw Stephanie stiffen slightly and soon determined the reason as Raoul joined them.

'The photographer was happy with everything today,' Stephanie continued, ignoring Raoul after offering him a fleeting polite smile. 'There will, of course,
be more taken tonight. However, we'll try to contain
it so it doesn't become too intrusive. Now, if you'll
excuse me?'

'You appear to have a disturbing effect on that
young woman,' Michel observed to his brother.

'I'll settle for disturb rather than disinterest,' Raoul
drawled in response, and Sandrine wrinkled her nose
at her husband, then turned to Raoul.

'Like that, is it?' she teased.

'She doesn't want to talk to me and she avoids my
calls.'

'I imagine you've arranged a few meetings with
marketing?' she posed musingly, and glimpsed the
gleam of humour evident in his expression. 'In
Michel's absence, in the name of business, of course.'

His smile held a certain wry amusement. 'Of
course.'

'Another rare young woman uninfluenced by the
Lanier wealth and social status?'

'I think we should go inside and take our seats,'

Michel indicated quizzically. 'Naturally you've arranged to sit at our table?'

'*Oui*,' Raoul agreed dryly, and Sandrine suppressed a chuckle as a committee member checked their tickets and indicated their table location.

The chairwoman's husband was the sole occupant, and upon introduction he explained that his wife was busy with last-minute details. Of Cait and Gregor there was no sign, and Sandrine suppressed the uncharitable thought that Cait was probably aiming to stage-manage a dramatic entrance.

She wasn't wrong. Just as the lights flickered, indicating the formalities were about to begin, Cait swept into the function room with Gregor and a photographer in tow.

In a gown that was backless, strapless and appeared moulded to her figure, the actress stepped towards them, pausing every now and then to pose as the camera lens focused on her.

'We're not late, are we?' The beautiful, sultry smile was at variance with the breathless little-girl voice.

Cait, the actress, playing to the audience, Sandrine perceived wryly. Of the remaining empty seats, Cait slid into the one between Raoul and Michel.

Sandrine kept a smile in place with difficulty and took a sip of chilled wine.

Stephanie slipped into her seat seconds before the evening's master of ceremonies stepped on stage to take the microphone.

There were introductions and speeches as the spotlight focused on Cait, Gregor and Tony, followed by a studio representative. The mayor said his piece, then a small army of waiters began serving the starter as music beat through sound speakers and a singer provided entertainment on stage.

Sandrine was supremely conscious of the man seated at her side. His enviable aura of power combined with a dramatic measure of primitive sensuality had a magnetic effect.

Cait resembled a feline who'd just swallowed a saucer of cream, Sandrine observed as she forked a morsel of the artistically arranged starter.

'Darling, you don't mind if I have a few photos taken with Michel, do you?' Cait queried, managing to make the request sound like a statement.

The female star and the man who'd rescued a movie from financial disaster, Sandrine reflected cynically, and wondered why she should feel like a possessive tigress. Protecting your interest, a tiny voice taunted. And her interest was Michel, her marriage.

'Mr Lanier has specified any photographs in which he appears must also include his wife,' Stephanie informed her with businesslike candour.

'A group photo, perhaps?' Raoul suggested in a slightly accented drawl. 'Including the marketing manager?'

Stephanie cast him a level glance. 'I don't think that's necessary.'

'Oh, but I think it is,' Raoul argued smoothly. 'Marketing is an integral part of any film production, *non*?'

Careful, Sandrine cautioned silently. Stephanie is a

steel magnolia, not a fragile violet. Baiting her won't achieve a thing.

'Marketing as a whole,' Stephanie agreed.

The chemistry between them sizzled, Sandrine mused. Raoul was a persistent and determined man. While Stephanie gave every indication of wanting to avoid him at any cost. Who would win?

Michel reached out a hand and threaded his fingers through her own. She turned towards him and caught the smouldering passion evident beneath his veiled gaze.

'My money's on Raoul,' she said quietly.

'Indeed,' Michel agreed. 'Although I doubt it'll be an easy victory.'

His thumb began a disturbing pattern across the sensitive veins inside her wrist, an action that played havoc with her equilibrium. As he intended it to do.

'I think I need to repair my make-up,' Sandrine ventured, and caught Michel's knowing smile. He realized the effect he had on her and precisely why she wanted a temporary escape.

'You look beautiful just the way you are.'

'Flattery won't get you anywhere,' she responded with a teasing smile, aware that she lied. She was so incredibly susceptible to everything about him. His voice, the softly spoken French he frequently lapsed into whenever he became lost in the throes of passion. The fluid movement of his body, his limbs, the way he smiled and those chiselled features softened when he looked at her.

She'd thought independence was important, but

nothing in her life held a candle to her love for Michel. He'd been right from the start. Why choose to be apart unless circumstances made it impossible to be together?

All those lonely nights she'd spent in her empty bed she'd longed for him to be beside her, to feel his touch. She'd enjoyed the part she'd played in the film, but that satisfaction didn't come close in compensation for being away from her husband.

Sandrine pushed open the door to the powder room and freshened up. Just as she was about to leave, Cait entered the vestibule.

One eyebrow slanted in recognition, and her mouth curved into a petulant smile. 'Really, darling, I'm surprised you could bear to leave Michel's side.'

Sandrine was heartily sick of the actress's game playing. 'It's a challenge, is it, Cait, to seduce another woman's husband?'

'Forbidden fruit, darling, tastes much sweeter than any that's readily available.' She raised a hand and placed the tip of a finger in her mouth. 'And it's always interesting to see if I can pluck the fruit from the tree.' She deliberately licked her finger, removed it, then offered Sandrine a sultry look. 'So to speak.'

Sandrine had had enough. She replaced her powder sponge and lipstick in her bag and closed the clasp. 'If you can succeed with Michel, you can have him.' She moved towards the door and paused momentarily at the sound of Cait's sultry drawl.

'Aren't you going to wish me good luck?'

'The hell I will,' she said inelegantly, and stepped quickly to the function room.

The buzz of voices hit her the moment she re-entered the large room, and she forced herself to walk slowly across the carpeted floor.

The chairwoman and her husband were absent from their table, as were Stephanie and Gregor. Only Michel and Raoul remained, and they appeared deep in conversation as she rejoined them.

Michel cast her a quick glance, glimpsed the faint edge of tension and accurately defined the reason for it.

'Cait?'

She managed a wry smile. 'She made it clear you're the target of her affections.'

'Indeed.'

He seemed amused, damn him.

'If you choose to play her game, then she can have you.'

He picked up her hand and lifted it to his lips, then kissed each finger in turn. 'Now why would I do that, *chérie*, hmm?' He grazed his teeth against her thumb, and saw her eyes flare. 'When all I want is you.'

'Perhaps you should tell Cait that.'

He brushed his mouth across the delicate veins inside her wrist, and Sandrine barely controlled the shiver that threatened to scud the length of her spine.

She could feel herself slowly drowning when she looked at him. The liquid warmth evident in his gaze rendered her bones to jelly, and she had to physically stop herself from leaning forward to place her lips against the sensuous curve of his mouth.

As crazy as it seemed, she could almost feel him inside her, relive the strength and the power of him as muscles deep inside clenched and unclenched in intimate spasms.

He knew. She could see by the glint of those dark eyes that he'd somehow detected the way she was inwardly reacting to him. She lowered her lashes and attempted to pull her hand free. To no avail, as he merely carried her hand to rest on his thigh.

An equally dangerous move, and she pressed the tips of her fingernails into hard muscle in silent warning.

'We've been invited to party on at the hotel's nightclub,' Michel relayed. 'Everyone else associated with the film and marketing will be there.'

She almost groaned out loud. 'Tell me our flight isn't the early-morning one,' she pleaded, and he gave a husky laugh.

'Eleven-thirty.'

'Breakfast before nine isn't an option,' she warned.

'Plan on sleeping in, *chérie*?'

She wrinkled her nose at him. '*Sleep* is the operative word.'

The photographer got his shots, several of them. Raoul very cleverly positioned himself beside Stephanie while Cait insinuated herself between Raoul and Michel. Gregor, bless him, wriggled his eyebrows at them all and flanked Stephanie.

It was after eleven when the evening began to wind

down, and half an hour later they wandered in groups towards the nightclub.

The DJ was spinning loud, funky music, the air was thick with noise, a cacophony of voices straining to be heard, and flashing strobe lighting provided a visual disturbance.

'Let's party, darling,' Gregor invited as he swept a glass of wine from the tray of a passing waitress.

'Why don't you ask Sandrine to dance?' Cait queried with a contrived pout. 'I want to play with the big boys.'

'Both of whom have their own women,' Gregor warned, regardless of her careless shrug. 'Don't do it, sweetheart.'

'Oh, stop trying to spoil my fun.'

Raoul turned towards Stephanie and indicated the crowded dance floor. 'Are you game to enter the fray?'

'With you?'

'Of course with me.'

'I'm not really into dancing.'

Cait placed a hand on Michel's forearm and used her fingers to apply a little pressure as she tilted her head and offered a provocative smile. 'Sandrine won't mind if I drag you away.' She turned towards Sandrine, openly daring her to object. 'Will you, darling?'

Michel covered Cait's hand with his own and transferred it to her side. His expression was polite, but there was an inflexible hardness apparent in his gaze. 'Regrettably, I do mind.'

Cait didn't bat an eyelash. 'I think the idea is for

everyone to loosen up a little now the film is in the can.'

'Define ''loosen up'',' Michel drawled.

Sandrine recognised the faint inflection in his voice and almost felt sorry for Cait.

'There's the party after the party, if you know what I mean,' the actress intimated with deliberate coquetry. 'A very *private* party.'

Was she aware just how brazen she sounded? And how damning? There was an edge apparent, a hyped overbrightness that hinted at substance enhancement. It left a sick feeling in Sandrine's stomach and provoked a degree of sadness.

'No.'

Cait's mouth formed a perfect bow. 'No?'

If she stayed another minute, she'd say something regrettable! 'Please, excuse me for a few minutes?'

'Do you mind if I join you?' Stephanie asked.

It took several minutes to weave their way through the nightclub patrons and locate the powder room. Once inside, the noise level diminished to a bearable level as they joined the queue waiting to use the facilities.

'Ten minutes, fifteen tops,' Stephanie commented as she examined her nails. 'Then I'm out of here, business and social obligations completed.'

'The suits won't have reason to complain,' Sandrine agreed with a quizzical smile, then saw the marketing manager visibly relax.

'It's all coming together well. The trailers are good, and the media blitz will gain the public's attention.'

The queue shifted, and they moved forward a few paces.

'I understand you're returning to Sydney tomorrow.'

Sandrine inclined her head. 'Just for a few days, then we fly home.'

'New York,' Stephanie murmured. 'I visited there once. Very fast, very cosmopolitan.'

'It has a beat all its own.'

'Distinctive.'

'Like the Lanier men.'

'One of them in particular,' Stephanie declared dryly.

Sandrine shot her a teasing smile. 'Persistent, is he?' she queried, and caught the other woman's wry grimace.

'You could say that.'

'Naturally, you don't like him.'

'He makes me feel uncomfortable.'

'Uncomfortable is good.'

'No,' Stephanie refuted. 'It's a pain in the neck.'

A light bubble of laughter rose to the surface. 'Good luck.'

'For Raoul to catch me? Or for me to escape unscathed?'

'Oh, I'll take a gamble and go for the first option,' Sandrine said wickedly.

'Not in this lifetime.'

There was a finality about those few words, and she wondered what, or rather *who* had damaged Stephanie's trust in men.

The music hit them in waves as they returned to the nightclub, and Stephanie joined a representative group from the marketing team as Sandrine crossed to rejoin Michel.

As she approached, Cait wound an arm round his neck and placed her mouth to his. It was a deliberate and calculated action, she knew, but one that angered her unbearably.

Michel showed restrained dignity as he broke the contact, and the actress turned towards Sandrine with a tantalising smile.

'You said I could have him, darling.'

'From where I stood, it didn't look as if he wanted you,' she managed in a remarkably even voice.

'Bitch.'

'I could say the same.'

Michel caught Sandrine's hand and linked his fingers through hers, applying a slight warning pressure. Which she ignored.

'Perhaps we should leave,' he suggested indolently, and suppressed a degree of amusement as Sandrine shot him a stunning smile.

'Why? I'm having so much fun.' She lifted his hand and brushed her lips across his knuckles. 'Ask me to dance.'

His eyes darkened and acquired a wicked gleam as he led her onto the dance floor. 'Minx,' he murmured close to her ear.

'Confrontation,' she mocked lightly. 'Works so much better than retreat.' A light gasp escaped her lips as he drew her in close. 'That might be a bit of overkill.' One hand cupped her bottom while the other slid to clasp her nape.

'You think so?' he drawled, enjoying the way her heart thudded into a quickened beat, the slight huskiness in her voice.

The music slowed, and they drifted together for several long minutes, only to break apart as the DJ switched discs and tempo.

By mutual consent they began circulating between the various business heads from marketing, the studio. Something that took a while, until they came at last to Raoul.

'Sleep well,' she bade as he brushed his lips to her cheek.

Minutes later they entered their suite, and Sandrine slipped off her shoes, then unfastened the zip and stepped out of her gown.

It had been a long day, and there was a sense of satisfaction that everything had come to a close.

She crossed to the en suite, removed her make-up, slipped on a silk nightshirt, then re-entered the bedroom and slid into bed.

Within seconds Michel joined her, snapped off the bedlamp, then caught her close.

It was heaven to lean against him, to feel the reassuring beat of his heart beneath her cheek. His lips touched her temple, then slid to her mouth to bestow a brief, warm kiss.

His chin rested against the top of her head, and she simply closed her eyes and drifted off to sleep within seconds.

CHAPTER TEN

SYDNEY looked achingly familiar, and the Double Bay apartment particularly welcoming. There were several things she wanted to do, a few loose ends she needed to tie up, and she wanted some time alone with her father.

Michel's cell phone rang as Sandrine began unpacking the few necessities required during the next day or two, and his voice faded into a muted sound as he took the call in the lounge.

He returned to the bedroom minutes later and began unpacking. 'Raoul has set up a meeting with the Enrique Corporation for tomorrow afternoon.'

A new deal, initiated by Raoul who had flown into Sydney the previous day, which, if it proved successful, would see a Lanier Corporation link in Australia.

'I'll ring Lucas and see if he's free to meet me for lunch.'

Michel handed her his cell phone. 'Do it now. We're meeting Raoul for dinner, and it might be late when we get back.'

She punched in the relevant numbers, greeted her father's availability with enthusiasm and agreed on a time and place to meet.

'All done,' Sandrine said with satisfaction. She had

twenty minutes in which to change and repair her make-up, and she managed it with a minute to spare.

Deep red evening trousers and a matching cropped evening jacket worn over a black silk camisole highlighted the texture of her skin and emphasised the lustrous colour of her hair. She left it loose to fall onto her shoulders, simply because there wasn't sufficient time to pin it up.

Raoul was booked into the Ritz-Carlton in Double Bay, and they joined him in the lounge at seven for a drink before entering the restaurant.

The maître d' led them to a table and snapped his fingers for the wine steward.

'Too premature for champagne?' Sandrine queried with a quizzical smile.

'Who needs a special occasion to drink champagne? Dom Pérignon,' Raoul instructed, and she observed the smooth approach of the waiter. Such synchronisation in service deserved a reward.

After they ordered a starter and main, deferring dessert, Sandrine spared a cursory glance at the room and its occupants as she sipped champagne from a crystal flute.

Michel and Raoul discussed strategy for the next day's meeting and finetuned arrangements over the starter.

They were part way through the main dish when something caught Sandrine's attention. The stark light of a flashbulb, followed by the glimpse of a familiar figure combined with a trill of laughter she'd hoped never to hear again.

For a moment she thought, *hoped*, she was mistaken, but no, there, making a grand entrance, was none other than Cait Lynden.

I don't believe this. She had known Cait and Gregor were due to fly out to the States this week, but of all the hotels in Sydney, was it coincidence Cait had chosen this one...or had she done some careful sleuthing?

Perhaps she wouldn't notice they were here?

Fat chance, Sandrine acknowledged in wry silence as she viewed Cait's performance. For it was a piece of superb acting, which didn't fool her in the slightest. Any more than it deceived Michel or Raoul as Cait approached their table.

'For heaven's sake,' Cait greeted with delighted enthusiasm, 'who would have thought we'd run into each other, *here*, of all places.'

The maître d' hovered, well used to the presence of celebrities in this exclusive hotel. He aimed to please and to serve, and Cait took flagrant advantage of his position.

'You don't mind if I join you?' She slid into the chair held out for her, then waved her hand in an elegant gesture to the wine steward. 'Bring another bottle of champagne.' When the waiter presented her with a menu, she scanned it quickly, then handed it back to him. 'Just a starter. The Caesar salad.'

'You're alone?' Raoul drawled in query, and Sandrine watched Cait weigh up which Lanier brother she'd attempt to captivate.

Just try it with Michel, she warned silently, and I'll scratch your eyes out!

The famous pout was a touch overdone. 'Gregor deserted me, the rat.' Her mouth formed a moue. 'I could have ordered room service, but I didn't feel like being alone.'

Cashing in on national publicity and revelling in the limelight, Sandrine perceived, then mentally chastised herself for being cynical.

'So, what are we celebrating?'

'Life,' Michel stated with studied indolence as he took hold of Sandrine's hand and lifted it to his lips. 'And love.' He kissed each fingertip in turn, then curled her hand within his.

Oh, my, that was about as blatant as you could get. Add to that the passionate gleam apparent in his eyes, the sensual curve of his lips. It was a combination that succeeded in melting her bones.

'Quite a change from when Michel first appeared on the scene a month ago,' Cait imputed with thinly veiled sarcasm. 'At Tony's apartment I could have sworn you were enemies instead of husband and wife.'

'If husbands and wives didn't experience a difference of opinion on occasion, the marriage would become boring,' Sandrine offered.

'Really?'

'Anyone for coffee?' Raoul intervened. 'I have a few calls to make.'

'Likewise I need to go on-line.' Michel succeeded in attracting the maître d's attention, then turned towards Cait. 'By all means stay on and finish the champagne.'

They weren't able to escape quite so easily. The

photographer appeared out of nowhere and reeled off a few shots, which, unless Sandrine was mistaken, would be sold to at least one of the national newspapers.

Michel muttered an imprecation beneath his breath, signed the proffered credit slip, then rose to his feet and pocketed his wallet.

'Safe flight, darlings,' Cait bade, again looking like a cat who'd just finished a bowl of cream.

'*Merci*.'

Michel curved an arm round Sandrine's waist as Raoul accompanied them to the main entrance, then waited as they slid into a taxi.

'Coincidence, do you think?' she posed as the taxi swiftly joined the traffic.

'Extremely doubtful,' Michel said dryly.

'Coffee?' Sandrine offered on entering the apartment five minutes later. 'We didn't have any, and if you need to work on-line…'

'The only thing I want to work closely with is *you*.'

A lazy grin widened her mouth, and her eyes sparkled as she turned towards him. 'I'm not sure I like being referred to as a *thing*.'

He crooked a finger in a beckoning gesture. 'Come here.'

Laughter bubbled up inside her, emerging as a delightful throaty sound. 'You'd better have a good reason for issuing orders.'

'Oh, I don't think you'll have reason to complain.'

She moved into his arms and felt them enfold her close. 'Really?'

'*Really*,' he mocked lightly, then proceeded to kiss her with such passion she went up in flames.

They made it to the bedroom, discarding clothes as they went, and it was a long time before she found the energy to do more than murmur her appreciation as she slipped close to the edge of sleep.

The taxi eased to a halt outside the Ritz-Carlton, and Michel paid the driver as Sandrine emerged from the vehicle.

Together they entered the main lobby, shared a coffee with Raoul, then Sandrine rose to her feet and brushed Michel's temple with a light kiss.

'Three o'clock?'

Michel's answering smile held warmth as he inclined his head. 'Have fun.'

Her mouth assumed a wicked curve. 'I intend to.' She wanted to select a special gift for his grandmother and she was due to meet her father at one.

Double Bay was a delightful place to browse and shop, and she found a beautiful Hermès silk scarf that was just perfect.

It was almost one when she entered the restaurant Lucas had recommended, and she was barely seated when the maître d' showed him to their table.

'Sandrine,' Lucas greeted with affection, 'this is a pleasure.'

She ordered wine, and they settled on a starter and main.

'It's regrettable this has to be brief, but I have a scheduled meeting at two-fifteen.'

'That's okay,' Sandrine voiced without hesitation.

He surveyed her over the rim of his glass. 'You have something on your mind you want to discuss with me?'

'Chantal.'

Lucas replaced his glass down on the table. 'You know your mother and I no longer maintain contact.'

She was aware of all the reasons why and had accepted them. 'I'm concerned for her.'

'And you expect me to share that concern?'

'She's my mother,' she said simply.

'Chantal is an emotional butterfly, always seeking something different and new. When life becomes boring, she moves on without too much thought for those left behind.' He paused as the waiter removed their plates. 'I rebuilt my life with a loving woman.'

A loving woman who was civil and superficially affectionate to her husband's daughter from his first marriage, but one who'd made it clear Sandrine had no place in her home or her heart.

Lucas placed a hand over hers. 'Your mother will never change. She's *Chantal*,' he declared with wry cynicism, as if that explained it all. 'You have Michel. Treasure that love and treat it with care.'

There was no point to pursuing the conversation, and she didn't even try. Instead, they spoke of Ivan's academic achievements and aspirations.

It was after two when they emerged from the restaurant, and Sandrine gave her father an affectionate hug in farewell.

She needed to make a few calls to friends, and she

strolled towards the hotel, settled herself comfortably in the lounge, ordered a cappuccino and punched a series of numbers into her cell phone.

She temporarily lost track of time, and it wasn't until she glanced at her watch after concluding the last of her calls that she realised it was after three.

Where was Michel? Sandrine checked her watch for the third time in fifteen minutes. It wasn't like him to be late.

'Can I get you anything else, ma'am?'

She cast the waitress a brief smile and shook her head. 'Thank you.'

A slight frown creased her forehead. She hadn't got the meeting place wrong because Michel had dropped her off outside this hotel more than three hours ago.

Perhaps he'd been held up. Yes, that was it. His meeting had run overtime.

The frown deepened. If that were true, why didn't he ring? She slipped the cell phone from her bag and checked it for any messages. There were none.

Okay, she'd ring him on his cell phone. A few words of reassurance were all she needed. Without further hesitation she punched in the numbers and waited, only to have the call switch to voice mail. She left a message, then slipped the phone into her bag.

Raoul. Maybe she could call Raoul, she thought, only to remember she hadn't keyed his number into her memory bank.

Business lunches were notorious for running late. Any minute now Michel would call, apologise and explain. Except he didn't, and a fist closed over her heart.

Several different scenarios played through her mind and she examined and discarded each of them.

The peal of the phone interrupted her increasing apprehension, and she plucked the unit from her bag and activated it.

'Raoul, Sandrine.'

'Michel—'

'Is okay,' Raoul assured her. 'There was a slight car accident, and the officers who attended the scene insisted everyone involved receive a medical examination.'

Dear heaven. 'Where?'

He named a private city hospital. 'Take a cab. I'll be waiting for you.'

A chill invaded her bones. 'I'm on my way.'

The ensuing fifteen minutes were the longest minutes of her life as she imagined a plethora of possibilities regarding Raoul's description of events.

'Okay, he's okay,' she repeated several times beneath her breath as the cab negotiated heavy city traffic.

What if Raoul wasn't telling her the truth? Dear Lord in heaven, what if the accident had been severe?

Sandrine froze. Images of horrific televised accident scenes flashed before her eyes. She pictured bodies being cut from crushed vehicles and transported by ambulance to hospital.

How much longer? She checked the location and estimated another five minutes should do it, providing there were no unexpected traffic snarls.

The cab made it in seven, and she hurriedly thrust

a note into the driver's hand, opened the door and waved away his move to give her change.

She ran down the concrete path and paused impatiently as she waited for the automatic glass doors of the main entrance to open.

Sandrine was oblivious to the nurses' station, the collection of waiting patients. All she saw was Raoul crossing the room towards her, and she rushed to his side.

'He's with the doctor,' Raoul soothed, taking hold of her elbow as he led her down a corridor. 'He's fine. The wound needs a few stitches.'

Her stomach clenched at the thought of torn flesh being stitched together. 'How bad is it?'

Raoul gave her arm a reassuring squeeze. 'A few scratches, some bruising.' He indicated a doorway to the right. 'He's in here.'

Sandrine's heart missed a beat, then thudded loudly in her chest as she stepped into the room. The attending doctor partly obscured Michel from her view, and she moved quickly to his side, her eyes sweeping over his features, his lengthy frame, in a bid to determine the extent of his injuries.

'*Michel*,' she breathed raggedly as she took in those flawless, broad-boned facial features, then roved over his bare chest.

No scratches, no visible bruising, she noted with relief. The doctor was working on Michel's left arm, stitching what looked to be a deep gash, and she paled at the sight of the needle suturing the wound.

'My wife,' Michel drawled as the doctor paused in his task to give her a quick glance.

'Your husband is fine. A few bruised ribs from the restraining seat belt, plus a gashed arm. I'll be done in a few minutes, then you can take him home.'

Sandrine felt the blood drain from her face as her vivid imagination envisaged the car screeching as Michel applied the brakes, the sickening crunch as two cars collided, the reflexive action at the moment of impact.

For one brief, infinitesimal second she experienced a mental flash of how it might have been, and the thought of what *could* have happened almost destroyed her. A life without Michel in it would be no life at all.

A hand curved round her nape as Michel pulled her towards him, and her hands instinctively clutched hold of his shoulders. Then his mouth was on hers in a brief, hard kiss that almost immediately softened to a light caress before he released her.

'Don't, *chérie*,' he chastised huskily, and uttered a muffled curse as he saw her lips tremble.

She tried to smile but didn't quite make it.

Michel's eyes darkened, and he caught her hand and held it. His thumb lightly caressed the veins inside her wrist, moving in a rhythmic pattern that stirred her senses. Just looking at him made her want to fling her arms around him and hold on tight.

Relief flooded her veins, closely followed by love. The deep, abiding-forever kind. Her heart, her emotions, belonged to this man, unequivocally. Nothing else held any importance.

'There, all done,' the doctor declared as he applied a dressing and secured it. 'Those stitches need to be removed in a week.'

Michel rose to his feet, grabbed his shirt from the back of the chair, shrugged it on and attended to the buttons before slipping into his jacket. 'Let's get out of here.'

'I'll organise the cab and drop you off on my way to the airport,' Raoul stated as they exited the building, and Sandrine gave him a brief, keen glance.

'You're flying back to the Gold Coast?'

He offered her a wry smile. 'Yes.'

'I see.'

'Do you?'

Her eyes held musing humour. 'Oh, yes.' Stephanie was in for a battle if she thought she could easily dismiss Raoul. The Lanier men fought for what they wanted. 'I recognise the signs.'

'Then wish me luck, Sandrine.'

'Do you need it?'

His expression assumed a faint bleakness.

So he wasn't so sure after all. Good, she decided silently. He'd appreciate Stephanie all the more for not providing him with an easy victory.

She lifted a hand and brushed her fingers down that firm cheek. 'You have it, Raoul.'

He offered her a smile that held warmth and affection. '*Merci.*'

CHAPTER ELEVEN

THERE was a rank of taxis outside the main entrance, and one moved forward at a flick from Michel's fingers.

Twenty minutes later the cab slid to a halt outside their apartment building, and they bade Raoul a quick farewell, then made their way through the foyer to the lift.

The instant the lift doors closed behind them, Michel punched the appropriate panel button, then he pulled her close and fastened his mouth over hers in a kiss that was all too brief as the doors slid open at their designated floor. They walked the few steps to their door and then entered the apartment.

For a few seconds she stood in dazed silence, her eyes large as she looked at him. There was so much she wanted to say, yet the words seemed caught in her throat.

He was so dear to her, so very special. Life itself. Without him, the flame within her would flicker and die.

Something flared in his eyes, and she stood perfectly still as he threaded his fingers into her hair and tilted her head.

'I couldn't bear to lose you,' she said simply, and saw his lips curve into a gentle smile.

'It isn't going to happen.'

'Today, just for a while, I thought it might have.'

As long as he lived, he'd never forget the expression in her eyes, the paleness of her features when she entered the emergency room. His thumb caressed the firm line of her jaw. 'I know.'

She swallowed, the expression in her eyes mirroring her emotions. 'You probably should rest,' she voiced huskily.

'You think so?'

'Michel…' She paused as his head lowered down to hers and his lips settled on one cheekbone, then began trailing a path down the slope of her jawbone to settle at the edge of her mouth.

'Hmm?'

'I can't think when you do that.'

'Is it so important that you think?'

One hand moved to the vee of her top and slid beneath it.

'I want…' Her breath hitched as his fingers brushed the slope of her breast, the touch infinitely erotic over the soft silk and lace of her bra.

His lips teased hers, light as a butterfly's wing, as they stroked over the sensuous lower curve, then he swept his tongue to taste the sweetness within.

This, *this*, was where she was meant to be. Held in the arms of the man who was her soul mate. Nothing else mattered.

'What is it you want, *chérie*?' Michel drawled gently.

'*You*,' she said simply. 'But first…' Her voice

climbed a few notches, then came to a sudden halt as
his fingers slid to unfasten the clip of her bra. The
sensitive peaks burgeoned in anticipation of his touch,
and heat arrowed from deep within as he began an
erotic, evocative stroking. It drove her wild, and she
groaned out loud as he pulled the knit top over her
head, discarded her bra, then lowered his mouth to one
highly sensitised peak.

She could feel herself begin to melt as her body
melded to his, aligning itself to allow him access as
her hands crept round his neck.

A long, heartfelt sigh whispered from her lips as he
shifted his attention to render a similar salutation to
its twin. For what seemed an age she exulted in the
sheer sensation his touch evoked, feeling every pore,
every nerve cell pulse into vibrant life.

It wasn't enough, and she murmured encouragement
when his fingers slipped to her waist and attended to
the zip fastening.

His clothes were an impossible barrier she sought
to remove with considerable care, and his gentle smile
almost completely undid her as he put her at arm's
length and finished the task.

Sandrine took in his muscled frame, the olive-toned
skin stretching over superb bone structure and honed
sinew. His shoulders were broad, his chest tightly
muscled and liberally sprinkled with dark, curling hair
that arrowed down to his waist, then flared into a geo-
metric vee at the juncture of his thighs.

He was an impressive, well-endowed man, a skilled
and exciting lover whose degree of *tendresse* melted

her bones, while his passion had the power to awe and overwhelm.

With one easy movement he swept an arm beneath her knees and lifted her high against his chest.

'Your arm,' she protested, and heard his husky laughter.

'Afraid it might hinder me?' Michel teased as he strode through to the bedroom.

'Hurt you,' she corrected as he pulled back the bed-clothes and drew her down with him onto the sheets.

He kissed her, deeply and with such soul-destroying intensity she lost track of time and place until he slowly released his mouth from her own.

She looked *kissed*, he saw with satisfaction. Her mouth was slightly swollen, and her eyes resembled huge liquid pools a man could drown in.

He wanted to savour the taste of her, skim his lips over every inch of her skin, suckle at her breasts with the ferocity of a newborn infant seeking succour. Except a man nurtured his woman's breasts to give her pleasure, for some of the most sensitised nerve endings were centred at those peaks.

Most of all he wanted to bury himself deep in her moist heat and become lost in the sweet sorcery that was *Sandrine*. His woman, his wife. His life.

From the moment he met her, he had only one agenda. It was instant, breathtaking desire. Yet it had been more than that, much more. Deep within the raw, primitive emotion had been the instinctive knowledge they were meant to be. Almost as if they'd known each other in a former existence.

Crazy, he dismissed with a mental shake of his head. He possessed a logical, analytical mind. Yet he was frighteningly aware of the timing and how, had he not been at a friend's home attending a party, he might never have met her. Equally, the slender thread of chance that led her to be persuaded to tag along to something she freely admitted hadn't been her first choice of an evening's entertainment.

Of the many women he'd met socially and in the business arena, there had been none who'd come close to the magic that was Sandrine.

Beautiful, with a gently curving slenderness that made her frame perfect for displaying designer clothes on various European catwalks. Fine-boned facial features, lovely, wide-spaced dark brown eyes, a generous mouth.

Rather than her physical appearance, it had been the genuine warmth of her smile, the expressive eyes and her *joie de vivre*. The way her chin tilted when she laughed, the faint twist of her head as she tossed her hair back over her shoulders. The sound of her voice, its faint huskiness when she became emotionally aroused. And because he was a man, the feel of her body in his arms, her mouth beneath his. The scent and essence that made her unique.

Destined to be, he mused, like two halves of a whole that fitted perfectly together as one.

'Michel?'

He looked down at her and tried to control the slight tremor that threatened to destroy the slim hold on his libido. 'You get to talk *after* we make love,' he teased

mercilessly, and felt his body go weak at the languorous humour evident in those beautiful dark eyes.

'You could make an exception.'

He trailed a finger down the slope of her nose. 'So
what is it you want to say that can't wait, hmm?'

She reached up a hand and pressed a finger to his
lips, stilling any words he might have added. '*I love
you*.' There was the prick of unshed tears, an ache
deep inside her heart.

He kissed each of her fingers in turn, and she almost
melted from the warmth evident in his gaze. '*Merci,
chérie*,' he said gently.

'I always have,' she assured him with such a depth
of feeling two tears materialised, clung to her lashes,
then spilled to run down her cheek in twin rivulets. 'I
always will.'

His thumb stroked away the dampness. 'Are you
done?'

She inclined her head and made an attempt to restore her composure. Her gaze speared his, and there
was a depth apparent that made him catch his breath.

'I have something for you.' He reached out and slid
open a drawer of the bedside pedestal, extracted something, then turned back to her and caught hold of her
left hand.

It was an exquisite diamond-studded ring, a perfect
complement to her existing rings.

'It's beautiful,' Sandrine breathed. 'Thank you.' A
circle symbolising eternity. She wanted to cry. 'I have
nothing for you.'

The passionate warmth evident in his gaze succeeded in melting her bones. 'You're wrong,' Michel said tenderly. '*You* are my gift. Infinitely more precious than anything you could give me. *Je t'aime, mon amour.*' His voice was husky as he curved her close against him. '*Je t'adore.*' His lips hovered fractionally above her own. 'You are my life, my love. Everything.'

Love was understanding, compassion and trust. And more, much more.

She linked her hands behind his head and pulled him down to her. '*Merci,*' she teased, and heard his husky growl an instant before his mouth closed over hers.

After the loving, she lay spent, curled in against his side, one arm flung across his midriff, her cheek resting on his chest.

The sun had shifted lower in the sky, and soon dusk would fall. Shadows danced slowly across the pale wall, creating an indecipherable pattern.

At last everything had fallen into place, she decided dreamily. The film was finished, publicity completed. Tomorrow she would board a flight with Michel bound for New York. A week later they'd embark on a holiday in France.

Paris in winter, drizzle, grey skies. But nothing would dull the magic of love in a city made for lovers. It was the appropriate city in which to try to conceive a child.

'Are you awake?'

She felt him shift slightly towards her. 'Want me to order in something to eat?'

'How do you feel about children?'

'In general?'

She waited a few seconds. 'Ours.'

Now she had his attention. 'Are you trying to tell me something?'

'There's nothing to tell…yet.'

He propped up his head as he leant towards her. 'The thought of your being pregnant with my child overwhelms me.'

She wrinkled her nose at him. 'Too overwhelming?'

He kissed her with lingering thoroughness. 'I think we should work on it.'

'Now?'

'You object?'

She didn't answer. Instead, she showed him just how she intended to work on it.

THE ROYAL HOUSE OF KAREDES

Two crowns, two islands, one legacy

Volume 1 – April 2009
BILLIONAIRE PRINCE, PREGNANT MISTRESS
by Sandra Marton

Volume 2 – May 2009
THE SHEIKH'S VIRGIN STABLE-GIRL
by Sharon Kendrick

Volume 3 – June 2009
THE PRINCE'S CAPTIVE WIFE
by Marion Lennox

Volume 4 – July 2009
THE SHEIKH'S FORBIDDEN VIRGIN
by Kate Hewitt

8 VOLUMES IN ALL TO COLLECT!

THE ROYAL HOUSE OF KAREDES

Two crowns, two islands, one legacy

Volume 5 – August 2009
THE GREEK BILLIONAIRE'S INNOCENT PRINCESS
by Chantelle Shaw

Volume 6 – September 2009
THE FUTURE KING'S LOVE-CHILD
by Melanie Milburne

Volume 7 – October 2009
RUTHLESS BOSS, ROYAL MISTRESS
by Natalie Anderson

Volume 8 – November 2009
THE DESERT KING'S HOUSEKEEPER BRIDE
by Carol Marinelli

8 VOLUMES IN ALL TO COLLECT!